Will touched her cheek, a whispered stroke shivering her to her heels.

"First," he said softly, "if I'm attracted to a woman, it's *who she is* that appeals. And—" his fingers slipped to her nape and tugged her forward "—caveman or not, I'm very *into* you. So let's see where it takes us, right?"

He would kiss her. *Oh, Lord.*

But no.

A buss against her forehead. A touch so light it mimicked the flit of a hummingbird's wing.

When had a man offered sensuality to that degree?

Not once. Not once in her memory.

Savanna watched him return to the stove. How was she to endure—*fight off*—the magnet that was Will Rubens over the next weeks?

Because he *was* a magnet, potent as a lightning storm.

Dear Reader,

Years ago, I saw a documentary about Alaska and was completely entranced by its wild untouched beauty. From that moment, I hoped to one day set a story somewhere amid its copious snowy mountains, dark green timber and lush wildlife. I wanted to see Alaska through my characters' eyes. What better way than to do it with a bush pilot, one of those brave and remarkable folk who fly helicopters and tiny four- and six-seater planes up and down the state's vast river valleys, lakes and mountain slopes?

May you enjoy the journey of dashing pilot Will Rubens and the woman who brings a special little boy into his life, as they conquer their own uncertainties within the sweeping glory of the Last Frontier.

Mary J. Forbes

PS In October 2007, look for *Red Wolf's Return,* in which a reclusive wilderness photographer reunites at long last with his childhood sweetheart in Montana.

HIS BROTHER'S GIFT

MARY J. FORBES

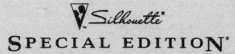

SPECIAL EDITION®

Published by Silhouette Books

America's Publisher of Contemporary Romance

SILHOUETTE BOOKS

ISBN-13: 978-0-373-24840-7
ISBN-10:   0-373-24840-7

HIS BROTHER'S GIFT

Copyright © 2007 by Mary J. Forbes

Books by Mary J. Forbes

MARY J. FORBES

grew up on a farm amid horses, cattle, crisp hay and broad blue skies. As a child, she drew and wrote of her surroundings, and in sixth grade composed her first story about a little lame pony. Years later, she worked as an accountant, then as a reporter-photographer for a small-town newspaper, before earning an honors degree in education to become a teacher. She has also written and published short fiction stories.

A romantic by nature, Mary loves walking along the ocean shoreline, sitting by the fire on snowy or rainy evenings and two-stepping around the dance floor to a good country song—all with her own real-life hero, of course. Mary would love to hear from her readers at www.maryjforbes.com.

*Wendy—here's to our "Alphie" sessions
in those Route 10 coffee shops!*

ACKNOWLEDGMENTS

My sincerest thanks go to Wendy Roberts and
Camille Netherton for sharing their personal
knowledge and experiences regarding autistic
spectrum disorders, although each child with
Asperger's syndrome and high-functioning autism
is unique and traits vary with each case. Also, many
thanks to Leanne Karella and Kevin Karella for their
help about helicopters and the geography of Alaska.
As with any work of fiction, I have taken license
with some facts on the above topics.

Chapter One

Starlight, Alaska
Early April

Will Rubens sank to the kitchen chair and stared at the phone on the counter.

Dennis was...*dead?* Impossible. His brother lived in Central America. He was busy saving lives....

A hazy image of a tall, blond man with glasses magnifying his brown eyes was all Will's brain conjured. Dennis, the last day they had seen each other face-to-face three years ago down in Washington state. *Jeez, Dennis.*

Will eyed the phone. The woman from Honduras had left three messages in the past hour. Urgent messages for him to call her. But he'd been with Josh, hitting fly balls, practicing for the upcoming Little League season.

Will didn't blame the kid for the missed calls. Josh

needed a big brother in Will and, truth be known, Will needed the boy. The eleven-year-old eased the decade of guilt Will carried because, if he'd been more disciplined in his actions, Elke and Dennis might have stayed in Alaska. Now three phone messages stamped another bruise over those his heart had accumulated. If the woman was right, what remained of his family was gone.

Gone as if they had never existed.

He wiped a shaky hand down his face. Stared at the phone. No, the woman had the correct number, the correct *owner* of that number.

He propped an elbow on the table, leaned his forehead against the base of his palm.

When was the last time he'd talked to Dennis? A year? Two? Yes…June, two years ago. Ten minutes of strained conversation that led nowhere. Strangers rather than brothers.

He raised his head, blinked into the April sunset spilling through the window above the sink and was surprised at the burn behind his eyes. *Dennis. What the hell was in Honduras that you couldn't have found in your own backyard?*

But Will knew why his brother had trekked to Central America for a decade. Why their relationship had petered to a phone call every couple years.

Elke had wanted it that way. Hell, could he blame her?

Rising, he again punched Play on the answering machine. Just to be sure. Just to know he hadn't misunderstood.

Grabbing a pen and slip of paper, he listened as the old machine whirred and clicked.

Beeep. "Hello. I have an urgent message for Will Rubens. This is Savanna Stowe, S-t-o-w-e, of Honduras. I hope I've reached the right residence. I'm staying here in town at the Shepherd Lodge. The phone number is…" The machine dated the message: Wednesday, 6:12 p.m.

First of all, why was she in Starlight? Why hadn't she simply called from whatever mud hut she'd set up house-keeping in down there?

Will wrote her name: Savanna Stowe.

She had an incredible voice. A hint of the South, slow and husky.

Beeep. "Mr. Rubens, I know you've returned from your flying trip today. I met a fellow at the airport who said you'd gone home to sleep because you were exhausted. I really need to talk to you. It's about your brother Dennis in Honduras. Please call me at the Shepherd Lodge anytime. Better yet, if at all possible, please come to the lodge and ask the desk clerk to ring my room. I'll meet you in the lobby." She repeated the number. The machine noted date and time: Wednesday, 7:05 p.m.

Beeep. "Mr. Rubens. I'm not sure why you're ignoring me. Maybe you aren't home, or maybe you don't care about your brother." Will snorted. Presumptuous of her. "Whatever the case, I'll try and explain why I'm here, though I'd wanted to do this in person. Your brother Dennis and his wife were killed in a plane crash in the mountains south of the Rio Catacamas on Sunday. Please, come to the Shepherd Lodge. It's urgent I speak with you." Wednesday, 8:23. The machine clicked off.

Will frowned. Dennis and Elke were dead. Okay, he'd got that the first time. But in his shock he'd missed one impor-tant fact. Savanna from Honduras had not mentioned the son.

Dennis's son.

The one conceived with Will's sperm in an Anchorage clinic eleven years ago.

Savanna set the receiver back in its cradle. Shane the desk clerk had called and informed her that Mr. Will Rubens was waiting in the lobby. Cautious as she'd become over the past seventeen years, she had asked Shane if he knew Rubens. He did. Very well. They'd fished together off and on over the years. Should he send Mr. Rubens up?

Give her ten minutes, she had told the man.

That was thirty seconds ago.

She looked through the bedroom door where ten-year-old Christopher sat crossed-legged in his pajamas on the flower-printed bed covers, flapping his left hand while inserting his right index finger into the tiny hole worn on the left heel of his sock. She could barely make out his low monotone murmur, "Thread can repair this fracture."

She let him mutter. The last two days had been Everests to climb for them both. Journeying across Honduras from Cedros to Tegucigalpa by car, then flying to LAX and on to Anchorage and finally, the short jaunt east to Starlight in a six-seater plane.

Through the sedative she'd had to administer to keep Christopher calm during the last forty-eight hours, she saw exhaustion in his down-turned mouth, the droop of his blue eyes. *Elke's eyes.* She hated dispensing medication, unless it was necessary. Traveling across a continent and a half made it a necessity. But tonight, thank God, he would sleep. He was worn-out, she knew.

She walked into the bedroom. "Christopher," she said softly.

He continued flapping and murmuring.

She moved into his line of vision.

Flap, flap.

On the night table lay the laminated agenda. She set it beside him on the bed where he could see the day's checkmarks.

"You've brushed your teeth, I see."

"Yeah."

"That's my boy. It's time for bed now. See…" She pointed to "Bedtime," which he had checked off earlier.

"Okay." He unwound his legs and crawled under the covers. Relieved, she returned the agenda to the table. Later she would slip onto the cot near the door. Strange places and beds upset him. Waking to them in the middle of the night traumatized him.

Leaning down, she kissed his youthful forehead. "Good night, buddy."

She didn't expect a response. Already he had zeroed in on a linear stain crossing the room's wall. Linear like his trains.

Quietly she turned out the night lamp, walked to the door. There she waited a few moments until she heard the tiny snore and knew he'd allowed sleep to usurp his mind.

Sweet dreams, honey-child. Slipping from the room, she pulled the door partially closed.

In the bathroom she checked her face. She did not want Will Rubens seeing her fatigue and assuming the child in her care received less than her best. Except the lines between her eyes and the dark circles beneath them were hard to extinguish. Well, she couldn't worry about these tokens she had earned, ensuring people had food on their tables and clean water to drink, an education to enlighten their minds.

Stifling a yawn, she tow-boated a brush through the shamble of her hair. Once, long ago, she would have wailed over its hectic red color, but living in Third-World countries had accented the difference between a bad hair day and a major crisis. Tangled, unwashed curls was not one.

Sleep, that's what she needed. About a month's worth.

But first Mr. Rubens. And Christopher.

What if this brother of Dennis's won't agree?

You'll stay the twelve weeks stipulated in the will to give the man his chance.

And if he still reneged after three months, she'd take Christopher back to Tennessee, as Dennis also stipulated, though that option was a last resort.

Inside her overnight case on the sink's scratched counter, she found her lipstick.

What was she doing? This was not a date. She was meeting Will Rubens about Christopher—and because of the last request left by two of the people she loved and respected most in the world next to Christopher.

A soft knock sounded on the suite's door.

Showtime. If not for Christopher needing a good night's sleep, she would have insisted on meeting Rubens in the lodge's lobby.

Or better yet, not at all.

Through the peephole, she glimpsed a tall man several feet back, hands in hip pockets, staring at something left of the door. Skewed as his face was through the magnifier, she felt a small shock at that ragged dark-blond hair, the same as Dennis's.

Then he turned his head, looked straight at her. In the obscure corridor lighting, she could not determine the color of his eyes, but it was their fierceness that stunned her. And suddenly he looked nothing like his brother.

Swallowing a knot of apprehension, she threw back the bolt and chain and opened the door.

"Mr. Rubens?"

Azure eyes. Slowly they widened. "Ms. Stowe?"

She stuck out her hand. "Pleased to meet you."

He nodded. His grip was firm, warm. She drew back quickly, and stepped aside. "I'm sorry I couldn't meet you below."

She gestured for him to enter the tiny suite, then closed the door. When she turned, he stood next to the coffee table, eliminating air and space by his tall, honed body.

"Won't you sit down?" she asked, keeping her gaze on the furniture rather than on him.

He sat. And for the first time, she noticed his black jeans and boots and the navy bomber-style jacket hanging open to a gray V-necked polo shirt. He looked up, and she saw sorrow deepen the hue of his eyes, and something shifted in her chest. "Would you like some coffee?" She motioned to the kitchenette.

"No, thanks." The darkness of his voice shivered across her skin. "If it's all the same to you, I'd like to know what happened to my brother." Imperceptibly his mouth softened. "Other than dying."

Savanna remained beside the TV cabinet. "He and Elke were heading for Comayagua. They had scheduled to meet with a doctor, an internist, an expert in colon problems. Dennis had a patient who needed part of his large intestine removed and this surgeon was one he trusted to do the operation."

She caught herself wringing her hands, and moved to sit in the chair across the coffee table, across from the man who was now, by all technicalities, Christopher's father. "Elke went along. Originally she had planned to stay home, but Dennis—" Savanna studied her fingernails; they needed clipping "—Dennis wanted them to have some time alone together, just the two of them. They were seldom able to get away as a couple. Life in Central America is not easy, Mr. Rubens. Especially not with…"

Christopher. She held his gaze, determined to impress on him that his brother and sister-in-law were neither whimsical nor flighty. Nor irresponsible.

Dennis was not like the man who sat four feet away—according to the tales she had heard from her best friend.

"The bodies?" he asked.

"The crash…" She swallowed hard. Concentrated on kinder images of her friends. "It burned." *To cinders.* "We held a small memorial yesterday."

For a long time he stared at his hands clasped between his knees. A black-banded wristwatch edged from the jacket's left cuff. "Where's the boy?"

She sensed Will Rubens wanted to get up and pace. Or leave the room. Go home.

"Christopher's sleeping." She inclined her head. "In there."

"He's here?" Rubens darted a look left. "You brought him to Alaska?" *Are you crazy?* His eyes burned with the words.

Savanna aligned her shoulders. "Yes, I brought him. *He's* the reason I'm here and why we're having this conversation. Your brother's last request was for Christopher to live with you in the event he and Elke—" *Oh, God.* "In the event they…died before their son was of an independent age."

Alarmed, Rubens sat back. "Are you kidding? I can't take the kid. I fly people into the wilderness all summer, and skiers and boarders up mountains in the winter. Who's going to look after him when I'm gone on those trips?" Abruptly he rose to pace from TV to hallway. Back and forth. Scraping a hand through his hair. Muttering, "I can't do it. The time schedule…"

"Mr. Rubens, if you could calm yourself…"

He barked a laugh. "Calm myself? Lady, first you inform me my brother and his wife are dead, then you tell me I've inherited their kid. How do you expect me to react?"

"With responsibility," she retorted.

His head jerked. "You think I'm not responsible? Do

you have any idea what it takes to fly into a mountain range with six people aboard a helicopter?"

The way Dennis and Elke had four days ago. "Yes," she said steadily. "I do. And, please. Could you speak with a normal tone? You'll wake Christopher with your shouting."

He stopped, once more running a hand through his shaggy hair. "I wasn't shouting."

"Your voice is raised."

"I wasn't shouting," he repeated stubbornly.

"Okay. We agree to disagree. Let that be the only thing."

A snort. She ignored it. "What matters at the moment is that you are now Christopher's guardian." *And father.*

He continued to pace. "Why the hell would Dennis make this—this request when I don't know the first thing about kids."

"But you do," she said patiently. If the situation hadn't been so serious, she might have laughed at his expression. "You used to volunteer for Big Brothers, although you stopped that a couple of years ago when you got involved coaching Little League teams during the daylight season."

His blue eyes pinned her. "Been busy, have you?"

Gossiping, his gaze accused. Except, she hadn't; she hated idle chatter. "Shane down at the desk volunteered the information." She lifted a brow. "Your fishing buddy?"

And Elke. Elke had told her more than Savanna wanted to know about the notorious freewheeling Will Rubens.

He grunted. "Shane's flapping his gums, as usual."

She had no idea what Shane's "usual" was. "Don't blame him. I made some inquiries before I set out on this trip." Like contacting Elke's grandmother and longtime resident, Georgia Martin, as well as Starlight's mayor, Max Shepherd. "I was not about transfer a ten-year-old from the only home he's known to this frozen tundra without investigating *who* he'd be living with for the next decade." She gestured to the rust-colored sofa. "Would you please sit down so we can go over the issues?"

"What are you, a teacher?" he grumbled, but did as she requested.

"Actually, I teach special-needs students, though I began in ESL—English as a second language." She hesitated, then decided if they were to get on the same page, he had to know the wheres and whys of her history with his family. "Elke and I were roommates at Stanford and became best friends. It didn't matter that she married Dennis, we continued to keep in touch through the years. Then I moved to Cedros and began teaching there." She paused, letting this brother absorb the information. "When Christopher went into third grade, Elke and Dennis asked me to set up a behavior intervention program for him."

"Behavior intervention?" Rubens shot a look toward the bedroom as if Christopher might appear, fangs bared. "Like those nannies on TV?"

"No, I assist children with Autistic Spectrum Disorders, or ASD as we know it."

His head came around slowly. "Autistic…?"

"Yes," she confirmed so there would be no mistake. "As you probably know, Christopher has Asperger's Syndrome. It's a form of ASD. A milder form," she added when he set his hands on his knees, ready to spring into a mode of action. "But autism nonetheless."

"Dennis never said anything about autism."

Savanna couldn't look away. "I'm sorry, Mr. Rubens. Maybe they were afraid to tell you."

"I'm his brother." He shook his head slightly. "*Was* his brother." Again the blueness of his eyes startled her. "He should have told me."

Oh, Dennis, she thought. *Why didn't you forewarn him? The child is his, after all.* "Yes, he should have." The omitted fact spoke more than she wanted to consider about Will Rubens.

Again, he scraped at his hair. The result left a rumpled look she imagined he saw in the mirror each morning. She looked away.

"Guess I had that coming," he continued. "Dennis and I…our relationship went by the wayside after— Ah, hell. Look, Ms. Stowe. I can't look after the boy…Christopher. My work takes me miles from home and it's dangerous. Anything can happen to a helicopter in the mountains. And besides, my place…my *life* isn't set up for kids, never mind one with problems. Have my brother's lawyer contact me and I'll arrange to give him complete permission to put the boy into foster care or adopted into a loving and trustworthy family."

"Mr. Rubens—"

"Will. Please." Suddenly his head swung left and his body jerked.

Christopher stood in the bedroom doorway, hands fluttering at his sides. He had removed his pajamas, put on the jeans and blue sweatshirt he'd worn during today's trip. His sneakers were laced.

A stream of accelerated speech poured from his mouth. "Anything-can-happen-to-a-helicopter-in-the-mountains."

Rubens released a throaty sound. The boy turned. "Daddy?"

Oh, God, he'd mistaken Will for Dennis. Savanna grabbed her copy of the laminated agenda and hurried to the boy. "Christopher. This is your Uncle Will. Remember I told you—" *a hundred times* "—that we were coming to Alaska to see your uncle? This is him."

As Christopher rushed forward to crowd her space and look straight into her eyes, a small thrill struck her heart. In the past two days he hadn't made eye contact with her once. He'd been anxious and worried and disoriented, wholly out of his routine.

"Savanna! How come Uncle Will looks like Dad?"

"Because he's his brother." *Even though he's much taller and bigger and his eyes are another color.* "We'll talk more in the morning, okay, pal? Now it's time for bed." She held up the agenda, pointed to the tenth number. "See. Bedtime. Take off your day clothes and put on your pajamas."

"Oh, yeah." He turned and disappeared back into the bedroom.

"Excuse us," she said to Rubens and followed Christopher.

She was helping the boy back under the covers when Dennis's brother came to the door. "Anything I can do?" he asked.

"We're almost done."

"He always like that?"

She shot him a look. "I'll be right out, Mr. Rubens. Then we'll talk."

Big and bold, he remained leaning in the doorway with those watchful eyes. She turned away, though the skin beneath her sweater grew uncomfortably warm. The man was like no other she'd met. Yes, she had known overconfident, arrogant males—she'd seen them in the Third World carrying guns—but Will Rubens needed no gun. His confidence stemmed from an innate source.

After tucking the covers around Christopher, she leaned down and whispered in his ear, "Go to sleep, pal. Get a good night's rest."

The boy closed his eyes. For several moments, she watched him, waiting. His mouth drooped, emitting the little snore; he was asleep.

She brushed back his hair—the aged-gold shade of his

father's—and dropped a kiss on the child's temple. Christopher disliked hugs and kisses unless he initiated them, so Savanna contented herself with these sweet furtive rituals.

"Wow, fast sleeper." Rubens spoke from the doorway where he still lounged. "Wish I was so lucky."

"He wasn't always as quick. Prior to his eighth birthday, he had a hard time falling asleep. The slightest noise would wake him." She walked to where Rubens stood backlit by the soft glow of the lamps in the living quarters. Hands in rear pockets, he leaned against the doorjamb, comfortable with studying her. She hugged her waist.

Quietly he said, "Never heard someone repeat entire sentences like that."

"He's very bright, Mr. Rubens. You might say he's gifted. But he's still autistic, which means his development is not the same as most children. For example, if you asked him to name a very small item, he might say the electrons around the nucleus of a helium atom."

"Really?" Awe gripped his voice.

"Really."

He looked past her. "Sounds like he's pretty special."

"He's incredible."

Ruben's attention reverted to Savanna. "You love him."

She didn't waver. "With all my heart."

For a long moment he held her in place with his eyes. "How long did you work for my brother?"

"Three years. Initially it was a couple times a week, but because Elke was like a sister…" She looked back at the bed. "When he was born, they asked me to be Chris's godmother."

He didn't respond. Not a flicker of an eyelash.

"Anyway," she continued, disquieted with his scrutiny, "Elke cut back her hours at the clinic to be with Christopher in the afternoon. I taught her how to handle his behaviors, to work with routines." And a thousand other strategies Savanna couldn't explain in one evening.

"Why did it take so long before he was diagnosed?"

"They suspected something was amiss when Chris was three. He hadn't started talking yet, and when he finally did, it was mostly repetitive. He also didn't play with your typical toys, like trucks and cars." She sighed. "At first, Elke tried to deal with the situation on her own, but she found it…exceedingly difficult." She released a heavy breath. "That's when I came into the picture."

Still he did not let her pass through the doorway, and his eyes snared her with that dawn-dusk blue. "I've never worked with kids like him," he said.

"Then you'll learn."

He pushed away, walked to the suite's entry door. "Have the lawyer contact me, Ms. Stowe. I'll make the arrangements for you to take the boy back to the Outside."

"Mr. Rubens—"

He turned, eyes hard. "You have my number. Call me in the morning and we'll discuss it further. Good night." Stepping into the hotel corridor, he pulled the door closed.

Savanna's heart thudded in her chest. From what she had observed, Will Rubens was not Dennis. He was not gentle or compassionate or caring. Instead she had brought Christopher into an environment far from conducive to his optimum upbringing. How could she leave him with this man, this brother who was the inversion of the one she'd come to respect and admire?

Dennis, how could you have been so reckless?

But she knew why he'd done it. She understood his reasoning to bring Christopher without warning.

Dennis had relied on his memories. On the one factor that made Will Rubens human. With Christopher, he'd gifted his brother part of his heart.

Chapter Two

Will tossed the keys to the SUV onto the kitchen counter. Beyond the window above the sink, a clear moon cut an icy hole in the starry night.

What was he going to do about the kid—hell, the *woman?* How could she have brought the boy so far north without checking with him first? And Dennis…what the hell was *he* thinking? *Had* been thinking…?

God, his brother. For two long minutes Will leaned his hands on the counter and hung his head, battling the tears, knowing grief and guilt would lie on his soul for years. Dennis, his lone sibling, the one person in the world who had taken a seventeen-year-old Will under his wing when their mother died. The last remaining part of Will's blood, the only part he had loved beyond words. Wasn't that why he'd offered the child when Dennis explained his sterility?

I love you, man, Will had told his brother the moment the notion entered his mind. *Let me do this for you, okay?*

And so they had. Amidst the fighting between Elke and her mother and grandmother. In the end, Elke had won, had conceived, but Dennis had taken her away from Alaska forever.

God almighty, why *hadn't* he been more communicative? Will thought for the millionth time. Called more often? Invited his brother back for some fishing or trail biking? Things they'd done in younger years.

Dammit, these days with e-mail and instant messaging the excuses were just that. Excuses.

And now it was too late. Too late for Will and Dennis— but worst of all, too late for the kid.

His phone blinked another message. He hit Play. "Hey Will," Josh's youthful voice exclaimed. "Thought you'd be home by now. Well…um…I had tons of fun tonight. Even though you yell and scream a lot and pitch like a girl." Will's mouth twitched. "Juuust kiddin'. Thanks, Will. See ya Saturday."

Saturday. Three days from now Will would be standing in the dugout with Josh's Little League team, coaching and handing out last-minute instructions and pep talks.

Sixty minutes, that's all Will had given Josh tonight.

Guilt, the damn gut clincher.

The kid hadn't said a word, but Will knew disappointment. Josh had hoped for more than a few practice pitches and hits in Starlight Park. He'd counted on Will taking him for a soda at Pete's Burgers. Instead Will opted to drop the boy off early at his mother's house. Which was another problem. Valerie had met him at the door with her hungry eyes and sweet, begging smile.

For her sake, he wished he felt the same.

The Stowe woman whipped through his mind. No sweet-

ness there, except for Christopher. That bun of red hair was
a dead ringer for her bristly spine and rigid rules. And those
eyes. Green as a jalapeño pepper with twice the bite.

He figured her to be in her late thirties. Her eyes were no
longer young or innocent. But then, living amidst Central
American poverty with merciless sun beating down on that
pale, freckled skin, he supposed she'd earned every one of
those creases.

No, she wasn't Valerie. Valerie of the tall, slim body she
worked incessantly to keep toned and trim. But neither was
he interested in Valerie, much to Josh's dismay. Will knew
the kid wished for a connection between the adults. Trouble
was, he wasn't drawn to neediness.

Tonight she had asked him inside and, as always, he'd
reneged. Being a big bro to Josh did not mean being a big
date for Valerie.

Not that he didn't date. He did. But mixing his volunteer
work with desperate women wasn't part of the picture.
Besides, he'd tried that last year with Valerie and it hadn't
worked—not for him.

He shrugged out of his jacket and tossed it onto a chair.
Before he fell over, he needed a shower. Josh. Old Harlan's
musty cabin clung to his T-shirt.

God, had it only been twelve hours since he'd flown up
the river?

He'd risen at dawn every day this week, flying his Jet
Ranger loaded with sports fishermen and hikers into the
Wrangell or Chugach mountains and chartering glacier
tours. Later, during the long daylight hours of summer, he'd
add fighting forest fires to the list.

Today, he'd flown up the Susitna River—Big Su to the
locals—to bring old Harlan supplies and make sure the old
man had survived another winter. After landing the bird in

a space wide as a thumbprint a hundred yards from Harlan's cabin, Will had spent the day with his friend chopping wood and digging a new hole for an outhouse. Tonight, his muscles whined at the slightest movement.

Sleep. His eyelids suddenly sagged. Bushed and filled with a bellyfull of sorrow, he stripped off his clothes and turned on the shower. Give him his bed and let him die for a week.

He was there when the phone rang again.

"Mr. Rubens, it's Savanna Stowe."

As if he'd need a reminder with that voice. He pushed up on the pillow. "Yeah?"

"Sorry to bother you so late, but I wonder if you'd like to have breakfast with us here at the lodge. My treat, of course."

He remembered her mouth. Fine and full. He imagined it holding a smile for his answer. "All right. What time?"

"Would eight o'clock work for you?"

Not eight, but eight *o'clock*. She was nothing like the women in Alaska or any he'd known elsewhere. "Sure. See you then."

"Thank you."

He hung up before she said good-night.

Good-night was personal and he wanted her and the boy on a plane back to the Outside tomorrow.

The minute he strode into the restaurant, she saw him. A man of sizable height and broad shoulders, his tarnished-gold hair askew from the wind, his cheeks ruddy from the crisp morning air. A brown suede jacket soft with creases and scuffs hung open to a sweater mirroring the Caribbean blue of his eyes. One day, she realized with a jolt, Christopher would replicate this man. Already, the long bone structure was in place, the dimpled cheeks.

"Sorry I'm late," Rubens said, slipping into the chair across the table from Savanna.

"No need to apologize. It's only seven minutes past."

He shot her a look, then slipped off the expensive jacket and hung it over the back of his chair. His gaze flicked to Christopher tracing a finger along an Alaskan river on the creased map he'd dug from his red and yellow knapsack.

"Chris," she said. "Remember your Uncle Will? He came to see us last night."

"Yeah." The boy remained focused on the charted page.

"Uncle Will is going to eat breakfast with us."

"You okay with this, boy?" Will asked.

This. That they were about to discuss his life. "Uh-huh," the child responded, intent on the highways of Alaska.

Savanna interjected, "Christopher knows why we've come to our most northern state, Mr. Rubens, and that you are now his legal guardian. We've talked about it many times."

"Many times," Christopher repeated, finger following the Tok Highway.

"Good." Rubens frowned. "Can we cut the formalities? Most folks call me Will. The other two percent call me names I'll leave with them." A lopsided grin spun through her middle.

The shapely brunette who had served Savanna coffee, approached with a fresh carafe. "Hey, Will. Thought you always caught breakfast at Lu's."

"Mindy." He held out his mug for her to fill. "As they say, a change is as good as a rest."

"Better not let Lu hear you say that." Her eyes fastened on his face. "Gonna be at the dance Saturday night?"

Eyes on Savanna, he took a sip of coffee. "Maybe."

"Haven't seen you there for a couple weeks." The woman gave him a McDreamy smile. "You work too hard. I was talking to Valerie, and she said you were up to Harlan's this week. How is he?"

"Grouchy as ever, but he's in good spirits—"

"Excuse me," Savanna interrupted. "Can we do the chitchat another time and order our breakfast?"

Unruffled, Will sat back with a slow crooked grin.

Mindy's mouth tightened. "Sure."

"For my boy, toast with the crusts cut off, and peanut butter and orange juice." Savanna almost laughed when Will's eyebrows aviated at her possessive words. "Cereal and fruit for me." She motioned across the table. "Will?"

He ordered the special: eggs over easy, sausages, sourdough toast, a rasher of hash browns and a triple decker of pancakes. After the waitress left, he remained relaxed in his chair. "*My* boy?"

Savanna sipped her coffee. "It's easier than explaining the situation."

Under the table his knee nudged hers, and they each shifted in their chairs. "Which is why we're here," he said. "Do you have the lawyer's number and my brother's will with you?"

She dug into her purse, drew out a business card. "I have a certified copy of the testament, yes. However, Mr. Silas will also send you a certified edition."

"Huh. Typical lawyer to take his sweet-ass time about what's important. Why didn't he send me one up-front or, better yet, contact me himself?"

Savanna hoped her eyes conveyed her irritation. "First, I'd appreciate you don't swear in front of Christopher. Second, Mr. Silas and I thought it best if I came and talked with you first."

"And bring along your…charge." His gaze took in Christopher, head bent low over Alaska. A blond lock grazed the tattered edge of the map.

"Yes." She handed him the card. "That's Mr. Silas's office and cell number." Next she slid the envelope across the table. "First page explains everything."

She watched him file the card in his wallet, then remove the document. She knew its words blindfolded. *In the event that both my wife, Elke, and I die, I appoint my brother William Faust Rubens of Starlight, Alaska, and owner/operator of Rubens Skylines and biological father of our son Christopher William Rubens (born March 4, 1997) as his own to rear and educate and parent until Christopher William Rubens reaches the age of maturity and self sufficiency.*

A clear and concise request.

He laid the sheet on the table before reading the next paragraph, the one outlining Dennis's instructions that if after every initiative had been taken and the transition between Christopher and Will still failed, she, Savanna Lee Stowe was to raise the child.

His eyes resembled the deep navy shadows along the glacial waters they had flown over yesterday. "Dennis should've warned me. This isn't fair."

"When is life fair? Do you think it's fair to—" She cast a sideways glance in Christopher's direction. Will's silence spurred her on. "Your brother didn't warn you, because he knew what your response would be."

"If he knew, why put it in writing?"

"Because," she said softly, "he never believed for one second this day would come."

His eyes held hers. And she saw again the blue wash of grief. He looked at Christopher, oblivious to the life-altering events surrounding him.

"It won't work," Will muttered. "I'm not parental material."

"I beg to differ. You've volunteered—"

"Key word. *Volunteered.*"

"Still. You're familiar with how children behave. You're good with them, even the toughest." That much Shane had told her when he'd noticed Christopher's restless hands down in the lobby.

Again a soft snort. "The toughest isn't anything like…"

Like Christopher, unpredictable and attuned to his own world. Weird to those who did not understand the underlying genius of the autistic or the quicksilver mood changes, the panics, the rages.

"I'm sure," she murmured. "But were they your own flesh and blood?"

Compact black lashes blinked. "What exactly are we talking about here, Ms. Stowe?"

A stain of warmth crept up her neck. "Elke mentioned the—" she peeked at Christopher "—procedure you undertook to help them eleven years ago."

He sat back. His foot bumped hers, and she carefully slid it beneath her chair. "Seems my life's been a regular open book."

"Elke didn't go into details. Just that Dennis was…" *Sterile.* "And about…your very generous…offering."

"I was young and stupid."

"You were a man who loved his brother," she countered. That caught him. He glanced away. "It was a long time ago."

"And you'd think twice before doing it today."

His eyes hardened. "Yes."

"Why? Because of the result or because of the consequences?"

He toyed with his mug. "Both. And because of the life I live now." He nodded toward the windows and Main Street with its one block of quaint Old West storefronts and mud-covered trucks parked along the curbs of a narrow strip of asphalt. "It's not easy in Alaska."

"And Central America is?"

"You don't give up, do you?"

"I'm Christopher's godmother. My responsibility is to him and to your brother and his wife. But most of all to you, Mr. Rubens."

"Me."

"Yes, you." Common sense said to take Christopher and leave, but she could not refuse the last wish of her friends. It was up to her to follow through with their request— incongruous as it seemed, given this man's goals and life-style. "Both Elke and Dennis wanted this. They gave me specific instructions—" *in case* "—to acquaint you with your nephew, and vice versa, to make sure you both have an equal chance."

"It won't work."

She sighed. She was getting nowhere with him. "Will—"

"Savanna." Elbows on the table's edge, he leaned in close. She saw individual whiskers on his upper lip and along his jaw. He hadn't shaved after rising from bed, and the male essence of that went through her like a streak of hot sunshine. "As soon as we're done eating," he continued, "I'm driving you both back to Anchorage and you're catching the first flight to the Lower 48."

Christopher lifted his head. "Back to Honduras?"

"No, pal," Savanna said, giving Will her best stern look. "We're staying in Starlight."

"Forever?"

"Hopefully for a long time."

Thankfully, Mindy the waitress arrived with their food. For several seconds Savanna watched Will and he watched her while the waitress doled out the plates, asking Christopher to move his map so she could set down his plate.

The boy disregarded her.

Savanna slid her hands gently beneath Christopher's, lifting him and the page free from the table's surface.

"Doesn't he hear?" Mindy asked.

"He has difficulty—"

"He's autistic," Will cut in.

"Awesome-tistic," Christopher corrected without raising his head from the map. "I'm awesome-tistic and you're an NT."

The waitress looked as if she'd swallowed a raw egg. "Sorry. Um, well... Holler if you need anything else." She scurried off.

Savanna picked up her cereal spoon. "Let's eat."

Will studied Christopher. "What's an NT?"

"Neurotypical," the boy said, checking both sides of his toast; finding them acceptable.

Savanna explained, "People who are not aspies, who don't have ASD, are sometimes called NTs." She winked at Will, hoping he would clue in and let the topic drop.

"You mean nor—"

"Yes. Exactly. But that's an old term."

"Sorry, didn't know."

"Now you do." She leveled her gaze across the plates of food. This was his child. His obligation according to Dennis's last request. Given the choice she never would have brought Christopher to Alaska, to this man with his wily handsome eyes. She would have taken Christopher to Tennessee, to her hometown where her brother and family lived, and reared the boy as her own.

But she had to give Will Rubens the conditional twelve weeks.

She turned to the boy. "It's time to eat your breakfast, buddy. You can study the map once you've finished your juice and toast."

"Triangles," he said.

She cut the bread into the geometric shapes; the boy chose one and bit off a corner. "Chris likes his food cut into precise pieces and I help him get it right." Over the table she caught Will's gaze. *Give the man something positive, Savanna.* "He's also a pro at drawing maps and trains."

"Trains." The boy munched his toast and latched on to his current pet topic. "They were once steam engines, y'know? People think they were invented by a Scotsman James Watt in 1769, but he only improved the mechanics and designed a separate condenser. The real inventor was Thomas Savery in 1698 in England."

"Yes," she conceded. "And you sketch those old engines with a lot of detail."

Christopher spread a pat of peanut butter from a tiny packet the waitress had set on the side of his plate.

Savanna glanced at Will. A little hammer tripped in her chest. It had been a long time since a man looked at her with such intensity. Softly she said, "I know this is all a shock to you, Mr. Rubens. However, Chris and I will remain at the lodge for the interim until I find a place to rent. It's important you and your…nephew begin the changeover as soon as possible."

The man across from her dug into his eggs. "There's a flight out of Anchorage this evening. I can have you there in two hours, then you can sleep on the way home, wherever that is."

"Tennessee." Savanna set her fork against her plate. "You might as well understand. We are not leaving."

Slowly he laid down his utensils. "Fine." From his hip

pocket he drew out his wallet; tossed down a twenty. "This conversation is over." Pushing back his chair, he offered her a nod, then walked out of the restaurant.

Well. That certainly was interesting. At least he hadn't said flat-out no.

Packing the New York businessmen's fishing gear into the storage compartment of the helicopter, Will thought long and hard about Savanna Stowe. Hell, he'd been thinking long and hard about the woman since he heard her message on his answering machine.

Five foot whatever of unadulterated obstinacy, that's what she was. Where did she come off figuring he could manage a kid who had those kinds of behaviors and learning problems—with him flying all over hell's half acre at the drop of a hat?

Kid is Dennis's.

Yeah, and the boy had *some* of his brother's DNA, but he also had Elke's gene pool running in his blood. And Will hadn't been a fan of Elke. After conceiving—an analytical experience he'd never go through again *for any reason*—she'd coaxed Dennis into that jungle. Where he had died in a fixed wing, a single-engine plane, not entirely different from the bird Will loaded.

Ah, Dennis.

Why hadn't he returned to Alaska after the boy was born? They needed doctors like him up here just the same as down there. But, no. Elke got that damned do-gooder notion in her head and thought Dennis, with his skills, could save more souls in those godforsaken jungles than in Alaska. As if they didn't have one-room shacks and diseases in this neck of the woods.

Truth be known, Elke hadn't wanted to live near her mother who had, by the way, considered Dennis' younger brother a "juvenile thrill seeker." So rather than stand up to Rose Jarvis, Elke chose to run and take Dennis along.

With a last shove, Will secured the expensive black tackle boxes the Henricks twins would use to fly-fish off the shores of the Big Su. This was the brothers' fifth trip to Alaska, and they always used Will as their pilot of choice. There were others—Ike Markham, Vince Forrest—but none flew the risky areas.

Only Will.

And Savanna Stowe wanted him to play Daddy.

He climbed from the helicopter's cargo area and motioned to his two passengers gazing out of the windows of the tiny airstrip's service station. Airtime.

The men, carrying shoulder packs, headed through the door, into the bright afternoon sun. As Will gave instructions, he settled them onboard.

A thousand feet up, the Talkeetna Mountains bumped along the western horizon and beyond them Denali, Alaska's highest rock, speared the sky like a chunk of white chocolate.

As always sky time was like touching heaven. For a moment Will imagined Dennis beside him with that crazy, slanted grin, eyes full of mischief—the way Christopher's had been when he'd said "awesometistic."

Will's heart thumped in his chest. God have mercy, what had he been thinking?

He couldn't let the boy go.

Christopher was the one piece, the final piece linking Will to his brother.

Your flesh and blood, she'd said.

My family, he thought. And suddenly his eyes stung, and a knot wedged in his throat. Since Aileen died he hadn't wanted family. Not in this lifetime, not in this *world.* And now here was the child of his brother, orphaned…

The bird swayed a little around a gust of air. Damn woman was right. He had to take the kid. Had to. Somehow.

Pulse rapid with the resolution, he wondered what she would say when he hunted her up later today. Likely she'd be pleased as a bear in a berry bush in August while *his* gut felt like he'd left it back on the helo pad.

Elke's grandmother Georgia Martin lived in a green clapboard house. Savanna had seen pictures of the place two years ago when the woman sent Elke a Christmas card straight out of the past.

"I haven't seen her in eleven years," Elke had said at the time as they studied the photographs of the small home amongst eighty-foot evergreens. "My mom hadn't wanted me to do what I did."

To clinically conceive a child. One from Dennis's eight-year younger brother and a man Elke had known growing up in Alaska. A man her mother, Rose, had labeled a diabolical daredevil who would one day end up killing himself or, worse, Dennis.

Georgia had told Rose to leave matters alone; the situation was between consenting adults.

The advice had fallen on deaf ears, and so to stop his mother-in-law's haranguing and save his brother's honor, Dennis had moved Elke to Washington state and eventually to Honduras.

Nevertheless, the pictures arriving out of the blue opened a door Elke had stepped through.

Now, with Christopher at her side, Savanna walked down a graveled road bordered by homes from an era that had fought World War Two, and which spruces, birch and willows all but sheltered from sight.

Last night's dusting of snow crunched beneath their footfalls. "Do you see it, Chris?" she asked the boy tapping his mittened fingertips together in time with each step. After Will left their breakfast table, she had taken Christopher to Larson's General to buy him a silver parka, along with a red polar fleece hat, scarf and mittens. Initially, she'd wanted wool, until he'd complained over its texture and weight. "Can you see a green house with a black roof?"

Through the trees she peered up trails winding to front doors of homes of various shapes and sizes and ambiances, like the two log cabins with moose racks hanging from porch roofs. Pickups and SUVs were parked on partially melted pathways.

"No. No." Christopher tapped his fingertips faster, his agitation about Georgia increasing. He disliked meeting new people, hated detours from his routine. "This could be the wrong street," he commented anxiously, his toe-rocking walk angling his body slightly forward.

"When I phoned this morning, Great-Nana said she lived on Mule Deer Road."

"Yeah, Mule Deer Road. We're meeting Great-Nana on Mule Deer Road." He looked straight ahead. "She lives in a green house on Mule Deer Road."

"Keep searching for it, pal."

Elke's grandmother had cried when she heard her great-grandson was three short blocks away. Savanna had insisted they walk the seven-minute distance rather than have Georgia pick them up at the lodge. Christopher needed the brisk air and exercise, and Savanna needed to scope out Starlight.

The town called to her. In some ways it reminded her of the Honduran villages, the camaraderie of its citizens. She wondered where Will lived, if his home resembled those on Mule Deer Road with its cozy down-home aspect that confirmed the door was always open, the coffee on the back burner.

Starlight citizens, she suspected, knew each other's lives as well as their own. The way Mindy the dancing waitress and Shane the salmon-fishing desk clerk knew Will.

And what would Georgia say about Mr. Will Rubens? Georgia, who had known Will as a child younger than Christopher?

"There it is." He pointed to a tiny olive house set amidst sturdy-trunked spruce and tall, elegant paper-barked birch at the road's end.

"Ready?" she asked, watching smoke curl from the brick chimney. Around them, lazy snowflakes spiraled from a slate sky and muffled their voices.

Christopher's fingertips tapped fast as pistons. "Uh-uh."

She touched his cheek and his eyes drew to hers. "Christopher. This is your great-nana's house. She is Mommy's grandmother."

"Mommy's not here. She'll never be here."

Oh, God. He's recalling the terrible news.

Fingers tapping, tapping. "Mom's in heaven with Dad."

Savanna's chest agonized. "Yes, darlin'."

"I don't want to go to heaven because then I can't go back home."

She blinked hard and stopped to zip up the coat he'd undone as they walked. His gaze fastened on the house. "Is Great-Nana's house a different home? Does she like maps?"

"Her home will be different because we haven't seen it yet. And you'll have to ask her if she likes maps." He'd spent hours on the plane studying the state's cities, towns, lakes, rivers, mountains. She gave him a quick hug. "Remember, be polite."

"Okay."

An ache ringed her heart. Elke should be here introducing her child to her family's oldest relative.

They started up the narrow trail through the trees, past the rusted white pickup and a dented wheelbarrow potted with last summer's annuals, to the front door.

The house had been given a coat of paint in the past year. White shutters bracketed the single front window. Before Savanna could knock on the door, it opened and a tiny woman in whitewashed jeans and a pink sweatshirt smiled at them. Silver curls sprang wildly around her head as her clear-sky eyes beamed happiness.

"Well, now," she exclaimed. "If this just don't beat all."

"Georgia Martin?" Savanna asked.

"And you're Savanna Stowe." She spotted Christopher flapping his hands and her expression filled with instant love. "Christopher…"

"Chris, say hello to Great-Nana."

"Hello, Great-Nana."

"Just call me Nana, Chris."

"Nana." His gaze riveted on a small oil painting of a tabby cat in the entranceway. He rocked on his feet. "Cats are dangerous. They digest rodents because they're carnivores, and they scratch your skin."

"Only if they're scared, Christopher," Georgia said gently. She stepped aside. "Won't you come in?"

Savanna spoke softly. "Would you mind taking the picture away, Georgia?" On the phone at the lodge, while Christopher brushed his teeth, she had given the woman a brief summary of what to expect with the boy, although Elke and Georgia had discussed autism at length in letter and phone exchanges. This morning the old woman had mentioned a Siberian husky but no cats.

"Of course." Georgia took down the picture, shoved it into the drawer of a small antiquated hall table. "Tabs was once my pet."

Christopher's flapping lessened to finger tapping again, and Savanna led him into the house. "I'm so sorry to barge in on you like this," she said.

"Oh, honey, I'm glad you did, but heartbroken over the circumstances." Her eyes filled for a moment. "I was planning a trip down to see my granddaughter this summer. She's—*was* my sole relative."

"Elke was so looking forward to your visit." Savanna touched the shoulder of the boy at her side and smiled. "You still have Christopher."

"I do." Georgia rolled her lips inward, blinked back tears and walked back to a tiny, cluttered kitchen. "Would you like some coffee?"

"I'm fine. We had a big breakfast, thank you. Georgia, I know this is very presumptuous of me, but I need your help."

"Anything, honey." She darted a look at Christopher. "Is Will adamant?"

Over the lodge phone, Savanna had briefed her on Will, as well. "I'm working on that. It'll take some time."

Georgia laughed. "I'd say you have your work cut out for you, then. That boy has a stubborn streak twenty miles wide. But a good heart. What is it you need?"

"A place to stay while he and Christopher get to know each other." She watched the child walk to the living room, where he sat yoga-style on a large round rag rug beside a husky, its tail slowly beating the floor. "Is your dog good around children?"

"Blue loves kids," Georgia assured. "But arthritis is eating his hips and he's half-blind. Now, he pretty much sleeps the day away. Chris is okay with dogs, then?"

"Yes," Savanna conceded, and for a moment they observed boy and canine. "Let's hope your Blue helps him adjust over the next twelve weeks—and I won't have to make a decision."

The old woman's eyes narrowed. "Decision?"

"To take Chris back to my hometown in Tennessee—if he and Will don't connect." Savanna pulled the copy of Dennis's will from her purse. "Georgia, your granddaughter and Dennis requested…" How to explain to this sweet elderly grandmother? "I was their second option to raise him," she whispered in a rush before clamping her mouth shut.

Georgia read the highlighted paragraphs, her curls quaking from the tiny tremor of her head. Was she in the initial stage of Parkinson's?

"I'm sorry," Savanna whispered, picturing the latter phase of the disease. "I can't imagine how you must feel." *On top of everything else.*

The stationary quivered in the old woman's hands. "No, they were right. I'm too old and…" She folded the testament carefully. "Well." Eyes sharp as a blade, she handed back the copy. "Do you love my grandson?"

"As if he'd come from my own body."

"That's good enough for me."

Savanna's shoulders relaxed.

"But," Georgia said with a wink, "three months is a long time. Will and I just might convince you to become an Alaskan."

Chapter Three

They arranged for Savanna and Christopher to temporarily move into Georgia's home. Savanna had argued against the offer, but the old woman would not budge. She wanted a chance to know her great-grandson, she said. And Savanna. She wanted to understand the woman her granddaughter trusted with life's most precious gift.

They used Georgia's old truck to move the suitcases from the lodge. Done, they drove to Starlight Elementary where Savanna registered Christopher in fifth grade for the remainder of the school year.

She was walking through the six-o'clock dusk, back to the house from Larson's General, with three king salmon steaks, when Will came up the street in a red Toyota 4Runner.

"Hey," he said through the open window. Slowing to a crawl, he drove with his right hand atop the steering wheel while his left arm sat jacked on the sill. "Lodge said you'd checked out."

She stopped, the grocery sack swinging against her leg. "We moved in with Georgia Martin."

His brows jumped. "Didn't know you were acquainted."

"She's Christopher's great-grandmother."

"I know who she is, Savanna. I just didn't know you two knew each other, is all." His eyes were ebony in the dusk.

"We didn't until about eight hours ago. I needed a place to stay. She offered, so…here we are."

He stopped the truck. "Get in and I'll give you a lift."

"What for? It's right there." She pointed a hundred feet up the street where lights welcomed the old lady's home among the trees.

"Because," he said, "we need to talk."

"If it's about us leaving, I'm not interested."

"It's about Christopher. I've changed my mind." He nodded to the passenger seat. "Get in. Please," he added.

The *please* went through her like butter, but she forced herself not to give in too quickly. "Are you always this charming?"

His grin rippled across her stomach. "Only with certain women."

Certain women. She could imagine the type. Tittering at his whim. Blinking doe eyes. Women like Mindy the waitress, dreaming of dancing with the local macho pilot. *Dirty* dancing. Eager *young* women. Not one skipping toward menopause with the next handful of birthdays.

She raised her chin. She had not spent twenty years in the Third World without earning her wrinkles, her tough spine. Nine years and Will Rubens might, *might,* catch up to her wisdom.

"I am not certain women," she said. "And I do not take

orders easily." *Definitely not from young hotshots with dimples.*

He laughed. "Feisty is good."

She walked on. "We can talk at the house."

"Savanna…"

"The house," she called back.

"Fine."

She heard gears grind as the truck detoured around her and roared ahead. He veered into Georgia's driveway and slammed to a stop. Before she could catch her breath, he was out of the cab, arms crossed and waiting like the headmaster of a nineteenth-century school.

She walked past him. He had some growing up to do.

"Damn it, Savanna." He wheeled to stride beside her. "You said the house."

"When you act your age, we'll talk."

He caught her arm, halting them midlane. "Where the hell do you get off talking like that? I'm not your student and for damn sure you're not my mother."

Her heart bumped her throat. She'd forgotten his size. They stood in a forest of trees, in the dark, and who in Starlight would come to her rescue against the fun-loving, dancing Will Rubens? "Please take your hand off me," she said quietly.

His mouth thinned, but he did as she asked. "I want Christopher."

For an indefinite moment, they stared at each other and she thought, *The shape's all wrong.* Christopher didn't have Elke's eyes. *Will* dominated both the shape and color of Christopher's eyes. A little ruffle stirred under her heart. "Why?" she finally managed.

"Why? This morning all you wanted was for me to take him, and now you ask why? How's this—because he's my brother's kid?"

"Not good enough."

His mouth gaped.

"First of all, blood does not make a parent. Second, last night *and* this morning you—"

He held up his hands. "Okay, okay. I can't deny what I said before, but I've been thinking on it all day and I want a chance." A heavy sigh. "He's all I have left of…of Dennis."

Again that little bump in the throat. *Dennis,* she reminded herself. She would do this for Dennis…and Elke. "All right. We can meet in the morning and figure out the arrangements."

He looked at the house with its inviting face. "Understood. Tomorrow it is." Then added softly, "Thank you."

He walked back to his truck, night shadows swaying through the trees to brush his shoulders. She tried to ignore the shadow stealing into her heart.

With one hand holding a thermos of coffee, Will knocked on Georgia's door at 7:30 the next morning.

He should be at the flight service station getting ready for the two hikers he was flying into the Talkeetna Mountains in a couple hours. He never understood people hiking when the weather was ornery and unpredictable. But who was he to argue? Their decisions and money put food on his table.

In the pale dawn light, he studied the front yard with its spruce and birch, frosted from the overnight temperature. The ambience resembled his own property on the next street. Except, when he'd bought, the original structure hosted rot and decay and he had torn it down to build a log cabin. This August would mark his seventh in the house, still ranked "new" by Starlight standards. It's what he loved about the village, this reluctance to massacre the environment in the name of progress.

When he'd returned to his hometown eight years ago, it was to lick his wounds. To flee a broken heart. Broken because of Aileen, dying for the same altruistic reasons as Dennis had last Monday. What Will hadn't understood then was you can't hide from memories, that it takes time— *sometimes never*—for the mind to evict its awful images.

Thanks to Harlan those images had faded, finally. Harlan, former Nam vet, teaching orphaned seventeen-year-old Will to fly helicopters—a boy who eventually grew into a man, flying rich folk around California and who, one day years later, would return and use those skills in the Alaskan wilderness to erase the memory of his murdered sweetheart. A woman like Savanna, journeying into areas where poverty and gangs were medians of survival.

The door opened. "Morning, Will," Georgia greeted.

"Nana Martin."

"I suppose you're here to see Savanna and Christopher?"

"Yes, ma'am. Savanna's expecting me."

"Come in, then." She walked back to the kitchen.

Entering, he smelled breakfast and coffee, and followed the morning odors. At his house, he had made a plate of eggs and toast; though he had no trouble brewing his own coffee, he sometimes left the task to Lu over at Lu's Table with her Starbucks franchise.

At the kitchen table, Christopher munched his toast triangles. His blue sweater was inside out. Savanna stood leaning against the counter, coffee mug cozy between her hands, green eyes on Will. She'd pulled *her* blue sweater on properly—and over breasts, he noticed, which were a nice ample package. Her jeans fit a damn fine package, too.

He offered a nod. "Savanna. Figured we could talk before I head out for the day. Don't know what time I'll be back."

"Where are you going?"

"Talkeetna Mountains. Hikers," he added.

She turned toward the window. Mounds of crusted snow lay among the trees. "People hike this time of year?"

He lifted a shoulder. "Almost May. Not as cold as it looks." If the wind stayed down.

Her look took in Christopher, and Will understood. "This won't take long," he said. "We can talk out on the porch." After the boy reiterated Will's words verbatim in the lodge's room, he'd rather ask questions and discuss his plans away from little ears.

"Let me get my coat."

Outside, day was beginning to arrive. Pale-gray patches stitched themselves into evergreen tops. Will stepped from the rear stoop to walk through the trees. Brittle brown grass and glassy snow crackled under their boots. He loved early morning best. The quiet, the peace. Before people cluttered the day.

Stopping, he lifted his thermos, took a deep swallow of dark roast. "Why didn't you tell me you knew Georgia?"

Hands buried deep in her parka's pockets, Savanna edged beside him as he stood on the path among the hulking black spruce. He could smell her, a clear, pure scent of summer in the mountains—blue skies and meadows filled with dogwood.

"You didn't give me a chance."

She had him there. "Suppose I didn't," he admitted. "So. What's the story? She know about the boy's problem?"

"Yes. Elke told her right after she and Georgia started communicating in 2005."

He looked down at the top of her head barely reaching his collarbones. "They had remained estranged all those years?"

She lifted a shoulder. "As I'm sure you know, the reasons were profound."

Yeah, he knew all about those reasons. Elke's mother thought him "foolish and stupid" putting his life on the line because he liked riding motorcycles and flying helicopters, sky-diving and whitewater kayaking—and dragging his brother along.

Dennis, wanting to be a doctor from his tenth birthday.

No, there hadn't been any love lost between Will and Rose.

But Elke was the woman his brother had chosen from the time they hit puberty. In Will's mind she'd been weak-kneed in the face of Rose. But Dennis loved Elke, and Will loved his brother, end of story.

"Who contacted who first?" he asked.

"Georgia. After Rose died."

"Two years ago."

"Yes. She wrote a letter of regret and apology on Rose's behalf, and Elke accepted. They corresponded several times a month."

"When did you tell her about the crash?" His throat tightened. Thinking of Dennis, God, it was a slug to the gut every time.

"Yesterday morning. After our breakfast."

So. Georgia wasn't first on Savanna's list any more than she was in Dennis's will. Oddly, Will felt satisfaction in that. As a result Savanna Stowe deemed him Priority One. She might have moved Christopher into Georgia's house, but she had kept her promise to Dennis.

"I'd like a chance with Christopher," he said. "I'll hire a nanny for the days I'm flying and can't be with him or," he looked back at the house, "I'll make arrangements with Georgia." Though he hoped that necessity wouldn't happen.

"Georgia isn't capable of watching Christopher for long stretches. She's eighty-six with a possible onset of Parkinson's. However, I *am* capable. As I've explained, I'll be staying in Starlight until I see that Christopher has adjusted to you and his new home. And," she paused, "until I feel confident you're able to care for him. If not, we'll both be on the next flight out."

Will stared at her. If she wasn't a woman and if his mother hadn't whupped respect into him before she died, he'd tell Savanna Stowe in no uncertain terms to take a long hike into the mountains. She was using that superior attitude again. Like he had no sense, no brains. The way Rose had classified him.

Okay, fine. He'd play along. He wanted the kid. If that meant singing her tune, he'd sing. "Tell me what you want."

She blinked, no doubt surprised he'd acquiesced without a murmur.

"You'll need to readjust your flying time to be home when Christopher is finished with his day. He'll need your attention then."

"Seems he does fine with his maps." He skipped another look toward the house. "I saw him with a Game Boy in there."

She scowled. "Those are fine for emergencies. Look, except for his learning and some specific behaviors, Christopher is just a little boy. He requires stability *and* routine like other children. But he also requires a lot of mental stimulation. Which you'll need to provide."

"And if I don't he'll throw a tantrum, rip down curtains?" Will tried to joke.

Her pupils pinpricked. "Possibly. Imagine ignoring an active, anxious toddler."

Will couldn't imagine. The youngest kid he had coached was six. An age when they talked and walked and went to the washroom alone. When they could entertain themselves with a Tonka truck.

"Maybe he'll like playing on a Little League team."

She blew a soft sigh. "Will, have you read anything about Autism Spectrum Disorder or Asperger's Syndrome?"

"Checked the Internet a bit last night." Her scrutiny had him itching to pace. "Before that—" He shrugged.

"The Internet is a start. There's also the library or bookstores."

"Fine. What about his education at school?"

"I talked to the principal and the fifth-grade teacher at Starlight Elementary yesterday. They're willing to let me volunteer as Christopher's assistant for now. However, as his guardian, your input will be considered first and foremost."

"Seems you have it under control."

"Because my dedication is to Christopher, who needs an immediate routine. And sometimes even that doesn't work as planned. Today he'll be anxious. He won't be familiar with the school or the kids. And he'll worry they'll stare and tease."

Something shifted inside Will. He studied the house. Inside was a child vulnerable to the panorama of life. The thought of Christopher huddling in a corner because of some cruel gesture or word had Will pressing his lips together. For the first time he realized how much Savanna knew about the boy and how much he did not.

"Is that how it's always been, kids teasing him?"

"No. Honduran children seem kinder than North American kids. Probably because in the Third World they already have so little, differences are not as evident."

"I'll make sure no one teases him."

A sad smile. "You won't be with him every minute of every day, Will. There are going to be times his behavior will draw stares. The way he walks. His humming."

Flapping his hands. Repeating sentences and words. Will moved down the path a short way, thinking hard on all she had said. What training did he have to handle a kid with differences? With restrictions? None. Maybe he should let the boy go back to the Lower 48, live with Savanna.

Through the window of the house, he saw Christopher sitting at the table, probably working that pocket toy or poring over his maps. An isolated little kid who had Dennis's wheat hair, Elke's serious face.

Damn it. He had to make this work. For his brother, even for Elke. But more significantly for Christopher.

With a sigh he turned to Savanna. Her spruce-green eyes were determined; his decision made not a whit of difference. Christopher was her focus. If the boy stayed, she would stay. If Will changed his mind, she'd have the kid out of Starlight within the hour.

Her indifference on his behalf bothered Will. He wanted Savanna Stowe to care about what he thought, what he felt. Mostly he wanted her support, and the logic of that made no sense. He lived his life the way he liked, without a woman's whims or approval.

"Does he like school?" he asked, slamming the door on his emotional analysis.

Amusement sparked her eyes. "Oh, he loves school. He just wishes the other kids weren't there."

Will chuckled. "Did he say that?"

"The first day of every school year. As I've said, he has no desire to be with his peers."

"Because of the teasing."

"Because of his genetic makeup."

That stung. "I didn't give him autism, Savanna."

"Maybe not." Elke had fretted over the same possibility. "What I meant is that his condition won't seem so different or odd once you understand the underlying factors."

"What causes it?"

"They believe it's how the brain develops. Specifically,

deficits and delays in those areas dealing with social and emotional behavior and reasoning."

"Delays. You mean he'll be normal, *typical,* one day?"

"Like you and me? Not entirely. But he'll have mastered life skills that will assist him as an adult." A smile touched her mouth. "It's believed Einstein, Sir Isaac Newton and Henry Cavendish, the scientist who discovered hydrogen, all had a form of Asperger's. If that helps."

It didn't.

A weak sun peeked through the gray-blue patches, dusting the frosted trees in glitter. For a few moments they stood silent, contemplating the emergence of spring.

Will said, "This isn't all, is it?"

A head shake. "We've barely touched the surface. But with each day I'll explain more when a particular behavior crops up."

Will pursed his lips. "Seems he likes maps."

"You'll find he's very possessive about certain items. Like his maps, his knapsack, the sketchbook. He'll draw trains for hours. But he's averse to taking direction. Not because he's belligerent, but because he relates it to negativism. He needs a lot of praise and encouragement."

"Terrific. So how do I tell him when he's done something wro—inappropriate?"

"Why don't we take it one day at a time?"

He was all for that. What she had given him had overloaded his brain.

He studied her while she surveyed their surroundings.

She was small and curvy, with hair that spiraled around the shoulders of her black coat the way forest fires whorled into a night sky. Genetics had given her a linear nose, a little on the long side with tiny nostrils—and well-shaped lips. Kissable if he had an inkling. Which he did not.

On the whole, she matched nothing of what he found appealing in women. Her brows and lashes were auburn, her chin small and narrow. And she was shorter than he preferred. However, her smile was sincere and kind and he wished she'd volunteer it more often.

Suddenly he wondered about her age and how long she'd worked on foreign soil. "How old are you?"

Her head turned slowly, eyes wide and dark. "That's rude, don't you think? To ask a woman her age?"

He shrugged. "I figure with you and Elke being best friends you know *my* age." Lifting his eyebrows, he cut her a grin. "Fair is fair. And it's not like we're interested in each other."

She regarded him for a moment. "Forty-two."

"This year?"

"No." Her eyes flashed; he curbed a laugh.

Forty-three this year. A separation of nine years. He'd already had his thirty-fourth birthday.

"I think," she said, moving down the path toward the house, "we're done here."

"Are you planning to live with Georgia for the duration?"

She hesitated. "I'll be looking for a place to rent. Georgia is kind enough to have us stay, but I'd prefer not to take advantage."

Not with a high-maintenance kid. Will nodded. "I'll see what I can do."

"I wasn't asking."

"I know." He shifted on his feet. "Thanks for the information about…"

"His name is Christopher."

Was she for real? "I know that. Look, it may take a few months to adjust my schedule. I'm already booked into June."

"He doesn't have a few months, Mr. Rubens, so I suppose

it depends on what's most important to you. Your job or your nephew."

Damn the woman. "My job," he said, breathing deep for control, "pays the bills. It'll keep the boy in clothes and food with a roof over his head and a babysitter at his beck and call—"

"Babysitter?" Two steps and she was back within his space, a compact bundle of tenacity. "Christopher needs someone specialized in working with autistic children, Will. He'll need a behavior interventionist to help reinforce strategies to curb his anxiety and frustrations, establish boundaries. He may require an SLP. And you'll need to participate in his IEP. There's also the respite worker—"

He threw up his hands. "Whoa. Speak English. An IEP and SPL?"

"SLP. Speech language pathologist. An IEP is an individualized educational plan the school requires for his workload."

"Okay, understood, but a respite worker?"

"As sweet as Christopher is, *you'll* need breaks. Respite workers are trained in special needs."

"And where am I supposed to dig out this nugget of gold?"

"I don't know. Maybe instead of going dancing or playing pool, spend the time doing research."

"What? Where the hell do you get this sh—Argh!" He headed down the frozen path. "Elke, right?" Swinging around, he jabbed a finger in Savanna's direction. "Well, let me tell you something, Ms. Stowe. Her mother ruled the roost in that family, so I told Dennis not to marry the daughter. I also begged him not to leave Alaska. He'd started a fledgling practice right here, did you know that? But he wanted her and she wanted to be rid of Rose. And now they're dead. Because of her." The pain of it all had him breathing like a winded sled dog. "And here's another newsflash. I gave up 'craziness'—" he dittoed the air with quotation marks and a scowl "—the day Christopher was born. I don't drink, I don't smoke and if I play pool, it's once a month with good, decent folk. And, damn it, *yes,* I like dancing. You ought to try it sometime. Might loosen that block sitting on your shoulder."

Turning sharply, he strode for the back gate and alley that led to his cabin. *Damn* it. Forty-eight hours and the woman had his temper in a knot more times than in ten years.

"Will!"

She rushed after him. He strode on.

"Will, stop a minute. Please." Her fingers brushed his coat sleeve. "I'm sorry. You're right, I'm making assumptions when I shouldn't. It's… It's been a very grueling week, and I know that's no excuse. I apologize. Can we start over?"

One street over, a diesel engine fired into the morning quiet, and he knew his neighbor Nate Burns, their local flight-service controller, was bound for the airport.

Will took a deep breath. "Are we gonna argue every time something doesn't go your way?"

"That I can't promise, but I can give you honesty. If it means Christopher's rights versus yours, I'll choose his. Each and every time."

A heavy moment passed as his eyes held hers. Far in the distance his mind registered her green irises as beautiful with sun-gold dots dappling the outer rims. His gaze dipped to her slightly parted lips emitting a wisp of breath to the frosted air, and he wondered about the degree of warmth he'd feel there if he were to bend down and—

"Here's the deal," he said, annoyed because she confused him and had his libido running roughshod over his gray matter. "While you're in Starlight I'll respect you're Christopher's parental figure. But my free time is none of your business. Clear?"

"Only if—"

"It affects Christopher. It won't."

"Yes."

Again the long look. Again he felt a tickle in his gut. "I'll see you tonight when I get in."

He left her as he had last night. Standing among shadows. It wasn't until he slammed into his house that his words tracked back. *I'll see you.* Not, I'll see Christopher.

Will shook his head. The woman had his insides on a see-saw. One minute he was admiring her mouth, the next he wanted her out of state. He decided to go for a run.

Escaping, Will?

Shut up and get your gear.

Chapter Four

Six days later, Christopher's teacher phoned and left a message on Will's answering machine. She wanted to discuss present and future educational goals for his nephew.

Must be the IEP Savanna mentioned, he thought, driving into the school parking lot a half hour after the home-time bell.

A few kids still hung around the yard, playing a game of basketball on a cemented pad. He remembered those days when he'd been twelve, *right here,* joshing around with his buddies after sitting in a desk for five hours.

Those had been good days. Kind days.

His parents had been alive then, his brother down at Stanford and Aileen…sweet Aileen…had sat on the grass and watched Will and his pals show off, dribbling the ball, tossing it over their shoulders, twirling it on their fingertips, sinking pointers into the ratty net. He'd been the star player then, his sprout of height lending him a five-inch advantage to the rest of the group.

He had laughed in those days. Laughed and sent Aileen all sorts of mischievous grins. And she had held her hand over her mouth, giggled with her friends, but he'd known, clear as a July sky, that he would marry her one day.

God, how naive he'd been then. Twelve years old and already he'd mapped the direction his life would take.

He hadn't counted on Aileen's sensitive heart, her need to help the underdog, to travel and teach in disadvantaged areas of the Outside. Like Savanna, and Dennis.

He pushed through the school doors and strode down the hall to the office. The smell of youth, sweaty bodies and chalk dust stung his nose, filtered into his memories. His boots echoed on the tiled floor.

Valerie sat inputting data on a computer. Her son drew silly faces with a blue erasable felt on a dry board next to a filing cabinet.

"Will!" the kid called.

"Hey, Josh." Will nodded to the woman. "Val." Her face lit like an ornamental lamp; he looked away.

Josh rushed over. "Whatcha doing here?"

"Got an appointment with Ms. Murphy."

"Cuza the new boy? I mean your…your nephew?"

Will flicked a look toward Valerie, and shame rose. He should have told Josh about Christopher. In all senses except bloodlines, Josh was his little brother.

But he knew why he'd kept Christopher to himself, why he hadn't been up-front with Josh, or anyone else for that matter.

Christopher was different.

Oh, hell, admit it, Will. You don't know what to make of the boy.

Jeez. He wanted to walk out of the school, out of Josh's life for fear his shame would touch the kid.

Sweat popped from Will's skin. Could he be any more of an ass? If Savanna knew how he felt…

"Yeah, sport, I'm here because of Christopher."

"Oh." A tone of resignation.

"Sorry, pal. I should've told you about Chris earlier. I will later, okay?"

Valerie had gone back to typing. As always, she wasn't getting involved. More loudly than necessary he said, "But right *now*, I need to speak with his teacher and Mr. Germaine."

Valerie's head turned. "Of course, Will," she murmured. "Follow me." She led him down a tiny hallway to another door, one he'd gone through more than once as a student and not always for praise. "Mr. Germaine, Will's here to see you." She gave him a hesitant smile, then bustled back to her desk.

Will nodded to the principal, "Harry," and shook the teacher's hand. "Ms. Murphy." The woman looked to be in her early twenties. He'd bet his helicopter that Starlight Elementary was her first teaching position. A neophyte in the business of education. And kids with Asperger's Syndrome.

Behind the desk, the man Will had flown up the Copper River for fly-fishing the past four summers gestured to the empty chair beside Ms. Murphy. "Thanks for coming, Will. Penny, here, wanted to discuss some possibilities for your nephew next year. Since she teaches a split fifth-sixth grade, he'll be in her class again come September. Penny, why don't you explain your concerns?"

The woman studied a notebook in her lap. "As you know, Memorial Day weekend and the end of the school term is only seven weeks away, Mr. Rubens. While Ms. Stowe has agreed to volunteer in class with Christopher for the interim, she's made it clear she won't be here in the fall."

Oddly, hearing the information from this girl-teacher made it more real than hearing it from Savanna. Will's gut clenched.

"Therefore, Mr. Germaine and I recommend Chris be placed in a specialized program in September."

"Specialized program?"

"A special needs class. There's a very good one in Palmer."

Will's heart pounded. They wanted Christopher to travel sixty miles to attend a class separate from his peers? The idea did not sit right with Will. Years ago, educators like Ms. Murphy had singled *him* out because he'd been three grades ahead in math. The geek in elementary school.

The daredevil in high school.

"Has he been in a special class before?" he asked calmly.

"Well, according to Ms. Stowe, no. But—"

"Then he's not going in one now."

"Mr. Rubens—"

"Will," Harry began.

"No," Will said, forcing his breathing to level. "I want Chris staying *here,* with the other kids. I don't care where you get the help, but he's not going into a class that'll make him feel more different than he is."

"Mr. Rubens." Ms. Murphy clenched her hands on top of her notebook. "I know Christopher has been in class only a week and I'm not completely familiar with his behaviors, but I've read that autistic children can be highly agitated if…if things don't go their way." Her knuckles paled with pressure. Will almost felt sorry for her. "They're also prone to being very focused."

And that was a problem? Didn't teachers want their students focused?

Suddenly his gut spun like a dryer. He had to step up to the plate. For Dennis—and that young math geek twenty years ago. But not without Savanna. He'd been wrong, thinking to send her back to the Lower 48.

You need her help.

"He's staying in your class, Ms. Murphy." Will regarded Harry with what he hoped was a take-no-prisoners look. "I won't have his routine interfered with. Meantime, get him to use an agenda. Ms. Stowe has one and he follows it to the minute." During the evenings at Georgia's, he'd witnessed Savanna model behavior through workable techniques by way of the agenda.

"It isn't that simple," Ms. Murphy stressed. "For example, Christopher will need assistance in switching tasks."

Will turned to her. "Isn't that your job?"

The woman flushed; Harry cleared his throat. "Penny has twenty-nine students in two grades, Will. Christopher takes up more time than one regular student. A smaller class would eliminate confusion for him."

"Chris is a bright kid," Will said stubbornly. *Like my brother.* "He's quick to catch onto routine." *Sort of.* "I've seen it at his grandmother's house. He doesn't need a special class."

Harry sighed. "Fine, but he will require testing to qualify for an assistant in the fall."

Tested. Like a guinea pig. Will could imagine what testing involved for a boy with Christopher's condition. Hadn't Will gone through similar rigors at six, ten, twelve, because the ratio of his age to his acumen didn't match?

Harry checked the file folder in front of him. "You're the boy's guardian, right?"

Would perspectives change if he admitted, *Biologically I'm his father?* "Yeah," he said, shifting uncomfortably on his chair. "Look, Harry. Give me a name and I'll hire her to help Christopher. I don't want him tested."

The principal laid down the file. "Can't do that, Will. First, the board would have my job for bringing in an outsider they haven't hired and second, the boy *will* need to be tested eventually for our own records. Best to do it now."

Hands on his knees, Will leaned forward. Softly he said, "Christopher was diagnosed three years ago. Since then, my brother had every test in the book tossed at the kid. Ask Ms. Stowe."

"We have, but we need current criteria since Christopher is older now."

Will considered. "Then have her do the testing." Savanna and the boy had a connection built on trust and love.

Harry shook his head. "Ms. Stowe is not a district employee."

Will stood. "Ms. Stowe can test my nephew," he insisted. "She knows Christopher inside and out." He opened the office door. "I'll have her here within twenty minutes and you can arrange it with her."

"Won't do any good, Will," Harry intoned. "Ms. Stowe understands our procedures."

"Well, maybe your *procedures* need reevaluating, Harry."

He strode from the building. *Damn bureaucrats.* He'd been up close and personal with some when Aileen needed his support in that emergency room—had cried for it—and they hadn't allowed him to sit at her bedside because he hadn't been her husband.

Not this time, dammit. He would not let some neophyte schoolteacher make life miserable for Dennis's boy. Savanna wanted Will to find assistance, okay, he'd find it. And if it took hauling her over to the school by the seat of her cute butt to give Harry Germaine the information he needed, then Will would get the job done.

He jumped into his truck and drove to Georgia's.

"Savanna's over at the library," the old gal told him when she opened the door.

Will peered over her shoulder. "Where's the boy?"

"In the kitchen with a map of Starlight. Everything okay?"

Will explained school policy.

Georgia snorted. "Never could see two sides of a coin to save his soul, that Harry. If you need me to stand at your back, call."

"Thanks, Nana."

Back in the truck, driving to the two-story 1940s building housing Starlight's library, he wondered what he would do if Savanna sided with the school. Where would that leave Christopher?

Will found her in the farthest corner of the library, tapping computer keys speedy as a professional. From a nearby table he pulled a chair. Sitting backward, arms along its spindled back, he attempted to appear casual while his heart pounded. "Hey."

She proceeded to type, e-mailing someone about Alaska's autism association. "You know it's not polite to read other people's mail," she informed him, intent on the screen.

"I'm not reading your mail." Okay, he was, but out of curiosity.

She hit Send and closed the program. When her eyes turned on him, Will lost his voice. She had incredible eyes. Why hadn't he noticed they were green as a quiet forest pool? He swallowed, looked away. Thinking about her eyes wasn't getting Christopher the help he required.

"They want to retest Chris," he said. "I'm not in favor unless you do it."

Their eyes met. Held.

He scrubbed a hand down his cheek, sighed. "What I really want is for you to convince them it's not necessary. Kid doesn't need retesting. Anyone with a brain can see he's not…"

"Quite normal?"

"Typical." He offered a small smile. *See,* he wanted to say, *I'm learning.*

Slowly the corners of her mouth tilted. "I think there's hope for you, Will Rubens."

"That mean you'll see Germaine with me—" he checked his wrist watch "—in ten minutes?"

"And lay it all out on the table for him?"

"Whatever it takes, baby."

She stood, reached for her jacket draped over the back of the chair. They walked out of the library to Will's truck. He held open the passenger door. When he was behind the wheel, she turned to him. "For the record, don't call me baby again."

Will hid a grin as he checked the street out the side window. "Yes, ma'am."

The lady had her likes and dislikes. Well, so did he.

They drove to the school in silence.

With a hand to the small of Savanna's back, Will ushered her into the school, past Valerie's desk and down the short hallway to Harry's office.

The principal touched his tie before motioning to the same chairs he and Ms. Murphy had used a half hour ago. "You definitely keep your word, Will," the man said without humor.

"Damn straight."

Taking a seat, Will liked how Savanna got to the point. "Mr. Germaine," she said in her cultured manner. "I understand you want Chris retested. Well, we're in luck." She proffered Will a smile. "A few minutes ago, I e-mailed a teaching associate, something I should have attended to before Chris and I left Honduras. However, under the circumstances, I'm sure you understand these past ten days have not been…easy for us."

"Of course."

"As I mentioned when I registered Christopher, a comprehensive test was done six months ago. My associate will FedEx the results. Will is right," she continued in her soft Southern drawl. "Further testing will only frustrate Christopher. He needs routine right now and time to adapt to this state. The climate alone is difficult for him."

"Difficult?" Harry blinked.

"For one, he's averse to wearing a lot of clothes. He constantly takes off his coat and mitts when he's outside."

"His teachers will make sure he keeps his clothes on."

Will pushed an exasperated hand through his hair. "Jeez, Harry. Don't you people have any clue about autism? These kids have trouble adjusting to unfamiliar—"

Savanna touched the fist bunched on his thigh. Four fingers leaving heat marks on his skin. She said, "If you wish, Mr. Germaine, I can retest him in a few of the more common areas."

"The district wouldn't be in favor of that," Harry said.

At that she placed her hands on the man's desk. "It isn't a matter of favoritism—" those warm Southern syllables were cold as icicles "—but a matter of what's *best* for the child."

"That's what we're hoping to achieve," he retorted.

Sitting back, she smiled as if he'd given her a bouquet of roses. "And *I'm* hoping that with your knowledge and guidance at this school, Chris will be in the best hands simply because you'll do everything to make his transition smooth as glass."

The man harrumphed. "'Course, I will. We have quality teachers on staff and—"

"Then you agree to let the testing stand until next fall?" Savanna asked.

Germaine flicked a look at Will. "I'll put in the paperwork to get someone in from Palmer or Anchorage sometime in September. The earlier the application, the better. Special education teachers are about as numerous as this up here." He touched his index finger to his thumb. *Zero.* His smile was restrained. "You wouldn't be interested in applying to our district, would you?"

Will held his breath. What the principal offered would solve a hundred problems.

Savanna shook her head. "I'm not making Alaska my home, sir, but thank you for the offer. And, for facilitating Christopher's case." She rose from her chair, nodded and walked out of the office.

One impasse resolved, another on deck, Will mused. Time to work on keeping her here. And not just for Christopher, he reflected, pursuing Savanna out of the school and appreciating the narrow line of her spine, the way she angled her chin with pit bull ferocity. Had she been a man, he would have followed her onto a battlefield.

But she wasn't a man. She was woman. *All* woman.

His fingers twitched at the thought of that red waterfall across her shoulders. Springy and smooth as Christmas ribbon. The picture of how one lone loop might twist around his left pinky shot a hot jolt straight to his groin.

Outside, he opened the truck door and helped her inside before rounding the hood and getting behind the wheel, where he sat a moment staring out the windshield. "Appreciate your help."

"I'd do anything for Christopher."

Their eyes caught and a current arced between them. He tamped down the impulse to lean over and lay his mouth against hers for an instant, her generous mouth with its lush lower lip that held the remnants of pink from the lipstick she had applied a few hours ago. He noticed she wore little makeup. No face powder, no eye liner. He wondered if she'd tried once long ago to cover those thousand freckles, then gave up.

She blinked and the slight action returned him to the present. *Christopher.* She had attended the meeting to rescue Dennis's son.

Not you, fool.

He turned the ignition, set the gear, pulled from the curb. "Want to go back to the library?"

"I'm done there."

"To Georgia's?"

Several seconds of silence passed. "To your house."

Electricity zapped up his thighs. "*My* house?"

"I'd like to see where Christopher will live and what he'll need before I leave in a few weeks." She eyed him. "Or did you plan to let Georgia keep him?"

"No."

Christopher again. Always Christopher. Will knew he should be glad her focus was on the boy; it was what Dennis had wanted and—if he was honest with himself—what Will needed, too. Still, for once he'd like her to think of *him.*

How, Will? As a woman would?

The question startled him. *Jeez, man. What the hell's gotten into you?*

But he knew. Ms. Savanna had sneaked under his skin.

Irritated that his libido bullied his brain, he groused, "You don't trust my house will meet the boy's expectations? Just so you know, I built it from the ground up when I returned to

Alaska. Got all the state-of-the-art necessities you could ask for, including hot and cold running water and indoor plumbing. And," he couldn't help the half grin, "I don't use outdated Sears catalogs in the bathroom. Mine are this year's."

Laughter, rich and full-bodied, rang through the cab of the truck. He'd never heard her laugh before and the sound traveled his blood like a flash fire.

"Well?" he asked when she turned pleased eyes on him. "Do I pass?"

"Let's wait and see." Her smile was an enigma.

Wait and see. He could do that for the boy. He would not consider what wait and see meant for himself and Savanna Stowe.

If she persevered with her goal as planned, in less than three months she would be gone from his life.

Will's happy mood stumbled a little.

Savanna gazed at Will's dual-leveled log house among the tall evergreens. A dirt trail, similar to the one leading to Georgia's home, wound three hundred feet to a broad-lipped, wraparound screened porch. For the bugs—in particular mosquitoes—she'd been told. But what intrigued her most were the two wood-stained rocking chairs and the cane-bottom glider set in a semicircle to the right of the front door.

She wondered how often he'd sat there with friends— a woman perhaps—enjoying an evening or a night bedecked in stars.

Near the porch steps, among patches of dirty snow, roses sported green signs of life. *Roses.* A macho bush pilot with *roses* sprouting along his front porch.

Will shut off the engine. "Home sweet home. Such as it is."

"It's incredible, Will." Beautiful and utterly suited to the encompassing wilderness.

"*I* like it," he said as though indifferent of her approval.

But she had seen his eyes in Harry Germaine's office. Her approval mattered.

"Come on," he said, opening the truck's door. "I'll show you around."

Standing inside the screened porch, Savanna experienced such a strong sense of homecoming she almost told Will to take her back to Georgia's. At least in the old lady's house, she could think without wishing and dreaming and...

He lived in a home Savanna had coveted from the time she was a child and read *Little House in the Big Woods*. At ten years old, she'd craved the Ingalls' children's life, their home, loving parents, but mostly their devotion to each other. Of course, she could do without the outdoor plumbing. But to live in a log house in the country with nature waiting beyond door and window?

The whimsy had painted itself on her heart. And the colors brightened the instant she saw the interior layout of Will's house.

A great room with a massive fireplace of river stone. A fifty-two-inch TV. Several pieces of futon furniture in warm burgundy cloth and oak. The kitchen was a woman's dream: island, pots and pans hanging overhead, a six-inch window ledge for herbs, a square booth table in a corner nook.

"Standard bedrooms down there." He motioned to a hallway right of the kitchen. "Master, office, two guests. I figure Christopher can use the biggest of the pair. Want to see?"

She did not want to go where Will slept. Where he'd likely taken women to bed. But saying no meant she cared. She nodded and he headed down a hallway that divvied into a T.

"The master," he said, pointing left. "Wanna take a peek?" His eyes gleamed.

"I'll pass," she said dryly.

His dimples winked. "This way, then." And he led her in the opposite direction to a door at the end of the hall.

The room was more spacious than any bedroom she'd seen. Larger than her childhood room and the size of entire homes in some of the impoverished countries she'd worked.

She walked to the windows, stared at the postcard display of forest and mountains. Christopher's view. Christopher, who would not care one way or another what the scenery offered beyond the glass.

She cared, however. The child was not from her body; instead, he was hers in a thousand other ways. And one day he might look out this window at those jagged mountains and perceive them as she did this instant.

"Think he'll like it?" Will's voice came over her shoulder.

Arms tight to her waist, she replied, "The spaciousness is perfect for his train set."

She turned. Will stood within *her* space, close enough to react to the heat of his body.

He had lashes black as the raven she'd seen on the tip of a spruce this morning. Watching the gray streaks darken in his irises, she moved a step back. Cooling the air.

"Dennis and Elke bought Christopher a model train set for his last birthday," she said. "It sat on a table Dennis built..." The memory of her friends' happiness filled her throat. *Oh, Elke. You would've loved this room for your son.*

Will frowned. "You okay?"

She pushed the memories aside. "Yes."

"Where's the model now?" he asked quietly.

"Being packed up like the rest of their furniture and clothes to be distributed in the villages Dennis and Elke worked. It's what they wanted." *What was in their testaments.*

"Who's looking after that process?"

"A couple of Dennis's colleagues. Will…I should have asked sooner if you wanted some of the clothes and things…I'm sorry."

"No, give them away."

"These friends are trustworthy people. They'll send the personal items, the photo albums and any heirlooms."

"There's only one heirloom in the family and he's already here. But the albums would be nice."

The swell of her heart forestalled an answer.

He went on. "I spoke to that lawyer, Silas. He's transferring the house sale to a fund I've set up for Christopher in Anchorage. It won't be touched until he's of age or unless there's an emergency."

"Thank you," Savanna managed. "That's very thoughtful."

"Not thoughtful. Necessary."

"Dennis," she said, working around the lump in her throat, "would be proud." *Beyond proud. He should be here, seeing this, hearing this.* An oxymoron, in its truest form. If Dennis were alive, Christopher would not be in Starlight.

And she wouldn't have met Will.

But Dennis and Elke had thought ahead, had arranged for this terrible possibility and Christopher's future in a big way. Savanna appraised the room. It was up to her to secure the boy's life in Will's hands the best way she knew how before flying home to Tennessee.

Her gaze wove back to the man. One hand hooked a hip pocket in an offhand stance. But Will Rubens, she was coming to recognize, was not an offhand type of guy. He was man, male and masculine to the nth quantity.

A pilot with roses.

She crossed the floor, cursing herself silently. *Hopeless, Savanna. So hopeless. One minute you sniffle over Dennis, the next you're practically in heat over his brother.*

And him nine years your junior.

In the doorway, she said, "I need to get back to Christopher." *And away from you.* From that stance, from her rouletting hormones.

She proceeded down the hallway, had stepped into the kitchen when he called her name.

Trim-hipped in black jeans, he stood in the junction of the hallway T, a man whose potency blew toward her like a sultry wind, leaving her weak in its wake.

"I'll take the alley," she managed. "It's only four houses."

He walked slowly down the hall. She knew she should turn, flee out the door, but her feet remained rooted.

The raised platform at the kitchen's entrance gave him six extra inches to his already tall frame.

"Would you have dinner with me tomorrow night?" His eyes gripped hers.

"I…" She shook her head. "It wouldn't be fair to Georgia to leave her with Christopher."

"If I find a respite worker, will you come then?"

"Is there one in Starlight? One with experience?" She didn't believe it.

"I'll bring one in from Palmer."

The next town over. Sixty miles west. He'd drive sixty miles back and forth to ensure a dinner with her. Was the female potential that disadvantaged in this village? What about the dancing Mindy? Or Valerie whose son Will coached in Little League, according to Georgia? Both women were his age.

Do you want him with Mindy or Valerie?

"All right," she said before she had time to reconsider the Mindy-Valerie dichotomy. "What time?"

"How about eight?"

"Isn't that a bit late?" She never ate past seven, not if she could help it.

His lips tweaked. "All right, seven-thirty."

"Will, this is not a good idea."

"Because…?"

"You and I need to keep our relationship professional."

A long pause, then, "When was the last time you ate an evening meal with a man, Savanna?"

"That's not the issue." She headed for the front door.

"Then what is the issue? Are you afraid we might talk about something other than Christopher?"

She turned. "Not at all." *Liar. I'm afraid we'll talk about things I haven't talked about in years. Not with a man.*

"Come on. Live a little." He walked across the great room. "You're so wrapped up in Chris's situation, you haven't given yourself any time off." He offered a lopsided grin. "I'm sure Dennis and Elke didn't have you working 24/7."

"That was different. They were still alive. Chris has only me, now." She caught herself. "And you. But until he understands that you're his mainstay, I need to be there for him."

Oh, that recalcitrant jaw!

"Understood. But everyone needs a little fun in life. What's the old saying? All work and no play makes Jack a dull boy. I figure this could be in Christopher's best interest." Levity and something else sparked in his eyes. "Be ready at seven-thirty."

"Will…"

He reached past her, opened the door. "I'll walk you home."

The late-afternoon hour had arrived on a cool, crisp wind.

Wishing she'd worn a scarf around her ears, Savanna slipped her gloved hands into her coat. Adjusting to the northern climate would take a few years, she suspected.

A few years.

She would be long gone before then, a vague dream in Christopher's mind. She wasn't fool enough to think she'd be anything but a foggy memory to Will, either.

The thought had her tucking her chin into her jacket's collar.

A few years down the road she'd be on the downhill slope of forty. Living alone. *Lonely.*

"Cold?" the man beside her asked.

"Not at all."

Chuckling, he draped an arm around her shoulders and pulled her close to his side. "Better?"

Yes, and thank God for the low light. Will this close rushed heat across her skin. "You do know how to charm women, Mr. Rubens."

"Am I charming you, Ms. Stowe?"

She released a soft snort. "You wish."

His chortle rang low and deep above her ear. "Careful, darlin'. Don't want that veneer of yours gettin' transparent."

At Georgia's back gate, he dropped his arm, and the wind swept away his warmth.

After unlatching the gate, he trailed her through the trees to the back door where she paused to say, "Thank you, Will. It really wasn't necessary to walk me home."

He gusted a breath. "Savanna, let yourself be a woman, okay?" At her gaped mouth, he strolled back through the trees. "By the way," he called over his shoulder. "Jeans'll do tomorrow."

She watched him go. *Young upstart,* she thought.

But deep in her belly she quivered.

Chapter Five

When she opened the door to him the next evening, Savanna couldn't find her voice.

He wore a suede jacket soft as bread dough and black chinos that fell in a sharp cut over black boots. Thank God she'd amended the jeans to gray dress slacks, a sunshiny sweater and boots with four-inch heels. A whiff of his cologne—citrus and spice—sent a silly urge through her fingers. One that would have her brushing the tawny Bon Jovi–like lock off Will's forehead, before pulling his head down and setting her mouth on his.

As though he'd read her mind, he bent forward slightly, a grin working his lips. "Savanna, this is Molly Avonde. She'll be watching Christopher for us over the next couple hours."

Surprised, Savanna's gaze flicked to the woman standing behind Will. The respite worker.

Told you I'd find one, his eyes humored.

She gathered her senses. "Let me introduce you to Georgia and Christopher," she said and stepped aside as the pair entered the house.

Fifteen minutes later, settled in Will's SUV, she asked, "Where is it we're going?"

"Airport. I want to show you where I work."

"Good place to start." She hid a smirk. *Macho as they come*.

"And I'm cooking supper."

Her head snapped around. "*Really?*"

With a chuckle he backed out of Georgia's lane. "You think men can't cook?"

"On the contrary. Most men I know can cook, including your brother. It's just…" What? Will flew helicopters, so he shouldn't be the kitchen-comfortable type? Why should he be different from his brother?

Because he *was* different.

They might look alike, but that's where the similarity ended. Where Dennis was serious, Will had an aura of amusement about him. Yet she'd seen him deal with Germaine at the school. No laughter there. He'd been all business and determination.

"It's just what?" The grin he shot her tripped across her heart.

"I didn't think you had time for culinary aspects."

"I need to eat, Savanna. Every day. And I like having good food on my plate when I do."

He drove one-handed, his right hand centered on the wheel, left arm on the windowsill, the tips of his fingers more of a balancing act against the wheel's rim. The maleness of the sight dove to the soles of her feet.

"Ah, damn." He slowed the truck as a tan pickup turned the corner of Mule Deer Road and approached.

"What is it?"

Valerie Jax, the school secretary, braked her vehicle and rolled down her window.

Pressing the electronic button on the 4Runner's window, Will muttered something about women on the hunt. "Hey, Val."

"Hi, Will." She peered around him. "Oh, I didn't realize that was you, Savanna."

"Hi, again, Valerie."

"Out for a drive?" the woman asked Will. She touched her brown hair in the ancient signal of female preening.

"I'm taking Savanna to dinner," he told her.

"Oh." Her hazel eyes flitted to Savanna. "Well, that's…that's nice." Again her gaze locked on Will, and in that instant Savanna recognized the unspoken nuances. Georgia was right: Valerie Jax was interested in Will. *Very* interested.

A twinge of sadness washed through Savanna. Valerie should be in this truck, going on a dinner date. She was Will's age, lived in the same town with a child Christopher's age. And she was not from the Outside.

"Well, see you around." Will lifted his foot off the brake, let the truck roll forward, the window slide closed. The woman's gaze chased him before the cab cut her from Savanna's sight.

Silence pursued them out of town.

She said, "Valerie's a good woman." *And a single mother.*

His attention remained beyond the windshield. "Yep."

Do you realize she likes you?

None of your business, Savanna.

She concentrated on the road dappled with the dusky glow of sunset. She'd forgotten the difference in daylight hours between Alaska and Honduras. There, night would have fallen, a blanket pulled over the earth.

Observing a rabbit bound across their path into the secrecy of the forest, she asked, "What's on the menu?"

"Not rabbit, if you're worried."

"God forbid."

Another chuckle. "Hungry?"

"Should I be?"

"It'd work best, yeah." He flashed her a full smile.

Oh, my. Was she in trouble? *Too much.*

"I like a woman who's a little hungry," he remarked with a wink. "Then my efforts aren't wasted."

The way he said "hungry" and "efforts" he wasn't talking food. She closed her mouth, focused on the wilderness beyond the truck.

A small wooden sign with Airport painted in white directed them onto a narrow access road winding several hundred yards inward. Evergreens shadowed the truck. Abruptly, a slim clear-cut rectangle opened to present the single runway she had arrived upon twelve days ago with Christopher.

Will drove past the two-bay hangar before pulling in front of a squat cabin with PILOTS' HOUSE in big black letters above its door.

He shut off the engine, reached behind the seat for a sack of groceries. Before she had time to react, he was out the door, striding around to her side.

"Welcome to the flight service station, my other home," he said, helping her from the truck's cab.

Her hand in his, they went up a dirt path, before he pushed open the door to the building that was, indeed, a house. There was a small sitting room on the left, an office on the right. Compact but fully equipped, the kitchen took up a rear quarter of the house where a garden-variety table had been pushed against the window overlooking the landing strip.

"That way—" Will set the groceries between the sink and tiny refrigerator and jutted his chin toward a mini hallway, "—is the washroom. First door. Bedroom's the second."

Bedroom. A thousand pictures roared through her mind, all with Will and the women he'd cooked for in this… "other home."

Unloading vegetables and chicken onto the counter, he had his back to her; she couldn't determine his expression.

He said, "Sometimes pilots need a place to catch a few hours sleep if they're on a layover from another area. Or during emergencies."

"What kind of emergencies?"

He gave her a leer, eyebrows jumping.

"Oh, for heaven's sake." But she couldn't help her own grin.

"Ah, finally. The woman has a funny bone. Here's the deal, Ms. Savanna. Tonight we switch roles. You laugh, and I'll be the serious one. How's that?"

Her mouth curved. "Don't get off topic. Emergencies…?"

"Forest fires, mostly. Guys will sack out for a couple hours if they've been flying for more than eight straight."

"I thought pilots were only allowed to fly six hours."

"Depends on the number of pilots we get up in the air."

She wandered to the window. Vacant, the landing strip lay like an elongated gray ruler amidst the forest.

"Is it always this quiet around here?" she asked.

He handed her a glass of Merlot, then resumed tossing peppers, cucumbers, bok choy, broccoli and cauliflower into a colander in the sink. "This time of year is the lull before the storm. Come Memorial Day weekend, the summer tourists start arriving by the truckload. Guys going fishing, hikers, flightseers."

"You love your job."

Both dimples winked. "That I do."

Pivoting, she watched him work with deft, swift movements, washing, tossing, dicing. He seasoned the chicken breasts, laid them into a heated skillet.

"And you enjoy cooking."

He had yet to flip the light switch and in the mellow light his eyes were the blue of a Steller's Jay. "Used to hate it."

"What changed?"

"I discovered I liked feeding my woman."

My woman. The words sparked every nerve ending. Deliberately, she snorted. "I'm hardly your woman, Mr. Rubens."

A lightning grin. "Twelve weeks is long enough, Ms. Stowe."

"For what? For you to make me that woman?" Savanna laughed.

"Go ahead, laugh all you want. Alaska can be a lonely place."

"And you're prepared to ensure I won't be."

He stopped dicing and looked across the counter separating them, eyes vivid as the North Star. "I like you, Savanna. Is that such a crime?"

"I'm also nine years older and here for three months. Possibly less if you and Christopher connect quickly. Those are just two factors of why I am not your woman." Her gaze held his. "And to set the record straight, I will *never* be someone's woman. The Cro-Magnon routine is highly passé."

"Ouch. That a slap on the wrist?"

She grinned. "Which you barely felt."

He flipped the chicken. "How would you know? All that age and caveman rhetoric, I'm probably scarred for life."

"That I severely doubt. You thrive on challenge, which puts me next in line because I'm not—" *Valerie or Mindy* "—fawning at your feet," she finished.

"Savanna, Savanna." He walked to where she stood by the window, captured by his solemn expression.

And that quick, the banter in her ebbed.

A voiceless *move away* rushed up, yet she remained motionless, and then he was in front of her, meat fork in one hand. "You wound me with your opinions."

"I doubt that." But her stomach leaped.

His free hand lifted, touched her cheek, a whispered stroke shivering to her heels. "First," he said softly, "age has never been an issue with me. If I'm attracted to a woman, it's *who she is* that appeals. Second, tact was never my forte, but I'll be more careful in the future. Third—" His fingers slipped to her nape and tugged her forward. "Third, caveman or not, I'm very *in*to you. So, let's see where it takes us, all right?"

He would kiss her. *Oh, Lord.*

But no.

A buss against her forehead. A touch so light it mimicked the flit of a hummingbird's wing.

When had a man offered sensuality to that degree?

Not once. Not once in her memory.

She watched him return to the stove. How was she to endure—*fight off*—the magnet that was Will Rubens over the next weeks? Because he *was* a magnet potent as a lightning storm.

Knees weak, she sat on one of the red vinyl chairs rounding the table. "Where did you train to fly?" she asked when her throat loosened. *Get him to talk about himself.* Didn't men take pride in hearing themselves?

"A friend taught me right here in Starlight. Now you." His eyes were keen over his bottle of beer. "How long have you worked on foreign soil?"

"Twenty years. Liberia was my first posting with the Peace Corps."

His stare unnerved. "You must have been very young. Straight out of college."

"I was." She smiled. "I'd received my graduate degree one day and flew to Africa three days later."

"Why?"

"Because I wanted to help people, make their lives a little more bearable, offer a little happiness."

"Aren't there thousands who need help in our own country?"

"I also wanted to see something of the world," she reasoned.

He shook his head. "Take a trip to New Zealand or Australia or, hell, Greenland. You don't need to go into gun-toting places."

"They're hardly gun toting, Will."

She thought of the gaunt, doe-eyed children with the bloated bellies of malnutrition. Men and women trying to find work to buy their families enough food for one day's meal. Of the disease and dirty water and fly-ridden faces of poverty. Of the shanties, the cardboard huts—havens for the crippled, the blind—on the side of the road. The lack of education for women.

"Many of those countries are impoverished because of corrupt governments, Savanna," Will said, interrupting her reverie. "Or they're ruled by insurgents and rebels."

"Some are." She knew *that* too well. Hadn't her own body suffered one of those atrocities? "But," she said, ruthless against the memory of that pain, "it's also much more. That's why we try to make a difference."

"We?"

"People like Dennis and Elke." *Me.*

"My brother should never have left the States. And for damn sure not after his wife got pregnant with Christopher."

Bitterness. It tugged his mouth downward. *What*

happened to you, Will? Something more than Dennis and Elke moving to Central America, Savanna surmised.

She said, "Dennis could have died in a plane here."

"Not if he'd been flying with me."

"Isn't that a bit arrogant?"

He shot her a look. "I know what I'm doing behind the controls. I'd never take flagrant risks."

Anymore. "This pilot didn't, either. He'd flown for thirty years in Honduras." She looked down at her Merlot. "I believe when it's your time, it's your time."

"What does a guy in Central America know about small aircraft?" he muttered, lifting the lid to the rice. Steam puffed against his face.

She understood. It was no longer ego, but grief speaking.

"He'd flown in Vietnam. Training doesn't get much better than that."

The line of his shoulders relaxed. "Touché." Picking up his beer, he toasted, "To pilots everywhere."

She raised her Merlot and, for a split second, craved to press her lips against those dimples. *You're drunk, Savanna. In June you'll be a scant thought. Remember that.*

Will was not a man to go long without female companionship. Hadn't she heard that men outnumbered women in Alaska? The Valeries and Mindys would be more than willing to fill his plate or whet his appetite with enticing delicacies.

Still, she was intrigued. "Why did you invite me here?"

"First, to get to know you. Second, to thank you for all you've done for my family, for Christopher."

"You're welcome, but anyone would have done the same considering the circumstances."

"Except it wasn't anyone. It was you."

Outside the window, night encroached upon dusk.

"And as I said, I'm attracted to you," he added.

She remained intent on the landscape, its black jagged tree line, the airstrip and its markers of yellow lights. "I don't want…this…to interfere in your connection with Christopher."

"Making you supper? Why would it?"

"I want your attention on him."

Will laughed, the sound kicking her pulse. "I can chew gum and walk at the same time, Savanna."

He swigged a good portion of the beer, eyeing her as his throat worked swallows. "Arrrgh. Nothing like the taste of fermented yeast to give the blood a boost."

The last thing he needed was alcohol to amplify his mood, she mused. But she said nothing. She preferred the cheerfulness in his eyes to the darkness she'd seen when he spoke of his brother.

He set aside the bottle, took her hand, pulled her from the chair. "Come. I want to show you something."

"What about the food?"

"It'll simmer. We won't be long."

He ushered her through the back door, down three wooden steps and across a patch of frozen turf to the edge of the field.

"Over there." He pointed right, to the horizon above the mountains, and she saw night dark as Honduran rum imbued with trillions of stars, and across its canvas, northern lights swirled and leaped, a cluster of giant fairies in iridescent greens, pinks and blues.

"Ohhh…"

"Thought you'd like it."

"I've never seen anything so lovely." Or classically Alaska. He had taken her breath. Again.

"Now I know why they called the village Starlight," she murmured.

"Hmm. Couple sourdoughs—guys that were frontier veterans—pitched their tents here about eighty years back. Figured there was enough starlight to do a day's work in."

"I can believe it." Everywhere she looked, the sky brushed its luminance across hill, mountain and tree.

"Check it out," Will said near her ear, and pointed left toward the tip of the airstrip.

Her eyes followed the line of his finger where a dark bulk briefly blotted a section of lights at the end of the runway.

"Grizzly," he whispered, and she shuddered inside her coat. She had never seen a real grizzly, had forgotten the type of wildlife enriching the state's environment.

"They're most dangerous this time of year because they're hungry. Sometimes they wander into town after hanging around the dump a mile up the road."

Christopher. Ten and in his own world. "What about children walking to school?"

"The rural kids take the bus. The rest are driven or walk in groups."

She wanted to say, *I'm taking Christopher back to Tennessee,* wanted to grasp at any excuse. Except *this* was his heritage. Alaska ran in Will's veins, in his heart. Christopher had the same genes. And whatever he lacked, Will would teach him.

She would see to it. She had to set her fears at bay for Christopher. And Will. Model calm and levelheadedness.

"Let's go eat," he said, guiding her back, arm around her waist, spreading heat up her torso. "We'll deal with bears later."

Fears and bears. One and the same.

She went inside and let him feed her. Walking away from this land one day, from Christopher, would require stamina.

A lot of stamina.

* * *

Will pulled into Valerie's lane as Josh rushed out the door in his maroon-and-gray baseball uniform, leather mitt in hand.

The boy's mother, dressed in pink jeans and a snug white top exhibiting her perky goods, stood on the stoop. She sent Will a little wave; he issued one in return.

"Ready for some action today, buddy?" he asked as the eleven-year-old climbed into the 4Runner.

Josh's excitement stretched ear to ear. "This season's gonna be so awesome! We're kicking butt, right, Will?"

"You bet, tiger." He waited until the boy fastened the seat belt and wondered if one day Christopher would be as animated about a practice. Savanna had said not to get his hopes up; the boy might never be "into" sports. Well, maybe he just needed a man to teach him the ropes.

Before he could put the SUV into gear, Valerie trotted off the stoop. *Damn*. Now he'd have to be polite. And pretend he didn't see hope in her eyes.

Tentative smile on her pink-painted lips, she opened the passenger door. "You listen to everything Will says, hear?" she told her son.

"I always do, Mom."

"Good boy. Hey, Will."

"Val." His fingers itched to crank the steering wheel so he could leave. But this was Josh's mother, and he couldn't embarrass the boy by telling the woman to get a life. Will knew what she wanted. Chitchat and a man's attention. Trouble was, he had no intention of falling prey to her criteria. Desperate women did not do it for him, and Valerie Jax was desperate.

"You going to the dance tonight?" she asked; smiled.

And there it was. Her reason for standing beside his truck in the cool April air without a jacket.

"Haven't decided yet." What he *had* decided was that he wanted Savanna. Over last night's meal, he'd enjoyed the sound of those slow Tennessee tones. He relished her intelligence, the way she listened with genuine interest. Mostly he craved her smile, how her eyes centered on him when she spoke of Christopher, of the life she had carved out for herself.

"Well." Valerie swerved him back to the present. "If you want to go, maybe we can hook up?"

"Mo-om." Josh darted a look at Will.

"All right." Her smile wobbled. "No pressure."

"We gotta go now." The boy tugged on the door, and Will's heart softened.

"I'll have Josh home in two hours," he said. "Mind if I take him to the store for a cone afterward?"

"That would be nice, Will. Thanks." She shut the door, but remained in the driveway until they drove down the street and out of sight. Will felt a twinge of regret for Valerie. A nice woman who'd had some tough breaks with her husband dying in a logging accident six years ago. Yes, he'd made Josh his "little brother," but that didn't mean Valerie was part of the package. It didn't automatically shoe in Will as her partner at the Saturday-night dances.

"You okay, bud?" he asked the boy focused on the scenery beyond the side window.

A shrug. "Sure."

"Look, about your mom—"

"She can be so lame."

Will ruffled Josh's dark hair. "She just likes dancing, buddy."

"Yeah, well…" The boy toyed with his catcher's mitt.

Will caught sight of reddened, chapped skin. "Mom make you wash your hands before leaving the house?"

"Yeah." Josh slipped both hands under the mitt. Hiding the evidence.

Will reached over, flicked open the glove box, drew out the familiar tube of cream.

"Thanks." Josh squeezed a quarter-size dollop onto his raw skin.

"No problem."

But it was a problem. Valerie needed a counselor to dig out the root of her obsessive compulsiveness—which included Will. By the time he'd reached the ball field his guilt had taken flight. In a couple of hours he would see Savanna again. Last night they had decided to take Christopher to his first theater movie.

Halfway through a scrimmage game, the twelve-year-old playing third clutched his chest and fell to his knees.

"Kenny's hurt!" shortstop, Todd Malloy yelled. "Coach, Kenny's hurt!"

Several teammates ran to the boy curled on the ground.

Will raced down the white line from home base, skidded in the dirt beside the kid. "Kenny, it's Coach. What happened, bud?"

The kid's lips were blue; he wasn't getting air.

"M-my ch-chest h-hurts."

Panic attack? "Take it easy, Ken. Slow and steady breaths."

The young ball player rolled his head. "My h-heart f-feels like it's got a nee-needle in it."

Tugging the uniform shirt up, Will's hands shook.

He set his ear to the boy's chest....

Heart bonging like a drum out of whack.

"Call 911," he ordered, hoping one of the parents clustered around them had a cell phone. "Kenny, hang on, pal." But the boy had slipped into unconsciousness. *Merciful*

God. Again Will checked the boy's pulse. Barely there and erratic. Palms to the child's chest, Will exercised the skills he had learned years ago in flight training.

The next hour blurred. He rode in the ambulance to the medical clinic, helping the paramedic stabilize the little third-baseman. At the clinic, Will met the boy's parents, tried to keep them calm while their son lay in Emergency on a stretcher.

Waiting in a small private room, Kenny's father tried to compose his wife. "He'll be all right," Clay Harding repeated. "The doctors are looking after him." The wife continued to cry.

Will sought out the clinic's cafeteria and bought three mugs of coffee. His pulse beat through his veins. *Kenny,* he thought. *What the hell happened back there?*

Mentally he filed through the hour and half on the ball field, pinpointing each moment leading to the boy's attack. Nothing out of the ordinary. Nothing indicating Kenny had heart problems. In fact, the previous summer the kid had emulated Mark McGwire, hitting the season's most home runs.

Coffees in a tray, he walked back to the waiting room. Mrs. Harding paced the vinyl floor. Clay sat on an ancient green Naugahyde sofa, elbows propped on his knees, head in his hands.

Will handed them each a paper cup.

"Thanks," the man said. "Doc hasn't come out yet."

"Ken's a tough nut," Will assured them.

"He had a hole in his heart when he was born, but they fixed it. Last six years he's been…normal…playing sports…hockey…ball. Not even so much as a niggle, y'know?"

Will didn't know. He wished to hell the parents had clued him in to their son's medical condition. If it hadn't been for his CPR training, God knows what might have happened back in that ball park.

He walked down the hall. In an alcove of pay phones, a woman sobbed into the receiver she clutched. Shoving off eight-year-old images of himself and Aileen—pregnant with his baby—in an L.A. hospital, he strode back to the waiting room. Clay had his arms around his wife; both were crying. Will slipped back to the hallway.

What if Kenny died? Just a kid, an only child.

Only child.

Like Christopher.

God in heaven. If the boy had a condition that could take him any second—

Will walked faster. *Savanna,* he thought. He needed to hear her voice, needed to ensure Christopher was all right. He had to hear the kid's voice.

Please. Give me a truckload of nonsense about trains and maps, I don't care. Just so I know you're okay.

Five minutes outside, that's all he required for his cell.

"Will," Clay Harding called from the waiting room.

Wheeling around, Will retraced his steps down the hall.

"Doc's given Kenny something to sleep," the man said. "He's stabilized, but they're flying him to Anchorage in an hour to do some tests, make sure things are okay." He held out a hand. "Thanks, man. Doc says if it hadn't been for you massaging his chest…"

Will nodded, lump in his throat. "He'll be fine, Clay. Give him a hug for me when he wakes."

He walked out of the hospital, headed for Starlight Park and his truck four blocks away. Josh, he knew, had gone home with one of the other parents. All the kids had been shuttled home the minute Will and Kenny left in the ambulance.

By the time he reached his truck, half the afternoon had

vanished. Three hours since the emergency occurred; two since he was to meet Savanna and Christopher. He drove straight to Georgia's.

Savanna met him at the door. "Christopher's involved with something else right now," she said calmly.

"I'm sorry." He rubbed his nape. "Something came up."

Her look told him that "something" shouldn't have taken precedent over the boy in the house.

"Look, I'll make it up to him, okay?"

She stepped onto the stoop, closed the door. "What happened, Will? You look sick."

"Nothing." He didn't want to go over the last hours, couldn't get past the crazy angst in his chest that Kenny might have died out there on the ball field. God, and if it had been Christopher lying there grabbing his chest…? "Look." He scrubbed a hand down his face. "I can't talk about it right now, okay?"

She studied him a moment. "All right. But when you say you'll take Christopher to a movie at two o'clock, and then you don't show up for two hours, it puts him into a tailspin."

"A tantrum, you mean."

"To put it mildly."

Her finger pointing got to him. She had no idea what he'd just gone through. Curbing the urge to put a fist through the wall, he said, "Well, crud happens. He'll have to get used to that sooner or later."

She stared at him as if he had grown an extra ear. "You don't get it, do you? Life with an autistic child is not the norm. They expect things to go as planned. And when they don't—" she lifted a hand "—I know it can't always be that way, but the least you could have done was phoned and let us know you weren't coming."

That ticked him off. "I was a little tied up at the time."

Her arms gripped her middle. "I think it's best that you go." Her expression softened. "Give him time to readjust, Will. Otherwise, he'll think you're here to take him to the movie anyway."

"Good. We'll get a video. I'll take him to my place, watch the big screen." He had a sixty-two inch screen in his office and another in the great room. Kid could take his pick.

"Perhaps next time."

"How about an ice cream cone?"

She sighed. "It doesn't work that way. The schedule changed when you didn't show up. He's settled now."

"Jeez, Savanna. Just tell him the schedule has been *re*-scheduled. Hell, make a new agenda."

"I'm sorry." Her eyes held sympathy.

"Fine." He leaped down the step. After the day he'd had, he didn't need an additional load of junk from a woman who didn't have an inkling about his life.

"Perhaps tomorrow," she called and hope lay in the words.

"Yeah. Maybe." And maybe she could fly to the moon.

Damn it, didn't *she* get it? He was trying, *really* trying to juggle his flying schedule, coach baseball *and* fit in the boy. A boy with some wrong DNA, not a boy who was broken.

Not like Kenny.

Tomorrow Christopher would be over his "tailspin." And Kenny Harding might be dead.

He stormed into his kitchen five minutes later to grab a soda from the refrigerator, and his conscience rose its flag of guilty gratitude.

If he had to choose, he'd take Savanna's disappointment and Christopher's tantrums anyday over a damaged heart.

Chapter Six

She needed to get out of the house for an hour. This afternoon Will had done exactly what she'd feared. By not phoning and letting her know, warning her, he had neglected his responsibility to Christopher.

He had crushed a little boy's hopes. And she'd had to deal with the result: Christopher crying, stamping his feet, batting his head with his fists, yelling loudly enough to send both Blue and Georgia to hide in the bedroom.

It had taken Savanna more than an hour to work through the behaviour tactics and calm the child. By the time Will stood on the doorstep, the worst was over and Christopher was quietly comparing the highways of Alaska to Honduras on his maps.

When he'd fallen asleep at nine, she'd left him in Georgia's care, grabbed her jacket and gone out the door.

Down the street, she heard a lively jitterbug of accordion,

guitar and piano. In Tennessee her grandfather would have called it mountain music.

Stars winked through the black oasis of night and to the left the northern lights reeled in opalescent greens.

Was Will reeling across the hardwood with Mindy the waitress…or Valerie?

Valerie, who yearned for his attention?

The music segued into a country ballad as she approached the rec center, a log cabin that served for council meetings, art displays and a myriad of annual events. Pickup trucks and SUVs lined the street and packed the tiny graveled parking lot. Through the open doors bursts of laughter punctuated the dark.

Several feet from the steps Savanna debated. Should she go inside? See what dancing in Starlight offered? She couldn't deny the magic of the music, of the town.

Or was it Will's magic slipping under her skin?

The cool night air brushed her hot cheeks. *Will, Will, Will.* The name patterned her footsteps. Why couldn't she get him out of her head? Why had she wandered down here, pretending to need a breath of fresh air? Had Georgia with her knitting in her lap and old Blue, the husky at her feet, seen through Savanna's motive?

If my old knees could handle it, I'd check out the dance myself, Georgia had said. *Give that Will a run for his money.* Then she'd giggled like a thirteen-year-old.

A run for his money. Right. Savanna wouldn't dream of chasing a man, least of all Will Rubens. The pilot was too young, too rash. Too everything that Savanna was not.

Is that so wrong? Let go, Savanna. Minimize your past and maximize your future. Just once.

At the hall's entrance, she checked for the few familiar faces she'd met over the past two and a half weeks.

Shane, the lodge clerk and Will's fishing buddy, danced

with Ms. Murphy. Valerie wheeled in and out of the throng of dancers with an older man. Her father? Not by the way he looked at her. Waitress Mindy chatted and danced with a craggy-faced man.

"Hey, Ms. Stowe."

Savanna turned to see Shane coming toward her, his moon-round face splitting on a grin. "Hello, Shane."

"Wanna dance?"

Where's the quick-footed Ms. Murphy? "Actually, I was out for a walk and heard the music."

"Great, you've come at the right time." Grabbing her hand, he pulled her onto the dance floor.

Savanna laughed. "You certainly don't waste time, do you?"

"No, ma'am. Can't afford to." He swung her into a two-step. "Not when the men in this state outnumber the ladies."

"Well, don't get your hopes up," she teased. "I'm not making this home."

His dark eyes held a glimmer of interest. "Too bad. You'd be value added to our school system."

"Is that what Ms. Murphy thinks?" Savanna watched the young woman with her arms around the sixth-grade teacher's neck. *So that's how the wind blows here.*

"Her and everyone else in town," Shane said, blind to the woman who'd hung on *his* neck minutes ago. "You've probably realized our special-education experts aren't that numerous here. There's Mrs. Wilkins, who's 110, and now you." His merriment was contagious. "If we want specific assessments done, we have to bring someone in from Palmer." He twirled her around. "You wouldn't consider staying?"

Savanna huffed a laugh. "You on the board of education?"

"Nah, but my sister's boy's having a lot of problems. She can't get anyone to assess him."

"In Starlight?"

"No, ma'am. In the Chugach Mountains. She home-schools."

"Whereabouts in the mountains?"

"In the bush. You know, the wilderness. They're sour-doughs."

Alaskan natives living for more than a year deep in the wild and beyond civilization.

Abruptly his eyes were grim. "Would you assess my nephew if we flew you in?"

Savanna didn't hesitate. "Behaviors?"

"Like your boy."

"You know about Christopher?"

"It's a small community, Ms. Stowe."

Of course it was. She'd read the sign entering the village: *Welcome to Starlight. 808 Souls Thriving under the Midnight Sun.*

"Ladies and gentlemen," a voice boomed.

The throng slowed to a stop and turned to the small stage where a man had taken the mike from the lead singer, a thir-tyish woman with long, dark hair. "Tonight is a special night. As many of us already know, little Kenny Harding was flown to Anchorage today."

Murmurs resounded. Nearby, a woman commented, "Poor Amy. Don't know I could deal with this."

The announcer went on. "The Hardings have asked me to give thanks to a very special person. But first we want to thank all of you for coming tonight. Your generous dona-tions to pay the medical expenses…" He pointed to a white cloth-covered table at the side of the stage where a woman and man seated on stools guarded a cardboard box. "At last check that box is almost full."

Applause, shouts, whistles.

"So thank you from the bottom of our hearts. Now, I'd like Will Rubens to come up here. Coach, where are you?"

For the first time, Savanna noticed his dark-golden hair in the crowd. He glanced her way once, then moved toward the stage and up its five wooden stairs. A woman about midtwenties trailed after him, but remained at the bottom step. Her eyes tracked Will's every move.

Hands on lean hips, feet planted apart, he stood center stage and nodded to the cheering crowd.

"Our hero," the announcer said, clapping him on the shoulder. "Will, Clay and Amy want the people of Starlight to know that if it hadn't been for you—" Savanna edged to the front of the crowded dance floor "—well…young Kenny wouldn't be where he is today, resting and healing under expert care." The man shook Will's hand. "All of us here want to give you our thanks by offering you a night of your choosing at our very own Shepherd Lodge."

Boots beat the floor, whistles shrilled louder, and the chant of "Go, Will" boomed against the rafters.

He took the mike, waited for the crowd to calm. "Thanks, folks." His deep voice resonated through the hall. "I was just lucky to be in the right spot at the right time."

"But you know CPR," someone shouted. "Don't sell yourself short."

He waved to the big-boned, steel-haired man, the one who had given Valerie *The Look*. "All in a day's work, Nate." His smile faltered when he caught Savanna's gaze. "I see a young lady I'd like to ask to dance." He walked to the singer, spoke to her, then jogged down the stage stairs.

The crowd clapped, the band began the song, and Will stopped to speak against the ear of Ms. Midtwenty. Giving the woman's shoulder a squeeze, he turned and crossed to Savanna.

She inhaled long and slow to compose jittery nerves. *Intense. His eyes are so intense.*

"Sorry to cut in, bud," Will told Shane. "Dance, Ms. Stowe?" Without hesitation he pulled her into his arms.

"Why didn't you tell me this afternoon?" she asked. He smelled wonderful. Wilderness and night.

One brow lifted. "That one of my ball players needed help?"

"Would it have been so difficult to explain?"

"I shouldn't have to explain, Savanna. My word should mean something. Short of death or an emergency, I keep it." He twirled her under his fingers, brought her against his chest. Her breasts pressed into his shirt; his breath fanned her forehead.

"Fine for these people." She glanced around. "They know your habits. I don't."

The dimples appeared. "But you *could.*"

He was flirting with her. The shuffling crowd and Will's closeness heated the skin along her collarbones and prickled her scalp with perspiration.

Disregarding those snapping eyes, she said, "There are women here who had read your habits better than me." *Like Ms. Midtwenty glaring at us with lips so taut they're white.*

"And I told you I'm not interested in those women," he said, weaving her to his side for two synchronized steps.

She laughed into his eyes when he brought her close again. Oh, yes, Pilot Rubens was a seasoned dancer.

"When was the last time anyone took you dancing?" He bent his head next to hers, and his lean, hard body aligned along each of Savanna's curves as they spun in a small circle.

"In college," she admitted. When she'd danced until one in the morning most weekends and none of her partners had been as light-footed as Will. When Liberia was still on the horizon.

"Then we're not missing a Saturday from this day on."

"Excuse me…Will?" a female voice interrupted. "Can I speak to you a minute?"

He continued to sway with Savanna. "Can it wait, Val?"

"It's about Josh."

His eyes zeroed in on the woman. "What about him?"

A fleeting look at Savanna. "Can we talk in private?"

"Val, unless he's in trouble, I'd like to finish this dance."

"Oh." Another swift look at Savanna. "Well…all right." She gave him a small smile and moved back into the crowd.

"Now, where were we?"

"Not sure," Savanna murmured into his shoulder. "Valerie has a crush on you."

"She has an obsession on me."

"Can you blame her? You're the father figure her son doesn't have." According to Georgia.

"Josh is a good kid. Couple years ago he needed a big brother and I volunteered. But I am not his father."

"'Course not. Instead you're a handsome man who loves to coach Little League. How could she lose?"

His full-of-mischief grin tickled her stomach. "Handsome, huh?"

"Don't let your head swell."

"Oooee, Ms. Stowe—a little double entendre?"

Savanna flushed. He would put it to sex.

"You're blushing," he whispered into her ear.

"You're rude."

He tossed back his head and laughed. "Your talk turns me on, Savanna." A twirl right, then left. Eyes of midnight blue. "What I was thinking," he said against her hair, "is I'd like to take you and Christopher up in the helicopter tomorrow. Think he'd be able to handle that?"

"I'll prepare him. However, if it's not his cup of tea—"

"We'll be fine," he assured. "But I'll give him some brochures on helicopters in the morning to get him acquainted."

"That would be great, Will."

"See, I'm not such a bad guy after all." The amber reflection of wall lamps gleamed on his skin.

"No," she admitted.

His lips twitched. "Forgive me?"

"There wasn't anything to forgive. You're a fine man, and eventually you'll be the father Christopher needs."

His enjoyment abated. "Let's hope."

"That's all anyone can do with kids."

The two-stepping song segued smoothly into a slow Faith Hill melody. Saying nothing, he swayed Savanna in one spot, and she imagined them attending hundreds of dances throughout the ensuing years. Dancing into old age.

He hummed in her ear, "Just breathe," and across the surface of her flesh a thousand miniature fires ignited and her blood sang to the strum of her pulse.

Too soon the melody ended; she opened her eyes to reality.

Will lifted her palm to his mouth. His eyes leached her breath. "Tomorrow," he murmured, then shouldered through the crowd, out the door and into the night.

Across the breakfast table, Savanna handed Christopher the day's agenda, pointed to the time Will was to pick them up to go to the airstrip in forty minutes.

"You'll have fun in the helicopter, Christopher." Georgia set a fried egg onto his plate.

He stared down at the food as if she'd plopped an enlarged pimple next to his toast. "Eeew, I don't eat eggs."

"You don't like them?"

Lifting the plate away, Savanna pushed back her chair before the boy fell into another bout of anger. "It's okay,

Georgia. For breakfast, Christopher eats only peanut butter and grape jelly toast." *Cut in triangles*. Savanna offered a smile to soften her words.

"Oh. I wish you had told me."

She'd explained the routine the first morning, but the old lady forgot things now and again. On her way to the counter, Savanna touched the other woman's shoulder. "It's nothing we can't rectify. Right, Chris?"

"I don't eat eggs," he said in his staccato voice, then began a tuneless hum.

"I know, honey." Savanna scraped the food into the trash under the sink and sent Georgia an apologetic look. "I'll make some new toast."

"I don't want breakfast. Uncle Will's taking me up in his Jet Ranger. I don't want to be late."

"We won't be late. Uncle Will's coming in thirty minutes. Plenty of time to eat your toast. Look at your watch."

The boy checked his wrist. "Okay. Twenty-eight minutes. I'll eat toast and PB and grape jelly. Can I read the helicopter brochures at the table that Will gave me?"

"Absolutely."

In the living room, Savanna retrieved the colorful brochures displaying information and photographs about Will's Skyline business and his blue-and-white helicopter. An hour ago, on his way to the airstrip to prep the machine, he'd dropped off the pamphlets.

"Did you know the Jet Ranger is the most versatile helicopter?" Christopher asked, when Savanna gave him the toast and he'd taken a bite.

"Chew and swallow first, Chris," Savanna advised. "Then speak."

"'Kay. Jet Rangers can cruise at 120 miles an hour and can carry seventy-six gallons of fuel."

Savanna laughed. "Way too much information for me to process right now. Why don't we wait until Uncle Will comes and then you can tell him all you've learned?"

Shoving his last piece of toast into his mouth, Christopher leaped from his chair, brochure clutched in hand. Old Blue trotting at his heels, he rushed into the living room, yelling, "Is Uncle Will here yet? It's ten past nine. He said he'd be here at quarter after."

"Give him another five minutes," Savanna called from the sink where she ran the water. "Why don't you put on your coat and mitts and your fleece hat?"

"I don't need a coat."

Savanna squirted soap into the sink while Georgia poured another coffee. "Put it on, Chris."

She could hear him moving about in the front entrance. "Where's my backpack?"

The infamous knapsack. Christopher went nowhere unless it hung from his shoulder. Which meant no one else left until the bag was found.

"I need my backpack for the brochures. And my maps. I need my maps." Panic rose.

"I'll go see." Georgia rose from the table.

"No, I'll go, Nana." Drying her hands on a towel, Savanna hurried into the living room. Flinging the cloth over her shoulder, she asked, "Have you checked your bedroom, Chris?"

"I always take my knapsack."

"Did you look in your bedroom, son?" she asked again.

"I can't leave here unless I have my knapsack." His voice rose in pitch. Old Blue nudged his snout against Christopher's hand.

Savanna sighed. "Hold on, honey. I'll see if I can find it." She walked to the bedroom they shared.

"Hurry," Christopher called. "I think Uncle Will's here."

The doorbell rang. *Thank God,* Savanna thought. No emergencies this morning. She heard Christopher ask Georgia, "Should I open it?"

"Yes, darlin', that's what you do when the doorbell rings."

"My dad said never to open the door without asking first. That's the rule."

"It's a good one. Open the door, Christopher."

The yellow-and-red knapsack sat behind the bedroom door. Will's voice drifted down the hallway. "Hey, tiger."

"I'm not a tiger. Tigers are cats and I don't like cats."

Will chuckled. "Well, you'd better not come to my house, then, because I own a cat."

Savanna paused on the bedroom's threshold. He owned a cat?

"Okay, I won't come to your house."

"Hey, I'm teasing, buddy." A deeper chuckle.

Christopher mumbled a reply Savanna didn't catch.

She hurried back. Will grin's twirled through her in a Snoopy dance. "He meant," she said to Christopher ignoring the man who looked like the hotshot pilot he was in Levi's and a black nylon flight jacket, his tawny hair tousled, "that when the cat's not *in* his house it's okay for you to come inside."

"I didn't…" Will began.

"Another time." Her eyes were direct. Had she known about the cat the other day, she would have told him about Chris's fear of felines. Worry rose. How on earth would she explain all that was Christopher to Will in a few short weeks?

"Are we going to the airport now?" the boy asked. "It's seventeen minutes after nine. We're two minutes late."

"On our way." Snatching her coat from the front closet, Savanna hurried to the kitchen with the towel. To Georgia she said, "I'll call when we get back around two or so."

"Have a wonderful time," the old woman said as Savanna hugged her before heading out the door. On the stoop, the grandmother watched them climb into Will's truck.

Savanna felt a flutter of regret. She suspected having Christopher around had brightened Georgia's days in a way that hadn't been there before.

The way Georgia's letters had brought peace to Elke.

Ah, girlfriend, I miss you. I miss our conversations, our laughs and how you thought Christopher was your shining star. Savanna vowed Will would clutch that same star before she left Alaska.

Belted in behind the driver's seat, Elke's son gazed out the side window. "Okay back there, pal?" Savanna asked.

"Yes, because I'm sitting in a Toyota 2004 4Runner SR5 with a brush guard on the grill and four spotlights on the roof and *Consumers Report* says they're very reliable and—"

Will laughed. "I take it you're into trains *and* cars."

"I'm not in a car. I'm in a four-wheel-drive SUV. I've never been inside a train or a helicopter. But I will be in a Jet Ranger real soon. Right?"

"Give us five minutes." Will shot a look at Savanna. "I'm glad you like machines, Chris."

"Last year he liked cars," Savanna pointed out. "Didn't you, buddy?"

"I like trains best. Helicopters are second best."

Will chuckled. "Wait until you go up in one."

"I am waiting."

Savanna reached back and patted Christopher's knee when his hands began flapping. "Remember, flying in Will's helicopter is like flying in the airplane, only the helicopter has bubble windows and it's not as big inside."

The flapping increased.

"We're almost there, honey," Savanna said when Will turned off the main road and started down the winding wilderness road. She glanced over. He checked the rearview mirror routinely.

He's worried. A spark of empathy touched Savanna. She recognized the symptoms of a new adventure in Christopher. If nothing else, the morning would relay insight to life with an autistic child for Will.

Parking the SUV in front of the hangar, he said, "Chris, today you're going up in your first set of fling wings."

"What are fling wings?"

"Helicopters. Fixed wings are airplanes."

Christopher thought a moment. "Oh! Whirly wings and stationary wings."

"Right." Will chuckled.

They climbed from the vehicle—Christopher hauling the knapsack—and followed Will inside the dark hangar where two small one-engine planes were parked.

"Where's your Jet Ranger?" Christopher asked.

"Ah. You've read the brochure."

"Uh-huh. The Jet Ranger can load 3,200 pounds. It flies one pilot, you, and four passengers, me and Savanna and other people, but not today. Its cruise speed is 120 miles an hour and it's one of the best light turbine helicopters."

"That all in the brochure?" Will said, around a laugh. "Seems I'll need to reread those pamphlets once in a while. Good work, pal." He ruffled the boy's hair; Christopher jerked aside.

"Whoa. Did I hurt you, Chris?"

Savanna caught Will's bewildered expression. "Chris, tell Will why you don't like people touching your head."

"It's the place of my thoughts. I don't want people touching my thoughts."

Will shot Savanna a glance. "Thanks for letting me know, buddy. I won't do it again."

"Chris also likes hugs," she said, "but he has to give them first. Right, Chris?"

"Uh-huh. I give the hugs. Where's the Jet Ranger?"

Will opened the back door. "There." He nodded toward the helicopter sitting a hundred feet away on a ragged patch of asphalt.

"Cool." The boy's eyes rounded. Dropping to his knees, he dug inside his knapsack and retrieved the brochure. "It's just like the photograph."

"Yep. It's the same bird."

"It isn't a bird. It's—"

"I know, Chris. Pilots often call their planes and helicopters birds, because we sort of soar through the clouds the way birds do."

"Oh."

Will's patience swelled the mother heart in Savanna. She had expected many traits from the swift-grinning pilot, but not this gentle forbearance with a needy little boy.

"Ready?" Will asked, but Christopher raced toward the helicopter yelling, "Wow, this is awesome!"

Savanna's stomach tightened. The machine looked small and confined. Elke and Dennis had died in a Cessna. In mountains as rugged as those tripping along the horizon.

She worried her bottom lip.

"Savanna." Will stepped beside her. "I know these mountains like the back of my hand."

"So did their pilot," she said, not hiding the thoughts he so accurately understood.

"But I'm not him. I would never take you or Christopher up if it wasn't safe."

She looked into his eyes. The dead pilot had probably re-iterated those exact words to his passengers at one time.

"Come on," Will coaxed softly. "Look at Christopher. He's enthralled with the thing."

Indeed, the boy rushed around the helicopter, eyes big as sourdough flapjacks, filing details into his receptive brain.

Will said, "Does he know how Dennis and Elke…?"

"I told him. Several times. But children with Asperger's often block information that overwhelms them."

Will observed the boy. "He'll remember them, won't he?"

"When he sees their pictures or when we talk about them."

"Did he cry?"

He'd huddled in a corner, rocking back and forth. Humming, humming, humming. The most pitiful sound she had heard in her life. And watching him on the bedroom floor, head buried in his knees, hands beating his skull… She'd had to give him an extra calming pill.

"Yes, he cried. Though not the way the average person does." Quietly she added, "Another day I'll explain."

Will gusted a breath. "I don't need to know how he took it."

"I disagree," Savanna said. She looked at his wind-blown hair. "You're his father, Will. It's your obligation to know. How else will you understand your son?"

How will you understand? Will glanced at the boy harnessed into the seat beside him, fluttering his hands like a bird with a broken wing. Something altered inside Will. Other than Savanna, *he* was the child's last hope, his final soft place to land, as the saying went.

Suddenly Will wanted nothing more than to take those quivering little fingers in his own, tell the boy not to worry—

the way Harlan had when Will first climbed into a helicopter seventeen summers before. He wished he could explain how he had felt, that he'd had butterflies in his stomach, but that he'd felt on top of the world, too. But he couldn't. The child was not like other children. Instead he was special and he needed Will's understanding above all.

"Okay, Chris," he said, swallowing back a swell of unfamiliar emotion and handing over the headgear. "I need you and Savanna to put on your headsets. Savanna, yours is attached to the back wall."

She found and secured the gear, while Will helped Christopher put on his set. "Can you both hear me?" Will asked, reaching for his black-rimmed aviators.

Christopher nodded enthusiastically. "Uh-huh!"

"Loud and clear," Savanna affirmed.

To Will she looked more nervous than the boy. "You okay?"

A hard nod. "Perfect."

Offering a reassuring smile, he pulled back the collective, slowly lifting the bird from the helo pad while confirming his coordinates with Nate Burns in the flight service station.

Behind him Savanna asked. "Can you tell us what you're going to do before you do it?"

"Sure." She'd want the boy prepped, in case he became distressed. *Makes two of us,* Will thought, wondering what the hell had possessed him to take an autistic kid up in a helicopter. Well, he'd take them to the end of the landing strip and back. Smiling at Christopher, he pointed to the instrument that looked like a joystick and said, "This is the collective. I'm going to use it to fly the helicopter. We'll go to the end of the runway and return."

As he actioned his words, the helicopter slowly lifted higher, then flew at a snail's pace along the paved line of the airstrip.

"I'm making a wide loop to circle back now. You'll feel us tilt a little to the left, then we'll level again." Carefully he made the turn, glancing at Christopher as he maneuvered the helicopter.

The boy sat with both hands on his thighs, not in a death grip, not flapping, but relaxed—with a rapt look on his face.

He likes it, Will thought on a surge of delight. "Okay, we're heading back to where we started. How's everyone doing?"

"Great," Savanna's voice was stronger than when they'd first climbed into the ship.

Flying problems. And hiding them from the boy. "Chris? You okay?"

"Awesome." He pointed at the front windscreen. "Can we go over there?"

"Toward the mountains?"

"Yes."

"Savanna?" Will scanned the forested landscape.

"For maybe ten minutes?" she suggested.

"Ten minutes it is."

Christopher pointed. "Can we go *to* the mountains?"

"Not quite, but where we're going they'll *look* closer."

The boy focused on a point ahead.

"Look to the right, guys. You'll see Starlight."

"I want to go to the mountains," Christopher repeated, intent on the horizon.

"Not today, bud."

"A bud is the stage of a flower or leaf before it opens in the spring."

Will laughed, relaxing more than he had all morning. "No grass growing under your feet, pal."

"For grass to grow under my feet—"

"Chris," Will patted the air, "it's just a saying. It means you're a swift thinker."

"Oh."

"Wouldn't you agree, Savanna?" Will grinned at the woman sitting rock rigid behind him.

"I agree completely. Christopher is one clever lad."

They flew for fifteen minutes toward the Talkeetna Mountains. Beyond their jagged rise, The High One, Denali, bumped the bright skyline, a snowy monarch over her crystalline kingdom.

Will gestured to the right. "That big tip is Mount Wrangell. And there's Sheep Mountain." He pointed left. "If we had time to fly farther west you'd see a spur of the Alaskan Railroad. It's 470 miles long."

"Cool."

"Savanna, you okay there?"

"Fine." A smile in her voice.

"No barf bag needed?" he teased.

"Not at the moment."

Will's shoulders eased. "That's what I like to hear."

They followed Glenn Highway for several minutes, before Will lifted the helicopter up over the trees again. He flew them across Tolsona Lake, its plate of ice breaking up like a busted windshield.

"Spring's on its way," he said, and later flew down the Nelchina River where ice chunks big as Volkswagens battered one another in the flowing waters. And later still, to a waterfall spangled with thousands upon thousands of raw diamonds.

They swept through a small forested valley as two eagles hung on an easy breeze. When he curved for home, he pointed out a patch of rusted deadwood. "Pine beetles."

"How sad," Savanna said. "I wish they could be stopped somehow."

"They're trying, but some say we need to stop tapping out the underground springs that feed the trees."

Christopher monotoned, "That's because the springs supply water to the trees and they make a sap that guards against bugs."

Will looked over. The kid never ceased to surprise him. "Where'd you learn that?"

"In a nature magazine."

"Well," Will said. "That's…awesometistic."

"Yep." Christopher agreed. Just the way Josh would.

Will curbed a laugh.

They returned to Starlight Airport fifty minutes later. Will talked through the landing as he maneuvered the helicopter toward the ground. As the engine died, he turned to Christopher. "So. Think you'll like helicopters as much as trains?"

"Helicopters are air machines. They're not the same."

A little pride drained from Will. "That mean you don't like them as much as trains?" He felt Savanna wait with him.

Christopher looked out the windscreen. "Helicopters are better than trains. They can go places trains can't. When can I go up again?"

Will removed his sunglasses. "Let's see how my agenda looks first, okay?"

"You have an agenda?"

"Couldn't live without it."

Christopher bobbed his chin in an exaggerated nod. "I understand."

Will winked at the woman seated behind them. He and the boy had found a diminutive commonality. Now all he had to do was transfer him from Georgia's house into the room he'd shown Savanna last week—and convince her to move in with them as the boy's nanny.

Chapter Seven

An hour before supper on Wednesday, Will was working up a sweat digging out a holly shrub at the corner of his house. Someone had given him the plant when he first moved in and over the years the roots had morphed into a creeping weed. About to swing the axe once more at the stubborn root core he'd unearthed a foot in the ground, he heard a vehicle pull into his driveway.

Valerie's beat-up Dodge Dakota.

Now what?

Blowing out a breath, he pushed back his cap and wiped the sweat from his brow. The woman was like a terrier, nabbing a pant leg and hanging on.

Suddenly Josh came to mind and Will's unlikable thoughts vanished. Axe in hand, he stepped out of the hole as she climbed from the pickup's cab. "Hey, Val."

"Will."

"Did I forget to pick up Josh or something?" He knew he hadn't. He surveyed his calendar every morning while drinking his first coffee. He wasn't seeing Josh until the weekend when the team met at the park diamond for practice.

"No. He's, um, at Roger's playing video games." She studied his house. "Your home is so beautiful, the way the sunlight comes through the trees and hits those logs."

Was there a point to this? "Yeah, I suppose."

Her cheeks turned pink and she inched into the shadow of an evergreen—as if she didn't want her embarrassment to show—and eyed him warily.

"You need something, Val?"

She took a deep breath, kicking at a clump of dirt. That's when it hit him. She was needing something all right, and it was *him*. Dammit, hadn't he made it clear at the dance he wasn't interested? Why was she putting herself through another bout of rejection from him? Because he would reject her, kindly, of course, but as far as he was concerned their day in the sun, so to speak, was done.

"I, uh…" A schoolgirl giggle.

Will tilted his head, waiting. He would not make it easy for her. If she couldn't read his body language, he was not going to explain it to her. She wasn't a clueless woman, just one on a mission. Unfortunately, that mission was him.

"Were you chopping wood?" she asked.

He held an axe, didn't he? Lifting his Red Sox ball cap, he scratched his damp scalp. "I'm clearing out a holly shrub. Roots are tenacious."

"I've heard that stuff can pop up everywhere."

Come on Val. Stop stammering. Let's be done with it. Will looked over his shoulder. The sun was fading fast and he wanted to get back to axing that shrub before night fell.

"I...need..."

He took a step back. Maybe it was about her son. "This about Josh?"

"No. No I...came here to see you." Her face turned a violent pink, her eyes begged him to invite, to understand.

"Why?"

For three breaths she looked at him, then shook her head. "Know what? This wasn't a good idea. Sorry to bother you," Purse tight under her arm, she hurried back to her truck.

Will sighed. "Val, if there's something I can help with—"

She whirled. "Would you go out with me again?"

Bingo. "Excuse me?" He couldn't help the semi laugh that pocked the quiet air.

She looked like the earth was about to swallow her whole. "Sorry," she repeated. "I must be losing it. Forget I asked." Grabbing the handle of the truck door, she yanked it open.

"Wait a second." Something inside Will loosened. He walked over as she stood half in and half out of the vehicle. "Never apologize for courage."

Her mid-section sagged in visible relief. "You mean you'll—you'll go out with me?"

"Val." He blew a breath. "I don't know what to s—"

Before he finished, she set her fingers against his mouth. His head jerked back.

"Oh, God, I'm sorry." Eyes round and worried, she hugged her purse to her breasts. "I shouldn't have asked but, see...Josh loves you like a dad and I thought you and I could try..."

A strip of sunlight struck her face and she turned her head, blinking hard. Will rubbed an eyebrow. "Val, you know I like Josh. I like him a lot, but you and I, we already..." *Did that scene.*

From the way she looked at him, she'd clearly read his mind. "As I said, forget it. I just thought we could have dinner one night. My treat for—for all you've done for Josh, and then, well, maybe we could…could see…"

Her words sparked a memory: Savanna's information about friendships and autistic children. Thinking hard, he nodded slowly. "Might be a good way for Chris and Josh to get acquainted."

"Chris?"

"My nephew. He'll be living with me." Within the next few days if he could arrange it with Savanna. "We go out to dinner, he comes along, Val." And that was a rule and he would not debate.

He could see her mind seesawing over his offer. Savanna had told Will that Josh seemed irritated at times by Chris's antics in class, especially when he repeated words the teacher said, or if she presented a lesson he didn't favor.

And then there was Josh. He knew the boy hadn't liked the fact Christopher was part of Will's life now. Just the other day, Josh had mentioned Chris constantly talking of helicopters. While the words were part of another conversation, Will caught a thread of jealousy.

His eyes narrowed at Valerie's silence. "If it's going to be a problem," he said, voice cool as the lengthening shadows, "I understand."

"No, no. Josh will love going with Christopher."

Yeah, he figured she'd make it happen come hell or high water. "Great. Decide on a date and time and we'll be there." He shouldered the axe. "Well, gotta get that shrub chopped out before it re-roots."

She gave him a timid smile. "I'll call you."

"Sure."

He watched her get in the truck, give a wave, then back

from the lane. Three seconds later she was gone. He walked back to the holly shrub. An evening for the boys might be exactly what Chris needed to develop a friendship. And with Savanna along...

Yep, dinner with the Jaxes wasn't looking so bad.

He was whistling when he swung the axe.

Throughout the next few days, while she worked with Christopher in class, Savanna thought about Will's words after the helicopter ride.

He wanted to begin the transition process and move Christopher into his home within the week. She knew he was right. The quicker it happened, the sooner Christopher would acclimatize to Will's home and the man himself.

And the process of goodbye begins, she thought during recess supervision while watching Christopher with Angela Germaine, the principal's daughter. From the onset, the little girl had taken Will's son under her motherly wing.

Today the pair stood out of the wind near the classroom windows while Christopher relegated his new-found passion: helicopters and flying over Alaska's terrain.

Every minute or two Angela would ask a question. Savanna could have hugged the girl. Ms. Murphy had been right. Angela came by her name honestly. A sweet, kind-hearted little soul, the genuine article.

A titter erupted from Angela at something Christopher related, but there was no sneer in the sound. Not the way there had been with some of the others in class.

Josh Jax, Valerie's son and a boy Will coached, was one of those others. Savanna kept an eye out as he and his friend Roger walked past the pair by the classroom.

"Hey, Angela," Josh called. "Aren't you sick of helicopters and trains yet?"

"Go away, Josh." Angela frowned. "You're not nice."

"Least I'm not a weirdo." Josh laughed.

Roger slapped Josh on the back. "Or a freak-o."

Christopher's hands began flailing. It was all Savanna could do not to walk over and tell the boys to treat people with decency.

But Angela set her fists on her hips, mother hen to the rescue. "Josh Jax, you should be ashamed of yourself. You, too, Roger." She glared at the taller boy whom Savanna had observed doodling in his notebook instead of completing his assignments. "You're both mean. Chris is very smart, you know."

"Yeah, he's so smart he can't talk about anything except trains and helicopters."

"And maps," Roger jeered. "Got your map, Chris? Maybe you should get it out so you can find your way back to class."

More laughter.

Christopher stared ahead, frozen to a spot beyond the children. Hands fluttering.

Enough. Savanna headed for the group. "Maybe you boys could find more constructive things to do?"

"You're not our teacher," Josh sneered.

"No," she said, "but Christopher is Will's nephew." She hated using that kind of clout, but this was Christopher. *Her* Christopher who, until today, hadn't encountered this brand of cruelty. "Think Will would like your behavior, Josh?"

Head bowed, the boy dug a sneaker in the dirt. "No-o," he said so quietly she almost missed the word.

"You're right. He'd be very hurt."

Eyes full of worry, Josh asked, "You gonna tell him?"

"Perhaps *you* should."

"*Me?* But—"

"Would you rather he find out from someone else?"

His eyes flicked to Christopher to Angela to Roger. "They won't tell."

How could she refute it? Too often kids bore the brunt of bullying years before they buckled under stress.

Her pause returned smugness to Josh's expression. "Will won't find out," he assured.

Before she could respond, the bell rang and the two boys ran off, laughter trailing in their wake.

"Come on, Chris." Angela caught Will's son by a quivering hand. "Time to go back to class."

He dug in his heels. "Don't want to."

"It's okay," she said. "I won't let anyone say mean things. I promise."

Flap, flap. "You were here when they called me a weirdo."

"And I told them it was wrong."

"I don't like school anymore."

Angela turned to face her new friend. "Some kids say bad things, Chris. But most of them are like me. Nice." She smiled. "Come on. We'll be late."

"Late?" Christopher checked his wrist watch. "It's time for math and ratios."

"Yup," Angela agreed. "You can help me 'cause I don't get them at all."

"They're easy," the boy said, and walked in his toe-rocking gait to the school's doors.

Expelling a long breath, Savanna walked behind the children. She'd need to explain what happened today to Will, prepare him for the difficulties Christopher would encounter with other students, other adults. As a parent of an autistic child, Will needed to discern pitfalls the future might bestow.

But first she needed to speak to Valerie about her son.

* * *

At 2:30, Savanna took Christopher home to Georgia.

Since the boy's first school day in Starlight almost three weeks ago, Savanna, Christopher and Georgia had fallen into a routine of snacking on the homemade cookies Georgia baked each afternoon. Christopher drank his glass of milk, Georgia brewed a pot of tea for herself and Savanna and they discussed the day while Christopher fed crumbs to Blue in the living room and watched Sponge Bob reruns.

Today, Savanna said to the boy, "I forgot something at school, Chris. I'll be right back, okay?"

"He'll be fine," Georgia said. "We'll have our snacks and watch Sponge Bob together."

Fifteen minutes later Savanna entered the school office. The secretary was pulling on her coat. "Valerie, can we talk a moment?"

Wary as a mouse in a corner, the woman hesitated.

Savanna asked, "Has Josh mentioned Chris to you today?"

"Should he have?"

Savanna explained the recess incident. "Please understand. It's very hard for Christopher to make friends and doubly hard for him to comprehend unkindness. Often he doesn't understand why, just that it's directed at him."

The secretary looked taken aback. "Are you saying my kid isn't kind?"

"Not unkind, but he does need to recognize that Christopher might perceive conversation differently and in a very literal sense."

Valerie took her purse from a drawer. "All kids tease," she said defensively. "It's part of childhood."

"Yes, but as you know not all kids handle teasing well.

And if they have Asperger's Syndrome it's a hundred times worse because these children often don't translate teasing."

Valerie frowned. "Is he really that bad?"

"Autism isn't bad," Savanna pointed out, hoping to reach this mother. "It's a condition. Christopher is high functioning, which means by learning certain coping skills, he should lead a fairly normal life. It's like you teaching Josh proper etiquette or to cross the street by first looking both ways."

"Josh isn't a bad boy."

"I know," Savanna agreed gently. She hesitated, then decided to lay the cards face-up on the table. "Could there be some jealousy with Josh because Chris is Will's nephew?"

Valerie looked away.

Okay, then. "I wonder," Savanna said, cautiously, "if the boys played together one evening after school, do you think that would help?"

Valerie brightened. "I'm having supper with Will and Christopher Friday night. I'll get Josh to ask Chris over an hour before, so they get used to each other."

Savanna's breath caught. Will had asked Valerie out? For a heartbeat, words failed. "That's wonderful. If you go someplace where the kids can play a video game, it'll help. Christopher loves video games."

Enthusiasm lit Valerie's eyes. "So does Josh. Okay, I'll speak to him. You're right. Christopher needs friends, not enemies. See you in the morning."

She left Savanna staring around the empty office.

Isn't that what you wanted? Will and Valerie together?

Yes, but...

You're leaving, remember? This is best. You know it is. Besides, Valerie is a nice woman.

Truths Savanna could not deny or that lessened the ache in her heart.

* * *

"Ready to move into my house, buddy?" Will asked Christopher inside Georgia's front door three nights later.

"Are we going for a helicopter ride first?" the boy asked.

"Soon, pal. But I need to finish some schedules before then."

"I have an agenda, too."

"I know." Will looked at Savanna standing behind Christopher. He had requested she move with the boy into the guest room as a sort of nanny. Now he wondered if she was relocating due to Dennis's last testament—or was there a small chance she found the idea of living in Will's house intriguing? He could only hope.

"Christopher," Georgia said, "you'll come visit me after school, won't you?"

"Every day," the boy responded looking at the door and fluttering his hands.

"I'm glad." Her smile was sad.

"I'm going to Uncle Will's place with Savanna."

"I know, honey." Georgia followed them out the door.

"Honey is what bees make in a hive." Christopher tiptoed off the stoop. "The worker bees fly all day collecting pollen—"

"Chris," Savanna called from the stoop. "Remember what I explained about endearments? How they're nice nicknames?"

"Oh. Yeah."

"That's what Nana meant."

"Okay." He walked to Will's truck without looking back or saying goodbye or giving Georgia a hug.

Savanna's heart ached for the great-grandmother. The child was leaving without a second thought. *It's not carelessness,* she wanted to clarify. Just part of the condition.

"We'll see you tomorrow around 2:45." She enfolded Georgia into her arms, offering the hug the woman had craved—needed—from her great-grandson.

Georgia's eyes clouded. "I shouldn't feel so emotional. You're only four houses down the alley, but I've gotten used to having noise in my house again."

Savanna kissed the old woman's papery cheek. "I'll call you the minute we're unpacked."

Will shoved their suitcases into the rear storage of the 4Runner as Savanna slipped into the passenger side. "Seat belt on, Chris," she directed the child sitting behind her.

Will jumped in, turned the ignition. "Georgia okay?"

"She's fine. A little teary, is all."

He put the truck into gear. "We could invite her for supper with Valerie."

"That would be nice." He had explained tonight's supper date when he visited Christopher yesterday following Savanna's chat with Valerie.

Savanna kept her gaze on the road. Though her heart sank a little, Will and Valerie would be good as a couple. The boys were close in age, but most of all Valerie was Will's age.

He sent her a lopsided grin. "It's not a date."

How did he do that, read her thoughts so easily? "Who you see, Will, is not my concern."

The corners of his mouth tensed. "Val thinks the boys should get to know each other better. I think with Josh living up the street, taking the boys for pizza is a good idea."

Savanna was tempted to say, "Ah, a family thing." Instead she said, "What do you think of that, Chris? You'll be eating your favorite food, pizza."

"Can't eat pizza," he said in his static voice. "Mom isn't here."

Elke. Who had constructed pizza with the finesse of an architect. Savanna could almost hear her laughter as she sliced olives, tomatoes, mushrooms and pepperoni.

Will turned into his lane, drove toward the beautiful structure that was his home. "Did your mother make pizza, son?"

Son. Savanna wondered if he realized how easily the word had tumbled from his mouth.

Fixated on the door of the house, Christopher repeated, "Mom isn't here."

"I know," Will said softly, shutting off the motor. "This is my home. And now it's yours."

"Mom isn't here," Christopher echoed, hands flapping.

Savanna wanted to explain to Will, *He doesn't mean Elke isn't in the house. He's remembering his mother is dead.*

Will opened the door of the truck. Worry darkened his eyes as they met Savanna's over the boy's ragamuffin head. "Ready to go inside, buddy? Get settled in your room?"

Anxiety ran cold through Savanna. Were they were doing the right thing, adding one more disruption this early in long rope of disruptions over the past weeks?

Perhaps, they should have waited, given both man and boy a couple of months to adapt, to connect.

And what about her and Will? Could they be a united front for the child in the interim? Will danced on Saturday nights. And flew down rivers and up mountains, sometimes remaining overnight.

She followed them into the cabin, her mind afire with options and worry. Standing inside the house with its burgundy furniture, its stone fireplace, its chef's kitchen, Savanna realized only one option mattered. Dad and son needed to live together. *This* was the "right" time, the only time.

Now or never.

"Chris." Will paused in the great room. Savanna had not seen his eyes so serious. "My house is your house," he said.

The child's fingertips tapped together. She would need to remind Will that the boy was intensely literal. 'My house is your house' could create a host of consequences.

"Really?" Christopher deadpanned.

"Really." Happiness rode his deep voice. "Come on, pal. Come see your room."

The one facing a calendar scene outside the window. The one with enough floor space to lay out a train set.

Fingers fidgeting, the child moved cautiously forward and down the hallway. Will stood inside the bedroom, excitement in his eyes. "So. What do you think, Chris?"

A spanking-new train track with two red engines and several cars of various colors cut an oval over the hardwood floor to the left of the bed.

"My trains!" Christopher fell to his knees beside the controls and immediately tugged the lever; one little engine tooted as the model slowly began a revolution around its track.

Behind Savanna, Will sighed, "Thank God."

He'd been uncertain how his gift would be received. The bones in her chest ached. "When did you buy it?"

"Picked it up last Tuesday when I flew a couple of glacier skiers back to Anchorage."

"You've made his day."

A black-and-white spotted cat twined around her ankles. "Oh…!" Savanna looked at Will. "Get it out of here," she whispered. *"Fast."*

Too late. Christopher caught sight of the feline and leaped to his feet. "Get away! Get away!" Clambering onto the bed, he crouched in the corner of wall and headboard. "Cats are related to jaguars and lions and cougars and pumas and leopards and—"

Will scooped up his pet. "Sorry, Chris. I forgot." He shot a harried look at Savanna. "I'm really sorry." And then he was gone.

Savanna hurried across the room. "Christopher, it's okay. Will's taken the cat away. It won't be here anymore. I promise." She touched his arm, but he huddled into the pillows, hiding his eyes. "Everything is going to be all right, honey. Christopher, it's all right."

She sat next to him, coaxing, soothing, until at last his restless hands quieted and he raised his head. Fear magnified his eyes. "The cat went away?"

"Yes, it did." How on earth had Will forgotten after she'd explained the phobia the night after the helicopter ride? "It won't be in your room again. Will won't let it come back."

"Didn't he know I'm afraid of cats?"

"Yes, but he forgot. But not on purpose." She smiled. "Christopher, remember when we talked about cats and played pretend games about cats to help you not be afraid?"

"We played the cat games in Honduras."

"Yes. What did I say you should do when you feel afraid?"

"Breathe slowly. And remember cats are pets, then think of something else." A loud sniff. "Does Will think I'm crazy?"

"No, honey. He's just very upset with himself for forgetting my explanation."

"Is he going to play the kitten games now?"

"One day. But right now, he's new at learning what you like." She nodded to the model train. "I think he got it right with the train set. Don't you?"

Christopher studied the complicated toy, then climbed gingerly from the bed. Another minute and he was lost in watching the train and manipulating its controls again.

The model had chugged its umpteenth course around the track when Will returned. From the rumpled bed, Savanna looked across the room. *Your son isn't like the Little League boys. He's different and precious and you'll need a lot of patience.*

Fingers in his rear pockets, Will leaned against the doorjamb, watching Christopher for several minutes before his worried gaze locked on Savanna.

"We're fine," she mouthed.

But their newfound pleasure in the toy train had vanished.

Chapter Eight

Will cursed silently and stared down at the boy playing with the model train he'd bought on impulse. Why hadn't he recalled the fear about the cat? *Damn it*, he should have remembered. Savanna had told him not six days ago—after their ride in the Jet Ranger—about a cat scratching Christopher's hand when he was eight and he'd needed two stitches. That the experience had terrified him.

Shows where your priorities are, Will. You're too damned busy planning your next flightseeing tour.

An image of Dennis flitted into Will's mind.

Dennis with sadness in his brown eyes. And disappointment.

You let your relationship with your brother slide, and in a heartbeat Dennis is gone. Forever. You going to blow this chance with Christopher, too?

Christopher, with Dennis's hair.

And my dimples.

The realization rocked Will back a step. Christopher, a mix of both brothers. *Dennis,* he thought, and a wave of grief and love so fierce swept through Will he gulped several breaths, *this was the son you loved.*

Time to step up to the plate, Will, put the boy number one. Every day. When his feet hit the hardwood beside the bed, his first thought had to be of Christopher.

Savanna had whispered, *We're fine.*

Fine until the next time he fumbled the ball. And, God help him, without the woman on the bed, he could see himself fumbling it over and over again.

Stepping into the hallway, he beckoned her to follow.

"It's okay, Will. Chris is calm now," she said when they were out of earshot.

He tossed back his head, stared at the ceiling. "Honest to God, I don't know how I forgot."

Her hand touched his arm. "Don't take it so hard. One thing to remember about Christopher—once the incident is over, it's history. Until the next time." Her smile was sad and sweet.

She was right; already the boy had lost himself in the train set, cat entirely forgotten.

"Where is it?" she whispered.

The cat. "I locked her in the laundry room. Guess I'll have to give her away."

"If you have a neighbor who can take her for a few days, that'll give me some time to work with Christopher. I've done some role playing with him in the past on this issue. We were almost at the acceptance stage when…"

"The crash happened."

She sighed. "Yes, and then less than a week later he saw a cat painting on the wall inside Georgia's door. She had to put it away before he would enter the house."

Will was silent for a moment. "His parents wanted you to fix every situation."

"I had the strategies, which I passed on to Elke and Dennis. But in this case both felt it was just easier not to have pets. It made sense. They each worked long hours and wanted to keep their time with Christopher upbeat and positive."

So the boy's parents left the teaching of life skills to Savanna. *What happened to you, Dennis, that you'd take the easy way out?*

Hell, Will wanted to stride into the bedroom, grab Christopher and hold him. Hold him until all the delays and difficulties and missing pieces in his young mind disappeared.

Hadn't Dennis wanted to do the same thing? Hadn't Elke?

Will studied the woman who had become Christopher's surrogate mother. She'd done three years of miracle work down in Honduras, he suspected. He couldn't imagine the child living without her. More so, Will couldn't imagine how he would manage without her. A small package of intelligence and compassion, that was Savanna.

You lucked out, Dennis.

Today she'd pulled her penny-red hair into a bun that accentuated the no-nonsense clarity in her green eyes. Tiny hoops of gold clung to her elegant ears.

His eyes trailed downward, along the lacy neckline of her mist-gray sweater, to where the knitted material molded her breasts—breasts large and round as grapefruits and soft, he imagined, as a kitten's fur.

When those breasts rose on a long, steady breath, his eyes shot upward. Her brows lifted, two graceful arches that held no surprise. He almost smiled.

"Are we finished talking about Christopher, Will?" she asked, looking down her dignified nose, which—

considering he had ten inches of height on her—might have been a neck-cricking feat for someone other than Savanna.

Once more he checked the bedroom. "He going to be okay for a few minutes?"

"For a couple hours." One side of her mouth lifted.

"Come with me." Taking her hand, he led her down the hall to the great room where he turned and faced her. "Stay."

"I'm not going anywhere."

"I mean stay for good, not just the twelve weeks. Christopher needs you and I need you to help me with him." When she opened her mouth, he shook his head. "Hear me out. You can teach, tutor or consult, Savanna. You've got years of experience. Even Harry Germaine at the school said they need people like you in the district. And I'll pay you to care for Christopher when I'm not here. You'll see him daily, he'll see you in the classroom *and* you'll get to do the work you love."

Her eyes had gold streaks near the pupils. "Will, I…"

He set the side of his palm against her lips. "Just think about it, okay? Don't make a decision yet. Promise you'll give it some honest thought."

She eased back from his touch. Her eyes seized his. "All right," she said slowly. "I'll think about it."

He wanted to kiss her, to swoop up her lovely feminine body, swing her around like a man celebrating a win. "Thank you." And then, before he could stop himself, he leaned down and set his mouth on hers.

A fistful of heartbeats passed as he waited for her to move away, and when she remained stationary, he pressed in closer. His fantasies had barely evoked what reality brought to fruition.

She was quiet moonlight.

She was a tender song.

She drifted through his veins.

A moan escaped her throat and his tongue gamboled along her lips. "Let me in, Savanna," he said, and her hands traveled his shirt, then up, up, around his neck.

Under the hem of her sweater, he found warm skin.

Her essence dizzied him. Her scent dazzled him.

He wanted to devour.

He wanted to kiss her blind.

He wanted to lay her on the rug under their feet. Take her. Hard. Easy. A thousand ways.

"Will, stop." A whisper.

He lifted his mouth from the junction of her shoulder and neck, where her skin teased like honey.

Eyes dark as moss. Lips lush and rich.

She eased away from his hands. Shook her head. Her eyes were woeful. "This is not right. I'm nine years ol—"

"Stop," he demanded, and kissed her again, a smacking kiss that rang through the great room. "You are not old, damn it. Stop thinking numbers, Savanna. Feel. *Feel*." He cupped her buttocks and pulled her close. "*That's* what you do to me."

She jerked away. "Don't be ridiculous."

"Ridiculous? Way I see it, it's a man's normal response to the woman he's interested in, the woman he's attracted to." He bent to her level. "And I *am* attracted here, Savanna. I want you in my bed. I want you under me. I want *you*."

Staring at him, she backed away, pushed her hands into the pockets of her brown corduroy jeans. "I'm sorry. I can't stay in this house." She nearly ran to the front door.

He was after her in a flash. "Why not?"

"I'm going back to Georgia's." Which didn't answer his question.

"What about Christopher?"

He saw her pause, cast a glance toward the hallway leading to the boy's room. "He'll be too engrossed to know I've left. Meantime, call the respite worker. We'll talk tomorrow."

And then she was gone.

Savanna shut Will's front door, hurried across the porch and pushed through its screened door. Before she reached the bottom step, she hesitated.

What am I doing?

She couldn't leave Christopher alone with Will. The man knew virtually nothing of his son's behaviors and habits—or how to deal with them.

And Christopher… Leaving him with Will was setting the boy up for a plethora of confusion.

She had to stay. The realization had her sitting down hard, head in hands. She shouldn't have kissed him, shouldn't have let herself feel what intellect had warned against.

Will Rubens was interested in her for one reason. Christopher. She was simply a sidebar, a convenience. She had to believe that. *Had* to. Contemplating more, that something *real* existed between them…

God, she was such a schmuck. *You see a pair of blue eyes and all your red flags fly off with the first wind.*

How many other women had fallen under Will's spell? Valerie, for one. Except Valerie was Will's age. She had a son Christopher's age. Single, and a genuinely decent person, Valerie was family. And pretty. Perfect for Will.

"You are an old maid, Savanna," she whispered. "Used and abused."

And so damned scared to let herself live, truly *live*, for a single moment.

A fissure traveled slowly over her locked heart, oozing

out a memory and, for the first time in seventeen years, she allowed herself a glimpse...

Of Liberia. Her first assignment in the Peace Corps. Where unrest ran like whitewater rapids. Where guns and guerrillas were as commonplace as cotton candy at a fair.

Young and educated, eager and determined, she'd been a consummate candidate for the corps's education program, for teaching ESL to children and parents, as well as directing them onto the path of improvement.

She'd thought nothing of journeying alone to communities ruled by disease and flies, hunger and stagnant water.

Until arrogance had caught her on a road between villages late at night. Her own arrogance—that corrupt politics could not stop her from assisting the helpless, the downtrodden. Children and mothers lost in poverty.

Sitting on Will's step, she whimpered. And remembered....

Hard, dark faces. Glittering black eyes. Surrounding her Jeep, surrounding her.

Guns jabbing her ribs. Boots pinning her arms. Zippers hissing. One, then another and another. Eight in all.

A night of rage, of defeat.

A Beyond Borders doctor traveling through the Lofa region had found her on the roadside at dawn. Had healed her. Offered truth: *The damage is too great.*

Dreams of bearing children—broken.

Dreams of family, gone.

A man would want family. A man like Will, who was slowly realizing he was a father. Who coached Little League and danced Saturday nights and flew through mountain canyons. What would he want with a woman unable to give him another child, a little girl, perhaps?

Palming cheeks that hadn't succumbed to tears in almost two decades, she raised her head.

Josh stood in Will's driveway. Savanna manufactured a smile. "Hey, Josh." Her voice rasped and she cleared her throat.

The boy flicked a look to the house. "Is Will home?"

"Yes. Go on inside."

"Shouldn't I knock?"

She pushed back unruly strands escaping the bun she'd twisted up that morning. "He won't mind."

"He was supposed to meet me'n mom for pizza a hour ago." Annoyance directed at Savanna traced his words.

"I'm sorry. We— There was a small crisis." *My little boy cowered from a cat. Will kissed me until I couldn't think.*

Valerie's son climbed the steps. "He should've called. Mom's been waiting, and I washed my hands three times."

"You don't have to wash your hands so often. It's actually not good for the skin."

"Mom hates germs. Washing your hands kills germs."

"Yes, it does."

He looked back. His hazel gaze was direct. "You should wash your face."

A laugh popped from her throat. "Just what a girl wants to hear." No doubt tears blotched her cheeks and gunk stuck under her nose. For a moment she thought he'd say more, then he climbed the steps to the screened door of the porch.

"What's going on here?" Will spoke from the cabin's door.

"Will!" Josh's glad note. "Didja forget about the pizza?"

"Not all, bud. Look, can you check on Christopher? He's playing with his new train set in his bedroom. Just give a holler. I'll be there in a couple minutes."

"Sure." The boy walked into the house.

Three strides and Will crossed the porch, shoved open the screened door. A creak, wood slapping closed, and then he was crouching beside Savanna, his hand cupping her cheek. "You stayed."

She drowned in his lake eyes. "Yes."

Will hurried to Christopher's bedroom.

God help him, he'd convinced Savanna to stay. And to come with him and Christopher, Josh and Valerie to Bob's Pizza.

Chris, she had said, loved spaghetti. In his mind Will saw a large pizza for the Jaxes, while and he, Christopher and Savanna ate big plates of meatballs; then later the boys would play a couple games on Bob's antiquated arcade machines.

Christopher still sat on the floor, wrangling the train's joy stick. In the middle of the oval track, Josh sat crossed-legged watching engines and cars revolve around the track. His eyes wove up to Will.

"Cool," he said with a wide grin. "Wish Mom would get me one of these."

"Come anytime," Will told him. "I'm sure Chris won't mind."

Josh looked at Christopher. "Can I, Chris?"

"Trains are for after school. Trains are not for anytime."

"That's what I meant," Josh said. His eyes darted to Will.

Savanna stepped into the room. "Christopher," she said. "Will and I would like to take you, along with Josh and his mom to have supper at a restaurant."

"I want to play with my train."

"You can play with your train when we get home."

He continued maneuvering the controls. "I want to play now."

Savanna knelt beside the boy. The red bun of hair listed to one side. "I'm hungry, Chris. It's time to eat."

Raising his head, he smiled at Savanna, and it went straight through Will's heart. The boy had Dennis's three-cornered smile.

"I get to play with my train after supper?"

"Yes." She gave him a quick, easy hug, one Will suddenly longed to offer. "After we come home from the restaurant."

"Is the cat gonna come in and scratch my train?"

"No. The cat is in her own room and the door is locked. And Will has the key."

Christopher stopped the train. A second's silence passed while Will held his breath.

"Okay." The boy climbed to his feet. "I want my door locked so the cat and Josh can't come in here."

"We can close the door," Will said. "Josh will be coming with us, buddy."

Christopher walked past the other boy. "I don't like Josh."

"Chris." Will gaped. "That wasn't very nice. How would you like it if somebody—"

"Christopher," Savanna interrupted. "What is it you don't like about Josh?"

"He likes carnivores."

"I do not," Josh protested.

"Yes, you do." Christopher glared at the other boy's shoulder. "You wear carnivore shirts."

Josh's mouth dropped open. "What?"

"You wear carnivore shirts."

"I do not!"

"Boys," Will interjected. What the hell was going on here?

"What type of carnivores?" Savanna asked quietly.

"Jaguars."

"That's my team," Josh protested. "Will—" a look of misery, "—sometimes I wear the Jaguars jersey to school."

Will bent on one knee in front of Dennis's son. "Chris, the jaguar shirt Josh has is part of a baseball uniform the Starlight Jaguars wear. He plays catcher for the team."

Christopher stared at Will's shoulder. "I want to eat spaghetti now."

"All right." Will rose, hand lifting to tousle the boy's hair, then dropping away. A yearning to earn the child's trust shot through Will. "Let's go have some supper."

After closing Christopher's door, they trooped down the hallway to the great room where the boy grabbed his knapsack from the welcome mat at the front door.

"You don't need a knapsack," Josh said.

"I like my knapsack."

"Well, I like my Jaguar jersey, so there."

Will sighed. "Boys, let's call a truce, huh?" At least until the evening ended. "Both of you get in the back seat and buckle up." Savanna pulled on her coat. She hadn't looked at him once since she told him she would stay.

Driving to Valerie's, Will wondered what waited for him at the restaurant. Christopher hated cats and disliked Josh. Savanna was only staying because of Christopher. And in a few minutes Valerie's eyes would implore Will to see her as The One.

Yep, the friggin' evening would be a piece of cake.

Savanna set tomorrow's agenda on the night table before tucking Christopher into his new bed, one he would sleep in every night until he was old enough to leave Will's care and forge a life of his own.

While the thought uplifted her, it was edged with sadness. Barring the worst, that something happened to Will, security would be Christopher's for the rest of his life. But along with that security, Savanna's days with the child were numbered.

Eventually Will would marry and Christopher would once again have the mother he needed.

And from what Savanna saw tonight, she knew Valerie wanted that, as well. The moment the woman stepped into Will's SUV, Savanna understood what it meant when they said people staked territory around their partners. While Valerie wasn't openly hostile, Savanna recognized the woman's disappointment when she saw who sat next to Will in the front seat.

Valerie had not expected Will to bring his nephew's care giver. Nor had she expected Will to explain, "Savanna's staying with me until Christopher's settled in."

At Bob's Pizza, she had purposely waited until Valerie took the spot beside Will in the booth, then sat across from the woman along with the boys.

Oh, yes, she'd caught Will's frown at the seating arrangement.

How could he not see Valerie's happiness? The woman had smiled through the whole meal, a pretty smile that any man would appreciate.

On the way home, Savanna switched places to sit in back with the boys while Valerie sat up front with Will.

He hadn't spoken to her since they walked into the house, and Savanna readied Christopher for bed.

After shutting off the night lamp, she waited for Christopher's slight snore, then brushed a kiss to his hair.

In the guest room, she found her suitcase on the floor beside the bed. Tomorrow she'd retrieve the remaining four suitcases from Georgia's and finally hang up Christopher's clothes. She wouldn't yet think of the chore granting permanency to Christopher's relocation.

It was what Dennis and Elke had bequeathed.

She'd finished shoving the empty suitcase into the closet

when Will spoke from the doorway. "I'll take that out to the garage." Stepping into the room, he picked up the bag. "Be right back."

A creature of habit, she shut off the bedside lamp before walking to the window. She loved looking out into the night. On Fox Avenue no pole lamps offered light for the late-night walker. As with most residences in Starlight, evergreens framed Will's house, their massive frames bumping the night sky.

By pushing open the window, she let in the clear, crisp air with its fragrance of sap and dank soil. A slight breeze swung a wind chime somewhere on the rear porch, the sound lovely and elusive in the dark.

"Room suit you?" From the doorway, Will's deep voice traveled through the shadows.

"Very much." She did not turn, but continued her vigilance out the window.

He walked to where she stood, felt him stop behind her. "By the way, I've taken my cat over to Valerie's for the interim."

"I'm sorry, Will. I wish there was another solution."

"I'll ask around town, see if anyone is interested in taking her. She's a sweet little thing. I found her out by the hangar last summer. No one knew where she'd come from. I figure someone had a last kitten they couldn't give away and dropped her off there, hoping a pilot would take her home."

She smiled. "One did." On a deep breath, she continued, "Sometimes it makes me wonder about people."

"Agreed."

She heard his hands rasp denim. *Probably slipping his fingers into those rear pockets.* A routine she had come to accept as pure Will.

"What were you trying to do tonight?" he asked.

"Eat a very tasty plate of spaghetti."

"Let's cut to the chase, Savanna. I mean what were you doing with Valerie and me? Playing matchmaker? I told you, I'm not interested in the woman."

"Maybe you should be. She's a good mother and she cares for you. She's pretty—"

"Whoa, stop right there." On her shoulders his hands were warm. "Listen carefully," he said, turning her around. "I am. Not. Interested. In Valerie. I coach her son, I do fun activities with him, eat ice cream with him, but I'm not going to be his daddy." His eyes were direct. "I *have* a boy to raise. He's about all I can handle right now."

"Josh would be good for Christopher."

"As a friend, not a brother. Savanna, I'll let you in on a little secret. Valerie has been giving me moon eyes for two years. Initially, we dated, but it didn't work out. She's… Look, I don't want to get into it, but she and I don't match. Okay?" He brushed a strand of hair from her eyes. Lightning zipped to her toes when his fingers lingered on her cheek. "Now you and I— You can't deny the chemistry between us." A semigrin cut a crease into his right cheek.

She pushed his hand away. "Will, I said I would stay to ease the transition for Christopher, but that does not mean you and I are playing house."

"Why not? We're over the age of eighteen. We like each other. We have something here. Let's see where it goes."

"It'll go nowhere. I'm not part of the package that comes with Christopher. Once he's settled, I'll be flying back to Tennessee. I haven't been home in many years and I think it's time I reconnect with my roots and my people."

"Who are your people?"

"My brother."

"Younger?"

"Two years older."

"Maybe he and his family could come up here for a visit."

"That won't happen."

"Why not? Every guy likes a bit of fly-fishing."

"Because he hates airports and road trips. And he doesn't enjoy fishing or hunting. He likes routines. Schedules." Her eyes latched on to his face, his deep-water eyes. "He has Asperger's, Will. Like Christopher."

Chapter Nine

He has Asperger's like Christopher.

The words hopscotched through Will's brain. He scanned the forested mountains ahead, maneuvering the Jet Ranger toward the Chugach Mountains, his passengers' destination.

Needing time alone, he'd left the house before Savanna and Christopher awoke, and gone to the airstrip to putter around his portion of the hangar, checking and rechecking instruments and gear.

When the four heli-skiers arrived at seven-thirty, excitement in their voices and gestures, Will had loaded the two men and two women and their gear into the bird, then taken off while the sunrise limned the mountains in translucent pinks and golds and tangerines.

He'd flown enough skiers to know these people were seasoned athletes. They conversed little; instead, looked out the windows at the rough and awesome landscape extending to the arc of the earth.

Thank God. Today, he wasn't into answering a pile of questions from first-timers.

Savanna had an autistic brother, the adult version of Christopher. *Not severe, Will. Asperger's is only a form of autism, remember that.*

Savanna's brother was married. With one child, a girl.

The thought had Will swallowing hard. Could that be Christopher one day? God, he hoped so.

The single thought surged up, choking him. More than anything in his life, he wanted Christopher to have what Savanna's brother, Gerald, had attained and accomplished.

The man worked as an accountant for a trucking firm, a job that lent him autonomy without appearing "antisocial" and "uncommunicative," as Savanna explained.

ASD characteristics.

Traits Christopher exhibited with Josh—and Will.

He swung the helicopter up the mountain where, in seven minutes, he would drop the skiers. For the hundredth time he asked a silent Why? *Why Christopher?*

The question rolled on a tide of regret, and guilt, as he flew over the brilliant white cusp of a ridge. His hands clenched the collective; the helicopter rocked momentarily.

"Wind current, guys," he lied. "Sorry."

Jeez, idiot. What the hell you doing?

Leveling the machine, he located the landing spot, then carefully lowered the helicopter. Within the next minute the four skiers dropped to the snow and began swooshing down a long slope of fresh powder.

Will lifted away from the sequined surface. Tomorrow afternoon he'd return to the base of the mountain where the group planned to set up camp tonight and hike the trails in the morning.

On the distant horizon, the sun crested. For miles, the wilderness lay in a panorama of white, green and gray, lidded by a sky of eye-stinging blue.

What had Christopher observed the day he'd flown with Will and Savanna? What had gone through the boy's mind? Would Will ever know? He figured Savanna had a better inkling.

Savanna. Her parting question last night had kept Will awake half the night: *Do you understand now why a relationship between us would never work?*

Later, lying in bed, thinking of those words... Her insinuation had forged a burst of annoyance. What did their bloodlines, their *DNA*, have to do with a relationship? He wasn't planning on marrying her. Hell, he wasn't planning on marrying *anyone*. He liked his life too well, enjoyed his freedom. Though, with Christopher freedom would alter some, he knew.

Still, marrying had never been on his radar. Not since Aileen, the only woman he'd ever loved, the only woman with whom he'd wanted to join his life.

But Aileen had died. And when Will had buried his memories and escaped back to Alaska, his desire for marriage and family had been locked in that grave with Aileen.

Aileen, advocate for the poor and oppressed.

A thought poleaxed him.

Damn it. Savanna knew.

Somehow, she had sensed his attraction to her was more than simple lust, more than a fling between the sheets.

Will nearly laughed aloud at the irony. She was like Aileen, whom he *had* wanted to marry. And without understanding the complexity of his past, without him breathing a word of it, Savanna had recognized his attraction to her for what it might offer.

A chance at family. A chance he'd rendered years ago to Lower 48 soil.

He snorted. *Dumb-ass. No wonder she'd ranted on about not being part of Christopher's package.*

Looping down toward the Starlight airport, Will's hand shook on the controls.

Family.

Christopher *was* his family. He'd been given to Dennis out of Will's love for his brother. The bond didn't get much tighter than that.

And, much as he wanted to dismiss the notion, much as *she* wanted to ignore it, Savanna was also part of that bond— through Christopher.

Kicking a stone along the way, Josh walked up the back alley to Angela's house. He'd always liked going to school, especially since he and Angela had gotten to be best friends.

She was cool. Like no other girl he'd known. Yeah, she was Mr. Germaine's daughter, but she was also fun and smart and she loved sports. Just like him. Best of all, she loved pitching for her softball team the way he loved playing catcher for the Jaguars.

Last summer they'd practiced playing catch in this alley almost every day. They would dress up in their uniforms and cages, put on their mitts and throw some really good balls.

Josh wished Angela played for his baseball team. She could outpitch Roger, and Roger was the best in Starlight's Junior League.

But Angela…man, she had an arm! She could throw curve balls that sometimes stung his hand.

Lately Angela didn't want to hang out with him

anymore. He knew why. That Christopher kid, Will's nephew. Angela was turning into a real stupid girl, always hanging around the guy.

Josh didn't get it. Sure, Christopher was smart and could do ninth-grade algebra in his head. Big deal. And, yeah, Angela was a whiz at math, too—the only thing Josh had always hated, because it made him feel like a dummy when she got a hundred on a test and he'd get a crappy fifty-six.

But did she have to be such a goody two-shoes around Christopher, helping him with every little thing and eating lunch with him? As if he was somebody special?

Strange was what the guy was. Everybody knew it.

Okay, not everybody, but most of the other guys, Ian and Ben and Roger, all agreed with Josh.

He pushed memories of last night's supper at Bob's Pizza out of his mind. No way was he admitting Christopher played those old arcade games like a pro, or that he was the best opponent Josh had gone against.

Even if he'd won by a measly two points.

For a few minutes there, Josh had been so excited at the challenge of winning he thought his heart would pop right out of his chest, it pounded that hard.

Afterward, Christopher had looked at the score and said, "You win by two points."

"Yeah, cool," Josh replied. Then felt as if he had to say something to take the frozen look off the guy's face. "But you gave me a good run."

"I didn't run anywhere."

Christopher was always saying dumb things like that. Like he didn't get it. So Josh had said, "No, but you kept your car—" he pointed to the machine, "—right on my bumper."

Christopher continued staring at the arcade screen where the game flashed to begin another round. "My car ran into the ditch," he said in that odd droning voice. "It rolled over thirteen times before it exploded. The motor was defective and the oil pump leaked."

Then he walked that weird rocking-on-his-toes walk back to the booth where Josh's mom and Will and Ms. Stowe were sitting.

Josh didn't believe the motor or the oil pump had anything wrong with them. It was just a game and the machine didn't bother explaining about broken motors. They were only excuses Christopher made up because Josh had whipped him. For a second he felt sorry for the guy. He really, really did not get it.

Approaching Will's backyard, Josh heard Angela's voice.

"Hey, Angela!" he called, thinking she was heading for the street side.

"Over here, Josh."

He searched through the trees and frowned. She came through Will's yard instead of her own, two houses down.

Christopher followed her like a puppy.

Great. Now they couldn't even walk to school without the geek tagging along. "What're you doing?" he asked. "I thought Ms. Stowe took him to school."

"Josh, stop talking as if Chris isn't here or doesn't understand what you're saying." She came through the gate, holding it open for the guy. "He's my neighbor now, and I think it'd be fun if we all walked to school together."

"He isn't my neighbor," Josh grumbled, falling in step beside Angela.

"Yes, he is, Josh. We all live on the same street. That makes Chris your neighbor *and* mine."

"Whatever. All he does is talk about helicopters."

"Like you talk about baseball?" She peeked over and her eyes had her usual fun look in them.

"I guess," he said.

"Will bought me a train set," Christopher offered. He looked straight ahead and his head bobbed as he walked. "But we can only play with it after school 'cause school's important. That's the rule."

"I hate rules," Josh grumbled, thinking if Will had bought *him* a train set, he'd be wanting to play with it all day, every day, and school would be the last thing on his mind.

"Did you know the Jet Ranger is a very versatile and user-friendly helicopter?" Christopher asked. For the first time he looked over at Josh.

"You mean Will's helicopter?" Josh wondered.

"Yup."

They walked out of the alley and onto the street that led toward Starlight Elementary, four blocks away.

A couple of other kids joined them, but Angela stayed at Christopher's side, listening to him talk on and on about helicopters. By the time the school came into sight, they all knew that Leonardo da Vinci had drawn diagrams of helicopterlike machines and that something called a swashplate lifted helicopters straight up and that by 1936 they had become practical and usable machines.

Christopher, Josh had to admit, knew tons about helicopters. But who *cared?*

"Hey, Chris. Can I play with your train set after school today?" he asked when they reached the school grounds.

"Maybe."

"When?"

"When you stop liking carnivores."

Josh laughed. "Okay." He glanced at his friends gathered around them. "I hate carnivores. Now can I play with your set?"

"Not until three o'clock."

"Great."

"Can I, too, Chris?" Roger asked.

"No. Just Josh and Angela at three o'clock. That's the rule."

Josh shot his best buddy a grin. "Christopher likes rules."

"Tomorrow, then?" Roger asked.

"Tomorrow isn't here yet," Christopher said.

"Come on, Chris," Angela said. "Let's walk around the school until the bell rings."

Josh watched them disappear around the corner of the building.

Roger said, "He really Coach's nephew?"

"Yeah." Josh's throat got tight the way it had when Will told him a couple of weeks ago. It wasn't fair. Christopher acted like he didn't even like Will. And Josh loved him.

Roger scuffed his toe in the dirt. "Think he'll put him on the team this year?"

Josh stared at his friend. Man. Not once had he thought of *that.* "Dunno."

Roger's grin was sly. "We could see if he's any good."

"Whatcha mean?"

"Pitch him a few balls one day. See if he can catch."

Josh hesitated. Roger was a cool guy, but sometimes he had a mean streak around certain kids. Especially the weak ones or those who said no to him. On top of that, Josh's gut warned that Christopher would be lousy at catching.

"Coach'll never know," Roger coaxed.

Suddenly the bell rang. "Oh, crap!" Josh said. "I forgot my science project. Ms. Murphy's gonna kill me!"

He ran for the school door.

He hadn't forgotten the project.

He hadn't liked what Roger was suggesting.

Two points for Christopher, Josh thought, pushing his way into the school among the rest of the kids.

* * *

At lunchtime the next day Savanna left Starlight Elementary and headed down Elk Street.

For the afternoon Ms. Murphy had organized two drawing projects, one in art and one in science. Christopher, the teacher assured, could work on his helicopter picture for science or his map of Starlight until home time.

This afternoon Savanna wanted see how Chris would do without her for a couple of hours. Baby-step preparations. For when she left Alaska forever.

During the last few days she had discussed this afternoon's absence with the boy, had written it on his agenda today and explained the plan before exiting the school.

"It's okay, Savanna," Christopher had said. "I'm going to help Angela with her map. You can go. I'll see you after school."

Thank God for Angela. The sixth-grader was a wonder. For whatever reason unbeknownst to Savanna or Penny Murphy, the child had taken Christopher under her sweet wing like a precious brother. Savanna knew the girl would keep Christopher occupied and children like Josh and Roger at bay. Still, Savanna had left her cell number with Penny. Just in case.

Walking down the town's only sidewalk, she breathed deep of the early-May air. Today Alaska smelled of spruce sap and ripening earth, mountains and snow. Fresh and clear, without the toxins that layered atmospheres in other parts of the world. Places like Tokyo, L.A. and Mexico City. Cities with hazy blue sheens sewn onto the summer air.

Today would be her first to explore Starlight, to check out the few quaint shops, feel their ambiance ring her shoulders. Sunshine touched her face, a warm gift after the residual coolness of April.

She wondered how Will saw the day, up in his helicopter, soaring through valleys and over lakes and timber.

Would he think of Christopher? Of her?

They had argued briefly last night after she fed Christopher his five-thirty supper of oven-baked chicken, sweetened mashed turnip and a small pile of sliced strawberries. A triangle of foods on his plate.

When Will entered the kitchen's back door at seven o'clock, Chris had already disappeared into his bedroom.

"Sorry I'm late," Will had said cheerfully.

"Another emergency?" She stood at the sink, washing the dishes. *Only emergencies would keep you from your son, right? Only they would keep you from calling to let us know.* The incident with Kenny had taught him that. Surely.

Plates and cutlery clinked under her hands.

A pause elapsed and weighted the room.

"Keeping track of my time now, Savanna?" In her peripheral vision she saw him remove his jacket, hang it by the door.

"You have a child living in your house, Will. Time is of essence." *Especially when that child is ten and lives by a rigid routine.*

He crossed the room, tossed his keys to the counter beside the telephone. "It *was* an emergency, if you must know. Another pilot asked if I could help tour three flightseers around Mount Drum. Just got back."

"And you didn't take your cell?" She hadn't meant to sound snide, but they were talking about Christopher. The little boy she would be leaving with the man standing ten feet away in a green sweatshirt and black Levi's.

A man she was starting to think too much about.

She lifted her head. Their eyes clung briefly.

After pulling the drain, Savanna dried her hands on the towel draped over the handle of the oven door.

"Will, I thought I explained that your schedule needed to change if this is to work. In less than eight weeks, I won't be here anymore. It'll be just you and Chris."

From the moment they arrived in Starlight, she had begun gearing the child up for a life with his new daddy, and readying for her departure.

Will's eyes narrowed. "You said you'd stay."

The day she'd sat on the porch. Remembering Liberia, remembering… She shivered. "If you recall," she began. "I went into the house and said I would *see to* Christopher. I didn't say I would *stay forever* with Christopher." *Or you.*

"So you'll leave us to fend for ourselves, that it?"

"Don't sound like a petulant child. I won't go *until* the two of you are on sturdy footing. I promise you that. Meantime, you need to take more responsibility in being around for him. He is not Josh, who you can see whenever it suits you. Chris is your *son*. Which means if you can't make it home on time, you need to make sure he knows, and that he has someone to care for him."

Ice-blue eyes. "Point taken. It won't happen again." He strode from the kitchen, down the hallway. Moments later she heard the door to his office close. He hadn't reappeared for the remainder of the evening.

This morning a note sat on the kitchen counter:

"S— Give me time. I'm well aware this is not an over-night bandage solution. W."

No, it's a lifelong operation, she thought, entering a small shop, Sage Secrets, at the end of the single-block merchants' street. And Will had barely cut the surface.

What if it takes longer than you've scheduled? a tiny voice inserted. Well, then, she'd stay as long as it took. A year, if necessary.

For Elke.

And Dennis. Dennis, trying and failing to assuage the fears, the shame his wife harbored about their son and herself. Dennis, requesting Savanna's aid to allow Elke breathing space.

"She needs some down time," he'd told Savanna that first month. "She's going crazy with worry something will go wrong, that she'll do something wrong and Christopher somehow will be damaged forever."

A genuine concern of any parent.

"Don't worry, Elke. I won't abandon your baby," Savanna murmured.

Standing in Sage Secrets, which offered a unique blend of cultural crafts, books and knickknacks, she browsed shelves and bins.

The video peeking out from under a batch of used CDs had her heart leaping in high gear. *Choo-Choo, The Train Cat*. Sixteen minutes of animation about a kitten called Choo-Choo and his admiration of trains.

Savanna closed her eyes, thanking fate and kismet and any god or angel nearby.

Hurrying, she paid for the CD and almost ran from the shop, heading for Will's house. There, in a corner of his living room, she slipped the video into the elaborate TV system.

The story was perfection. A lilting song. Colorful props and background. Delightful characters.

And an artistic cat named Choo-Choo that played with a small boy's red toy train while he was at school. Within minutes, train and cat became friends, and in the end the boy, owner of both, discovered a new and adventurous world awaiting him after a long day laboring over assignments at his desk.

Savanna sat on the couch and pressed her fingers against her eyes, against the sudden burning.

The video, played and replayed, would be the jewel Christopher needed to help master his deep-seated cat phobia. And maybe, just maybe, in a few weeks or months Will could retrieve his spotted feline from Valerie's house.

One small step at a time.

The kitchen phone rang, squealing through her hope and excitement. She hastened from the sofa. *Christopher.* The name trembled through her mind as she snatched up the receiver. "Yes?"

"Oh, thank God, you're there. Savanna, this is Penny Murphy. I don't know how to say this—"

A mountain wind funneled ice through her veins. "What's happened to Christopher?"

"He didn't come in after lunch. We've searched all over the schoolyard and looked through every classroom and in all the washrooms and closets, even the furnace room. Savanna, we can't find him."

Will guided the Jet Ranger over the last rise of timbered hills, and aimed for the Starlight Airport two miles in the distance. The clock on the instrument panel read 1:50. Thirty minutes early.

Today he'd be home well before schedule and, thankfully, before the dark wall of rain blowing in from the west hit the area.

He spoke to Nate Burns manning the radio in the Pilot's House. "Nate, this is Skyline One. ETA is five minutes."

"Copy, Skyline One. No one's off ground."

In other words, Will was the only pilot in the air from Starlight at the moment. He swung the craft left, down the air strip and toward the asphalt oval beside the hangar.

Nate crackled into his ear. "Skyline One, we just got a call from a Savanna Stowe. Your nephew disappeared from school during lunch hour and hasn't been seen since. Ms. Stowe contacted the police and is organizing a search. Would like you to meet her at Starlight Elementary ASAP."

Will's breathing stopped. *Christopher disappeared?* A thousand scenarios bounded through his mind.

A stranger lured the boy off the grounds.

Chris decided to go home early and got turned around downtown.

No...not with those maps...the kid loved geography!

God, maybe he'd wandered onto the other side of the school fence into the bush and a cougar—

No! Will's hands trembled on the collective. The boy was somewhere in town, close to the school. Had to be. There was no other answer. He wouldn't accept anything else.

He checked the clock. The boy had been gone an hour at most. How fast did a ten-year-old walk? How *far* could he travel in sixty minutes?

Will swallowed down the knot lodged at the base of his tongue. "Nate." Incredible the calm in his voice as he lifted the Jet Ranger over the trees. "I'm taking a look from above. Maybe I can spot him."

"Copy, Sky One. Hope you find him soon."

"Ditto."

He swept the helicopter down the road that trekked through the dense forest hemming the town and forced himself not to think of the wildlife lurking in the underbrush. Predators....bobcats, cougars, bears. Hungry to feed after a long winter. Hungry to feed their spring-born young.

I don't like carnivores. Christopher's words pounded with Will's heart. Please, Chris.

Please, stay on the streets in town where we can find you.

Skimming the treetops, Will slowed the ship to a crawl

and scanned the winding narrow road leading north from the east-west Glenn Highway.

Abruptly the day's brightness vanished; big drops of rain streaked the windscreen. Below, the road fell into a black ribbon curling among the hulking mountains and trees.

He wove back and forth over the access. Ahead the highway looped flat and dark as cable wire.

What had Christopher worn to school this morning? His silver parka? Had he removed the coat at lunch, left the building wearing a sweatshirt? *Savanna would know.* The thought eased the crazed beat of Will's heart. Savanna. God, he wished he could speak to her, thank her for…hell, for being here. In Starlight. With him.

Look for the red-and-yellow knapsack. Will could almost hear her voice the words. *He never goes a step without it hanging on his shoulder.*

Through the peppering rain, the town's rooftops loomed. To the right stood the school. A large group of people, some with umbrellas over their heads, huddled near the entrance. The town's one police cruiser, its blue and red lights swirling through the downpour, sat parked on the graveled roadside.

A woman, her chestnut hair a drenched straggle, talked to Officer Bowers. *Savanna.*

Will closed in, lowered the helicopter to twenty feet off the ground. Across a hundred feet of wet day, their eyes met, and his heart crashed against her angst.

He attempted to signal: *I'm checking the streets first. I'll be back,* before veering upward and away.

Village more than town, Starlight nestled against the gentle slope of a foothill. Three minutes to sweep up and down seven streets. The elementary sat at the northern end of town, the airport at the other.

Retracing the route to Airport Road, Will cruised the

valley floor. *There!* Within the trees, a flicker of yellow. Accelerating, he flew toward the splash of color. Sweat popped from his pores. His heart rammed his chest.

Again the yellow flash. Fifty yards into the trees.

Will tipped the helicopter. The boy crouched among the trees, hands over his ears.

"Christopher," Will whispered. "Thank God."

Swooping past, he watched the child cover his head against the roar of the Jet Ranger. *He hates loud noises,* Savanna had told Will one night at Georgia's.

But the kid loved trains. And helicopters. And maps.

Will laughed. "Cover your ears, son. I'm coming for you."

At the delta of road opening to the air strip, he lowered to the pavement. "Nate, I've found him. He was walking up Airport. Contact the police."

"Copy, Sky One."

Shutting down the engine, Will took a long relieved breath, removed the headgear and flung open the door. He hit the pavement running.

Back through the trees. Back to his son.

Son.

Oh, God, yes. Chris was of his DNA. *His.*

Will's vision blurred. All the similarities were there. The dimples, the height, the quick smile. Even how he loved machines. Hadn't Will loved them from the time he could ride a bicycle? Hadn't he read about motorcycles and airplanes until his mother had had to cart the books away in order for him to focus on schoolwork? How had he forgotten?

Christopher was his. Oh, God, in too many ways to count. And he'd almost lost him today. *Almost lost him.*

The possibility shot Will's heart into his throat. His teeth clamped his bottom lip. *I'm coming, boy.*

Branches slapping his face, he tore through the brush. In his chest his heart thrashed. And then that tiny spot of yellow poked through the leaves. *My son.*

"Christopher." *I love you.* Will lifted the sopping child into his arms, not caring that his son disliked touching unless it was his choice. "What are you doing out here?" *I found him, Savanna. I found our boy.*

"I wanted to draw a map of Starlight," Christopher reasoned. "I needed to walk down all the streets and the road to the airport. I needed to see the houses and the mountains and where Glenn Highway was so I could make a map that's better than the one at Shepherd's Lodge."

Laughing, Will set him on his feet. "That's great, Chris, but you should be at school. Do you know Savanna is very worried about you?"

"I told Angela."

Angela. Harry Germaine's kid who lived two houses down the street and walked Christopher to school each weekday morning.

"I told her I was making a map," the boy said. Rain dripped from his nose as he gazed at the helicopter through the drizzle. "And I'm coming to ride in the helicopter to see the geography around Starlight for the map, and because you promised I could take another ride soon."

"Chris." Will knelt in the mud. "When I said soon, I didn't mean today. I meant…" He sighed. God, how to explain such a simple word?

"Soon," the boy's fixed voice pierced Will's heart a thousandth time, "can be anytime in the near future. It can be today or tomorrow or the next day. Soon is not years from now. I choose soon to be today."

"Well, son. I choose differently. I'm not taking you up today. It's raining for one thing. But most important, you need to ask permission to leave home or school. You cannot leave without permission. That's the rule," Will added, recalling Savanna's account on how autistic children loved rules. *They're like little policemen when it comes to rules.*

Will continued, "Is a helicopter ride on your agenda?"

A deadpan stare at the machine.

"Chris, what's on your agenda for this afternoon?"

"Drawing maps and helicopters."

"And why aren't you at school drawing them?"

"I told you. I needed to make a better map and I needed to ride in your helicopter because—"

"Stop," Will said gently. "Listen carefully, Chris. I will not give you a ride in a helicopter until you understand the rule about asking permission to leave home and the school. Do you understand?"

"Yes. But can I ride in the helicopter soon?"

Simplify your answers. Savanna's advice. "No. But I will tell you when you can ride in one. All right?"

A long pause. "Okay."

"Good. Now, let's go to the Pilots' House and wait for Savanna."

"Are you mad, Uncle Will?" Christopher asked as they walked side by side through the rain, mud sticking to their boots.

Will found it hard to swallow. The boy had used his name. His child had recognized him. "No, son," Will said. "I'm not mad. But we were very, very worried."

"Okay."

Okay. And that was that.

Will wanted to laugh with joy.

Chapter Ten

"Savanna!" Christopher rushed forward as Will let her into the Pilots' House. The second the police had informed her of his safety, she'd driven like a mad woman to the airport.

"How are you, Chris?" Her heart sighed at the sight of him: damp hair, pink cheeks, deep-set eyes. Will's eyes—though, more often than not, lacking the ever-ready gleam.

He was safe. Will had found him.

The boy threw his arms around her waist for a brief hug.

"I'm great, Savanna, but I wasn't lost. I knew where I was going. Starlight is a small place, but Alaska has a lot of mountains and evergreens, and there aren't that many roads and highways and there's only one way that goes south of Starlight and that's Hill Street and it hooks up with Glenn Highway and then I walked to the junction of Airport Road and here I am."

She let Christopher prattle his geographic directions while, over his head, her eyes caught Will's. He had worried; the crease above his nose was deeper than usual, but he said nothing and his mouth remained a stern line.

Was he angry? Did he want her to reprimand the boy?

"Will flew right over me *twice*," Christopher exclaimed as Savanna brushed the hair from his eyes. "A lot of high-amplitude sound waves were impinging on my eardrums."

"Yes," she said, smiling. "I imagine they were."

"Will said I should always ask permission to leave the school and home. Are you mad, Savanna?"

"I couldn't find you, Chris. But now we know where you are, so no, I'm not mad. Are you ready to go home?"

"Back to Honduras?"

To where he'd last seen his parents. "No, honey. Back to Uncle Will's house."

"Forever?"

"Until you grow up big like Uncle Will."

"I want to fly helicopters like Uncle Will."

Again her gaze went to the man standing in chilly silence behind Christopher. She would not lie to his son. Or to him. "Let's wait and see. It's a long time before then, and you might change your mind." *And realize flying helicopters might be impossible for you.*

"Never," Christopher said. Carrying his knapsack, he walked to the door. "Okay, I'm ready to go home."

"I have some paperwork to complete," Will said as Savanna turned to follow Christopher out the door of the Pilot's House. "I'll be along in a bit."

It was 2:15 p.m. No doubt he had things to finish before he drove back to Starlight. Or he was disappointed with Chris. She stepped outside.

"Savanna." Will gripped the door above his head.

"Yes?"

Deep as ocean waters, his eyes fastened onto her face. "I've never been so scared."

Tension whispered from her lungs. Not disappointed; he'd experienced a father's angst.

Will funneled fingers over his scalp. "He doesn't understand the repercussions. To him it was just a fun trip to the airport. Damn fool kid. He's soaked clean to the bone. Wouldn't surprise me if he comes down with pneumonia."

"I'll make him a warm bath and get some hot chocolate into him. He'll be fine, Will. See you later."

The rain had blown past and she walked down the stepping-stone path to the four-vehicle parking lot. Already Christopher sat inside Georgia's pickup playing his Game Boy, the day's adventure replaced by one on the miniboard.

As she climbed behind the wheel, Will stood on the stoop, gazing at his son, no doubt wishing the boy would raise his head and wave.

Don't hope. Then you won't expect it.

She drove away with Will in the rearview mirror, watching, waiting. Anticipating a sign his son had not forgotten his rescuer.

An ache, as large as the one for Elke's and Dennis's deaths, bloomed in Savanna's chest.

That evening, when Christopher was in bed and asleep, she sought out Will. She had never ventured into his wing of the house, the wing with his bedroom and office.

Walking quietly down the hallway, she saw a slim rectangle of lamplight on the hall wall from a partially opened door. Office or bedroom?

She would turn away, escape to her own room if it was the latter.

Focusing, she took a long soft breath and pushed the door gently. His office. And he lay on a cushiony hunter-green sofa, arm under his head, long legs stretched, socked feet propped on the opposite end. Eyes closed to the murmur of a sitcom.

From the minute he had walked through the kitchen door and set his keys on the counter, he'd been uncommunicative, sitting through supper—it had been her turn to cook tonight—speaking maybe ten words. Afterward, he and Christopher had done the dishes, the boy drying two cups through a comparative narrative about time zones and highways and roadways in Alaska and Honduras.

Warily she stood in the doorway.

"Come in, Savanna," Will said without opening his eyes.

Naturally, he'd be sensitive to strange sounds in his house—like her slippered feet on the hardwood.

She walked to the umber armchair adjacent to the sofa and sank into feather softness.

"Chris asleep?" Will lay relaxed as a lion in the African sun.

She wasn't fooled. Tension flickered across his closed eyelids. "Out like a light."

"I'd've put him to bed."

Was that what bothered him? That she preempted his duties by taking over the nightly ritual?

She crossed her arms, shielding her soul. "Sorry. I should've called you. Since Dennis and Elke died, I've wrapped my life around Christopher, which isn't the best thing to do sometimes."

He remained motionless, except for his eyes, which opened and stared at the ceiling. "You didn't today."

She held herself very still. "Are you accusing me of neglecting my duties to Christopher by leaving the school early this afternoon?"

Swinging his feet to the floor, Will rubbed the back of his neck. A sigh puffed out. "No."

"Then…?"

Torment pulsed in his eyes. "You can't be there all the time. Hell, *I* can't be there all the time. And that scares me, Savanna. It scares me to death, because it'll just be him and me soon. And I don't have a bloody clue how I'm going to deal with his condition, his behaviors, his reactions to things that happen to pop up in an ordinary day. Especially if I'm flying to the Wrangells or Talkeetnas or the Chugaches and won't be home until late at night or the next morning."

She rose to perch on the couch beside him, close enough that her knee touched his thigh, and forced herself to ignore the contact, the zip of heat.

"Will, for the moment try not to think too far down the road. It'll overwhelm you. Instead, focus on the day's agenda—yours and Chris's—and concentrate on what you can accomplish when you're together."

"Easier said than done."

"It is," she conceded, "but thank God for the old adage 'Time passes slowly.' Let the day evolve. That doesn't mean you shouldn't prepare and take careful steps. You'd do that with any child. Chris is no different."

His head turned, eyes on hers. "He's not like other kids."

"You're comparing him to Josh again. Don't. Chris isn't Josh any more than I'm Valerie or you're your fishing pal, Shane."

A smile tugged his mouth. "You're definitely not Valerie." Lifting a finger, he stroked her cheek…eye down to her mouth. Corner to corner. A leisurely journey that fired an excess of nerve endings under her skin.

"You're strong and independent—" his voice lowered; his gaze darkened "—confident and passionate."

"You're getting off topic." But she stayed statue still, her own breath tight in her lungs. She could not edge away or push aside that caressing finger, that finger slipping along her chin, down her neck and up again.

It had been so long. *So long.*

"Today took a year off my life, Savanna." Through the worry, she saw the edge of hunger in his eyes. "We need to diverge for a few minutes."

"How?" But she knew.

"Haven't you heard about people reaffirming life in the face of death?" he asked.

Yes. Oh, yes. "Christopher didn't get lost or—"

He straightened, cupped her face. Against her forehead his breath wisped, warm and sultry as morning coffee. "Thank God he didn't. But I keep thinking, 'What if?' What if next time I don't find him right away? What if something *worse* happens?"

Releasing her, he rose to pace the office. "I can't do this." The light dipped into his hair, grooved from restless fingers. "Not alone."

She went to him. "You're not alone. I'm here."

"But not forever."

"I said I'd stay until we work out a routine, until Christopher feels at home with you. I won't abandon him, Will. I won't abandon *you*." Under her hand, his heart beat, violent as a fist. "I won't," she whispered as a shiver rippled across her body, as his fear, his what ifs meshed with her own.

What if he was right?

What if he couldn't cope with Christopher once she returned to Tennessee?

What if her decision to leave the boy in Alaska resulted in disaster?

No negative thoughts, Savanna. Think positive.

Closing her eyes, she concentrated. And remembered Christopher's excitement about Will's helicopter. She recalled Will's grin when the boy first saw the train model. And Angela's kind voice, her need to be Chris's friend.

Oh, Lord. The girl had blamed herself today for running to the washroom during lunch hour while Chris sat in his sunny spot along the schoolyard fence.

She'd searched the entire area before telling Ms. Murphy.

Later, it had taken Savanna a full half hour to calm the child, explain it wasn't her fault, that no one was to blame for Chris's choices.

No one, except me. I should have been there. I should have stayed at school.

But she'd gone shopping. Shopping—for crying out loud!—to buy a stupid cat video, which Christopher likely would never watch.

"Heyyy." Will canted up her chin. "What's this?" His fingertip found a tear below her eye.

"If I'd stayed at the school—"

"Enough." He tugged her to his chest. "As you said, he's safe. And tomorrow's another day."

Up and down his hand stroked her spine, lulling away her tears. Long moments ticked by. Outside, a night rain tapped the window while breath by breath his scent eddied through her veins. And, against her belly, his arousal grew firm.

"Will," she said into the knit of his navy sweater. "We need to stop."

His hand wove through her hair, kept her harbored against the strength of his body. "Let yourself be, Savanna. Don't think. Don't analyze. Just be."

Just be. When had she just been? Never, if she were to examine her life.

Oh, she'd had a couple of relationships since Liberia. Men

who were safe, men who were devoted to their careers, who pranced around the continent, spending time with her when time was convenient. One had been a foreign correspondent, rushing off to wars and disasters, the other a doctor, hurrying between villages steeped in poverty and sickness.

Neither lover had voiced the word *stay* the way Will had last week, or in that tone she remembered, that deep, personal tone that spoke of desire and things she did not want to consider.

Hadn't she wanted it that way? Hadn't she wanted those men to leave her so there would be no ties, no connection. No family. *No children.*

Will had a child, one she loved, one she wanted to nurture and help toward maturity, help toward a life outside these walls someday.

Except she was not Chris's mother and she was not Will's wife. She was a spinster schoolteacher, settled in habits, routines and disposition. *An older woman.*

She said, "I don't think I'm capable of just being. It's not in my nature to…to go about something frivolously."

His head lifted, eyes gleaming. His hips rotated. Slow, carnal, provocative. Deep between her pelvic bones a spark flared, blazed.

"I wouldn't call *this* frivolous," he murmured.

"That," she said, and couldn't hide her smile, "is persistence."

He sobered, touched the corner of her eyebrow. "Savanna."

Oh, the blue of his eyes! She might step to their edges, dive down and down and down. Misplace her soul.

She studied his face: cheeks, hair, the configuration of his jaw, the way the tip of his nose bent ever so slightly to the left.

His lips were masculine, artistically shaped. And young. Almost a decade younger than hers. Which were not as full as when she was twenty or thirty, and to which another decade down the road might induce lipstick bleeding.

Flings were frivolous, and he would be a fling. Younger man, older woman.

Lord, she should walk away, back to her bedroom. Stop this silly thinking, this fantasizing. He was the father, the "uncle" protector of Christopher.

A few short months and she would be gone.

Gone from the boy she loved as a son, gone from Will, the first man to hasten her pulse and liquefy her thighs with a simple look.

He watched her study him, said quietly, "You're comparing, sweetheart. You're thinking of the years between us. For tonight—" he dipped his head, hovered over her mouth "—for a few hours—" lips touching, slipping away "—let your—" a second touch "—mind go."

Then he settled. His lips framed hers, a gentle commencement. Moving toward arousal. Slants and tongues. Deepening, ever deepening, kiss on top of kiss.

Hands reshaped hair.

Delved under sweaters, sought skin. Warm, warm skin.

Somewhere in the night, she heard a groan. And knew it surfaced from her throat.

His taste wrote poems on her flesh.

A first, a beginning, a salute to her womanhood.

Somehow he carried her into his bedroom, into his bed, a playing field of green and white and pale gold with thick pillows and a headboard of carved wood. Blinds shrouded floor-to-ceiling windows, and when he reached to turn on the night lamp she glimpsed wooden frames of quiet forests and sunsets among trees decorating the walls.

He whispered, "Don't move," and went to a small square table where a CD player waited. Moments later the song, the Faith Hill one they had danced in sync to, swayed in rhythm to at the rec center, spun quietly. And then he was in bed again, hovering over her. His eyes were the dark mountains, the glistening snow, the eagle soaring in the blue yonder. Softly, he sang, "Just breathe."

And she did.

And the kissing, the touching, the need to be closer, ever closer, continued and continued, their bodies in tune, one seeking the other. Rolling here, curling there.

She removed his sweater, pants, shorts—and, oh, my, what a hard, solid, *long* body!—while he removed her sweater and slacks, reached for her under things.

"Will, wait." She emerged from a dizzying sensuality to stay his fingers on her bra strap. Around her middle, she wrapped her other arm, concealing her forty-two-year-old flesh.

She wanted to say, *I didn't believe this would happen so I didn't bring protection.*

For my body.

For me.

But he kissed her mouth with such tenderness that her throat stung. In the next moment he reached to the night stand for the sealed box, bringing it onto the bed with a slow, crooked smile. "I figure this should get us started." His eyes were the aura borealis.

She trembled at his touch, at his look.

"Savanna." He kissed her nose. "Don't be shy. I want *you*. Please. No hiding." Gently, he tugged her arm free.

"My skin isn't toned as it once was, and no matter how much you ignore it or how often I work out in a gym, it'll never be *your* age."

He rested his forehead on hers. "Honey, you have to believe me when I say you're beautiful. *Beautiful.* If all I wanted was something frivolous, I would not be here in this room. I would not have pursued you since the second I laid eyes on you. I would not have done this…"

A soft kiss.

"I would not have been dying to touch you here…"

A gentle palming of her left breast.

"Or here."

Between her legs where she dampened his fingers.

"Savanna." A whisper. "Let me love you the way I've wanted to for more than a month."

She fell into his wooing, into him. Age dropped away with the last of her clothes and she lay before him, naked, transparent.

Her eyes impounded his. *My breasts are not perky. My middle isn't an hourglass.* "What you see is what you get," she said, levity failing miserably.

"What I see is what I want." Moving over her, he took their hands and clasped them on the pillows.

And then he was done with talking and she was done with shyness, and the night revealed its mystery and wonder.

Will lay with her in the crook of his arm. Mentally he cataloged each area sweat sealed their skin. Calves, thighs, hips. Chest to breast…

Ah, those lush, soft breasts. The left one pressed his ribs, the right one lay against his wrist. He stroked his thumb, back and forth, across its tender bell shape and felt his groin hurry. Again.

Three condoms before midnight. And he wanted her *again*. When had he wanted a woman as much?

Aileen had been the last. Eight years later and here was Savanna, so unlike the tall, lanky girl he'd fallen in love with, but having the same sheltering heart for the impoverished, the casualties of systems.

Yet he hadn't wanted Aileen the way he wanted Savanna.

He knew the moment he broke his own rule and told the woman in his arms about his long-ago dreams. He'd never told a single soul before tonight. Never told how Aileen had filled his dreams with whimsy; how he'd put her on a pedestal, the queen in his fantasy of the good life; how she had allowed him to place her there, sweet angel of mercy, delivering the world of its sadness.

And where had it gotten her?

Dead. Because her benevolent spirit refused to let her give up on those gangs, on the anger she saw in their eyes, the pain they inflicted on each other. In the end they had repaid her with the very violence she'd worked day and night to curb.

He'd told it all tonight, word after word vomiting from his mouth until he was spent and Savanna was holding him, whispering calm assurances in her slow Southern style.

He'd kept the part about the social worker to himself, the stupid one who had told him later that Aileen was a sacrifice for peace, because the gang had dissolved shortly thereafter. *Because.* Will had punched the man.

A sacrifice for peace. God almighty. If that was the case, he'd offered three. Aileen, Dennis, Elke.

Instinctively his arms tightened around Savanna and she snuffled in her sleep, slightly shifting her head under his chin. The scent of her lay in his nostrils, the taste of her on his tongue.

His heart bounded in his chest. Soon she'd be back in the Lower 48. But for how long? How long before the urge to *dedicate* took her to another Honduras, Congo, Kenya?

How long before she became his fourth *sacrifice?*

Closing his eyes, Will set his mouth to the confusion of her hair. Somehow he had to save her as he hadn't saved Aileen.

But how?

* * *

She heard Christopher's voice through her slumber. They were in the schoolyard and he ran toward her, eyes bright, laughter bubbling from his lips, sunshine tipping gold into his hair. *Will's hair.*

"Hey, Chris." She knelt on the grass, opened her arms.

"Savanna!" He rushed into her embrace without qualm, without hesitation, eager to tell her about his day. "Savanna," he called again.

"I'm here, honey." She spoke calmly, looking into his serious face. "No need to yell."

"Savanna!"

She bucked awake, eyes blinking in the dark. A warm, hard body slid along her skin under the blankets and she remembered. She slept in Will's bed.

"Wha'izit?" he murmured above her ear, snuggling closer.

"I thought I heard Christopher."

They lay without breathing, listening for the night's exaggeration of the smallest sound.

And then she caught it, the padding of bare feet on the hardwood in a distant part of the house.

"Something's wrong." She tossed back the covers. "Darn, where are my clothes?"

Will switched on the night lamp. The clock read 3:39.

"Easy, honey," he said, reaching for the heap of his inside-out jeans on the rag rug next to the bed. "Grab my robe behind the door."

Flinging on the navy terry robe, she bunched it under the too-long belt to keep it off the floor, and hastened from the bedroom.

Christopher stood in the kitchen, hands shaking as though they were wet.

"Hey, pal," Savanna said softly. Her heart knocked her

rib cage. He hadn't had a restless night in two weeks. "It's the middle of the night. You should be asleep. What're you doing in the kitchen?"

Through the dark he looked at the stove where she halted. "I couldn't find you."

"Oh, sweetie." He'd gone to her bedroom, found it empty.

"I thought you left me. Mom and Dad did."

"No, Christopher." Slowly she walked toward him; crouched on the floor, took his hands. "I was in a different part of the house. I was down the other hallway where Uncle Will has his office." A tiny lie, but…

Will walked into the kitchen. He wore jeans and a white T-shirt. "We were talking, Chris," he said.

"Why are you wearing a housecoat?" the boy asked Savanna. His gaze clung to her shoulder.

"Because it's nighttime."

"I was sleeping and then I couldn't find you," he repeated.

"I know. But now you've found me." Holding his hand, she climbed to her feet. "Let's go back to bed, Chris. It's not time to wake for school yet."

"Tomorrow I have to show Angela my helicopters book. I got it from the Starlight library yesterday before I went out to map the town."

She hadn't known that. "Chris, promise us you won't go to the Starlight library or leave the schoolyard without permission from Uncle Will or me."

"Okay."

"It's a very important rule, buddy."

As they walked from the kitchen, Will followed her to the boy's room. They saw him into bed, Savanna tugging up the covers. "'Night, honey."

Will touched the child's hair, a butterfly's stroke. "Catch you in the morning, son."

He wanted to hug the boy, Savanna saw, but held back, unsure yet of his son's reaction. Her heart ached. *One day at a time, Will. It'll happen.*

When Christopher was asleep again, they returned to the kitchen. The range light projected a muted glow.

Hugging the robe that smelled of him, Savanna faced Will. She refused to let her gaze fall to his chest, to the muscles she had traced under her palms, where she'd lain her cheek and listened to the thump of his heart.

"We can't let that happen again," she said.

"We won't," he agreed. "We'll make sure we go to our own beds afterward."

"No, Will. I mean we can't sleep together again. We can't take the chance he'll wake up while we're in the middle of…of…"

Having sex. She saw him finish the sentence with eyes dark as the night around them. "It's a natural part of life, Savanna. I'm sure Dennis and Elke made love."

Made love. Two words she found unfamiliar and incongruent to the experiences of her life. Was that how Will saw what they'd done in his bedroom? She didn't believe it.

Just words. Falling from his mouth.

"Elke and Dennis were Christopher's parents. You and I aren't even a couple."

"No?" His voice was calm, but his mouth tightened. Hiking his chin toward the hallway leading to his room, he asked, "Then what was that?"

"A temporary lapse of my good judgment. I'm here for Christopher, to ensure he connects with you. I can't and won't put myself—or you—first."

For a weighty moment he said nothing. Then he walked

across the room to where she stood fisting her fingers in the lapels of his robe. "Marry me, Savanna."

"What?"

"You heard. Live here in this house, in Starlight. Be a mother to Chris. Be my wife. Let's make the three of us a family. I'm— Look, I care for you, all right. More than I have any woman in a very long time. We'd make a great team, honey. An awesome team for Christopher."

"No," she whispered, disbelieving. *An awesome team? And what about love? Where does that fit in?*

He wove a strand of her hair behind her ear. "I know it's sudden, but where else would you rather be than with Christopher? You've said he's like your own. I'm asking you to *be* his mother. Permanently."

Oh, God. His solemn mouth, those blue, blue eyes. He wasn't joking. Tears burned.

To be Christopher's mother...

Of course. All he wanted was a mother for his son. How convenient. He'd take her, forty-two years old, over Valerie, because she, *Savanna Stowe,* understood kids like Christopher.

"No," she repeated, stronger now, shaking her head. "You're confusing what you *think* you feel with what you want for Christopher. I won't be a stand-in, Will."

His nostrils puffed indiscernibly on a hard intake of air. "You've got it wrong."

"I've got it right. You need a mother for your son, and I'm your best bet. How dare you play on my emotions for that boy." Anger lifted her chin, hardened her voice.

"That's not it at all. My feelings for you are real. They have nothing to do with Christopher. They never did."

Her eyes stung. He was offering a treasure she'd hidden from for two decades. Family was not in her future. Children would never be in her future. Seventeen years she had spent adapting to that fact, and now this…

She wanted to weep. To bang her fists on the wall. She had come to Starlight for one reason and that was to see Christopher in a safe and loving environment. She had no doubt Will loved his son; all she had to do was look at his face when he was with the boy.

"I'm not your answer, Will," she said. Turning on a heel, she started for her room.

"Savanna."

Keeping her face away from those piercing eyes, she halted.

"Can we at least try?" he asked.

Spinning around, she glared at him. "I will not put a child through angst while you and I 'try' something for the sake of some grand resolution. How do you think Chris would feel in a year's time when you and I call it quits because you've met a young woman who can give him a brother or sister?"

She heard the fridge thrum while his eyes confiscated hers. A small thrill rushed along her nerves. In the dimness of the kitchen, he appeared semi dangerous standing still as stone. Slowly he said, "Seems you've got it all worked out in that pretty head of yours."

"Don't talk to me as if I'm a bimbo."

"You're making a mountain out of a molehill. I meant what I said, Savanna. It's you I want, no one else."

Inside she died a little. "Then maybe this will clear *your* head. In Liberia I was gang raped. The damage was irreparable. I can't have children, Will. Ever."

With that, she left him to find his way back to his room, back to the bed where she had discovered, for the first time in her life, a soulful connection.

Chapter Eleven

Hands stacked behind his head, Will lay alone under the covers and stared through the dark.

Gang raped. His heart billowed with her pain, her suffering. This was worse than Aileen. Aileen had not wakened from her injury, hadn't carried the wound for years or been forced to hold up her head under its intolerable weight.

Aw, Savanna. Wetness tickled his temple and he realized with a small shock that he was crying. Not even with Aileen had he cried. Instead he'd raged and ranted and cursed.

Savanna, he thought again. Swiping away the tear, he rolled onto his side. The pillow smelled of her hair. The sheets held the scent of their sex.

She gave like no woman he knew. A fury of generosity, passion, of dizzying desire and abandonment. Hell, at one point, he thought they'd roll right off the bed.

And the intensity. He'd felt it sear the palms of his hands, the soles of his feet. No woman had lost him in her soul before. He wanted her back in his bed.

He wanted her in his life.

But after she'd spoken the words, those words that drenched her eyes, she had fled to her own room. She hadn't waited for a response, for him to say, *It doesn't matter.*

She would not have believed him.

He had never wanted kids. Once, maybe, with Aileen, but that dream had died with her on a street of East L.A. She'd been two months pregnant with his child, and he'd wanted her to quit her quest to fix ghettos, to remove young gang kids from the streets.

He'd wanted her to work in an office—or at least choose a field where she could help the downtrodden from a safe distance—so they could make a home, have their family. But then she'd died, shot in the chest by a stray bullet, trying to stop a gang fight.

The senseless killing had ended Will's desire for kids.

Not that he didn't like kids; he did.

When Dennis had come with his request because of sterility, Will had agreed. Because Dennis was his brother. And brothers did for each other. No matter the consequences.

Will wasn't so sure he would agree today, and it had nothing to do with Christopher's AS. It had to do with Will himself.

With the advent of unrest in the world these days—the wars, diseases, pollution, disasters, crime rates—he could not see bringing one more innocent into the fray.

But you have. You brought Christopher.

A fact he could not ignore. That the boy had been legally Dennis's son was not the issue. Without Will, Christopher would not be sleeping under this roof tonight.

And without Christopher, Savanna would be in a different city or town or country. Unknown to Will.

And, if Dennis hadn't died…

God, Will thought. His son…he wouldn't know his son as he did now, wouldn't *love* his son with this incredible do-or-die emotion.

The domino effect of his life.

He could imagine Savanna's beliefs. He could imagine all those silly platitudes she'd amass for him to understand, for him to *get* when they discussed this again. And they would.

Trouble was, he had no idea how to change her mind, how to move beyond both their histories.

As dawn winked over the mountains, Will rendered the night's sleep and headed for the shower. Twenty minutes later he filled his mug to the brim.

Savanna, wrapped in his robe, padded into the kitchen, her cheeks pink.

"Hi," she said softly.

"Hey," he returned and thought he had yet to see a woman more alluring. He wanted to hold her, protect her. "Want some?" he asked, presenting his cup.

The question roused her from a trance, and she walked to the cupboard to find a mug. While she stood next to where he leaned against the counter, he wondered if she had gotten any sleep the past two hours or if she'd lain, as he had, ruminating over their last conversation.

Forget conversation…

This close, he could smell the sultry sweetness of sleep in the tangle of her hair. He wanted to tell her how she looked without makeup, that her lips were rosy and plump and kissable, that her freckles were fairy dust and her burnished hair a mass made for his fingers.

He wanted run his fingertip down the tiny pillow crease

along her temple. Slip his hand into the minicave the robe made around the soft nakedness of her breasts.

Voice gravelly, he said, "I'd like to take you out to dinner tomorrow night. Think we can get Georgia to watch Chris for a couple hours?"

She poured the coffee. Slowly. "We've already done dinner out. Twice."

He sipped his coffee, said, "This is different. This is a date, Savanna. Me asking you out. Boyfriend-girlfriend kind of stuff."

That brought her head around. "What happened last night isn't going to change things. Why force something that will never work, Will?" She sighed into her cup. "Look, last night was—"

"The best."

Again her head snapped up. "I don't mean the sex."

"Neither do I." Anger slipped under his skin. "I'm talking about two people finding each other. *I* was found in that bed, Savanna. By *you*." He rubbed a hand over his hair. "I've never had that with a woman."

Clutching her mug between her palms, she stepped away from the counter. "I need to get Christopher ready for school."

"It doesn't matter, you know," he said to her back.

She hesitated, her eyes threading back to him.

He spoke quietly. "I don't want more children."

She shook her head. "Now you're talking like the young and foolish. Don't do that. It's not necessary."

He set aside his mug and walked across the kitchen. Stopping within her space, he tipped up her chin.

"It is necessary, and while I may be young according to *your* standards, I haven't been foolish for more than fifteen years. I'm not a boy, Savanna. I'm a man. One who coaxed three orgasms from you last night."

He bent and kissed her mouth. A quick, tender stamp to her heart. "But more important, I'm the man who found your boy yesterday and helped put him to bed two hours ago. We're good for each other, you and I. Think about that today."

Oh, she thought about his words, his offer, all right.

All day at school, helping Christopher through his transitions, she thought about Will. About the way he touched her in the night, of the whispered endearments, the encouragements when she would have held back, shy and uncertain.

She thought about the love in his eyes when he'd said, "Catch you in the morning, son," to a little boy frightened in the night.

Yet each time, she stumbled at the junction, *I don't want more children.*

Why didn't he want another child? Because of Christopher? Because he was afraid another son would inherit his first son's condition?

Or because *she* couldn't have children? Heaven help her. Had he said those things out of some sort of skewed *pity* for her? *No,* she reasoned. Will was not insensitive. She wouldn't allow herself to consider such a notion. He might have a reckless sense of responsibility, but her instincts told her he was not dishonorable.

The more she mulled over his statement, the more confused she became.

She couldn't refute the fact she was attracted to him. More than attracted. Maybe a little in love…. Lord, could it be true? After all these years of holding back gut-deep emotions, of keeping a cool and wary distance, could her heart be creaking open its rusty door? Letting in some light? He was young, handsome, energetic, intelligent, but more significantly he was demonstrating fathering skills. No doubt about it, Will Rubens was a catch.

And he wanted her.

No, he wanted her for his son, that was all.

So, what should she do? What could she do?

Eating in the staff lunch room, she tried to respond to questions the first-grade teacher asked about a special-needs student in her class. Time and again, Savanna's gaze wandered to Valerie at the other end of the table.

The secretary was perfect for Will. Her son walked to class with Christopher and Angela each morning.

A few days ago the boy had come to Will's house with Angela and the two played with Christopher's train set. Chris hadn't engaged in the play, instead read his helicopter books, but at least Josh was showing signs of becoming a friend. Thanks to little Angela.

"If you'd like," she said to the first-grade teacher, "I can come in and help your little guy this afternoon. I'll tell Chris I'll be out of class but still in school until home time. He'll be okay with that."

"I can't imagine what you went through yesterday," Penny Murphy said. Her eyes were sympathetic.

"Definitely in panic mode," Savanna replied around a half smile.

"We were all worried," Valerie put in. "Christopher's uncle was beside himself. He came over to talk to Josh and me later and asked if we'd keep an eye out for his nephew at the school whenever Savanna wants some relief time. I said we would." Her gaze darted around the table. "Just like we're taking care of his cat for a while because Christopher is afraid of cats."

A silence fell across the room. Everyone stared at their lunches.

Savanna spoke into the quiet. "I'm very grateful for that, Valerie. And so his Chris's uncle, I'm sure. However, I'm hoping with a little coaxing, Christopher will eventually overcome his fears and Will can bring the cat home."

"Well, if it doesn't happen, Josh and I'll be happy to look after it for him."

"Thank you." Forcing a smile, Savanna gathered up her lunch and pushed back her chair. "See you all later," she said, then left the room.

She could not look at Valerie's yearning eyes without remembering Will in the night.

In their classroom group, Josh watched Christopher working on his map of Starlight. Yesterday the guy got a ton of attention because he'd run away from school.

Josh didn't believe that bit about how he had to walk up and down the streets to draw a stupid map of the village. There was Caribou Street and three roads on one side and another three crisscrossing those. No big deal. Josh could draw them in his dreams.

He figured Christopher just liked attention. He was always wanting to do things his way.

What Angela saw in the guy, Josh didn't get. He knew she was the class helper and everybody really liked her, but she was also really smart, yet around Christopher she acted as if she didn't know beans.

Josh would bet his Jaguars jersey she knew as much if not more than Christopher. Except she didn't go around bragging about everything she knew.

Like right now. Christopher had his head down over his map, putting in stop signs on his map assignment. He'd even drawn a directional arrow pointing to the Arctic Circle. How weird was that! Starlight was *miles* from the Arctic Circle.

That was just it. The guy went way crazy when he got something in his head. And there was Angela, telling him it was the best map she'd ever seen.

Okay, it was pretty good with all the mountain ranges and trees and rivers and stuff, but it wasn't *that* good.

Josh caught Roger rolling his eyes. Smirking, his friend snuck Josh a slip of paper.

Hiding it from the teacher, Josh opened the note under his desk: "Loony-toony Chris."

Josh shoved the paper among his books.

Thank goodness Ms. Murphy walked past their group. Her presence gave Josh the excuse not to look at Roger.

"All done with your map, Josh?" Ms. Murphy asked.

Shaking his head, he reached for a blue pencil crayon and pretended to fix the outline of his title.

He didn't know what to do.

Chris was related to Will, and what Roger was saying wasn't right. But Roger had been his friend since kindergarten and Josh wanted to be on his side, too.

He pressed down on the pencil, hard, wishing Christopher *had* gotten lost yesterday. Or better yet, that he'd leave Starlight and never come back. Then all this stupid confusion would go away.

Moving about the first-grade classroom, Savanna worked with several children, surreptitiously noting the behavior and habits of the six-year-old student the teacher had concerns about. The child, a boy, would do well with several behavior-adjustment strategies. After discussing those with the teacher while the class worked on a writing project, Savanna promised to meet with the woman the following week to establish a more comprehensive program.

At 2:40 she walked down to Christopher's classroom.

"Savanna!" His gaze caught hers as he came through the door, the familiar yellow-and-red knapsack, the *lifesaving* knapsack, slung around his thin shoulders.

"Hey, pal." Her heart gave a painful lurch. One day she would not be standing at this door; instead it would be Will or a respite worker. "Ready to go to Nana's house and visit Blue for an hour?"

"Yeah, I like Nana's peanut butter cookies."

"So do I, honey." Ah, the burn of tears. For the first time, the mention of Blue had not prompted a monologue about Siberian huskies and the Iditarod. "Nana will have a fresh batch coming out of the oven the minute we get there." *Bless the old gal's heart.*

They walked from the school, heading down the street. Christopher rambled on about Jet Rangers and Will's flyby yesterday. Details, mechanics, statistics.

Savanna let him talk. Today she didn't have the heart to steer him onto other topics or into a two-way conversation. Today she simply wanted to enjoy *Christopher.*

Ten minutes later, they walked through Georgia's back gate. Trowel in hand, Elke's grandmother knelt on a foam pad beside the back stoop, loosening the soil around a cluster of dandelions poking through the fertile spring earth.

As they did every day, the woman's eyes lit up. Today, they glimmered. Savanna had no doubt Georgia was recalling the horror twenty-four hours ago. "Well, if it isn't my favorite boy."

"Hi, Nana." Christopher crouched beside Blue dozing in a spot of sun nearby. "Did you make cookies?"

Hands to knees, Georgia ascended slowly to her feet. "You bet." She gave the boy a light, quick hug. "Come inside and see. How was your day, Savanna?"

"Busy, but definitely better than yesterday."

"Anything is better than yesterday." Neither blame nor accusation lay in her eyes.

They entered the kitchen, where the scent of baked peanut butter sifted through the warmth. Without removing his knapsack, Christopher rushed to the counter.

"Ask politely," Savanna reminded him gently.

Turning, the boy watched Blue shuffling toward the living room. "Can I please have one, Nana?"

"Of course you can. But first take off your knapsack. Then you can get a bread plate and take two cookies." Pouring a glass of milk, she exchanged a smile with Savanna. Both knew the boy would slip the extra treat to Blue.

When Christopher disappeared into the living room, dog in tow, Georgia set the kettle on to boil for their afternoon tea. "That boy's the jewel of my heart," she said. "And," she glanced at Savanna removing the usual pair of Royal Albert teacups from the cupboard, "I suspect yours, too."

"It makes me ill to think what might have happened to him yesterday," she admitted. "I thought… Oh, Georgia. It was awful. Thank God for Will and his helicopter."

Georgia set a hand on Savanna's shoulder. "Don't sell yourself short, honey. You amassed half the town into a search. Someone would have found Chris."

She had to believe that. "Valerie Jax thinks Will is a hero and so do I. Like everyone does," she added hurriedly. Why had she mentioned Valerie?

Georgia snorted. "I don't doubt your integrity. But Valerie Jax has been chasing Will from the moment he started coaching her son's baseball team three years ago. If he rescued a cat from a tree limb, she'd think the man walked on water to do it."

"Well," Savanna said, glumly. "She's rescued *his* cat."

Georgia pursed her lips. "That'll change once we get little Chris convinced cats aren't the tigers he believes."

Savanna frowned. "While Christopher was walking away from school yesterday, I was in a store buying a video about a cartoon cat and a train. I'd hoped it would help ease the transition for him with Will's cat."

"Do you still have the video in your purse?"

"It's at Will's."

"Bring it tomorrow and we'll get Blue to sit with Chris while he watches it. That old dog knows when someone's stressed. He'll calm the boy."

Yes, Savanna thought. The husky had been a balm over the past month, its quiet acceptance eliminating some of Christopher's anxiety. Along the way, the child had grown accustomed to Georgia's gentle manners. *Oh, yes.* Not only was the great-grandmother exactly what the boy needed, she would be an enormous supporter for Will when the time came for Savanna to entrust Christopher into his hands before she left for Tennessee.

Lord, she wanted to weep. To leave Christopher…and this lovely, kind woman…and *Will.*

He'd asked her to marry him.

He said they could make a new family for Christopher. A loving family. *But without love in the marriage bed.*

"You look like you've lost your best friend," Georgia said, retrieving the whistling kettle to prepare the tea.

Savanna pressed her lips together. "I'll miss him." *Both of them.*

"Then stay." Georgia reached over, clasped Savanna's hand.

Stay. Will's word.

She looked away from Georgia's all-knowing eyes.

The older woman set the teapot on the table, pulled out a chair. "What's waiting for you in that other part of the world? Yes," she said, filling the cups with her golden vanilla-flavored Rooibos. "I know you plan to visit your brother and his family, but, child, he's got his own life now."

Savanna looked straight at the woman she had come to trust as much as Elke. "Will asked me to marry him last night."

"Well now," Georgia beamed. "Isn't that just plain wonderful? I hope you said yes."

Savanna released a shaky laugh. "No."

"No? You told him no?"

"Oh, Georgia. He only asked for Christopher's sake. It has nothing to do with…with…"

"Love?" Her eyebrows rose. "Is that what he implied?"

"No, but—"

"Listen here, girl. I've known Will Rubens all his life and I've seen girls trail him at school and around dance floors. I've seen them make calf eyes at him across the street. A few even snagged his attention for a month or two. But not one moved into that lovely house he built seven years ago. Until now."

"That's only because of Chris."

"Yes. But in all this time, I've also never seen him look at a woman the way he looks at you."

"What about Aileen?" Savanna knew all about the young woman who had died carrying Will's baby—and it broke her heart. That night when Will had loved her so tenderly, more than a window to their pasts had been opened. The door to her heart had been flung wide.

"Aileen was his first crush," Georgia said. "He saw her through a boy's eyes. He's seeing you through the eyes of a man."

Propping her elbows on the table, Savanna pressed her fingers against her forehead. "I'm so confused."

"Do you love him?"

"I don't know. I don't want to love him, but every time I

see him…" She raised her head, looked through the window to the backyard where a wind tiptoed through evergreen branches. "He has my heart doing flip-flops." Her eyes returned to Georgia. "But he's so young."

"Pfsst. He's a man."

Oh, yes. He is that. Around a rueful half-smile, Savanna said, "So he continues to tell me."

Leaning forward, Georgia slid her palms over the surface of the table. "Then listen to your heart, girl. Age is just a couple of numbers. When you don't look over your shoulder, you don't see them creeping up."

Savanna released a short laugh. "You do know how to put things in perspective, Georgia."

"Live the day for what it is, honey." She rose when the phone on the wall beside the refrigerator shrilled. "That's all any of us can do." Patting Savanna's hand, she picked up the receiver.

Savanna went to the living room to check Christopher.

He sat on the floor next to Blue, watching another Sponge Bob episode. Cookies and milk gone, Christopher had his Alaska map spread across his lap. An edge looped over the dog's shoulders. Same ritual every day. Sponge Bob, Blue, map. *Oh, my sweet boy,* she thought. *How will I get through the day without you?*

"Savanna," Georgia said quietly from the archway. "It's for you." She indicated the receiver resting on the counter.

Will. Heart skipping, she picked up the phone. "Hello."

"Ms. Stowe?" Not Will. "This is Max Shepherd, mayor of Starlight. Don't know if you remember me?"

"I do, sir." She had contacted the man about Will before leaving Central America. "We talked a month or so ago."

"We did, and I hope what I relayed at the time has been to your advantage, as well as the boy's?"

"Yes, it has." *And now I've fallen in love.* "Thank you."

"Ms. Stowe, you've met my son Shane over at the lodge?"

Shane, the desk clerk who danced with her, then laughed when Will boldly whisked her out of his hands.

"I met him the first day, Mr. Shepherd. He's not a bad dancer, you know."

He laughed. "Well, this is going to sound a little odd, but do you recall the conversation you had with Shane about his sister?"

The woman eking out a life with her husband and children deep in the state's wilderness. A modern-day pioneer wife with three children, the youngest of whom seemed incapable of focusing on the subjects of a home-school program.

"He mentioned a sister, yes."

A long sigh traveled through the line. "I've just come from the school, and Harry Germaine feels you might be able to help my daughter."

"What's wrong with her?"

"It's not her as much as it's my grandson. The boy is getting out of hand. He won't listen to his parents and he cowers when his daddy gets after him for not doing what he's told. The kid obsesses over crazy things like car parts and woodworking tools. He's taken their generator apart and put it back together a half dozen times. Not something you want in the dead of winter, for sure."

"True." She pictured frost-lined windows, frozen water pipes, eight-foot drifts. "How old is he?"

"Eleven. I've told them a thousand times to stop trying to play Grizzly Adams with those kids and move back to civilization, but they're both stubborn as a two-headed donkey. My son-in-law figures living like a sourdough will grant the kids a *pure* perspective of the world and teach them how to save it one day." Max snorted. "Idiots, both of them."

"How can I help?"

"Could you and I discuss some approaches Nadine could implement to get a handle on young Jeff? Better yet, I could fly you to their place, let you assess the situation yourself."

"Mr. Shepherd, assessments should be done through official agencies."

The man snorted. "Don't have time for a bunch of red tape. Hell, Jeff'll be an adult before someone gets the nod to go down there from some *agency*." The last word was spat out. "Look, Germaine at the school said you've got enough credentials to set up your own business, if you want."

Harry had said that?

Shepherd went on. "I'll make it very worth your while. Pay is no object. I own the lodge and have been flying my own float plane for nearly twenty-five years—if that will set your mind at ease. Ms. Stowe, Jeff is driving my Nadine crazy. Please, will you help them?"

How could she refuse? This was why she had worked in Africa and Central America. Why she loved children desperate for a chance to succeed.

And why she adored Christopher beyond reason.

"All right, Mr. Shepherd," she said. "I'll fly into your wilderness."

At 9:15 that night, Will shut down his home computer.

From the moment Savanna had made the announcement during supper about her impending trip into the Chugach Mountains, Will had kept quiet. In contrast, Christopher immediately rushed to his ever-ready knapsack and pulled out his map of Alaska.

On the kitchen floor, he'd rambled on about the flight

path she would take, the topography the plane would cover, the glaciers, individual mountains, the highway to follow and the lakes and rivers she would cross.

With the last dish put away, Will had escaped to his office for some checking of his own with Nate Burns. In particular, the southern weather pattern for the upcoming three days.

A front he didn't like was building over the Gulf of Alaska. He pushed back his chair and headed for the great room.

Savanna sat curled in a corner of the sofa, reading. Tiny granny glasses perched on the end of her nose, and all he could think was that he wanted to pluck them off, kiss some sense into her. He did not want her flying in Max Shepherd's thirty-year-old float plane.

"Chris in bed?" he asked.

She raised her head, her green eyes soft in the evening light spilling through the windows. "A few minutes ago."

Nodding once, he made his way down the hall. Will loved this part of the evening, this ritual of tucking in his child. Sometimes he wished Dennis could know how much Will had come to love Christopher. Of course, if Dennis could know *anything,* the child propped against the pillows with the state map supported by his up-drawn knees would not be living under Will's roof.

"Hey, buddy." Will crossed the threshold. The model train he had brought home that first moving day had been disassembled and stacked in a box at the foot of the bed.

Topic closed.

Fling wings now held his son's avid interest. Books about helicopters lay scattered across the floor and were piled on the night table. Will smiled. Machines and maps. Christopher's world.

"Did you get your homework done?" Will asked, sitting carefully on the edge of the bed.

"Uh-huh. Look at this, Uncle Will." Chris's finger journeyed down the page. "Savanna is going over the Nelchina River and past Tazlina Lake."

"She is," Will agreed, using the excuse to examine the trail as a way to move closer, to move shoulder to shoulder with his son.

"In a float plane it should take only an hour. If you go by air, Mr. Shepherd's daughter lives about ninety miles from here because a mile equals eighty-seven percent of a nautical mile. If you go by road—" He prattled on, until Will had to end the boy's monologue.

"Buddy," he said, reluctantly moving away from the cozy warmth of his son. "It's time for bed."

"But I haven't finished looking at the map. Savanna needs to know where she's going. I have to tell her the route so she can tell Mr. Shepherd."

"Check your agenda, son." Will picked up the laminated copy from the night table. "See, nine o'clock, lights-out time. Time to get some sleep. It's now 9:13. You're thirteen minutes late."

"I'm late?" Christopher threw the map onto the floor. Tears sprang into his eyes as he slipped under the covers. "I'm late. I hate being late. Late is not a good thing. Late means I don't get enough sleep."

"Easy, son." Will stroked the covers near Christopher's shoulder, soothing, calming as Savanna had taught him. "You'll get lots of sleep. Thirteen minutes is nothing. It's the time it takes to dream. We can pretend you had a dream, okay?"

Bottom lip trembling, the boy stared at the ceiling.

"You're okay, Chris. I'm not going to let time get away from you," Will assured. "You'll catch up while you sleep." He leaned over to shut off the light.

Gently he touched the boy's hair. "I love you, son. You're the best kid." *Any parent could have.*

Christopher's breathing eased. "You're nice, too, Uncle Will."

Will's heart tumbled. Such a huge first. They would make it, he and the boy. "Sweet dreams, son."

"Tomorrow Savanna won't be here."

A small chill went through Will. "Only for a few hours. She'll be back in time for supper."

Chris considered. "That's nine hours from when I go to school."

"But think of the descriptions she can give you for your map when she gets back."

The boy's gaze slowly came around to Will, then returned to the ceiling. "She can take pictures from the plane, right? It'll make the map more authentic because I'll have a lot to add."

"You bet. Now, go to sleep, Chris," he said gently.

The boy turned onto his side. "'Night, Unc' Will."

Heart pressing his ribs, Will waited for the little snort as Savanna had tutored. "'Night, little man," he whispered.

Back in the great room, he slipped the book from Savanna's hands, eased the glasses from her nose and tugged her to her feet. "Come with me," he said, leading her to the kitchen's door. After slinging a jacket around her shoulders and shrugging into another himself, he ushered her out onto the screened rear porch.

The evening air brimmed with the scent of birthing leaves and grasses poking slender green fingers through the earth. A handful of mosquitoes whined at the screens. Far beyond, the sorbet-washed mountains hunkered beneath a canopy of dusk.

"Will, what is it?" Savanna turned her face up to his.

He couldn't wait any longer. Pulling her against him,

sheltering her within his coat, he dipped his head and kissed her the way he had in bed. With every beat of his heart. A long moment later he touched a knuckle to her cheek.

"I want to fly you there tomorrow."

"That's silly. Max said he'd take me in his float plane. The family lives on a lake and he travels the route a half dozen times a year. I need you to stay with Christopher."

He studied her eyes. He didn't want her to go. Not because of his son, but because he didn't trust anyone but himself to fly her over Alaska's terrain.

"Don't worry," she said. "I'm only going for the day. Max is flying me up right after Chris leaves for school and I'll be back shortly after he gets home." She endowed him with one of her rare crooked smiles that had his stomach skipping. "Penny will have an aide to help Chris through the day. He'll be okay, Will. Chris and I discussed it at length tonight. And I've included my trip on tomorrow's agenda."

"It's not him I'm worried about. Max's plane is three decades old and there's a storm moving in from the coast."

Savanna moved out of his arms, walked to the railing. "Please, don't feel responsible for me. The other night happened because we were both overwhelmed."

Turning, she crossed her arms. Her lips were straight as the Jet Ranger's altitude indicator on the instrument panel. Will wanted to shake her and kiss her in the same breath. Had their shared words, those intimate life revealing words, meant nothing to her?

Inside the pockets of his jacket, his fingers curved. "Have you given any thought to my question?"

Their eyes locked for five long seconds. Over her shoulder, a soft wind soughed through the darkening evergreens.

She said, "I've thought of little else."

By degrees his body loosened. She hadn't tossed out a

reflexive no. Cultivating a grin he didn't feel, he said, "Well, that's good, I guess."

"It is and it isn't." Unhappiness shaded her eyes. "Will, you're a good man. You and Christopher are going to—"

He slung up a hand. "Don't. Not tonight, Savanna." His chest hurt. Goddammit, he did not need to hear the reasons again. He cared for her. More than he'd cared for a woman in nearly two decades. If she couldn't believe that—

Two paces and he loomed over her. "You're wrong. Christopher and I need you, and you need us. We can make it work, if you gave it one chance. That's all. One chance."

Vexed with her inflexibility, and with himself for his lack of sense around her, he shoved through the porch's screen door and stormed off through the pink-sponged trees.

Chapter Twelve

Slouching in his desk, pretending he knew what he was doing with this stupid math problem, Josh kept shooting glares at Christopher. The geek had his nose almost on the page of his notebook.

Okay, so he was a math genius. So he could do ninth-grade problems and in fifth grade. Big deal.

Bet you can't throw a baseball, Josh fumed as he stared at Christopher, hoping the guy would look his way.

Josh could throw a baseball farther than anyone on the team. He could catch curves quicker than most of the senior catchers. He was a star. His team loved him.

So why did he feel like a complete dumbbell right now?

Because of nerdy Christopher. Nerdy Christopher who always got the attention. Who was Angela's favorite and Will's nephew.

Will barely bothered with Josh anymore. Thinking about

that made him want to cry. Will was his big brother. He'd said so, hadn't he? *Josh, you can be my little bro anytime.* That's what he'd said three years ago when Josh had asked him if it was all right, because Josh didn't have a dad anymore or a brother and he'd felt so lost and lonely.

He knew his mom still felt lonely. He wished Will would see how nice she was and what a great cook she was and how hard she worked.

Now he'd never notice. Because of Christopher. Everything changed because of Christopher.

He looked over at Angela. What did she see in the guy? All he ever talked about was his stupid maps or helicopters. First trains, now helicopters. Because of Will.

The point on Josh's pencil broke. Stupid pencil. He hated math. He hated school. Well, not really, but right now he just wanted things back to the way they were before Christopher.

The recess bell rang.

"Yay," he whispered and slapped his notebook shut. He couldn't wait to get outside, away from all these bad thoughts in his head.

Roger poked him in the back. "Meet me out by the swings."

Today the intermediate kids were allowed on the activity center.

Coats half-zipped, everyone tumbled out the classroom's back door, racing for a turn on the swings, jungle gym, slides and teeter-totters.

Roger stood waiting beside the ball pole.

"Why didn't you grab a couple swings?" Josh asked, anger rising. All eight were taken.

His friend tugged him away from the center. "Let's find something else."

"Like what? I wanted a swing."

"Like that." Roger pointed toward the classroom door.

Christopher knelt on the ground, digging in his knapsack. Man. Couldn't the guy go *anywhere* without that thing?

"What about him?" Josh felt a pinch in his stomach. Roger had a smile on his face that wasn't nice.

His pal pulled a baseball from his coat pocket. "Let's see if he's getting on the team this year."

"Nah, let's not bother. Let's go see what Adam and Craig are doing over by the jungle gym."

"We will," Roger said, walking toward Christopher. "In a bit. Hey, Christopher!"

The guy looked up.

"Whatcha doin'?" Roger asked.

"Savanna is flying to the Chugach mountains today."

"Yeah?"

"She's going in a float plane."

That caught Josh's interest. "Will's not flying her?"

"No, I said she's going in a float plane. Mr. Shepherd is flying her to the Chugach range to see his daughter."

"How come?" Josh wanted to know.

"Hey, Chris." Roger bumped Josh with his elbow. "Wanna play some catch?"

"Catch?" The guy hauled out a map with tattered creases and ripped edges. Dirt streaked down one side.

"Yeah, you know? We toss the ball around and catch it?"

"Is it fun?"

"Tons."

"A ton is a measure of weight."

Man, Josh thought. *This guy's dumb with a capital* D. "Tons also means *a lot,*" he explained. "Playing catch is a lot of fun."

"Does this mean I'm your friend?" Christopher asked, and Josh saw a light go on in the guy's eyes.

"Sure," Roger said. "We'll all be pals. But you gotta put your map away first."

Christopher shoved the page back into his knapsack. He jumped to his feet and danced on his toes. "Okay! Okay, I'm ready to have tons!"

Roger's giggle didn't sound funny. "Stand over there," he ordered, pointing to a spot about twenty feet away from the classroom. "Josh, you stand here."

"Shouldn't we move over a bit?"

"Just go, Josh," Roger snapped.

"All *right*. Geez." He hated when Roger ordered him around. He moved to the spot while his friend walked to another spot.

Christopher yelled, "Hey, we're in a triangle."

"Yeah," Roger agreed. "It's the best way to play catch."

"How do you play?" Christopher wanted to know and Josh rolled his eyes. The guy couldn't be *that* dumb.

"Watch me'n Josh." Roger tossed the ball to Josh who tossed it back. Simple as pie.

"Okay, now I'll toss it to you." He did. Christopher's arms waved like tree branches in a strong wind. He missed by a mile. "Go get it," Roger demanded.

Josh watched the guy run after the ball. Roger laughed. "He even runs like a geek."

Shame trickled into Josh's stomach. He didn't like the way Roger was acting with Will's nephew. "Rog, let's not—"

"Here it comes," Christopher yelled and threw the ball.

It flew like a crazy thing to the right. Josh raced to get into its path.

Too late. The ball slammed into one of the classroom's windows. Glass shattered everywhere.

Josh's mouth dropped open. "Holy cow! You broke the window!" He swung around and stared at Christopher.

The guy stood blinking and rocking on his heels, hands batting like broken wings against his legs.

"Chris, it's okay." Josh started toward him. Oh, man. What had they done?

Roger swore. "Let's get out of here." He grabbed Josh's sleeve. Other kids were running toward them. Everyone was talking and pointing at the window and asking questions. Someone had run to get a teacher.

Angela was suddenly beside Christopher. "It's okay, Chris," she said over and over. "It was an accident. You didn't know the rule."

Tears ran down Christopher's cheeks. "What rule, Angela? I didn't know about the rule and now the window has a hole and cracks all over." He rocked back and forth. "Will glass have to be manufactured at a factory for the window?"

"Yeah," Angela said. "But that's okay, Chris. The window was old anyway. We needed a new one." She looked at Josh like he was a gutted bug on a windshield.

Then Mr. Germaine, the principal, ran over.

Gingerly Savanna looked out the cockpit window of the Piper float plane to the rugged landscape ahead. The Chugach Range. She squeezed back a thread of fear.

Beside her, Max confirmed his coordinates with Nate Burns back at Starlight. They had taken off from a small lake three miles east of the town. She was not a nervous flier…in large aircraft. Or, she'd discovered, in Will's helicopter, flying a few hundred feet above ground. But sitting in a single-engine four-seater float plane, similar to the one Elke and Dennis had taken through the Honduran mountains, had her pushing down a surge of nausea.

"This your first time in a little ship?" Max's voice came into her headset over the droning plane.

"How can you tell?"

He chuckled. "Your eyes."

Dennis had once told her she wore her heart on her face. She wondered about the heart Will had seen last night.

He wanted her to make a family with him and Christopher, but he didn't love her. He'd said, "I care for you more than I have any woman in a very long time." Since Aileen, she assumed but hadn't asked, hadn't pinned him to the wall.

Twelve hours ago he'd been angry and she had gone to bed alone and confused. He was right, of course. Christopher would hate it when she left. So much in these past weeks had changed for the child, so much taken away.

Could she remove one more constant?

She had no other choice. She was a woman beyond the age of prime, a woman unable to bear children, which, no matter how much Will tried to convince her, would make a difference at some point. Especially if theirs was a marriage for the sake of a child.

And that was the crux of her dilemma. If she stayed, Will's novelty with her would surely unravel into a backlash that, in the end, would leave its mark on his son. *And leaving in a few weeks won't hurt him as much?*

She did not want to picture Christopher's bewilderment. She did not want to think of his actions, the head batting, the humming, the curled fetal position.

"Feeling a little better?" Max asked, steering her rumination back into the cockpit of the droning plane.

She checked the terrain below and nodded.

"Keep your eyes on the distance. Don't look down until your stomach feels confident." Max's smile held sympathy.

Far beyond, the mountains spread, vivacious in white and brown, and speckled with spring green. On the line of the southern horizon, Savanna caught the spear of blue that was Prince William Sound.

Alaska in its splendor. Christopher had told her the state had twice the land mass of Texas.

Christopher and his facts and his maps.

Before breakfast this morning he'd offered his rendition of what he believed would be their route into the mountains.

"I drew the way, Savanna," he'd said, handing her the sheet of paper upon entering the kitchen as she prepared his three toasty triangles. Will had already left for a day of maintenance on his helicopter, though she suspected he'd escaped because of her.

Filled with mountains and lakes and rivers and elevation numbers, Chris's page tracked the float plane's destination in a bold yellow line to a point halfway between Starlight and Valdez. Exactly where Max had told her they were bound.

Remembering, she pulled the map from her jacket pocket.

"Looks like someone isn't taking chances," Max remarked, glancing over.

"My— Will's nephew drew it." She nearly said *my son*.

Because in every way but one, he is your son. You've thought of him as your son for over a month.

"Kid's good," Max said. "He the one who's autistic?"

"High-functioning autistic."

Max guided the plane into a wide, deep valley. "I've been doing some reading on the condition. I think that's my grandson's problem." His brown eyes were serious. "Would you know by observing him?"

"Not for certain, Max. I'm not a specialist, but I can ask some relevant questions that might help steer his parents in the right direction."

"That's all I can ask." He nodded to the map on her

knees. "Will's lucky to have a boy in the family with that kind of grasp on geography. Especially in this territory and him being a pilot."

"Yes." *Christopher is Will's lucky charm.*

Will got the call from the school at 10:45.

He'd been working inside the hangar greasing the Jet Ranger's rotors when Hewlett, one of the two mechanics, walked over and said, "School's on the phone."

Wiping his hands on a rag, Will headed for the small cluttered office with its stagnant scent of grease and coffee at the back of the building.

By the time he picked up the receiver, his heart was a caged wild bird behind his tongue. The last time he'd been called by the school….

He cleared his throat. "Rubens here."

"Will, it's Valerie. There's been an accident. Nothing serious, but I think you need to come to the school."

Nothing serious. He latched on to that, forced his body not to shake. "What happened?"

Valerie explained. A game of catch at recess with Josh and Roger. A broken classroom window. Christopher inconsolable. Crying over shattered glass.

"I'm on my way." He hung up.

Leaving Hewlett to finish the rotors, Will loped to his truck. The drive took less than five minutes. He rushed into the school, paced down the hall to the office. Roger Maize and Josh sat on a wooden bench along the outer wall. If someone said their pet dogs had died, Will would have believed it. Tears swam in the kids' eyes.

Josh said, "I'm sorry, Will. I didn't mean it, honest."

The broken window. "We'll talk later, bud." He strode into the office.

Valerie jumped from her chair. "Chris is in here." She led Will to the medical room across from the principal's office.

Hands drumming his little thighs, Christopher sat rocking back and forth on a chair. Tears streamed from his eyes, snot ran out of his nose. A woman Will didn't recognize knelt in front of the boy. Harry Germaine sat on another chair, trying to explain that what the boy had done was not his fault. Protector and defender, little Angela stood beside Christopher on the other side.

Both children's heads snapped up as Will entered.

"Uncle Will!" Chris leaped from the chair and ran to fling his arms around Will's waist. "The window is broke, Uncle Will," he cried. "It's smashed to pieces!"

Will's heart hurt. For the first time, his son had connected with him physically. Kneeling on the floor, he took the boy's shoulders gently in his hands and pulled him into a hug. "Chris, take it easy, son. Windows can be fixed."

Christopher shook his head; mangled a bunch of tissues between his hands. "But *this* window is ruined!"

Oh, God. What would Savanna say? How would she approach the topic to calm his son?

Will looked to Harry Germaine and the woman, their faces marked with worry and sympathy. Harry began, "We can't get him to understand it's not his fault."

"I told you, Daddy," Angela interjected, looking at the principal with big eyes. "Chris isn't to blame." She offered a tissue box to Will and he wiped his son's tears and nose.

She added, "He didn't know the rule about not throwing balls near the school."

Rules again. Everywhere rules. Will's heart rolled over for his little boy whose entire world revolved around rules and routines and schedules. "Chris," he said gently, brushing the hair out of those red-rimmed eyes. "Do you know why the rule Angela is talking about was put in place?"

A sniff. "No."

"Well, when this school was first built fifty years ago, they didn't have the rule and kids used to play around the grounds and near the building all the time."

He wasn't sure if this was true, but he needed some tangible fact to get through to the boy.

"Anyway, the kids would play catch and baseball and all kinds of games. Then windows started getting broken because some of these balls went through them. After that happened a few times, the teachers and principals had to put in the rule. But the fact is, Chris, many of the windows have been broken and replaced already. The school is old and when things are old, they need to be fixed or replaced."

Another sniff. "Like when my shoelace breaks?"

Will grinned. "Exactly! When your shoelace breaks, Savanna—or me—will need to buy you a new pair. It's the same with the window. The glass is broken and now it has to be replaced."

"Am I stupid for not knowing the rule?"

"Absolutely not." Will cast a glance at Germaine. "Did someone say you were stupid, Chris?"

"Some of the kids think I'm stupid."

Oh, hell. Savanna, I need you. "Did they say so?"

"No, but I know they don't want to be my friend."

Angela stepped beside the boy. "I'm your friend, Chris."

Will smiled at the girl. *You're a godsend, little one.*

Angela went on, "I think other kids are a bit afraid of you, Chris, because you talk about things they don't know. Like the history of helicopters, and you're great at math and can read maps like a wizard. You're really smart." She gave him a sweet smile. "And *my* friends? They think you're really cute."

He turned a baffled look on her. "They do?"

"Uh-huh. Want to get to know them?"

The boy stared at Will's shoulder. "What if they laugh at me and think I'm crazy?"

"They won't," Angela assured. To her father she said, "Can we be excused now, Dad?"

Clearly relieved, the man nodded. "Sure. You kids run along. There are still ten minutes before bell."

Will called, "See you after school, Chris."

"Okay. And then Savanna comes home?"

"Yes, Savanna'll be home later." Will felt a disquieting shiver run through him.

When the kids left, he rose to his feet. "He should be all right for the rest of the day. But if not—" he handed the man a business card "—it's got my cell number."

"Appreciate it. Thanks for coming, Will."

In the doorway he paused. "Look, Harry. In case I'm out of town next time, and Savanna isn't available, please get Georgia Martin. She's the boy's great-grandmother. I don't want him feeling abandoned when he's this upset."

"I'll make sure she's on the emergency list."

"Do that. Mind if I talk to Josh and Roger for a minute?"

"Send them in to see me when you're done."

Will headed back to the office. Valerie sat typing on her computer. He said, "I'd like to talk Josh, Val. Just want to hear his side of the story."

She rose from her chair. "I'll come with you."

He understood; Josh was her son, after all. Together they went out into the hallway where Will squatted in front of the two boys. "Hey, Josh."

"Hey, Will."

"Want to tell me what happened out there with Chris?"

"It wasn't me," the kid blurted. "It was Roger's idea."

"Was not!" Roger glared at Josh.

Will held up a hand. "Hold on, guys. I'm not looking to blame anyone. Josh, all I need from you is what happened." He looked at Roger. "You'll get your turn."

Josh darted a worried peek at Roger who picked at a scab on his thumb. "Roger said we should see if Chris could catch because he figured you'd put him on the team. We didn't mean nothing by it, Will. We didn't know Chris couldn't catch or throw."

"But you knew not to play near the windows."

"Yeah, but—"

"Did you tell Chris about the rule?"

"No," Josh said quietly. "We should've told him on account he's new'n all."

"Yeah, that would've been a good decision." Will looked from one to the other. How could he fix the problem? He didn't want the kids thinking his son was odd or crazy or different. He didn't want to lay blame at their feet when clearly they had set Christopher up for failure.

Will decided to go with honesty. "Look, guys. Chris has a disability which makes him anxious sometimes, especially with strangers and other kids."

"He does?" they asked in unison.

"Yeah. He's autistic, which means he sometimes does and says things you're not quite used to. But that's because he sees things differently. However, he does want to be your friend. Think you can give him a chance at that?"

"Like how?" Josh wanted to know.

"Well, if he starts getting on a topic like helicopters and you don't want to hear it, just say, 'Hey, Chris, we're not interested right now in helicopters. We want to talk about this or that.' He'll understand. He's a pretty smart kid."

"He does advanced math," Josh agreed.

Will smiled. "There you go. If you're having trouble with a problem one day, ask him for help. He'll be happy to show you the steps." Knees cracking, Will stood.

Josh looked up. "Are you gonna bench us at the game?"

The season's first game was in ten days. "No." He glanced at Valerie clasping her hands to her chest. "But I'll be bringing Christopher. I think he'd make a great team manager. What do you guys think?"

Both nodded eagerly.

"Good. I need to explain the position to him first, though, so this is a secret among us, okay?"

Josh made a motion to seal his lips and toss the key. Roger followed. Will nodded. The kids would be okay. "You boys go in and see Mr. Germaine. He's waiting."

When the boys had left, Will headed for the school's entrance.

"Will, wait." Valerie caught up to him. "Can I talk to you a sec?" She motioned to the door, and they walked into the May sunshine.

Tension lifted from his shoulders. Today he'd been a father. He'd handled his son's situation like a real dad. He couldn't wait to tell Savanna.

"Will," Valerie said, interrupting his contentment. "Josh is worried you won't be his big brother after today."

"Nothing's changed, Val, other than Chris being added to the mix."

"You'll still come around the house to see us?"

"Sure, but it'll always be with Christopher now." He wanted that perfectly clear.

"That's okay." A tentative smile. "I want Josh and Chris to be friends, too."

But not for the same reasons I do. "Look, Val. I've asked

Savanna to marry me. She hasn't said yes yet," he added when her jaw fell. "But neither has she said no."

"You...you love her?"

Did he? Hell, he liked Savanna-more than he should admit.

He cared for her, needed her there for his boy. And, yes, dammit, Will wanted her under him in the depth of night.

But...

Do you love her?

Anger bubbled in his chest. Where did Valerie come off poking at his business, his heart?

"That," he said decisively, "is between Savanna and me."

Minutes later he sat in his truck, wrists slung over the steering wheel. He'd handled a crisis with Christopher and they'd come through it fine. The world hadn't ended. He could *be* the father Savanna wanted for the boy. And if she chose to leave, he and Chris would survive.

So why did he feel his world had become a sink hole?

Graceful as an ice skater, the plane skimmed the lake. For a few moments Savanna caught sight of a cabin sheltered by budding deciduous forests at the edge of the water before the building disappeared from view.

They had made the journey without a hitch. Her stomach remained intact, her palms had quit their cold sweat.

Max taxied the plane toward the long wooden toe of pier reaching into the lake. Three children dressed in jeans and sweatshirts stood waving. The eldest child, about thirteen, hauled a rope from a thick wooden pylon in preparation for anchoring the aircraft.

The boy opened the Piper's door the moment all was secure. "Hi, Grandpa."

"Ralph." Max's smile was wide as he took in the other

two children, one who stood clapping his hands and dancing on his toes, and a little girl of about six. "Jeff, Adele."

"Hey, Grandpa," Jeff shouted. He ran to the old man, pushing himself into his space, pushing his nose within inches of Max's face. "You're here! You made it! We missed you!"

"Jeff, give me some room, okay, tiger?"

"Okay! It's been three weeks, six days and fourteen hours since you were here last, Grandpa!"

"No need to shout, Jeffy."

"Okay." Suddenly the child noticed Savanna. "Who is that lady? Her hair's like carrots. Is she your girlfriend, Grandpa?"

Max laughed. "No, she's a friend. Now let's go up to the house and see mom and dad."

"Okay." The boy raced ahead yelling, "Nadine! Nadine, Grandpa is here!"

"Sorry about that." He hoisted the elfin girl into his arms. "Hey, rosebud. How's my favorite granddaughter today?"

"Oh, Grampy." Her giggles were like the sunny speckles on the lake. "I'm your *only* granddaughter."

"That you are, sunshine. That you are."

They headed for the sprawling cabin where a woman opened the screen door to greet them. She wiped her hands on the granny apron hanging from her neck.

Introductions were made, and within minutes Savanna found herself in a cramped, cluttered kitchen with dirty dishes stacked on the counter and in the sink. Several flies buzzed over congealed left-overs. A mosquito landed on her arm and she slapped it before swiping the insect into a tissue.

Max asked Nadine about her husband.

"He's in the lake cove, fishing," she said. "Won't be back till he's caught a couple trout for supper."

Savanna suspected the man was avoiding Jeffery's "assessment." According to Max, his son-in-law believed Jeffery, the middle child, was simply going through an "obsessive" stage trying to fit between his siblings; Max's and Nadine's concerns were "damned ridiculous."

Savanna had heard similar words from Elke before Dennis had Christopher assessed in L.A. And hadn't a kernel of doubt shown in Will's eyes when she'd told him about Christopher that first night?

At the table Savanna pulled several folders from the briefcase she'd brought. Throughout the next several hours, she asked Nadine numerous questions, including those from the famous ratings scale for children with Asperger's Syndrome outlined by Australian autism expert Dr. Tony Attwood. She noted Jeffery's interaction with his siblings, his mother, his environment, convinced with each passing minute that inroads could be made for the family, a path toward relief and help could be set.

By four o'clock when she walked, exhausted but satisfied, with Max to the dock to untie the float plane, storm clouds had pressed onto the southern horizon. Savanna shivered in a gust of cool wind.

"Wind's behind us," Max noted as they harnessed into the plane. "We'll be back home in no time."

Back home.

Yes, Starlight *had* become home....

Because of Georgia and Christopher and the children at school, and even Valerie.

And Will. Will with his mischievous blue eyes and a laugh that tickled her stomach. Will with his gentle touch. Who said all the right things.

Except the one that counted.

Deep in her pocket, her fingers touched the page of Christopher's map once more.

Such a simple route from such a complex little boy.

As the plane's single prop roared and buzzed and the pontoons bounced across the lake's surface, Savanna prayed Christopher's day had gone well.

Because, God help her, she needed this all-day absence to broach the end of her time in Alaska.

Chapter Thirteen

Will sat in his SUV watching the sky across the little lake where Max's plane should have landed fifteen minutes ago.

Dark clouds hung over the water's surface and raindrops had begun to splat the windshield.

From the passenger seat, Christopher asked, "When is Savanna coming?"

"Should be arriving any minute." Will pointed toward the southeast. "Watch over those trees on the other side of the lake. See that tall spruce?"

"Yeah."

"The plane's light should come over the top of it."

"Like a star," the boy said, his hands rapping his knees. "At night, planes have lights that look like stars shining on the horizon. Savanna's coming soon, right?"

Will glanced at his son. The boy's eyes were riveted to the tree line a quarter mile away.

"She is, Chris." Checking his wristwatch, Will tapped the steering wheel, then caught himself and shoved his hand into his jacket pocket. Last thing he needed was Christopher picking up on his nerves.

Where the hell was Max?

Wind gusted against the truck, rocking it gently. The rain increased; drops struck the roof and streaked the glass with an urgency familiar to Alaskan weather.

Damn it, Shepherd. Come on.

Will wondered if the old man had decided to wait out the storm at his daughter's place, or if he had attempted to fly ahead of its approach. With a tail wind, the pilot would have made excellent time. Ten-minutes-early time.

Christopher pressed his nose against the side glass. "This lake is where Savanna's landing in the float plane, right, Uncle Will?"

"Right, son."

More thigh thumping. "Did you know there are about three million lakes in Alaska?"

Three million. And Savanna was flying over several. *She is not in one.* "That's a lot of lakes."

"Uh-huh. And the plane flies over nine. I mapped out the route."

Only nine. With rain hanging over this one like a wet navy blanket. Along the surface, whitecaps rolled to shore and surged against the dock's weathered pylons.

Will's gut fishtailed. No way could that old Piper land on the water now. Max would have to detour out of the storm system, find another spot of water, a quiet spot, to bring down the little ship.

"Planes are late because there are problems." Christopher said into the descending darkness. "Like engine troubles."

"Sometimes." Will wouldn't allow the thought to form. She was okay. She was still at that bush cabin. Max wouldn't have left if the storm front reached them before takeoff. *If.*

"Planes crash because of engine problems." Christopher's hands thumped his thighs. "Mom and Dad aren't here because their plane crashed in the mountains."

"Chris, Savanna's okay." God, how he hoped.

Do you love her? Valerie's question tumbled through him for the thousandth time, and looking at the turbulent lake, the ominous sky, he knew.

He loved Savanna more than he could begin to describe. From the moment he'd looked into those green eyes in that room at the lodge, he'd fallen for her like a sky-diver, hard, fast.

She *had* to come home. She had to come home so he could tell her. His chest ached with the words, with the enormity of knowing that he loved her, only her, and that his chance might have passed.

"Wait here," he told Christopher, flinging open the truck door. A wet wind whipped off the lake and slapped his face. Hurrying around to the rear of the vehicle, Will unhooked his cell and punched three, Nate's speed dial.

"Nate," the controller answered on the first ring.

"Will here, Nate. Have you heard from Max Shepherd?"

"About ten minutes ago, Will. He called in a May Day on a lake east of Matanuska Glacier. Apparently had engine trouble."

Sweet mercy. Will forced composure into his voice. "Any communication since?"

"None. Sorry, man. Search and Rescue from Palmer are heading out first chance, but this storm right now…"

"Yeah, I know." No sense losing another plane to the Chugaches. "I'll be up soon as I get my boy settled."

"You can't go up until the front's passed, Will. Weather's formed an ice storm across the range. Won't be finished until midnight. Too risky with low clouds and—"

"Does he have a GPS on board?" A Global Positioning System would pinpoint his location with strict clarity.

"No, he's been talking about getting one, but—"

"Damned old fool."

Slapping the phone shut, Will stared into the gray wall of rain. *Hang on, Savanna. I'm coming for you.*

The cold shook her bones and rattled her teeth.

Scrunching into a ball on the narrow seat, she hoarded meager heat from the blanket Max had offered the moment he realized the plane could be used as a refuge from the relentless snow and sleet.

When the prop died suddenly midflight, he'd been a master at piloting the silent craft down in a glide toward the small lake in the valley of the mountains, piloting it toward the shoreline for safety. Deep water, she knew, meant almost certain drowning.

A shoreline meant a chance.

The plane had bounced and skimmed, rattling its frame over fretful waves, then striking a pontoon against a submerged boulder and spinning the craft to a stop thirty feet from the rocky shore.

She had no idea where they were; nor was she sure Max knew.

A migraine pounded into her every nerve ending.

Her right wrist throbbed. Broken, most likely. She remembered excruciating pain the moment she'd tried to protect herself, flinging her hand against the glass for purchase as the plane's pontoon barged into the wall of rock concealed by the restless waters.

"You all right, Savanna?" Max's voice came out of the pitch-black night.

"I'm fine, Max," she replied. "How's your knee?" She recalled he had banged it upon landing.

"No worse for wear."

"How long have we been here?"

"Few hours. You… You slept for a while."

Passed out, likely. She wondered if the migraine meant a mild concussion.

Christopher, she thought. How was her little guy holding up? Was Will looking after him? Keeping him calm?

Hours ago they would have recognized something was wrong.

Would she ever see them again?

Lord, it was cold.

She should not have been so hung up on her age. Life was too short. Hadn't she seen *how* short in Liberia, Kenya, Honduras?

Will had seen it on the streets of L.A.

She should've taken a chance because now the chance might be gone, blown away with icy snow on the shore of a dark and desolate lake.

God, they could have died instantly or lain wounded beyond survival.

She needed his arms, his warm, strong arms. *Your feet are cold. Let me warm them up.* His hands, rubbing her heels, her toes. Warming, warming in the night with his strength, his body, his words.

Had she said yes to him she would have had a window of happiness—for an hour, a few more nights.

And this morning she would have kissed him goodbye.

Instead she had said to Christopher, with Will standing ten feet away, "Have a good day at school, honey," and walked out the door—without a glance or a word for his father. Because they'd argued. Again. Over stupidity. Him wanting chances. Her wanting words.

Now the words wouldn't stop. I'm sorry for what I didn't do, didn't say...don't have regrets, please...take care of Chris...I'm crazy in love with you...forgive me for not saying yes....

"Savanna." Max's voice.

"I'm okay."

A water bottle tipped to her lips. "Sip a little. Don't dehydrate."

"Will they find us?"

"In the morning. When the weather clears."

"What if they don't?"

"We're on open water. And Nate's got my coordinates and flight plan." In the glow of the tiny camp heater he had lit, his worried eyes smiled. "The plane won't be hard to spot from the air. Get some rest, if you can."

She closed her eyes, attempted to shut out the head pain, the ache in her wrist. Attempted to remember Will's eyes. His oceanic eyes.

She swam into murkiness.

Sitting on the bed in Christopher's room, Will waited for the boy to brush his teeth in the bathroom down the hall.

A first, this night. The boy would go to sleep without Savanna pulling the covers up to his chin. Without her comfort, her stability.

He'd asked a bazillion questions, all leading to or revolving around *when will Savanna be home?*

Will wished for an exact answer. In three minutes. By eleven tonight. Tomorrow at nine. He wished his mind could shut off images of the downed plane. He wished Alaska was less wild, less *lake filled*.

Restless, he rose from the bed and, agenda in hand, walked to the washroom.

"Ready, son?"

Christopher's cheeks were flushed from the washcloth, his eyes fixated. Taking the agenda, he checked off Washed Hands/Face, Brushed Teeth. "Is Savanna here yet?"

"No." Will led the child to bed.

Christopher climbed in. "Plane crashes kill people."

"Sometimes."

"But helicopters are safer. They don't crash as often as planes."

Will pulled up the covers. "That's because there are less helicopters than planes."

"Trains are safe. You can ride a train for ten thousand miles and never get killed."

"You can also fly an airplane the same distance without harm, Chris. Now, it's time for sleep. Savanna will be here in the morning." *Smart move. Give him a promise you might not be able to keep.*

The boy pointed to his desk. "I drew a map you can use."

"Did you now?" Will smiled.

"I drew one for Savanna. She won't be lost with it."

Emotion jamming words, Will clicked off the light. He kissed the boy's hair, smelled rain. Was it drenching her hair, her lovely red hair?

Hang on, honey. I'll bring you home to our boy at first light.

Standing in the hallway, he heard murmurs in the kitchen. Nate and the other pilots, figuring out a rescue mission. He should be there. He couldn't look into Georgia's distressed eyes. Georgia who had come the moment he'd told her.

Savanna's door stood open. Inside he flicked the light, stood studying the room.

Her things were neatly placed. Two stacks of books on the desk, pink slippers on the throw rug beside the bed, a green-patterned sweater on the back of the desk chair.

He walked over, removed the garment, pressed it against his nose. *Summer in the mountains.* Her scent streamed through his senses, a waterfall of memories.

Tonight she was in those mountains. Somewhere. With snow and rain and wind and icy temperatures. *But not in a lake.*

Turning to leave, he spotted the cartoon video on her night table. *Choo-Choo, the Train Cat.* The video she'd picked up the day Chris walked away from the school.

A video to help him conquer his fear.

Cautiously Will returned the movie to the night-stand.

In his head he had his own video of fear.

He flew the helicopter low as possible over the coordinates Max had radioed in on his Mayday call yesterday afternoon.

The area was a small glacial lake, about ten acres long— enough for a float plane to skim—in a valley east of the Matanuska Glacier and edging the northern boundary of the Chugach range.

As the crow flies, twenty minutes from home.

Twenty minutes. Twenty years.

He had not been able to rescue Aileen. But, dammit, he would rescue Savanna. He would.

This was not a recovery mission.

Think rescue. Only rescue.

The lake appeared unbroken, an oval path of ash-pink tipped by fog and a dawn yet to break over the butt of the horizon.

He'd been first to leave. First up in his bird.

Unable to sleep, Will had prowled the house half the night, waiting for the weather to lift, reviewing Max's flight plan and staring at the map Christopher had drawn of the terrain and route the Piper would have flown.

The kid was a wonder. He'd spent hours last night in his bedroom, laboring over the map. Hours, while Will and Georgia, along with Nate and the Starlight pilots, chugged coffee and discussed a search plan.

At 4:00 a.m., long after the others had left and before the search would begin at 5:30, Will left a note for Georgia on the kitchen counter. "I'm heading out. Tell Chris not to worry. I'll be back with Savanna. W."

He lowered the helicopter, crawling the lake's surface at fifty knots, straining to read the shoreline blotted by remnants of mist hanging in the timber.

Please, please, let them be here. Let them be okay.

On his second lap down the water's length, he saw the flare spear the violet sky from the northern bank.

Thank mercy.

"Hear that?" Max asked.

Holding her breath within sore lungs, she listened, ears cocked to the incredible silence.

Sometime in the night the snow and wind had quit, turning to rain and then leaving behind an icy silence broken by the drip of water and an owl hunting prey.

Now, into the distance another sound.

Whop-whop-whop.

Helicopter blades. Whirling slowly. *Will.*

She peered through glass streaked with dirt and bits of algae that had splashed up from the lurch over the boulder. Beyond, fog and low clouds concealed most of the lake in a smudge of pearl gray. Her heart sank. He would not see them.

"Gotta get a flare!" The plane rocked as Max jumped from the cockpit.

Shouting. Splashing in the lake.

Will, she thought. *Wait for us.*

Heart roaring in his chest, he veered toward the site of the flare. And then he saw it, the yellow Piper tilted at a shallow angle near shore, its left wingtip submerged.

Max stood thigh deep in the lake, waving his arms next to the craft's nose.

Seeing a spot to land the Jet Ranger, Will called in the location to Nate and the Palmer Airport.

Where was Savanna? *Let her be okay, let her be okay. Please, please.* Pleading, begging, praying.

He hadn't breathed words of the kind since his twenty-sixth year and Aileen lay dying in the UCLA Medical Center. Then he'd been more angry than anxious, angry at the risks she'd taken.

He told himself flying with Max had not been a brazen risk on her part. Had she known the plane's motor would die, Savanna would not have climbed aboard.

Max thrashed through the water, stumbling over rocks toward shore as Will flung off his headgear and jumped from the bird. "Where is she?" he shouted to the man staggering toward him.

"In the plane. She's okay, Will."

But he was already bounding through the water. "Savanna!"

The door of the plane hung open, slanted above the surface of the lake. Like a wild man, he scrambled up inside and over the pilot's chair. Clutching the blanket to her neck with bruised fingers, she lay huddled in the cargo hold. Her green eyes riveted on his. "Will," she whispered hoarsely. "You came."

"Savanna. Oh, baby." He squeezed into the narrow confines, wrapped her gently in his arms. "I'm here, honey. Thank the Almighty. You're safe, you're—" Tears, barred his words. "I thought—" He kissed her forehead, her eyes, nose. "Savanna…I thought I'd lost you."

Icy fingers touched his cheek. "I'm fine. Just hurt my wrist."

He sputtered a giddy laugh, leaned his forehead to hers, tenderly kissed her lips, the badly swollen wrist, her cold, cold fingers. "I'm taking you home, honey. How's that sound?"

"Like heaven."

Their eyes held. *I would die for you,* he wanted to say, but tears swarmed his throat. Instead, he enfolded her tenderly against his chest and inhaled the ether that was Savanna.

The Starlight doctor, a young determined man, wanted to keep her overnight at the four-bed medical clinic.

For observation, he said. Concussions of any kind—and she'd sustained a mild one—should never be taken lightly. Hers had been caused by whiplash and the plane's window.

And then there was the matter of the fractured ulna and lunate bones in her right wrist. The swelling needed to decrease before a cast could be fitted.

So she lay in the narrow bed at the medical clinic, fighting nausea and fatigue, tracking shapes in the stippled ceiling and wondering about Christopher in Will's home.

Was he happy Will had found her? Had he been anxious?

Was he asking to see her?

Do you miss me, little man?

She drifted into sleep imagining Will and his son surviving. Surviving in that lovely, warm cabin.

Without her.

They had set her wrist in a tiny cast, bandaged the scratch on her forehead and untangled her hair.

He watched her come awake in stages.

A twitch of the eyelash, an unfocused peep, finally a slow raising of the lids. Her green eyes inched left, caught his. At the bed's guardrail, he eased out a breath.

"Hey, baby." His voice rasped. "How you feelin'?"

Her chapped lips parted. "Like I've been in a plane crash?"

The stab at humor broke him. "Savanna." His hands found her free one, and he lifted it to his mouth before closing his eyes. Her pale skin tore him apart. "Don't do this to me again," he whispered.

Her eyes hooked him. "Can I ask you the same?"

To stop flying. "All right. If you must fly, I'm your pilot. This isn't open for discussion, honey. In Alaska, I'm the one." *And for everywhere else.*

Her gaze drifted toward the window where the afternoon sun spangled the trees. "How's Christopher?"

"Great. Georgia has him, they're watching that video you bought." It was Saturday, after all. "Chris watched it four times this morning already." Again he kissed her fingers. "He's kind of taken a liking to Choo-Choo."

"Oh, Will. That's good. Won't be long and you'll be able to reintroduce him to your cat, maybe bring her home."

"We'll see. If not, Val's willing to give it a home." He didn't want to talk about Valerie. "Chris was up half the night reading maps and drawing them." A corner of his mouth lifted. "Kid's nuts about Alaskan geography."

"He drew me a flight path before I left."

"I know. He gave me one as well." *He wanted us to find each other.*

In her eyes a smile, as if she'd read his thoughts. She said, "It sounds like you've both connected. That's so good," she whispered. "It'll make things easier when I leave."

His heart raced. "We'll talk later."

What he wanted was to tell her he loved her, except fear rolled across his heart. She had rejected him once before. But not this minute, not while he lowered the guardrail, slipped his arms around her fragile shoulders, lay his head on her pillow. Not while their pulses drummed together and he set soft kisses on her mouth, and her hair braided around his fingers.

She called Georgia at seven o'clock the next morning when she knew Will was scheduled to take four wildlife photographers up the Copper River and Christopher would be dropped off at his great-grandmother's house until his father returned.

"Don't bother to pick me up from the hospital," she told Georgia. "I'll get Valerie to do it once the doctor has made his rounds."

"Are you sure?" Georgia asked, and Savanna heard relief in the old lady's voice.

"It'll be better for Chris. I think he's had enough disruption in his life over the past three days." The school window, which Will had told her about yesterday; her plane crashing.

"He's handled the past three days like a trooper." Georgia remarked.

Savanna pulled the clinic's robe tighter around her middle. Twenty-four hours and she felt much better. A residual niggle remained of the migraine. Her neck, shoulders and wrist were numbed through painkillers. But her decision was made.

"Chris is a wonderful boy," she put in. "He's learned so

much these past two months. I can see a real bond between him and Will."

"There is," Georgia agreed. "Savanna, what's going on?"

"What do you mean?"

"You sound different. Like you're…far away."

"Must be the connection."

But she knew what it was: her putting time and distance between them, preparing Georgia to see this moment weeks from now and recognize its definition.

"I'll see you later." *Much later*. Savanna set the receiver into the telephone cradle.

The homey warmth of Will's house nearly caved her resolution. She stood in the entranceway, scanning the great room with its kid clutter.

Maps, a toy helicopter and a dozen aviation books lay strewn over the square rug. Three train cars lined the edge of the coffee table. The *Choo-Choo* video case lay on the floor in front of the TV. The movie was currently at Georgia's.

Three days of change. Three days of moving forward, one moment at a time.

Her briefcase with its notes about Jeffery stood on the mat at the front door where she assumed Will had left it after driving her to the Medical Clinic yesterday.

She walked to the overstuffed chair. Will's chair, though since she and Christopher moved in, Savanna hadn't seen him use it once. He preferred lying on the rug with his son to watch Discovery Channel or, from evidence today, engage in map speak and model engine action.

Yesterday he had lain on the narrow hospital mattress and secured her in his arms. Kissed her and then kissed her some more. Whispered endearments, told her he'd shivered through a thousand deaths while rain and wind and sleet stormed the starless night around his house, around her.

"Worry was my middle name," he'd breathed in her ear. "Savanna, Savanna. Lady of my heart."

Lady of his heart. Yet the words, those three specific words, had not journeyed over his lips.

She walked past the disordered living area into the kitchen. A half pot of cold coffee sat on its percolator pad; two breakfast plates, a glass and the Midnight Sun mug were stacked in the sink. Christopher's gray sweatshirt hung beside Will's at the back door.

The home of *family*.

A family she was not part of, would never be part of because Will would not love her for the reasons that counted between a man and a woman, and she could not get past her age and damaged interior, and the fact that one day he might change his mind and desire another child.

Time to stop the moaning and go, Savanna.

Upstairs she packed her two suitcases and overnight bag. From the bathroom she retrieved her accessories. Thick with minty paste, Christopher's blue toothbrush stood in its holder. The sight hurt. Such a small thing and it hurt as if she'd been punched. After today, her mothering instincts would end. She rinsed the bristles under a flow of hot water. The towel he'd used after his shower and left in a heap on the edge of the tub, she shook out and hung loosely on the bar.

Last time. I'm being a mother for the last time.

The tears came swiftly, staining her vision, dripping from her chin. *It's better this way. In another day, he'll have placed me behind that secret door with Dennis and Elke. The door he keeps locked.*

She carried the suitcases downstairs, set them by the front entrance. Valerie would be here soon.

Rummaging through the kitchen drawers, she hunted for a sheet of paper, a pen to leave a note. Something for Will to understand. Something for Christopher, if he sought to remember. Unable to locate what she needed, Savanna headed for Will's office.

His bedroom with its open door invited her first.

The duvet had been pulled straight, the pillows stacked against the headboard. She walked to the bed, stared down at the place she had loved him body, heart, soul.

Given her all.

Without seventeen-year-old memories of Liberia interfering.

Without guilt or self-reproach.

She raised her head to the north window where snowy-peaked St. Elias ascended between green drapes.

A last look at Will's wilderness. *Will's Alaska.*

The room smelled of him, of the soap he used.

A discarded black shirt hung over the wing chair in the corner, where at one point during *that night* she had ridden his lap, ageless and free and deliciously wanton.

She spun around and hurried down the hall to his office, found a page and pen, scribbled a note for him, "Thank you for giving me back my life," she began; then to Christopher, "You'll always be my favorite little boy."

Two minutes later she waited with her bags on the front porch for Valerie's tan pickup to appear.

Later tonight Savanna would be back home, surprising her brother in Tennessee. And Alaska would be behind her, another exodus in her life, another memory to forget.

Chapter Fourteen

"You're making a mistake," Valerie told her en route to the Starlight Airport. "You should have at least told Georgia. She'll be mega disappointed you didn't say goodbye."

Savanna watched the village disappear through the passenger window; the airstrip lay a mile and a half from the town's outskirts.

"I'm terrible at goodbyes." She looked across the cab. "You tell her for me, Val."

"What about Will and Christopher?"

You'll all make a great team. "I left them each a letter." Five lines for Will, three for Chris. *I love love love you both.* So much.

"That should go over well." Valerie shot her a frown.

"It's my business, Val."

"Hmm. That's what Will said, too."

She turned her head. "When?"

"When I asked him if he loved you." Valerie's eyes were soft. "He does, you know. I saw it the other night when…your plane went down. I've never known Will Rubens to lose it. That night he did."

"He'd worry about any friend lost in the mountains."

"It wasn't only worry. He went slightly crazy. At one point Nate caught him pacing the front porch and…"

A tiny chill went through Savanna. "And?"

"Shivering."

Worry was my *middle name.* Feigning indifference, she replied, "Well, there *was* a storm that night. The temperature fell to thirty." Cold that burrowed into her marrow on that lake.

Valerie signaled left for Airport Road. "I've seen Will work outside in a T-shirt in lower temperatures. He's practically immune to cold. This…this was more."

Let me warm your ice cubes. Her feet between his calves in bed. Warm, strong body. Warm, strong Will. Still, Valerie's reasoning meant nothing because he hadn't uttered the words—not then, not in the clinic when he climbed beside her and held her as though she were a rare rainforest flower.

But a knot formed in her stomach.

What if Valerie was right?

With every sky mile back to Starlight, Will's jaw clenched harder.

Damn her pretty little head. What was she thinking, sneaking off this way? Why hadn't she told him her plans yesterday in the hospital?

And what the hell was *he* thinking? He should've been there to retrieve her from the hospital today. He should've given today's trip to one of the other pilots.

He checked the time. Two minutes before the airstrip

came into view. Nate said Vince was planning to fly her out at 10:45. *Less than five minutes.*

If Nate hadn't radioed Valerie's information, Will would have been miles up the Copper River with the photographers. Thank God, the two couples had understood and agreed to fly out of Glenallen with another pilot.

As the Jet Ranger crested the small mountain east of town, he spoke into the headset. "Nate, this is four-two-five-niner, ready for landing."

"Roger, four-two-five-niner. All clear." Pause. "By the way, Vince hasn't left yet."

"What's his status?"

"On the tarmac."

Will could see Vince's dark-blue Cessna and a pair of figures near its open door. "Copy. Out."

He flew toward the twin-engine plane. *Brave woman, Savanna, to fly in another mini fixed wing so soon.* But then, courage had been her ally for twenty years in countries where survival purported selection of the fittest.

Courage was *her* middle name.

Closer, he saw Vince lift his head, eye Will's bird. *Yeah, man. It's me and I'm coming for her.*

He saw Savanna appear at the top of the plane's stairs, speak to Vince, likely telling him to hurry to make sure Will couldn't interrupt her flight.

Momentarily she studied the dropping helicopter, then she disappeared inside again. Will put the Jet Ranger on the pad beside the hangar, shut down the engine, unbuckled his harness. Her name was on his lips as he slung open the door.

The other pilot continued to load her baggage. "Don't bother with that, Vince," Will shouted, sprinting toward the Cessna. "She's not going to Anchorage with you."

"Back off, Will," the other man said, shoving the last suitcase through the door. "She's flying."

"Let me in there."

Vince blocked the door. "You're not getting on my plane."

Will narrowed his eyes. He'd known Vince half his life, but he'd deck the man to get inside the plane to the woman he loved.

"Savanna," he called.

In the cockpit, she gave him her stubborn spine. Will walked around the nose, rapped on the glass. "Savanna, come out here. We need to talk."

Her nose lifted.

"You are not leaving until we talk."

She ignored him.

"Woman, if you don't come out of that plane, I swear I'll come in and haul you out over my shoulder."

Angry green eyes bored into his. "Go home, Will."

Vince walked around his plane. "Look, man, this—"

"Take a hike, Vince."

The pilot shrugged. "Fine. But I'm flying out of here in three minutes."

"This'll be done in two. Savanna…" Will rapped on the windscreen again. "Please."

She sprang from the copilot seat; he loped to the door. "This, what you're doing," he said as she popped into the frame of the opening. "It's wrong. Just plain wrong."

Her copper hair drifted past her shoulders, loose, curly, beautiful. A tiny pink line marked the scratch on her pale forehead. Yesterday his lips had touched the spot, a healing kiss. His gaze dropped to the cast on her wrist. Another spot he'd kissed.

She said, "I told you I'd leave Starlight one day. This is the day."

He swallowed back his ire, his fear. Thickly he asked, "Without telling us? Without saying goodbye?"

"Oh, Will. Goodbyes are overstated." She half turned back into the plane. "I'll write."

His heart hurt. "I never took you for a coward, Savanna Stowe." Hands planted low on his hips, Will glared up at her.

Slowly she turned. Her eyes were emeralds. "A coward?"

"Isn't that what *this* is?" He gestured toward the Cessna. "You running off to someplace where there's no worry of putting your heart on the line?"

She moved down the steps, stopped directly in front of him. "Like I told you a dozen times before, Will. I *am* leaving Alaska. *That's* what this is."

But her chin quivered.

Softly he said, "All I want is a goodbye."

Seconds passed. An hour. Eternity. She had lived in his soul ten thousand years. He repeated, "Say it. Say goodbye."

Her lips parted without sound. He read, "Goodbye."

Before she could swing around, climb the steps into the plane, Will caught her against his chest. "No," he said. "This is goodbye."

And then he kissed her. Full-mouthed and turbulent. A kiss that sealed the air in his lungs—and destroyed them both. When it was done, he cupped her face, whispered against her lips, "I have two things to say, Savanna. First and foremost, I love you. Without you, I'd be lost in a deeper wilderness than your downed plane."

"Will…" Her eyes were wet.

He hugged her tight, whispered into her hair. "You've rescued me. You and Christopher. I love you, honey. More than I could ever say. If you leave, you'll take my heart, my soul." He smiled into her lovely eyes. "I can't let that happen to our little boy."

She began to cry in earnest, wetting his throat. Then she was laughing through her tears. "You don't play fair."

"I wasn't playing, Savanna."

A sigh. "All right, you win."

"You'll stay?"

"I'll stay."

He brushed a damp curl from her cheek. "And make us a family? No more talking about age and whatever other worry is in that sweet head of yours?"

She clamped her lip, nodded.

"And here's the second thing, honey." Gently he kissed her wrist cast. "If you want to adopt another child, that's what we'll do."

"Oh, Will," she whispered, and her smile trembled. "Are you sure?"

A blaze of northern lights danced over his heart. "As sure as I'm standing here, babe."

One auburn eyebrow elevated. "'Babe'?"

"I know. I'm a Neanderthal." Grinning, he shrugged a careless shoulder. "Think I'll have changed by our fiftieth anniversary?"

She laughed. "I sure hope not."

July, the Daylight Hours…

Watching Will send the Starlight Jaguars out into the field, Savanna worried the gold bands on the ring finger of her left hand. The sixth inning and their team was up 5-4 against the tough Grizzlies from Palmer.

Their team. Sitting on a plastic lawn chair near the Jaguars' bench, she smiled. The team *had* become hers and Will's and Christopher's over the past two months.

In the chair beside her, Valerie waved to Josh playing

catcher. "Don't fret. They're gonna win. Will and Chris have it under control."

"Hmm. They do, don't they?"

"I can't believe Chris made all those graphs and grids of what the other teams have done. The kid's downright awesome as a manager."

"He's the best." Savanna's heart felt moon big as she listened to Christopher, wearing a maroon-and-gray uniform, explain the latest page of stats in a pedantic speech to Will. Stats on each team: who attained the most hits, home runs; who'd been walked by which pitcher; how many outs on first and home base; how many fly balls, foul balls, grounders, punts… The list went on.

Over Chris's head, Will threw her a wink. In return she blew him a kiss.

So much had happened since that day on Starlight's tarmac. Unable to wait, they had married in June. Chris had been Will's best man, Georgia Savanna's matron of honor.

Could she be any happier? *Not in this lifetime*, she mused and knew it to be true.

Like any family they had their ups and downs, but overriding those moments was the abiding love they had for each other and Christopher. Day by day the child achieved a stride. Savanna remembered last week when Christopher finally shed his fear of felines and went with Will to bring home the sleek little ball of purring fur from Val's house.

They had celebrated with Chris's favored treat: a triad of strawberries, blueberries and grapes topped with whipping cream.

The bat cracked, whipping Savanna back to the game.

The Grizzly hitter raced for first. Roger caught the grounder, threw it to the baseman.

"Out!" yelled the umpire.

"Yes!" Savanna bounced in her chair.

And then it happened.

The next batter hit a foul, arcing the ball high and to the left before it plummeted—a slow motion event—straight toward Christopher staring upward.

He crossed his arms over his chest.

Gripped in his left hand, the book of graphs and grids fluttered with the hot July breeze.

A half second later the ball struck.

Christopher landed on his rump.

Savanna leaped to her feet. *"Chris!"* Down the third baseline Will raced for his child.

"Son!" Will knelt beside the boy. "Where does it hurt, Chris? Tell me where!"

The boy shook his head. "Doesn't." Then his gaze lifted. He looked straight at Will and laughed. "I caught it. I caught the ball!"

Sure enough, within the crook of his arms nestled the team baseball.

"Mom, Dad! Did you see? Did you see me catch the ball!" *Mom. Dad.*

"Oh, honey." Savanna's pulse spun. "We're so proud."

Clutching the baseball, Christopher jumped to his feet. All at once, the Jaguars swarmed him, cheering, patting his back, jumping up and down. At the sidelines, parents clapped and whistled.

Will caught Savanna's hand. Eyes blue as Alaska's forget-me-nots blinked twice in the shadow of his ball cap's visor. "Well, little mother," he said, voice thick. "What do you say about our kid, huh?"

Sunshine—or maybe tears?—stung her eyes. "I say I'm

a fortunate woman indeed. The two most remarkable men on earth are right here in this ballpark and they're mine to love."

In her heart, Elke and Dennis smiled.

* * * * *

Don't miss Mary J. Forbes's next book,
Red Wolf's Return,
on sale October 2007
wherever Silhouette Books are sold.

Award-winning author Stevi Mittman delivers
another hysterical mystery, featuring Teddi Bayer, an
irrepressible heroine, and her to-die-for hero, Detective Drew Scoones. After all, life on Long Island can
be murder!

*Turn the page for a sneak peek at the warm
and funny fourth book,
WHOSE NUMBER IS UP, ANYWAY?,
in the Teddi Bayer series,
by STEVI MITTMAN.
On sale August 7*

"Before redecorating a room, I always advise my clients to empty it of everything but one chair. Then I suggest they move that chair from place to place, sitting in it, until the placement feels right. Trust your instincts when deciding on furniture placement. Your room should "feel right."

—TipsFromTeddi.com

Gut feelings. You know, that gnawing in the pit of your stomach that warns you that you are about to do the absolute stupidest thing you could do? Something that will ruin life as you know it?

I've got one now, standing at the butcher counter in King

Kullen, the grocery store in the same strip mall as L.I. Lanes, the bowling alley cum billiard parlor I'm in the process of redecorating for its "Grand Opening."

I realize being in the wrong supermarket probably doesn't sound exactly dire to you, but you aren't the one buying your father a brisket at a store your mother will somehow know isn't Waldbaum's.

And then, June Bayer isn't your mother.

The woman behind the counter has agreed to go into the freezer to find a brisket for me, since there aren't any in the case. There are packages of pork tenderloin, piles of spare ribs and rolls of sausage, but no briskets.

Warning Number Two, right? I should be so out of here.

But no, I'm still in the same spot when she comes back out, brisketless, her face ashen. She opens her mouth as if she is going to scream, but only a gurgle comes out.

And then she pinballs out from behind the counter, knocking bottles of Peter Luger Steak Sauce to the floor on her way, now hitting the tower of cans at the end of the prepared foods aisle and sending them sprawling, now making her way down the aisle, careening from side to side as she goes.

Finally, from a distance, I hear her shout, "He's deeeeeeaaaad! Joey's deeeeeaaaad."

My first thought is *You should always trust your gut.*

My second thought is that now, somehow, my mother will know I was in King Kullen. For weeks I will have to hear "What did you expect?" as though whenever you go to King Kullen someone turns up dead. And if the detective investigating the case turns out to be Detective Drew Scoones…well, I'll never hear the end of that from her, either.

She still suspects I murdered the guy who was found dead on my doorstep last Halloween just to get Drew back into my life.

Several people head for the butcher's freezer and I position myself to block them. If there's one thing I've learned from finding people dead—and the guy on my doorstep wasn't the first one—it's that the police get very testy when you mess with their murder scenes.

"You can't go in there until the police get here," I say, stationing myself at the end of the butcher's counter and in front of the Employees Only door, acting as if I'm some sort of authority. "You'll contaminate the evidence if it turns out to be murder."

Shouts and chaos. You'd think I'd know better than to throw the word *murder* around. Cell phones are flipping open and tongues are wagging.

I amend my statement quickly. "Which, of course, it probably isn't. Murder, I mean. People die all the time, and it's not always in hospitals or their own beds, or…" I babble when I'm nervous, and the idea of someone dead on the other side of the freezer door makes me very nervous.

So does the idea of seeing Drew Scoones again. Drew and I have this on-again, off-again sort of thing…that I kind of turned off.

Who knew he'd take it so personally when he tried to get serious and I responded by saying we could talk about *us* tomorrow—and then caught a plane to my parents' condo in Boca the next day? In July. In the middle of a job.

For some crazy reason, he took that to mean that I was avoiding him and the subject of *us*.

That was three months ago. I haven't seen him since.

The manager, who identifies himself and points to his nameplate in case I don't believe him, says he has to go into *his cooler*. "Maybe Joey's not dead," he says. "Maybe he can be saved, and you're letting him die in there. Did you ever think of that?"

In fact, I hadn't. But I had thought that the murderer might try to go back in to make sure his tracks were covered, so I say that I will go in and check.

Which means that the manager and I couple up and go in together while everyone pushes against the doorway to peer in, erasing any chance of finding clean prints on that Employee Only door.

I expect to find carcasses of dead animals hanging from hooks, and maybe Joey hanging from one, too. I think it's going to be very creepy and I steel myself, only to find a rather benign series of shelves with large slabs of meat laid out carefully on them, along with boxes and boxes marked simply Chicken.

Nothing scary here, unless you count the body of a middle-aged man with graying hair sprawled faceup on the floor. His eyes are wide open and unblinking. His shirt is stiff. His pants are stiff. His body is stiff. And his expression, you should forgive the pun—is frozen. Bill-the-manager crosses himself and stands mute while I pronounce the guy dead in a sort of *happy now?* tone.

"We should not be in here," I say, and he nods his head emphatically and helps me push people out of the doorway just in time to hear the police sirens and see the cop cars pull up outside the big store windows.

Bobbie Lyons, my partner in Teddi Bayer Interior Designs (and also my neighbor, my best friend and my private fashion police), and Mark, our carpenter (and my dogsitter, confidant, and ego booster), rush in from next door. They beat the cops by a half step and shout out my name. People point in my direction.

After all the publicity that followed the unfortunate incident during which I shot my ex-husband, Rio Gallo, and then the subsequent murder of my first client—which

I solved, I might add—it seems like the whole world, or at least all of Long Island, knows who I am.

Mark asks if I'm all right. (Did I remember to mention that the man is drop-dead-gorgeous-but-a-decade-too-young-for-me-yet-too-old-for-my-daughter-thank-god?) I don't get a chance to answer him because the police are quickly closing in on the store manager and me.

"The woman—" I begin telling the police. Then I have to pause for the manager to fill in her name, which he does: *Fran*.

I continue. "Right. Fran. Fran went into the freezer to get a brisket. A moment later she came out and screamed that Joey was dead. So I'd say she was the one who discovered the body."

"And you are…?" the cop asks me. It comes out a bit like who do I *think* I am, rather than who am I really?

"An innocent bystander," Bobbie, hair perfect, makeup just right, says, carefully placing her body between the cop and me.

"And she was just leaving," Mark adds. They each take one of my arms.

Fran comes into the inner circle surrounding the cops. In case it isn't obvious from the hairnet and bloodstained white apron with Fran embroidered on it, I explain that she was the butcher who was going for the brisket. Mark and Bobbie take that as a signal that I've done my job and they can now get me out of there. They twist around, with me in the middle, as if we're a Rockettes line, until we are facing away from the butcher counter. They've managed to propel me a few steps toward the exit when disaster—in the form of a Mazda RX7 pulling up at the loading curb—strikes.

Mark's grip on my arm tightens like a vise. "Too late," he says.

Bobbie's expletive is unprintable. "Maybe there's a back door," she suggests, but Mark is right. It's too late.

I've laid my eyes on Detective Scoones. And while my gut is trying to warn me that my heart shouldn't go there, regions farther south are melting at just the sight of him.

"Walk," Bobbie orders me.

And I try to. Really.

Walk, I tell my feet. *Just put one foot in front of the other.*

I can do this because I know, in my heart of hearts, that if Drew Scoones was still interested in me, he'd have gotten in touch with me after I returned from Boca. And he didn't.

Since he's a detective, Drew doesn't have to wear one of those dark blue Nassau County Police uniforms. Instead, he's got on jeans, a tight-fitting T-shirt and a tweedy sports jacket. If you think that sounds good, you should see him. Chiseled features, cleft chin, brown hair that's naturally a little sandy in the front, a smile that…well, that doesn't matter. He isn't smiling now.

He walks up to me, tucks his sunglasses into his breast pocket and looks me over from head to toe.

"Well, if it isn't Miss Cut and Run," he says. "Aren't you supposed to be somewhere in Florida or something?" He looks at Mark accusingly, as if he was covering for me when he told Drew I was gone.

"Detective Scoones?" one of the uniforms says. "The stiff's in the cooler and the woman who found him is over there." He jerks his head in Fran's direction.

Drew continues to stare at me.

You know how when you were young, your mother always told you to wear clean underwear in case you were in an accident? And how, a little farther on, she told you not to go out in hair rollers because you never knew who you might see—or who might see you? And how now your best friend says she wouldn't be caught dead without makeup and suggests you shouldn't either?

Okay, today, *finally*, in my overalls and Converse sneakers, I get it.

I brush my hair out of my eyes. "Well, I'm back," I say. As if he hasn't known my exact whereabouts. The man is a detective, for heaven's sake. "Been back awhile."

Bobbie has watched the exchange and apparently decided she's given Drew all the time he deserves. "And we've got work to do, so…" she says, grabbing my arm and giving Drew a little two-fingered wave goodbye.

As I back up a foot or two, the store manager sees his chance and places himself in front of Drew, trying to get his attention. Maybe what makes Drew such a good detective is his ability to focus.

Only what he's focusing on is me.

"Phone broken? Carrier pigeon died?" he asks me, taking in Fran, the manager, the meat counter and that Employees Only door, all without taking his eyes off me.

Mark tries to break the spell. "We've got work to do there, you've got work to do here, Scoones," Mark says to him, gesturing toward next door. "So it's back to the alley for us."

Drew's lip twitches. "You working the alley now?" he says.

"If you'd like to follow me," Bill-the-manager, clearly exasperated, says to Drew—who doesn't respond. It's as if waiting for my answer is all he has to do.

So, fine. "You knew I was back," I say.

The man has known my whereabouts every hour of the day for as long as I've known him. And my mother's not the only one who won't buy that he "just happened" to answer this particular call. In fact, I'm willing to bet my children's lunch money that he's taken every call within ten miles of my home since the day I got back.

And now he's gotten lucky.

"*You* could have called *me*," I say.

"You're the one who said *tomorrow* for our talk and then flew the coop, chickie," he says. "I figured the ball was in your court."

"Detective?" the uniform says. "There's something you ought to see in here."

Drew gives me a look that amounts to *in or out?*

He could be talking about the investigation, or about our relationship.

Bobbie tries to steer me away. Mark's fists are balled. Drew waits me out, knowing I won't be able to resist what might be a murder investigation.

Finally he turns and heads for the cooler.

And, like a puppy dog, I follow.

Bobbie grabs the back of my shirt and pulls me to a halt.

"I'm just going to show him something," I say, yanking away.

"Yeah," Bobbie says, pointedly looking at the buttons on my blouse. The two at breast level have popped. "That's what I'm afraid of."

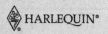

REQUEST YOUR FREE BOOKS!
2 FREE NOVELS PLUS 2 FREE GIFTS!

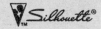

SPECIAL EDITION®
Life, Love and Family!

YES! Please send me 2 FREE Silhouette Special Edition® novels and my 2 FREE gifts. After receiving them, if I don't wish to receive any more books, I can return the shipping statement marked "cancel." If I don't cancel, I will receive 6 brand-new novels every month and be billed just $4.24 per book in the U.S., or $4.99 per book in Canada, plus 25¢ shipping and handling per book and applicable taxes, if any*. That's a savings of at least 15% off the cover price! I understand that accepting the 2 free books and gifts places me under no obligation to buy anything. I can always return a shipment and cancel at any time. Even if I never buy another book from Silhouette, the two free books and gifts are mine to keep forever.

235 SDN EEYU   335 SDN EEY6

Name _____ (PLEASE PRINT) _____

Address _____ Apt. _____

City _____ State/Prov. _____ Zip/Postal Code _____

Signature (if under 18, a parent or guardian must sign) _____

Mail to the **Silhouette Reader Service**™:
IN U.S.A.: P.O. Box 1867, Buffalo, NY 14240-1867
IN CANADA: P.O. Box 609, Fort Erie, Ontario L2A 5X3

Not valid to current Silhouette Special Edition subscribers.

Want to try two free books from another line?
Call 1-800-873-8635 or visit www.morefreebooks.com.

* Terms and prices subject to change without notice. NY residents add applicable sales tax. Canadian residents will be charged applicable provincial taxes and GST. This offer is limited to one order per household. All orders subject to approval. Credit or debit balances in a customer's account(s) may be offset by any other outstanding balance owed by or to the customer. Please allow 4 to 6 weeks for delivery.

Your Privacy: Silhouette is committed to protecting your privacy. Our Privacy Policy is available online at www.eHarlequin.com or upon request from the Reader Service. From time to time we make our lists of customers available to reputable firms who may have a product or service of interest to you. If you would prefer we not share your name and address, please check here. ☐

SSE07

SPECIAL EDITION™

Look for

THE BILLIONAIRE NEXT DOOR

by **Jessica Bird**

For Wall Street hotshot Sean O'Banyon, going home to south Boston brought back bad memories. But Lizzie Bond, his father's sweet, girl-next-door caretaker, was there to ease the pain. It was instant attraction—until Sean found out she was named sole heir, and wondered what her motives really were....

THE O'BANYON BROTHERS

On sale August 2007.

COMING NEXT MONTH

#1843 PAGING DR. RIGHT—Stella Bagwell
Montana Mavericks: Striking It Rich
Mia Smith came to Thunder Canyon Resort for some peace and quiet, but with her recent inheritance, other guests took her for a wealthy socialite and wouldn't leave her be. At least she found comfort with the resort's handsome staff doctor Marshall Cates, but would her painful past and humble beginnings nip their budding romance?

#1844 THE BILLIONAIRE NEXT DOOR—Jessica Bird
The O'Banyon Brothers
For Wall Street hot shot Sean O'Banyon, going home to South Boston after his abusive father's death brought back miserable memories. But Lizzie Bond, his father's sweet, girl-next-door caretaker, was there to ease the pain. It was instant attraction—and then Sean found out she was named sole heir, and he began to wonder what her motives really were....

#1845 REMODELING THE BACHELOR—Marie Ferrarella
The Sons of Lily Moreau
Son of a famous, though flighty artist, Philippe Zabelle had grown up to be a set-in-his-ways bachelor. Yet when the successful software developer hired J. D. Wyatt to do some home repairs, something clicked. J.D. was a single mother with a flair for fixing anything... even Philippe's long-broken heart.

#1846 THE COWBOY AND THE CEO—Christine Wenger
She was city. He was country. But on a trip to a Wyoming ranch that made disabled children's dreams come true, driven business owner Susan Collins fell hard for caring cowboy Clint Skully. Having been left at the altar once before, would Clint risk the farm on love this time around?

#1847 ACCIDENTALLY EXPECTING—Michelle Celmer
In one corner, attorney Miranda Reed, who wrote the definitive guide to divorce and the modern woman. In the other, Zackery Jameson, staunch supporter of traditional family values. When these polar opposites sparred on a radio talk show, neither yielded any ground. So how did it come to pass that Miranda was now expecting Zack's baby?

#1848 A FAMILY PRACTICE—Gayle Kasper
After personal tragedy struck, Dr. Luke Phillips took off on a road trip. But when he crashed his motorcycle in the Arizona desert, it was local holistic healer Mariah Cade who got him to stop running. Whether it was in her tender touch or her gentle way with her daughter, Mariah was the miracle cure for all that ailed the good doctor.

SSECNM0707

la courte échelle

Les éditions de la courte échelle inc.

Chrystine Brouillet

Née en 1958, à Québec, Chrystine Brouillet habite maintenant Montréal et Paris. En 1982, elle publie un premier roman, pour lequel elle reçoit le prix Robert-Cliche.

Chrystine Brouillet est l'un des rares auteurs québécois à faire du roman policier. Elle a d'ailleurs mis en scène un personnage de détective féminin, Maud Graham, que l'on retrouve, entre autres, dans *Le Collectionneur*. Elle a également écrit une saga historique franco-québécoise en trois tomes, *Marie LaFlamme*, *Nouvelle-France* et *La Renarde*.

En 1985, elle reçoit le prix Alvine-Bélisle, qui couronne le meilleur livre jeunesse de l'année pour *Le complot*. En 1991, elle obtient le prix des Clubs de la Livromanie pour *Un jeu dangereux* et, en 1992, elle gagne le prix des Clubs de la Livromagie pour *Le vol du siècle*. En 1993 et 1994, elle remporte le prix du Signet d'Or, catégorie auteur jeunesse, dans laquelle, par vote populaire, les jeunes l'ont désignée comme leur auteur préféré. Certains de ses romans sont traduits en chinois, en italien et en arabe. *Un bonheur terrifiant* est le dix-huitième roman pour les jeunes qu'elle publie à la courte échelle.

De la même auteure, à la courte échelle

Collection Roman Jeunesse

Le complot
Le caméléon
La montagne Noire
Le Corbeau
Le vol du siècle
Les pirates
Mystères de Chine
Pas d'orchidées pour Miss Andréa!
Les chevaux enchantés
La veuve noire
Secrets d'Afrique
Le ventre du serpent

Collection Roman+

Un jeu dangereux
Une plage trop chaude
Une nuit très longue
Un rendez-vous troublant
Un crime audacieux

Chrystine Brouillet

Un bonheur terrifiant

la courte échelle
Les éditions de la courte échelle inc.

Les éditions de la courte échelle inc.
5243, boul. Saint-Laurent
Montréal (Québec) H2T 1S4

Illustration de la couverture:
Stéphane Jorisch

Conception graphique:
Derome design inc.

Révision des textes:
Pierre Phaneuf

Dépôt légal, 3ᵉ trimestre 1996
Bibliothèque nationale du Québec

Données de catalogage avant publication (Canada)

Brouillet, Chrystine

    Un bonheur terrifiant

    (Roman+; R+42)

    ISBN 2-89021-273-4

    I. Titre.

PS8553.R6846B65 1996   jC843'.54   C96-940266-X
PS9553.R6846B65 1996
PZ23.B76Bo 1996

À Christina Parent Roberts

Chapitre 1

Le bel Antoine

— Je suis découragée! ai-je dit à Alexis. Pierre est vraiment... bizarre.

Alexis a repoussé son assiette de frites avant de soupirer longuement; il était aussi inquiet que moi. Pierre s'éloignait de nous depuis quelques semaines. Tout avait commencé par sa rupture avec Adélaïde. Enfin. Façon de parler. On ne pouvait pas dire que mon cousin l'avait vraiment fréquentée: Adélaïde l'avait laissé tomber à leur cinquième rencontre.

L'attitude d'Adélaïde m'avait pourtant surprise; cette fille m'était sympathique. Elle était intelligente et drôle. Qu'était-il arrivé pour qu'elle rejette Pierre si brusquement?

— J'aurais envie de parler à Adélaïde, ai-je confié à Alexis. Pour comprendre ce qui s'est passé entre eux. Ou pour la faire changer d'idée.

— Je pense qu'elle sort maintenant avec Antoine. Je les ai vus ensemble plusieurs fois.

— Antoine? Antoine Brisson? Depuis quand?

Je me sentais idiote. Comment n'avais-je rien deviné? J'aurais dû comprendre que le bel Antoine était entré dans la troupe de théâtre pour rencontrer la merveilleuse Adélaïde.

— Depuis le party d'Halloween. En tout cas, sois discrète si tu parles de Pierre à Adélaïde. S'il l'apprenait, il se sentirait trahi.

— Je ne sais pas comment l'aider, ai-je avoué. Tu sais que sa mère est dépressive. Si c'était héréditaire? Je ne veux pas qu'il ait la même vie que ma tante! Je le sens malheureux. Et si distant. Il refuse notre aide. Je sais bien que le temps guérit les chagrins d'amour...

— Il n'a pourtant vu Adélaïde que cinq petites fois! a protesté Alexis. Je n'en fais pas un drame, moi, quand on me plaque.

— Moi non plus.

— C'est facile... Oh! excuse-moi, Nat, je ne voulais pas...

J'ai rougi. Alexis avait raison: comment pourrais-je me plaindre, puisque je ne fréquente jamais personne? J'enviais presque Pierre d'avoir une peine d'amour: au moins, lui, il avait une vie sentimentale. Mon problème, c'est que les garçons qui me plaisent me considèrent comme une bonne copine. Celle à qui on confie ses histoires de coeur. Agréable, non? J'avais beau me répéter qu'il faut être patiente, je commençais à me demander si je rencontrerais quelqu'un avant la fin de mes études.

— C'est parce que tu ne vois rien que tu es seule, a fait Alexis.

— Tu dis ça pour atténuer ta gaffe.

Il secoua la tête vivement.

— Non. Tu ne te rends même pas compte qu'Antoine fréquente Adélaïde juste pour te rendre jalouse?

Antoine? Mon coeur s'est mis à battre un peu plus vite.

— Il t'intéresse, ne me dis pas le contraire. Alors parle-lui avant que ça devienne trop sérieux avec Adélaïde.

Parler à Antoine? Pour lui dire quoi? «Bonjour, mon chéri, j'aimerais ça qu'on sorte ensemble»? J'étais trop gênée.

Alexis a éclaté de rire.

— J'adore te voir aussi embarrassée, a-t-il expliqué.

— Je ne le suis pas et, de toute manière, ce n'est pas de moi qu'il est question aujourd'hui, mais de Pierre. Je suis vraiment inquiète. Il ne mange même plus avec nous.

— Je sais, il m'a dit que je m'intoxiquais avec les hot-dogs. Je serais mort depuis longtemps si c'était vrai.

— Il ne court plus avec Sébastien. Il prétend qu'il n'a plus le temps.

— Pierre a-t-il déjà eu ce genre de comportement avant? Était-il aussi renfermé quand il était petit?

J'ai haussé les épaules. Pierre n'avait jamais été un enfant joyeux. Il était fils unique, élevé par une mère qui passait la moitié de ses journées allongée et un père dévoré par ses affaires. Mon oncle s'était occupé de Pierre un peu plus quand il avait compris que sa femme était vraiment malade, mais il devait souvent s'absenter pour son travail. Pierre venait alors chez moi. J'ai plusieurs cousins de mon âge, mais il est mon préféré.

Et mon confident. Et voilà que le silence s'était installé entre nous.

— Au moins, il répète encore, a remarqué Alexis. Tout n'est pas perdu.

— Tant mieux!

Alexis, Hector et Pierre jouaient ensemble: Hector était batteur, Alexis guitariste, et Pierre saxophoniste. Ils devaient bientôt participer à un concours; les gagnants recevraient une bourse de cinq cents dollars et prendraient part à une finale nationale.

S'ils remportaient cette deuxième épreuve, ils se verraient décerner le premier prix à l'occasion d'un grand concert rock auquel ils assisteraient dans une loge privée, en compagnie des amis des musiciens du groupe. Bien sûr, des dizaines de jeunes participaient à ce concours. Il y avait des solos, des duos, des trios, des quatuors et même une chorale!

Malgré tout, mes amis avaient de bonnes chances.

— J'ai le trac, Natasha. Pierre est le meilleur du trio, mais il était tellement distrait aux dernières répétitions.

— Vraiment?

— Je t'assure.

Alexis est allé chercher une orangeade. Le restaurant se vidait peu à peu, les cours allaient bientôt débuter. On avait juste le temps de payer nos hamburgers.

— Qu'est-ce qu'on va faire avec Pierre? a demandé Alexis.

— Je l'ignore. Je ne peux quand même pas en parler à mes parents. Ils répéteraient tout à mon oncle.

— Eugénie pense que Pierre était bizarre avant même de rencontrer Adélaïde.

— Comment?

Alexis m'a expliqué que sa blonde suivait tous ses cours avec Pierre et qu'elle trouvait qu'il avait beaucoup changé depuis le début de l'année.

— Rappelle-toi, à son anniversaire, il était déjà plus froid avec nous.

J'allais répondre quand j'ai aperçu Antoine. Alexis m'a fait un clin d'oeil et, avant que j'aie le temps de réagir, il s'est dirigé vers lui. Je l'aurais étranglé! Antoine a hoché la tête deux fois, l'air grave, puis il est venu vers moi.

— Il paraît que tu t'en fais pour Pierre?

— Je ne sais pas pourquoi Alexis t'a parlé de ça.

— Parce que je devais faire un travail en équipe avec ton cousin, mais il a trouvé une excuse à la dernière minute. Et il s'est joint à Justin Carmichael et à Julie Longpré.

— Quoi?

— C'est curieux, car je crois qu'il ne les aime pas tellement.

— Qui les aimerait?

C'étaient les élèves les plus énervants de tout le secondaire: deux prétentieux de la pire espèce qui se donnaient des grands airs d'aristocrates.

— Je ne comprends plus rien...

On a entendu la cloche, Antoine m'a tapoté l'épaule.

— On peut en reparler à la fin des cours si tu veux.

J'ai battu des paupières tandis qu'il me fixait rendez-vous à l'auditorium.

— On aura le temps de discuter avant de répéter la pièce.

Il aurait dû me dire ça après le contrôle de maths! J'ai eu toutes les peines du monde à me concentrer. Je pensais à Antoine et je me rappelais la chaleur de sa voix, la douceur de sa main sur mon épaule, la caresse de son regard.

J'allais sûrement couler mon examen...

J'ai oublié ce détail dès que j'ai revu Antoine. Il m'a semblé qu'il embellissait d'heure en heure. Il avait un sourire aussi magique qu'un arc-en-ciel.

On s'est assis dans la rangée A. Comme Antoine, comme Amour. Comme Amitié? J'ai frémi; Antoine voulait sûrement me rencontrer pour me parler de son histoire avec Adélaïde... Et je jouerais encore l'éternelle confidente! J'avais envie de pleurer.

— Qu'est-ce qui se passe? a questionné Antoine.

— Je suis angoissée en pensant à Pierre.

— Justement, j'en ai parlé avec Adélaïde.

— Ah oui! c'est vrai, tu sors avec elle.

Antoine m'a dévisagée, l'air étonné.

— Adélaïde? Non, nous sommes amis depuis dix ans! Mais c'est ma première année ici, et je ne connais pas grand monde. C'est pour ça que je la vois. Elle m'a convaincu de faire partie de la troupe de théâtre: elle voulait que je rencontre ses amis. Elle t'estime beaucoup.

— Ah bon?

— Il paraît que tu es plutôt courageuse.

Peut-être avec des gangsters ou des meurtriers, mais certainement pas avec Antoine! J'avais les jambes en compote si je le regardais dans les yeux plus de cinq secondes.

— Pas... pas tant que ça, ai-je bredouillé, lamentablement.

— C'est ce que j'aime chez toi, tu n'es pas

orgueilleuse.

Comme il se trompait! C'était justement parce que j'étais très fière que je ne m'avouais jamais vaincue. Mais je n'allais pas le contredire. Je me suis contentée de sourire. Un petit sourire niais, probablement. Heureusement que l'auditorium est mal éclairé.

— Adélaïde m'a expliqué qu'elle ne voulait plus sortir avec Pierre parce qu'il l'effrayait.

— Pierre? C'est le type le plus gentil que je connaisse. Il ne ferait pas de mal à une mouche. Il est même un peu mou, parfois. Il veut toujours plaire à tout le monde.

— Elle l'a trouvé très rigide. Et elle n'a pas apprécié ses remarques. Il lui a reproché de porter des vêtements rouges. Et de manger de la viande.

— Qu'est-ce que tu me chantes là?

— La vérité. Tu demanderas à Adélaïde. Même si elle m'a dit qu'elle ne voulait plus jamais entendre parler de Pierre.

Je me suis mordu les lèvres; mon cousin était vraiment déboussolé pour tenir des propos si étranges.

— Je ne sais pas quoi faire, ai-je avoué.

— Il doit être devenu végétarien.

— Mais il pourrait nous en parler. Ce

n'est pas un défaut. Il a bien le droit de manger ce qu'il veut tant qu'il ne nous demande pas de l'imiter. Je suis pour la liberté d'opinion. Il le sait.

Antoine avait l'air navré pour moi. Il allait me passer la main dans les cheveux lorsqu'on a entendu des voix: Adélaïde, Jordan et Marilou nous rejoignaient pour répéter.

Je pense que j'ai été aussi distraite durant le cours de théâtre que pendant l'examen de mathématiques. Heureusement que j'ai un tout petit rôle! Mon cerveau disjonctait quand j'étais trop près d'Antoine. Il devait vraiment me prendre pour une imbécile! Ou il était aussi idiot que moi, ou il ne s'intéresserait pas longtemps à une pareille sotte...

***

Alexis ne s'est pas privé de me taquiner quand il a su que j'étais allée au cinéma avec Antoine.

— Je parie que tu ne pourrais même pas me raconter le film!

J'ai protesté mollement; j'avoue que je n'avais pas porté une grande attention à ce qui se déroulait sur l'écran. J'étais beaucoup trop bouleversée par la présence d'Antoine à mes côtés pour m'intéresser au sort des membres d'un vaisseau spatial. C'est à peine si j'avais sursauté quand il avait explosé.

J'étais tout de même contente que le capitaine survive, car je ne voulais pas que le film se termine si vite! J'aurais bien passé toute la journée au cinéma avec Antoine, mais il devait aider son père à couvrir leurs cèdres avant la première neige.

— J'en ai pour le reste de l'après-midi. Je me demande pourquoi mes parents ont planté tant d'arbres! Je t'appellerai quand j'aurai fini.

Lorsque le téléphone avait sonné, je m'étais ruée sur l'appareil. J'avais remarqué l'air inquisiteur de mon frère, mais je lui avais tourné le dos avant qu'il s'amuse de mon trouble. Il n'y a rien de plus énervant au monde qu'un aîné qui vous agace à propos de votre vie amoureuse.

Sauf un faux numéro, peut-être. J'avais raccroché avec une telle violence que j'avais ensuite vérifié trois fois si l'appareil fonctionnait toujours. En début de soirée, je me demandais combien de cèdres devaient être protégés des intempéries sur le terrain des Brisson. Au moins une centaine, sinon Antoine m'aurait appelée avant.

Nouvelle sonnerie. Mon coeur allait flancher. Au troisième coup, j'avais trouvé assez de courage pour répondre.

C'était Alexis.

J'avais essayé de ne pas trop montrer ma déception, mais il l'avait devinée. Et maintenant, il me taquinait...

— Tu pensais que c'était ton bel Antoine?

— Non. Oui. Pourquoi m'appelles-tu?

— Pour avoir de tes nouvelles. On ne s'est pas vus depuis que je t'ai trouvé un prétexte pour parler à Antoine.

— On est allés au cinéma.

— Tous les jours de la semaine?

J'ai reconnu que je l'avais un peu négligé. Mais il ne pouvait pas me le reprocher, car il en avait fait autant quand il avait rencontré Eugénie.

— Je sais. Je ne m'inquiète pas. Ce n'est pas comme avec Pierre. Il faut qu'on se voie, Nat. Il est vraiment trop étrange. Il a choisi une autre pièce musicale pour le concours.

— Mais c'est la semaine prochaine!

— Je sais.

— Viens me rejoindre ici. Il n'y a que mon frère ce soir.

J'étais contente qu'Alexis passe la soirée avec moi. Je n'avais pas envie d'être seule si

Antoine m'oubliait. J'étais en train de fouiller dans le réfrigérateur, sans grand enthousiasme, lorsque Antoine a téléphoné. Il s'est excusé; il avait eu la visite d'un voisin et n'avait pas vu l'heure filer.

On a continué à parler quelques minutes. Antoine m'a conseillé d'interroger Adélaïde sur sa rupture avec Pierre, puis il m'a promis de me rappeler le lendemain matin.

J'allais faire de beaux rêves...

Pas tant que ça, finalement.

Les propos d'Alexis étaient troublants. On a plaisanté en préparant le repas, mais le coeur n'y était pas. Je coupais les morceaux de poulet, les tomates et la laitue avec un sentiment d'angoisse oppressant. On a mangé nos *tacos* en silence puis on s'est installés au sous-sol pour discuter tranquillement. Il ne fallait pas que Nicolas nous entende. Mon frère adore Pierre et il s'en serait mêlé.

— Pierre n'a pas voulu répéter avec nous. Eugénie m'a appris qu'il passait ses soirées à la bibliothèque. Il y est allé trois fois cette semaine. Il n'est pas dans son état normal!

— Est-ce qu'il ne serait pas tombé amoureux de la nouvelle qui travaille à la bibliothèque?

— Non. Il y va vraiment pour lire.

Eugénie l'a vu fouiner dans les rayons des sciences sociales. Elle croit qu'il a emprunté des livres d'anthropologie.

— Pierre? Elle doit se tromper!

— Elle est formelle. Et elle a de bons yeux. N'oublie pas qu'elle est championne de tir à l'arc.

— Mais que cherche Pierre? Je devrais suivre les conseils d'Antoine.

— Appeler Adélaïde? Tu sais qu'elle ne veut plus parler de Pierre.

— Est-ce que je m'avoue vaincue si facilement, Alexis?

Mon ami a secoué la tête. On a téléphoné à Eugénie pour qu'elle donne rendez-vous à Adélaïde à la patinoire. Puis on les y a rejointes. Adélaïde a semblé mécontente de nous voir et s'est tournée vers Eugénie avec colère:

— Tu n'es qu'une traîtresse!

— Écoute-les, au moins, a plaidé Eugénie. Ils sont inquiets au sujet de Pierre.

— Je ne veux rien savoir de lui! a lancé Adélaïde. Ni y penser. Encore moins en parler.

— Mais pourquoi?

— Pourquoi est-ce que je lui rendrais service? Il m'a traitée comme une pestiférée.

— Quoi? Pierre? Mon cousin était amoureux de toi! Il y a sûrement un malentendu.

— Ah oui? Il n'a pas cessé de me critiquer. Il n'aimait ni ce que je portais, ni ce que je mangeais, ni ce que j'écoutais. Pourquoi a-t-il insisté pour qu'on sorte ensemble si c'était pour me faire des reproches? J'ai assez de ma mère pour ça!

— Pierre te critiquait?

— Oui, il a même dit que je dépensais mon argent pour des bêtises, que je devrais le garder pour partir en voyage.

— En voyage? Avec lui?

— Je trouvais l'idée romantique, mais il a ajouté que ça n'avait pas d'importance qu'on parte ensemble ou non. Il fallait seulement que j'économise mes sous. Je ne fréquente pas un garçon pour parler d'argent!

Si elle disait vrai, je ne pouvais reprocher à Adélaïde d'avoir cessé de fréquenter Pierre.

Mais c'était tellement étonnant...

Sur le chemin du retour, Alexis pensait à voix haute, et ses idées rejoignaient les miennes: dans quelle histoire Pierre s'était-il encore fourré?

— Est-ce que ton oncle a des problèmes d'argent?

— Non, tu sais bien qu'il vient juste

d'acheter un chalet dans le Nord. Pour qu'on fasse du ski cet hiver.

— Pierre ne m'en a pas parlé!

— Et oncle Martin lui a offert un nouveau saxophone la semaine dernière, pour le concours. Si mon oncle a un problème, il n'est pas d'ordre matériel.

— Alors quoi? Pourquoi Pierre s'intéresse-t-il à l'argent? Et de quel voyage s'agit-il?

Que de questions sans réponses!

Il fallait pourtant découvrir ce qui hantait mon cousin. Ce qui le minait, le détruisait.

— On va suivre Pierre pour tenter d'en savoir plus.

— L'espionner?

— On n'a pas le choix.

Chapitre 2

Les métamorphoses de Pierre

Je dois avouer que j'étais gênée de suivre mon cousin, et j'ai bien failli renoncer à ces filatures. Mais quand j'ai vu Pierre parler avec Gordon, je me suis félicitée d'avoir poursuivi mes investigations. Même si ce que je venais de découvrir m'inquiétait au plus haut point. J'ai immédiatement communiqué avec Alexis. Il m'a retrouvée au Café Z avec Eugénie.

— Quoi? a dit celle-ci. Il discutait avec Gordon?

— Ils avaient l'air très complices.

— Misère! On doit raisonner Pierre! Ça va trop loin!

J'approuvais Alexis. Si Pierre avait été dans son état normal, je l'aurais trouvé simplement gentil de s'intéresser à Gordon, mais maintenant...

Gordon était plus vieux que nous. Il aurait dû terminer son secondaire cette année. Puis il y avait eu «l'accident». Tout le monde en avait parlé sur le moment. Mais, à la rentrée, on aurait dit que le sujet était tabou. On faisait comme si de rien n'était.

Moi-même, j'avais eu envie de poser des questions à Gordon, et Pierre avait essayé de l'interroger, mais il avait préféré ne pas en parler. Ce n'était pas pour apprendre des détails sordides que j'avais voulu parler à Gordon. Non, j'aurais aimé comprendre ce qui l'avait poussé à se suicider.

En tout cas, à essayer.

Pourquoi avait-il voulu mourir? Lors de l'accident, j'avais pensé à Charlie Dulong, qui circule en fauteuil roulant mais qui rit tout le temps malgré sa maladie. Ou à Deborah, dont le père avait quitté la maison quand elle avait sept ans et qui était la fille la plus enjouée de l'école. Et même à mon cousin Pierre, dont la vie familiale est chaotique. Eux, selon moi, auraient eu de meilleures raisons que Gordon de vouloir mourir.

Gordon était beau, adorable, drôle et intelligent. Premier de classe et capitaine de l'équipe de water-polo. Toutes les filles étaient à ses pieds, et seul un manque de confiance en moi m'avait empêchée de me mettre sur les rangs... Tous les gars voulaient être ses amis.

Que lui manquait-il? Ses intimes disaient que sa famille était formidable. Il avait un superbe dalmatien. Même ses voisins étaient charmants. Alors?

J'avais éclairci bien des mystères dans ma vie, mais ce qui avait poussé Gordon à commettre un geste d'une telle gravité m'échappait totalement. J'avais tenté d'en discuter avec Pierre et Alexis, sans succès; Pierre semblait embarrassé de parler de la tentative de suicide de Gordon, Alexis, lui, était en colère. Ils n'avaient aucune réponse à mes questions.

Mais existe-t-il des réponses quand il s'agit de la mort?

On avait pensé à une peine d'amour, puisque Gordon avait fait sa tentative le jour de la Saint-Valentin. On avait enquêté sans trouver quoi que ce soit: pas de petite amie secrète, pas de rupture douloureuse, pas d'amour déçu. On n'avait pas revu Gordon. Cette année, il était de retour parmi nous.

Il souriait toujours autant, il avait de nouveau des tas d'amis, mais je ne croyais plus à sa gaieté. Je pensais qu'une peine incommensurable lui rongeait le coeur et que le silence sur son geste était aussi empoisonnant que les raisons qui l'avaient poussé à tenter de se suicider.

Mais je m'étais tue. Comme les autres.

Je me demandais maintenant si j'étais lâche. Ce n'est pas facile de parler de la mort. Encore moins à quelqu'un qui l'a vue de près.

Maintenant que Pierre s'intéressait à lui, je ne pouvais plus me cacher la vérité; j'avais peur que mon cousin soit attiré par Gordon parce qu'il avait frôlé la mort. Et Alexis résumait très bien ma pensée en me parlant de pacte de suicide.

— J'espère que ce n'est pas ça qui les unit, a murmuré mon ami.

— Il faut s'en assurer. Je préfère être maladroite ou même indiscrète plutôt que de paraître indifférente.

— Mais Pierre ne veut rien savoir de nous! Il ne m'a pas adressé la parole quand nous avons répété, hier matin. C'est sûr qu'on va perdre le concours s'il ne met pas plus de coeur à jouer.

J'ai juré. Je me sentais coupable. Je savais

aussi que je m'étais moins souciée de mon cousin ces derniers jours, car Antoine occupait toutes mes pensées. Il était temps de passer à l'action.

— Ça ne nous ressemble pas de perdre du temps à nous demander quoi faire, ai-je déclaré à Alexis.

— Mais il vous évite, a fait remarquer Eugénie. On dirait même qu'il se méfie de moi.

— S'il se méfie, c'est qu'il prépare quelque chose, a lancé Alexis.

— On va le coincer quand il sortira de la bibliothèque. On va l'obliger à nous parler!

Eugénie ne nous a pas accompagnés. Elle pensait qu'il valait mieux qu'on soit seuls avec Pierre.

— Vous êtes très près de lui. Pas moi. Il est préférable que je reste un peu en dehors de cette affaire. Je vous serai plus utile si Pierre ne sait pas que j'y suis directement mêlée.

Eugénie m'était de plus en plus sympathique. Je l'avais mal jugée. Au début, je la trouvais un peu snob, ou du moins distante, mais je pense qu'elle était simplement timide. Pierre, Alexis et moi formions un trio parfait. Je ne voulais pas qu'on détruise notre amitié. Et peut-être que je redoutais qu'elle nous enlève Alexis.

Mais c'était Pierre qui s'éloignait de nous. Et voilà qu'au lieu d'aller faire de l'escalade, Alexis et moi suivions Pierre. On l'a vu entrer à l'auditorium, sortir son saxophone de son étui, porter le bec à ses lèvres.

— Mais qu'est-ce qu'il joue là? s'est étonné Alexis.

On entendait les notes s'envoler, se heurter, se confronter, s'arrondir ou s'intensifier avant de s'évanouir. La pièce était très différente de ce que mon cousin jouait habituellement; c'était lancinant, plus répétitif et plus agressif. Si ça correspondait à son état d'esprit, son âme devait souffrir d'une mégamigraine! Ça me donnait mal à la tête d'écouter cette musique, même si je reconnaissais le talent de Pierre dans sa manière de jouer le refrain.

— Ça ne lui ressemble pas, a constaté Alexis. C'est bizarre. Tu crois que c'est une de ses compositions?

— Je ne sais pas. En tout cas, il ne gagnera pas de concours avec ça.

— Ni avec notre pièce! Il n'a pas le temps de jouer avec nous, mais il en trouve pour jouer seul. Il va devoir s'expliquer! On est

déjà assez défavorisés par le fait que
M. Jackson est président du jury.

M. Jackson était un professeur très con-
servateur qui ne jurait que par Chopin ou
Mozart. J'aime parfois la musique classique,
mais il n'y a pas que ça dans la vie. Même
M. Chanteclerc, qui est assez vieux, pense
comme moi. Il écoute du jazz, du rock, du
rap, et il a promis de m'enseigner le tango
quand il viendrait à Montréal. À condition
que je me décide à l'appeler par son prénom,
Horace. J'ai peur d'éclater de rire les premières fois...

La musique s'est évanouie. Pierre était
tellement absorbé par ses pensées qu'il ne
nous a même pas vus.

— Pierre!

— Pierre!

Il s'est retourné vers nous, a paru surpris.

— Oui?

— On est venus t'écouter, ai-je menti.
C'est... c'est nouveau, cette pièce?

— Oui.

— C'est toi qui l'as composée?

— Oui.

— Qu'est-ce qui t'a inspiré cette mélo-
die?

— Tout.

Était-il encore capable de faire une phrase complète?

— Tout quoi? s'est impatienté Alexis. Explique-nous.

— Je ne pense pas que... Oh! tu le sauras de toute manière: je ne participerai pas au concours avec vous. Je préfère y jouer seul.

— Quoi?

— Tu le diras à Hector. Maintenant, je dois rentrer.

J'ai protesté et j'ai réussi à convaincre mon cousin de nous accompagner au Café Z. J'ai dû lui promettre qu'on ne resterait pas plus de trente minutes.

— Tu as un rendez-vous? ai-je demandé.

— Non. Oui.

— Est-ce qu'on *la* connaît?

Pierre m'a regardée d'un air... supérieur:

— Il n'y a pas que les filles dans la vie. Il y a les femmes. La femme et l'homme qui savent s'unir pour le bien de l'avenir.

— Pardon?

Pierre n'a pas répété. Suzanne, la serveuse, nous apportait des jus de fruits. Pierre avait, à notre grande surprise, choisi un jus de raisin.

— Tu aimes ça, maintenant?

— Oui.

— Veux-tu devenir télégraphiste?

— Quoi?

— Tu fais des phrases hyper-courtes.

— La vie est courte. Enfin, cette vie-ci.

Je n'aimais pas le ton que prenait cette conversation... Alexis non plus. Il a posé une main sur l'épaule de Pierre et lui a dit franchement qu'on s'inquiétait pour lui:

— Je suis en colère, mais ce n'est pas uniquement pour le concert. Tu nous dois des explications.

— Je suis maître de ma vie. De mon cercle intérieur.

De quoi?

Alexis était à tel point désorienté par le discours de Pierre qu'il en oubliait momentanément sa rage.

— Je ne sais pas pourquoi tu nous rejettes, Pierre. Je ne comprends plus rien. Qu'est-ce que tu veux dire par «la vie est courte», «mon cercle intérieur»?

— Et tu fréquentes Gordon, on le sait, ai-je ajouté. Pourquoi?

Pierre nous a dévisagés comme si on était des... imbéciles.

— Je m'entends bien avec lui. Il a accédé à une forme d'élévation.

— Peut-être, ai-je concédé, mais ça lui a

coûté très cher.

— Il y a un prix à payer pour tout.

— Même la vie?

Pierre a haussé les épaules. Je le sentais très tendu et absent tout à la fois.

— Pierre, ai-je murmuré, penses-tu à un pacte de suicide avec Gordon?

Il m'a regardée d'un air ahuri puis a éclaté de rire. Un rire un peu trop fort, mais un rire tout de même. Ça m'a légèrement rassurée.

— J'ai trop de choses à accomplir pour me suicider, Nat. Surtout maintenant.

— Que veux-tu dire?

Pierre s'est refermé comme une huître.

— Parle-nous, ai-je supplié.

J'ai expliqué à mon cousin qu'il se sentait peut-être mis à l'écart, puisque son histoire avec Adélaïde n'avait pas eu un dénouement heureux.

— Je n'y pense même plus, a rétorqué Pierre d'un ton si détaché qu'on devait le croire.

— Alors? Qu'est-ce qu'on a fait pour que tu nous boudes? Pour que tu refuses de jouer avec nous au concert? Quand Hector va apprendre que tu nous plaques, il va être...

— C'est mieux ainsi. On n'avançait plus. J'ai besoin de me réaliser ailleurs. Je ne vous

boude pas. Je vous trouve seulement un peu...
jeunes.

Jeunes?

Je ne suis pas susceptible, mais il y a des
limites! Pierre a quatre mois de plus que moi!
JEUNES!

— Gordon n'est pas beaucoup plus âgé
que nous, a rétorqué Alexis.

— Non, mais ses amis le sont. Et j'apprends beaucoup d'eux.

— Tu apprends quoi?

— Tout ce qu'on doit savoir. Les grands
mystères.

— Eh! Les mystères, on est habitués à les
résoudre ensemble. Pourquoi nous caches-tu
tes nouvelles enquêtes?

— Parce qu'il ne s'agit pas d'enquête,
mais de quête.

J'avais l'impression de parler à quelqu'un
que je ne connaissais pas. Pierre s'exprimait
avec des phrases toutes faites. Même sa voix
avait des tonalités mécaniques. Il me regardait droit dans les yeux, mais je ne réussis-
sais pas à sonder son âme. Je le sentais très
très loin de moi. Une vague de tristesse m'a
submergée: un courant très puissant entraî-
nait Pierre sur des rivages dangereux. Je ne
savais pas contre quoi je devrais lutter, mais

la menace était presque palpable.

Je devais pourtant comprendre ce que vivait mon cousin. Malgré ma peur, ma peine, j'ai fait preuve de patience.

— Explique-nous un peu tout cela. Peut-être que ça va nous intéresser. On est plus jeunes que toi, c'est vrai, mais on n'est pas idiots.

Pierre a hésité, puis acquiescé.

Il s'est rapproché de nous, a baissé la voix et nous a appris que Gordon faisait partie du mouvement éodien.

Du mouvement éodien?

— C'est...

Alexis allait dire «une secte», mais je l'ai interrompu:

— C'est récent? Il est dans ce... dans ce groupe depuis longtemps?

— Depuis six mois. Il est heureux maintenant. Il n'a plus jamais parlé de suicide.

— C'est... bien, suis-je parvenue à bredouiller. J'en suis contente. C'est trop triste de voir quelqu'un comme Gordon, avec un tel potentiel, qui refuse de vivre.

Le visage de Pierre s'est éclairé.

— C'est ce que Gordon lui-même a dit quand il m'a expliqué toute l'aide que lui avait apportée le mouvement éodien.

— Et toi? Ça... t'intéresse aussi? a balbutié Alexis.

Il ne pensait plus du tout au concert! J'aurais parié qu'il serrait les poings, sous la table. Il devait se retenir pour ne pas secouer
Pierre comme un prunier afin de le ramener
à la raison.

— Je suis curieux, s'est contenté de répondre Pierre. Pourquoi refuser la nouveau-
té, fermer son esprit à la différence? Je ne
vois que des effets positifs chez Gordon.
C'est un type vraiment bien, vous savez. Ses
amis aussi.

— Pour le concours, tu ne changes pas
d'idée? a insisté Alexis. En tout cas, c'est toi
qui l'apprendras à Hector. C'est ta décision.

— Tu es sûr de ce que tu fais? ai-je demandé.

— Oui.

— C'est bientôt, le concours. Tu dois avoir
le trac.

— Non, pourquoi?

«Non, pourquoi?» Je détestais ce détachement. Je ne voulais pas d'un cousin aussi
froid qu'un androïde! J'ai changé de sujet.
On a parlé un peu des cours, des examens tri-
mestriels, puis on est partis.

J'avais la mort dans l'âme et la rage au

coeur. Une secte! Mon cousin voulait faire partie d'une secte!

Comment l'en empêcher?

Chapitre 3

Le concours

L'auditorium était plein à craquer. Alexis s'était finalement décidé à assister au concert.

J'avais eu du mal à le convaincre. Il répétait qu'il n'avait pas du tout envie d'entendre Pierre.

— Il nous a trahis. Je n'ai pas fait de drame quand il nous a abandonnés, mais de là à venir l'encourager!

— Les juges ne voteront jamais pour lui et sa nouvelle chanson subliminale! Il va perdre. C'est M. Jackson qui préside le jury... On doit être là pour le consoler.

— On n'est plus ses amis. Il ne nous

verra même pas. Il ne m'a pas reparlé depuis des jours...

— Je sais, mais on ne doit pas le lâcher. Il n'est plus responsable de ce qu'il fait. De ce qu'il pense. Tu as lu la revue que je t'ai prêtée?

J'avais fait quelques recherches sur les sectes, ceux qui les dirigent, ceux qui y adhèrent. Et ces lectures ne m'avaient pas du tout rassurée. Pierre était une proie tout indiquée.

— Oui, a répondu Alexis. Ça m'a fait froid dans le dos. Ton oncle devrait intervenir.

— Ce n'est pas si simple. Il faut être prudent, sinon Pierre coupera les ponts. On le perdra définitivement si on le trahit. Il faut que tu viennes au concert.

On discutait de Pierre avec Antoine et Eugénie. On s'est assis dans la rangée F de l'auditorium. Peut-être que mon cousin nous verrait et peut-être que notre présence lui ferait tout de même plaisir. Je n'avais jamais été aussi désemparée. Antoine l'a senti et m'a embrassée dans le cou en me disant que tout allait s'arranger.

— Pierre est intelligent. Il va se réveiller et voir que le mouvement éodien n'est que de la fumisterie.

— Justement, la plupart des gens qui font

partie d'une secte sont intelligents. Mais ils sont fragiles sur le plan émotif.

— Sois patiente. Ça ne sert à rien de brusquer les choses.

— Il aura besoin de nous après le concert. Il est certain de gagner.

— Pas toi?

— Non. Il a changé radicalement de style. Je ne sais pas à qui ça plaira. Moi, je n'aime pas. Alexis non plus. Ni les copains qui faisaient de la musique avec lui auparavant.

On devait tous manquer de goût: Pierre a obtenu le premier prix!

Je l'ai observé alors qu'on lui remettait son chèque et un certificat qui lui permettrait de participer aux finales nationales. S'il remportait encore la victoire, il irait au concert rock. Il n'avait même pas l'air surpris.

Ni heureux.

Un robot. Mon cousin s'était transformé en robot.

Juste après qu'il eut quitté la scène, j'ai remarqué la présence d'un homme et d'une femme vêtus de bleu ciel, qui ne cessaient de sourire à Pierre. Gordon était assis entre eux.

Un frisson m'a parcouru l'échine. J'ai regardé attentivement ces visages faussement angéliques; je leur aurais bien craché dessus!

— Qu'est-ce que tu as? m'a demandé Antoine.

— J'ai vu des vautours. Et même si leurs plumes étaient bleues, j'ai su les reconnaître.

Il m'a pressée contre lui et a chuchoté qu'on trouverait une solution. Eugénie aussi avait aperçu les disciples éodiens. Elle est meilleure comédienne que moi: elle a réussi à leur sourire quand on les a croisés dans l'allée alors qu'on se dirigeait vers la scène pour féliciter Pierre.

J'ai embrassé mon cousin, mais il m'a remerciée d'une façon automatique. Il réservait ses gentillesses à Gordon et à ces deux oiseaux de malheur. Ils avaient beau avoir emprunté les couleurs du geai bleu, ils ne m'abusaient pas! Je me demandais simplement pourquoi ils avaient opté pour ce ton azur.

On regagnait la sortie après avoir proposé vainement à Pierre de venir manger une pizza avec nous, lorsque M. Jackson m'a bousculée. Il a échappé sa serviette remplie de documents. Je l'ai aidé à les ramasser malgré ses protestations.

J'ai eu le temps de voir la fiche concernant mon cousin. Contrairement à celles des autres concurrents, elle était propre, sans bavures, sans ratures, sans remarques dans les marges. M. Jackson avait inscrit la note 20 avec une assurance étonnante. Je lui ai caché que j'avais découvert cette fiche en la glissant parmi d'autres feuilles. Quand M. Jackson m'a remerciée, je lui ai demandé pourquoi il avait aimé la pièce de Pierre.

— C'est... c'est nouveau, a-t-il balbutié.

— Mais un peu répétitif, non?

— Le *Boléro* de Ravel aussi est répétitif. Ça n'a rien à voir.

Il m'a répondu d'un ton sec. On aurait dit que je l'avais incommodé avec ma question. Pourtant, sur la scène, il avait vanté les mérites de Pierre avec insistance. Lui aussi était bizarre.

En sortant de l'auditorium, j'ai entendu un des membres du jury parler de M. Jackson. Il disait qu'il avait un comportement étrange:

— Je ne sais pas pour quelle raison il nous a imposé ce gagnant. Jackson déteste ce genre de musique! Je n'ai rien compris à son attitude.

L'homme s'est tu en me reconnaissant, mais je lui ai souri comme si je n'avais rien entendu.

Ses réflexions méritaient néanmoins qu'on

en débatte. J'ai tout répété à mes amis tandis qu'on attendait notre pizza.

On n'a évidemment pas découvert les motifs qui avaient poussé M. Jackson à désigner Pierre comme gagnant. Mais le surlendemain, quand on a appris qu'il abandonnait son poste de professeur et prenait un long congé de maladie, on s'est dit que ce concours avait des conséquences plutôt surprenantes.

Alexis et moi avons décidé d'interroger M. Jackson. Pourquoi, subitement, admirait-il mon cousin? Y avait-il un lien avec les nouvelles fréquentations de Pierre? Faisait-il partie du mouvement éodien?

On n'a pas pu discuter avec M. Jackson. Il avait quitté le pays.

Ce départ n'était-il pas un tantinet précipité? Ce voyage ressemblait drôlement à une fuite.

— Tu n'as aucune preuve pour étayer cette hypothèse, m'ont déclaré Antoine et Alexis.

J'ai soupiré; ils avaient raison. Pierre aurait pu répondre à nos questions, mais il ne nous parlait plus. Ma mère m'avait interrogée à son sujet, mais j'avais été évasive.

Un mois plus tard, Pierre remportait le prix

en finale nationale. Pourtant, il faisait face à un concurrent très sérieux, mais ce dernier avait abandonné en deuxième partie. On avait annoncé qu'il était malade et qu'il se retirait. Ce qui consacrait la victoire de Pierre.

Cette fois-ci, il avait l'air content.

Ses amis «bleutés» et Gordon furent les premiers à le féliciter. J'ai remarqué que Gordon portait un jeans bleu ciel et une chemise de la même couleur; il n'arborait pas encore les vêtements typiques des disciples éodiens, mais il en avait adopté les couleurs. Puis, j'ai vu la femme glisser une sorte de médaille dans la main de Pierre, dont le visage s'est illuminé.

J'ai su alors que mon cousin faisait partie de cette secte.

Je n'ai pas pu aller le féliciter. Que lui aurais-je dit?

Je ne pouvais tout de même pas mentir et prétendre que j'aimais sa pièce musicale: chaque fois que je l'entendais, elle me donnait mal à la tête. Elle m'angoissait.

On rentrait doucement à la maison, quand Antoine m'a dit que la maladie subite du concurrent de Pierre l'intriguait.

— Il paraissait tout à fait bien quand il a

présenté la première partie de sa trilogie musicale.

— Il a dû avoir une crise d'angoisse. À cause du stress.

J'essayais de trouver un motif à cette défection, mais je sentais qu'Antoine avait raison.

— Qu'est-ce qui l'aurait poussé à abandonner?

— Je ne sais pas.

— On ne le connaît pas. Il n'est même pas d'ici. Comment pourrait-il être mêlé à un... un complot?

— Quelqu'un doit l'avoir incité à se retirer, a dit Alexis. Je crois qu'Antoine a flairé quelque chose.

Mais quoi?

— Il faut rencontrer ce gars. Avant qu'il quitte Montréal. Avant qu'il s'évanouisse dans la nature, comme M. Jackson!

Nous sommes retournés à la salle de spectacle pour obtenir des informations sur Jonathan Gervais.

— Il a quitté la salle après qu'on a annoncé son retrait de la compétition, nous a appris le portier.

— Vous savez où nous pouvons le joindre?

— Que lui voulez-vous?

— C'est un ami d'enfance, lui a répondu Eugénie.

Elle avait une manière si candide de battre des cils que le pape lui aurait donné le bon Dieu sans confession.

— J'ai été tellement surprise de le voir ici. J'aimerais lui parler. Je sais qu'il est malade, mais ça lui fera sûrement du bien de retrouver une vieille amie.

— C'est que je ne...

— S'il vous plaît, monsieur.

L'homme a hésité, puis nous a demandé de l'attendre. Il est revenu avec une liste sur laquelle était inscrit le nom de l'hôtel où séjournait Jonathan Gervais.

— Vous êtes un amour! a déclaré Eugénie.

Elle a fait un petit geste très gracieux de la main, puis nous avons couru jusqu'à l'arrêt d'autobus.

Rendus à destination, nous avons aperçu Jonathan sortir de l'hôtel en souriant. Il avait l'air plutôt en forme.

— Qu'est-ce que ça signifie?

— Suivons-le!

Nous avons vu Jonathan Gervais se diriger vers le boulevard Saint-Laurent. Il est entré dans un pub. Antoine allait y pénétrer à son tour quand Jonathan en est ressorti. Il était accompagné d'un grand type avec qui il plaisantait.

— Je le reconnais! me suis-je écriée. C'est un des organisateurs du concours. Je l'ai remarqué: il ressemble à mon oncle Roland.

La rencontre entre cet organisateur et le concurrent nous semblait aussi louche que la disparition de M. Jackson. Et quand on a vu un des disciples du mouvement éodien rejoindre Jonathan et l'organisateur, nos doutes se sont mués en certitudes: ce concours recelait bien des zones d'ombre. Des ombres qui n'annonçaient rien de bon.

— Il faut se renseigner sur cet événement, a dit Eugénie. Savoir qui a créé ce prix, qui s'en occupe, qui gère le budget, d'où viennent les fonds...

— Oui, c'est sa première année d'existence. On n'a jamais entendu parler de ce concours avant le début de l'année.

— Je vais demander à mon ancien prof de guitare, a proposé Alexis. Peut-être qu'il pourra nous aider.

— Et moi, je vais faire semblant d'être attirée par le mouvement éodien.

Antoine s'est alarmé:

— Je n'aime pas que tu...

— Ne t'inquiète pas, je n'ai aucune envie d'entrer dans une secte. Et je ne suis pas candidate au lavage de cerveau. Mais c'est la seule manière de me rapprocher de Pierre. On a essayé de discuter avec lui, sans succès. On ne peut pas l'atteindre, à moins d'entrer dans son jeu.

— Drôle de jeu, a gémi Alexis. Tu ferais mieux de parler d'univers parallèle. Je vais avoir de la difficulté à duper Pierre.

— Tu ne lui mentiras pas. Je serai seule à m'intéresser à cette secte. Je vais même lui dire que je me détache de toi parce que je trouve que tu manques de profondeur, que tu ne cherches pas les vraies valeurs.

— Eh! N'exagère pas!

Alexis m'a donné une bourrade affectueuse. Ça m'a fait du bien. Nous avions besoin d'affirmer notre amitié, de nous taquiner un peu pour atténuer notre angoisse. On a reparlé des articles que j'avais lus sur les victimes des sectes.

— Je savais déjà qu'il faut éviter de demander à Pierre de choisir entre ses nouveaux amis et nous, a dit Eugénie. Mais ça m'a attristée d'imaginer qu'il peut nous considérer comme ses ennemis. Qu'on lui veut du mal parce qu'il est dans une secte.

— Ne jamais prononcer le mot «secte». Pierre est persuadé qu'il a trouvé un nouveau mode de vie. Le mot «secte» semble toujours suspect. Chaque fois, je parlerai du «mouvement».

— Ça ne me plaît pas que tu fréquentes ses amis, a avoué Antoine. J'ai peur qu'ils ne soient pas tous des illuminés, comme ils le paraissent. Il y a des têtes dirigeantes dans chaque groupe. Celui-ci n'y échappe pas. Les chefs ont des intérêts, des buts précis.

— Oui, amasser de l'argent, a approuvé Alexis. C'est toujours l'argent qui les intéresse, quelle que soit la secte. Ils parlent de vérité, mais ils ont un coffre-fort rempli par leurs victimes!

— L'argent les fascine, a affirmé Eugénie, mais je crois que le pouvoir agit sur eux comme une drogue. Ils se croient les maîtres du monde. Pensez aux derniers suicides collectifs...

L'Ordre du Temple solaire, Waco, Jonestown, autant de noms qui évoquaient des morts tragiques, le sacrifice de centaines d'innocents. Je ne savais pas si le mouvement éodien était aussi dangereux que ceux-là, mais j'étais persuadée que Pierre y perdrait sa personnalité. Ça ressemblait à un suicide: si Pierre cessait d'être Pierre, il serait mort, en quelque sorte.

On devait le ramener au royaume des vivants!

On s'est réparti les tâches. Antoine, Eugénie et Alexis tenteraient d'en apprendre davantage sur le concours. Antoine chercherait des informations auprès des organismes de spectacles, Eugénie verrait du côté des organisations étudiantes: y avait-il des collèges, des écoles, des cégeps qui avaient parrainé de pareilles rencontres?

On savait que c'était le premier concours qui portait ce nom, mais peut-être que des épreuves similaires avaient été organisées au cours des années précédentes. Quels en avaient été les résultats? Avait-on remarqué des aspects inquiétants, des conséquences tragiques?

Quant à Alexis, il prendrait rendez-vous avec son professeur de musique. Mais en attendant, il continuerait de surveiller Jonathan. Enfin, il essaierait. On l'avait vu s'engouffrer dans une voiture avec ses amis. Reviendrait-il à l'hôtel?

— Je vais patienter dans le hall, a précisé Alexis. J'espère que Jonathan reviendra. Je pourrais essayer de discuter avec lui. Il ne me connaît pas, il ne se méfiera pas de moi.

— Que lui diras-tu?

— Je ne sais pas, j'improviserai. Je le ferai parler de lui. Les gens aiment toujours parler d'eux...

C'était vrai. Et j'ai décidé d'amener Antoine à se confier davantage: il me trouverait plus intéressante. Je me demandais encore pourquoi il sortait avec moi. Tout s'était passé si vite! Depuis qu'Alexis lui avait parlé de moi, on ne s'était plus quittés.

Mes parents ne me permettaient évidemment pas de sortir tous les soirs, mais je voyais Antoine à l'école chaque jour. Je vous jure que ça aide à apprécier les cours... Et j'étais résolue à obtenir de bonnes notes; ainsi, mes parents ne pourraient jamais dire que mes fréquentations nuisaient à mon travail scolaire. J'étais prête à tout pour protéger notre amour! Même à avoir un B en physique.

***

La nuit tombait sur la ville. Les lumières s'allumaient les unes après les autres, formant une étrange galaxie de planètes incandescentes. J'aime cette heure où Montréal étincelle. Ce soir-là, toutefois, je pensais avec mélancolie à tous les gens qui souffrent de solitude et qui restent dans le noir, regardant la ville s'animer sans eux.

J'ai secoué ces pensées; l'action me convient davantage! Tandis que mes amis enquêtaient de leur côté, je tentais de joindre mon cousin.

Plus facile à dire qu'à faire! Pierre n'était jamais chez lui. Je ne le voyais même pas à l'école. Je lui ai laissé un million de messages sur son répondeur, et il a fini par me rappeler le mercredi soir. J'ai usé de tout mon pouvoir de persuasion pour qu'il accepte de me voir le soir même.

J'ai marché jusque chez lui. Le bruit des feuilles mortes qui crissaient sous mes pas, l'odeur de fumée qui flottait dans l'atmosphère et le léger brouillard qui nimbait les lampadaires d'un nuage opalescent m'ont aidée à retrouver une certaine sérénité.

Je devais être prête à entendre les pires folies si je voulais aider Pierre.

Je ne devais pas manifester la moindre opposition à ses idées.

Je ne savais pas que ce serait si difficile.

Chapitre 4

Les Éodiens

Mon cousin semblait très contrarié par ma visite; c'est uniquement parce que j'avais presque pleuré au téléphone qu'il avait consenti à me recevoir.

— Entre, m'a-t-il dit d'un ton ennuyé.

— Excuse-moi de m'imposer, mais je ne sais plus où j'en suis.

Il m'a fait signe de m'asseoir. Dans le salon. Habituellement, on descendait au sous-sol pour bavarder en écoutant de la musique. On se préparait un lunch, on se bourrait de chips et on discutait des heures durant de notre avenir: Pierre serait un grand musicien, et moi... avocate en droit criminel, journaliste ou détective privée.

On parlait de tout et de rien, de nos amours et de nos absences d'amour, de nos amitiés et de nos antipathies. Mais jamais dans le salon.

Ce soir-là, Pierre avait l'air de régner sur les lieux. C'était sa maison, bien sûr, mais on aurait dit qu'il l'avait construite de ses propres mains. Qu'il l'avait payée et pouvait en disposer à son gré. Il avait d'ailleurs déplacé les meubles.

— Ton père n'est pas là?

— Dans le Sud avec ma mère. Comme si ça pouvait lui faire du bien...

— On ne sait pas toujours ce qui peut nous aider.

Après en avoir discuté avec Antoine, j'avais choisi de m'exprimer avec des phrases aussi générales ou banales que celles de mon cousin. Si mes propos étaient vagues, il les interpréterait plus volontiers dans le sens qu'il le désirait. Enfin, c'est ce que j'espérais.

C'était une bonne méthode.

— Tu sais, Pierre, tu m'as parlé des bienfaits que le mouvement éodien a apportés à Gordon. Je l'ai observé attentivement ces derniers jours, et je dois avouer que tu as raison. Il est épanoui, sûr de lui. Je... je l'envie. Je pense que ça ne me nuirait pas d'en savoir plus sur le groupe.

— Toi?

— J'ai des problèmes, Pierre.

Je dois être une très bonne comédienne, car j'ai même réussi à verser quelques larmes. Peut-être que la peur m'y aidait aussi. Pierre a enfin réagi comme je le souhaitais.

— Quels problèmes?

J'ai inventé un malaise face à l'existence, aux questions qui restaient sans réponses, à ma vie qui n'avait pas de but, à ma jeunesse que je gaspillais au lieu d'apprendre à me dépasser. Bref, le genre de salade qui pouvait lui plaire.

— Toi-même, tu as l'air plus mûr que nous, que moi. Si c'est parce que tu es dans le mouvement, je veux en faire partie aussi. J'ai déjà perdu trop de temps.

— Natasha!

Là, j'aurais pleuré pour vrai. C'était le premier sourire que mon cousin m'adressait depuis des semaines. Il rayonnait de tendresse. Parce que je voulais entrer dans cette sale secte!

— Ça me fait plaisir d'entendre ça, a dit Pierre. Qu'est-ce qui t'a fait évoluer si vite?

Redevenait-il méfiant? Il fallait le rassurer

immédiatement.

— J'ai eu une sorte de flash en lisant la rubrique nécrologique. J'ai pensé que je ne pouvais pas me rendre à soixante-dix ans sans trouver les réponses à mes questions. Je me suis dit que la vie ne ressemblait pas à ce que je vivais. Ça ne peut pas être si vide, non?

— Non.

— Parle-moi du mouvement. Est-ce qu'on m'accepterait?

— Je vais demander à Gordon de nous rejoindre, veux-tu? Il sait en parler encore mieux que moi.

Je ne me suis pas opposée à sa visite même si je craignais que Gordon voie clair dans mon jeu.

Je m'inquiétais pour rien: Gordon était conditionné par le mouvement à un point tel qu'il n'avait plus aucun jugement. Quand il a commencé à parler, Pierre s'est calé dans un fauteuil, comme s'il allait écouter le plus beau chant du monde.

J'ai entendu les pires âneries du monde.

Imaginez que votre meilleur ami vous dise qu'il déménagera sur Pluton l'été prochain. Qu'en penseriez-vous?

Pierre et Gordon me tenaient un discours

aussi dément! Ils m'ont expliqué que les Éodiens voulaient rétablir la justice sur Terre! Beau contrat!

— On réussira, a affirmé Pierre d'un ton grave. Car le mouvement s'inspire des mythes les plus anciens. Nous retournons aux sources premières et nous intervenons dès qu'elles prennent ces mauvais plis qui font que notre monde est en plein chaos.

— C'est vrai, on est en plein chaos, ai-je répété.

Mais je pensais plutôt au désordre qui régnait dans l'esprit de Pierre.

— Tu trouves ça, aussi?

— C'est évident. Mais je ne pensais pas qu'on pouvait changer des choses... à l'étendue planétaire.

— Tout est possible quand on a la foi, a affirmé Gordon. Et nous l'avons. Parce que nous savons.

Ils pouvaient m'expliquer pourquoi il y avait des guerres, pourquoi des gens naissaient avec une infirmité, pourquoi des femmes ne connaîtraient jamais l'amour, pourquoi des hommes seraient assassinés sans raison, au détour d'une rue, par un beau soir de printemps.

Pourquoi des enfants se prostituaient et se

droguaient pour supporter cet avilissement. Pourquoi des fous torturaient des animaux. Pourquoi j'étais née dans un pays riche et paisible, alors que des centaines d'adolescentes devaient se battre pour survivre dans des régions arides.

Ils savaient pourquoi la vie était si injuste et comment changer tout cela. Comment remédier aux injustices.

Par quel sortilège avait-on pu leur faire avaler pareilles couleuvres?

— Tu vois, Nat, notre mouvement est un mouvement d'avenir basé sur le passé ancestral.

Les yeux de Pierre brillaient d'une lueur étrange chaque fois qu'il disait «notre mouvement».

Était-il trop tard pour le ramener à notre réalité? Et si le lavage de cerveau était irréversible?

— Le passé? Parles-tu de millénaires?

— Exactement. Le berceau de la civilisation, c'est la Grèce. Tout le monde sait ça. Mais on s'est éloignés des principes qui géraient le monde antique. Nous, nous le recréons.

Il m'a parlé des dieux et des déesses qui s'occupaient chacun de son domaine. «Le

Panthéon était une sorte d'assemblée nationale.»

Pitié! Allait-il détruire toute la beauté de la mythologie grecque? Et comparer les voyages d'Ulysse à une tournée référendaire?

— Le Panthéon vous inspire? ai-je balbutié.

— Nous inspire, oui. Mais nous allons plus loin. Le Maître a recréé un nouvel ordre. Nous communiquons avec les éléments. Nous sommes leurs enfants. Les parents doivent aimer leurs enfants, ils doivent les protéger, non? Alors les éléments nous apportent leur appui, leur soutien. Le Soleil parle à la Terre, l'Air intervient auprès du Feu.

Je devais avoir l'air un peu perdue. Gordon m'a donné un exemple:

— La faim dans le monde sera un mauvais souvenir quand la Terre se sera fait entendre du Soleil: il brillera moins. Il n'y aura plus de sécheresse, et les peuples mangeront à leur faim.

— Vous... priez le Soleil et la Terre, c'est ça?

— Plus encore. Nous sommes une partie des éléments. D'où nos noms de cellules.

— De cellules.

— Je fais partie de la cellule URADÉO, dit Pierre. Je suis un Uradien, c'est-à-dire que je suis en contact plus direct avec le Ciel. La personnification du Ciel dans la mythologie grecque, c'est Ouranos.

— Moi, c'est le Soleil, lance Gordon. Je suis un Hélien, de la cellule HÉLIDÉO. Tu n'as pas remarqué que mes cheveux sont de plus en plus dorés?

Et que les yeux de Pierre virent à l'azur?

J'ai failli me pincer pour être certaine que je ne rêvais pas et que j'entendais vraiment ces discours incroyables.

— Il y a aussi des Géodiens, des Gydiens, des Hydrodiens. Notre famille compte des centaines de membres. En l'an 2000, nous aurons atteint le chiffre sacré que le Maître Myria nous a révélé.

— Nous aurons quintuplé le millénaire, a ajouté Pierre, nous serons enfin des Myriadiens. Nous serons dix mille entités prêtes à aborder le Nouvel Âge avec la sagesse des Anciens. Nous triompherons de la vie.

J'ai hoché la tête, incapable de prononcer un mot: mon cousin était vraiment devenu fou. J'avais l'impression que le sol se dérobait sous mes pieds, que j'étais entraînée dans un gouffre noir et froid, que j'étais aspirée par de la boue ou des sables mouvants. J'avais mal au coeur.

— Tu es toute pâle, Natasha, a dit Gordon.

— C'est que je suis... bouleversée. C'est tellement extraordinaire! Personne n'a jamais compris notre univers de cette manière. Votre maître doit être un génie.

Pierre et Gordon m'ont souri en acquiesçant.

— Pouvez-vous m'expliquer la signification du nom du mouvement?

— Éodien vient simplement d'*êôs*, qui signifie «aurore» en grec. Par exemple, le mot «éocène» fait référence à la catégorie la plus ancienne des terrains du tertiaire. De plus, l'aurore est le début du jour. Nous sommes au début de nos projets, de notre vie d'Éodiens. Il y aura une mouvance vers l'an 2000. Nos noms, nos cellules évolueront.

J'ai posé d'autres questions sur le fonctionnement du groupe, la méthode de recrutement des membres, les devoirs de ces derniers, la fréquence des réunions. Je manifestais un tel intérêt que Gordon a répondu avec enthousiasme.

En le regardant s'emballer quand il me décrivait le monde merveilleux auquel les Éodiens allaient accéder, j'ai remarqué qu'il avait maigri. Son visage était plus long, ses épaules moins larges; il ne flottait pas encore dans ses vêtements bleus, mais il avait sûrement perdu du poids.

Gordon m'a parlé des devoirs des membres: les réunions, les chants et la lecture des textes du Maître. De plus, il devait exécuter quelques travaux pour entretenir les locaux où vivaient plusieurs Éodiens.

Des travaux d'esclave?

— Il me semble que tu as maigri, Gordon, n'ai-je pu m'empêcher de dire.

Il a semblé ravi par mon commentaire.

— Oui. Enfin!

— Mais tu n'as jamais eu de problème de poids!

— Peut-être en apparence, mais je me sentais si lourd. J'avais l'impression d'avoir des roches aux pieds avant de devenir Éodien. J'étais aspiré par les entrailles de la Terre, tout me pesait. Le régime me régénère, c'est fantastique!

— Le régime?

— C'est superorganisé, a dit Pierre. Je sais comme tu es gourmande, mais tu verras que c'est très amusant. On mange selon des codes de couleurs.

Il m'a expliqué qu'on groupait les aliments selon leur luminosité: de très pâle à très sombre. Dans la gamme chromatique des jaunes et des verts. Jamais de rouge. Le rouge était une couleur agressive; les tomates, fraises et framboises ainsi que la viande — bien évidemment — étaient bannies de l'alimentation des Éodiens.

— Et le poulet?

— Le poulet aussi, même si la chair est blanche. Car le poulet saigne.

— C'est logique, ai-je trouvé à répondre.

Qu'est-ce que j'aurais pu ajouter? J'étais dépassée par les événements... J'en avais assez entendu pour cette fois. J'ai remercié Gordon et Pierre de leur confiance et je les ai assurés de ma discrétion.

— J'ai vraiment envie d'en apprendre davantage sur le mouvement éodien. J'ai toujours été fascinée par la mythologie grecque. Si on peut retrouver le mode de vie des Anciens et améliorer leur travail, je veux en être!

— C'est vrai? a demandé Gordon.

— Oui, a confirmé Pierre. Nat a toujours aimé les légendes. Depuis qu'on est tout petits.

Il y a eu un silence, puis mon cousin a ajouté, l'air... illuminé:

— On ne pensait pas alors qu'on pourrait les intégrer à notre univers, hein, Nat?

— On n'avait pas assez d'imagination pour ça.

— Maître Myria est un visionnaire, a conclu Gordon. On parlera de lui dans l'univers entier.

— On va aller partout dans le monde, a dit Pierre.

— Vous avez prévu faire des voyages?

Mon cousin et Gordon ont poussé des petits cris d'enthousiasme et m'ont raconté que le Maître trouvait qu'il était sain que les Éodiens voient du pays. Des pays. Plusieurs membres avaient déjà séjourné aux États-Unis ou en Amérique du Sud. Certains s'y étaient même installés pour fonder une cellule éodienne.

— J'ai toujours aimé bouger, ai-je affirmé avec assurance.

— Tu auras peut-être ta chance...

Pierre m'a raccompagnée jusque chez moi. Il n'est resté que quelques minutes, ce qui a intrigué mes parents.

— Il n'a pas l'air dans son assiette, a décrété papa. Qu'est-ce qui se passe?

— Je ne sais pas. J'essaie d'en savoir plus.

— Une peine d'amour? a suggéré maman.

— Ce n'est pas si simple...

— Est-ce qu'on peut faire quelque chose? Je vais en parler à mon frère, si tu veux.

— Non, maman, attends un peu. Tout va rentrer dans l'ordre.

Maman m'a passé la main dans les cheveux. Ça m'agaçait un peu, mais je pensais à mon cousin dont la mère était toujours allongée ou absente et j'ai souri à la mienne.

— Toi aussi, tu as une petite mine, ma belle. Qu'est-ce que vous avez donc tous?

— Ce n'est pas une histoire de drogue, si ça peut te rassurer.

Je savais que maman était obsédée par ce problème. J'avais beau lui dire que ça ne m'intéressait pas, elle m'interrogeait souvent sur ce sujet.

— C'est Antoine? m'a-t-elle demandé.

— Quoi, Antoine?

Je voulais bien être compréhensive, mais il ne fallait pas exagérer! Maman n'avait pas à mêler mon chum à ses angoisses. Mon ton devait être sec, car elle s'est contentée de dire que l'adolescence était décidément un âge difficile à comprendre.

J'aurais aimé téléphoner à Alexis, mais il était trop tard. J'ai bu un verre de lait en mangeant mes biscuits au chocolat, et je suis montée me coucher. J'ai mis du temps à trouver le sommeil. «Les bras de Morphée», comme on dit si joliment. Le dieu grec des rêves... J'ai souhaité que les Éodiens ne l'aient pas récupéré, lui aussi; mes songes seraient sûrement épouvantables!

Je n'ai pas rêvé mais, en me réveillant, j'ai pensé que mes hypothétiques cauchemars ne pouvaient pas être pires que la réalité: mon cousin était embrigadé dans une secte.

J'ai téléphoné à Antoine avant même de boire mon jus d'orange. Il m'a écoutée attentivement, puis il a tenté de me rassurer, sans conviction.

— On doit faire le point, a dit Antoine. Rendez-vous chez moi à midi avec Alexis et Eugénie. Mes parents vont magasiner.

J'ai raccroché en soupirant; quelle chance j'avais de connaître Antoine. Il était merveilleux, charmant, beau, gentil, drôle, romantique, serviable... Le dictionnaire ne contenait pas assez d'adjectifs pour décrire mon amoureux. Je me demandais pourquoi Antoine m'avait choisie au lieu de s'intéresser à une plus belle fille. Il n'en manquait pas à l'école, hélas! J'espérais qu'Antoine ne change pas d'idée et que notre histoire dure très longtemps...

Alexis et Eugénie venaient tout juste d'arriver quand j'ai sonné à la porte. Antoine a ouvert et m'a serrée dans ses bras. Il sentait bon, c'était doux et chaud. J'avais l'impression d'être un oisillon dans un nid douillet. J'aurais voulu rester là durant des siècles et oublier tous les problèmes que nous causait Pierre. Mais je n'avais pas le droit de l'abandonner.

J'ai raconté tout ce que mon cousin et Gordon m'avaient révélé. Je lisais la consternation dans le regard de mes amis.

— Pierre est pourtant intelligent! a tonné Alexis. Comment peut-il adhérer à un mouvement aussi... fou?

Eugénie a tenté de le calmer en lui expliquant que ce n'était pas une question d'intelligence, mais de fragilité. Elle nous a confié qu'elle avait déjà eu des problèmes, plus jeune, et qu'elle comprenait un peu ce que Pierre pouvait ressentir.

J'avais envie de savoir de quels problèmes il s'agissait, mais je ne voulais pas me montrer indiscrète. J'admirais seulement davantage Eugénie; je n'aurais jamais cru qu'une fille comme elle ait pu vivre des choses difficiles.

Alexis nous a appris qu'il avait suivi

Jonathan Gervais jusqu'à sa chambre d'hôtel, mais que ce dernier n'était jamais seul et qu'il avait dû renoncer à lui parler. Il nous a ensuite raconté que son professeur de guitare n'avait jamais entendu parler du concours avant la rentrée scolaire. Il avait été très étonné par l'ampleur de l'événement. Et, paradoxalement, par le manque d'informations à son sujet.

— Mon prof a reçu une lettre où on lui proposait d'encourager ses meilleurs étudiants à s'inscrire. Ça ne coûtait pas un sou et «pouvait révéler de grands talents au monde entier», disait la brochure. C'est comme ça que je me suis inscrit, avec Pierre et Hector. Puis Pierre a fait cavalier seul... Je ne suis pas assez bon musicien pour jouer en solo.

— Mais tu es tellement drôle! a lancé Eugénie. Je peux écouter des disques, mais personne ne me fait rire comme toi.

Alexis a battu des paupières. Ah! il commençait à prendre les tics de sa copine! Est-ce que je faisais maintenant des choses comme Antoine?

Alexis a ajouté que son professeur n'en savait pas davantage mais qu'il avait promis de se renseigner.

Eugénie, elle, n'avait trouvé aucune trace

des activités des organisateurs dans le passé. Elle avait téléphoné à toutes les commissions scolaires de la province, sans succès. Tout le monde avait entendu parler de ce concours pour la première fois cette année. Et tout le monde s'en était réjoui; les organisateurs payaient la location de la salle et la publicité, et ils offraient cinquante billets pour assister au concert rock.

— Tous les animateurs scolaires à qui j'ai parlé ont fait le même commentaire: ils étaient surpris de tant de générosité. Il y a une femme, Mme Dubois, qui m'a confié que le nom d'une des organisatrices ne lui était pas inconnu. Mais elle ne pouvait me parler à ce moment. Elle a promis de me téléphoner plus tard.

— En tout cas, les organisateurs du concours avaient l'air de vraiment tenir à ce qu'il ait lieu, a dit Alexis.

— Je me demande quel est leur intérêt, a marmonné Antoine. Personne n'a entendu parler d'eux dans le monde du spectacle. J'ai discuté avec des agents, j'ai téléphoné à des maisons de disques: rien. On dirait que le concours est apparu comme par magie.

— Mais on sait que des Éodiens s'y intéressent...

— Qu'est-ce que vous proposez? ai-je demandé.

— Il faut que tu continues à infiltrer le mouvement.

— Je vous répète que je n'aime pas ça, a protesté Antoine. C'est une bande de tordus!

— C'est mon cousin, tout de même! Il ne me ferait pas de mal!

— Mais il est devenu fou!

J'essayais de trouver une réplique brillante et convaincante, mais Antoine avait raison; Pierre nageait en plein délire.

— Excuse-moi, Natasha, je ne voulais pas te blesser... Je crois que j'ai une meilleure idée.

— Chut, a fait Eugénie. Écoutez!

Elle a quitté la table pour augmenter le volume de la radio.

Un attentat. Il y avait eu un attentat contre une certaine Germaine Aubin.

Chapitre 5

Exsecte brûle!

— Un attentat contre Germaine Aubin! s'est exclamée Eugénie.

— Germaine Aubin? Qui est-ce?

— Chut! Je veux savoir ce qui s'est passé.

Un journaliste expliquait qu'un incendie d'origine criminelle avait ravagé les locaux d'Exsecte durant la nuit. Germaine Aubin, qui s'était endormie dans son bureau, avait été sauvée par son chien. La bête avait tiré sa maîtresse de son sommeil en aboyant. Mme Aubin avait eu tout juste le temps d'emporter ses dossiers les plus importants avant de fuir la fournaise.

— Mme Aubin est la directrice d'Exsecte!

J'allais justement vous en parler, a affirmé Eugénie.

Exsecte est un organisme qui combat les sectes. Les familles d'une victime peuvent recourir à ses services pour retrouver un enfant, un frère ou une soeur.

— Je m'étais dit qu'on devrait la consulter. Elle peut sûrement nous conseiller!

— L'attentat prouve qu'elle gêne certaines personnes. Elle doit faire un bon travail pour susciter tant d'inquiétude.

— Il faut lui parler! s'est écrié Antoine.

— Pas aujourd'hui, en tout cas. Elle doit se remettre du choc. Et les policiers vont lui poser un million de questions.

— Elle n'aura pas vraiment le temps de nous recevoir, ai-je conclu.

— Continuons à observer Pierre, a proposé Alexis. On verra Mme Aubin la semaine prochaine.

***

Les jours suivants se sont écoulés sans incident notable. J'ai téléphoné à Pierre deux fois pour lui dire que j'avais été très impressionnée par la philosophie du mouvement éodien. Je l'ai prié de parler de moi à ses amis;

ferais-je une bonne recrue?

— Il y a des épreuves à passer. Des tests, a répondu Pierre. Ce n'est pas si simple. Tu ne t'inscris pas à un club vidéo, Nat. C'est une démarche qui peut changer ta vie.

— Quelle était ton épreuve?

— Je n'ai pas le droit d'en parler à une non-initiée. Mais je suis fier d'avoir gagné la confiance du Maître.

J'ai raccroché en tremblant. En repoussant de toutes mes forces la vilaine idée qui germait dans mon esprit. Qui poussait, qui prenait toute la place: Pierre avait-il participé à l'attentat contre Germaine Aubin?

Mon cousin était-il devenu un terroriste?

Je n'osais même pas en parler à Alexis. Mais mon ami me connaît depuis longtemps: il a deviné que j'étais bouleversée et m'a forcée à tout lui raconter.

— Tu sautes très vite aux conclusions, a-t-il protesté.

— On l'aura entraîné. Influencé. Il ne réfléchit même plus par lui-même!

— Ils n'auraient pas confié une mission si importante à un nouveau membre.

— Tu dois avoir raison.

À ce moment, le téléphone a sonné: Eugénie avait reçu un appel de Mme Dubois, l'organisatrice scolaire dont elle avait parlé l'autre jour.

— Viens nous rejoindre, lui ai-je dit, j'appelle Antoine.

Le quatuor réuni, j'ai espéré qu'on soit aussi efficaces que les mousquetaires du roi. Je me serais volontiers battue en duel contre les anges de malheur qui avaient ravi l'âme de Pierre. Ils auraient mérité de se retrouver dans les griffes de Milady.

— Mme Dubois m'a dit qu'elle avait connu une certaine Jeannine Hurtubise, qui s'appelait Jeannine Waresky, à l'époque. Elle m'a raconté que la femme avait beaucoup changé, mais qu'elle l'avait reconnue. Elle était bénévole dans un centre d'aide aux jeunes. Mais les jeunes ne l'aimaient pas trop. Elle leur faisait des sermons et elle essayait de les convertir à ses idées. Finalement, on ne l'a plus revue.

— Il faudrait savoir si elle a changé de nom parce qu'elle s'est mariée ou parce qu'elle a divorcé et repris son nom de jeune fille.

— Pourquoi?

J'ai expliqué à Alexis que si Jeannine Hurtubise avait divorcé, son ex-époux accepterait peut-être de nous parler d'elle.

— Même *contre* elle. Et s'il avait des révélations à nous faire? On n'a pas d'autre piste, de toute manière.

— On est chanceux qu'elle se soit appelée Waresky plutôt que Tremblay; on n'aura pas à téléphoner à cent personnes avant de tomber sur le bon M. Waresky.

— Je peux me charger de cette mission, a dit Eugénie. Nat a déjà assez à faire avec Pierre.

Maman est rentrée à ce moment, les bras chargés de paquets. Antoine s'est empressé de l'aider. Il fait vraiment tout pour rentrer dans ses bonnes grâces, et elle commence à s'habituer à lui.

— J'ai dévalisé le supermarché. Qu'est-ce que vous diriez d'un spaghetti?

J'étais très étonnée de la proposition de maman: l'improvisation n'est pas tellement dans ses habitudes. Elle est gentille avec mes amis quand ils viennent et il m'arrive de les inviter à manger chez nous, mais jamais à l'improviste. Je me demandais bien ce qui avait motivé ma mère à recevoir ma gang.

Elle voulait probablement «communiquer» avec moi.

Elle devait avoir lu un article sur l'adolescence dans une de ses revues de psychologie et voulait mettre les conseils en pratique. «Parlez avec votre jeune.» «Établissez des priorités.» «Intéressez-vous à ses amis.» J'avais l'impression, quand je jetais un coup d'oeil à ces articles, que nous formions une race à part, bizarroïde et menaçante. Les ados semblaient effrayer davantage les adultes qu'une invasion d'extraterrestres.

Je n'ai pourtant pas le sentiment d'être étrange... Mes parents le sont bien davantage!

Ça doit être ça, le fossé des générations; on roule dans une nuit noire et on tombe dans le fossé sans avoir compris quoi que ce soit à ce qui nous arrive. Et on patauge longtemps pour s'extirper de cette situation inconfortable...

Les spaghettis étaient délicieux, et j'éprouvais un sentiment très ambigu en regardant maman rire avec mes amis. Ça m'énervait qu'elle soit aussi gentille avec eux, comme si elle voulait être leur copine, mais en même temps j'étais contente d'avoir une mère accueillante.

Et malheureusement trop intuitive... Elle a regretté que Pierre soit absent. On s'est tous tus pendant un instant, puis on s'est remis à parler de tant d'autres sujets à la fois qu'elle nous a dévisagés l'un après l'autre avant de nous dire qu'elle se demandait ce que devenait mon cousin.

— Pierre passait la moitié de sa vie ici, a continué maman. On ne le voit plus. J'aimerais savoir ce qui est arrivé. Pourquoi êtes-vous fâchés?

— On n'est pas en colère contre lui, madame, a répondu Antoine. On vous le jure!

— Alors?

— Il a changé, a laissé tomber Alexis. C'est lui qui n'a plus envie de nous voir.

— Il nous tolère, c'est tout, ai-je ajouté. Il nous trouve bébés! C'est ce qu'il a dit! Il a seulement quatre mois de plus que moi.

Maman a souri. Ouf! J'avais trouvé un motif qui semblait la contenter pour l'instant.

— Il fait sa crise d'adolescence, a cru bon d'ajouter Alexis.

Maman a eu un petit hoquet de surprise, puis elle s'est mise à rire sans pouvoir s'arrêter. On a tous ri aussi, sans savoir vraiment ce qu'il y avait de drôle. On en avait seulement besoin...

Papa est arrivé à ce moment-là, mais personne n'a pu lui expliquer pourquoi on riait. Il s'est servi des pâtes en disant qu'il était heureux de nous voir de si belle humeur. Je ne l'ai pas détrompé, même si je me sentais un peu hypocrite.

Après le repas, j'ai fait une longue promenade avec Antoine. J'aurais marché jusqu'au bout du monde avec lui, jusqu'au bout de l'univers. Il me semblait que la galaxie n'était pas assez grande pour contenir notre amour. Je comprenais Orphée, qui avait voulu sauver Eurydice des Enfers; je suivrais Antoine n'importe où.

En pensant au musicien grec, j'ai songé de nouveau à Pierre et à cette secte qui avait perverti la plus belle des mythologies pour servir ses intérêts.

Antoine m'a tapoté l'épaule.

— C'est l'heure.

On a couru pour attraper l'autobus. On avait rendez-vous avec Germaine Aubin. Alexis avait eu du mal à la convaincre de nous recevoir mais, quand il avait mentionné le mouvement éodien, Mme Aubin avait accepté.

Mme Aubin était une brune de taille moyenne, avec des lunettes en imitation d'écaille. Elle aurait été banale si ce n'avait été de son regard. Perçant, intense: on avait l'impression qu'elle lisait au fond de nous. Ses ennemis devaient la craindre.

Cela dit, ils étaient nombreux... et Mme Aubin avait l'air épuisée malgré sa détermination. Elle nous a expliqué en quoi consistait son travail, puis elle nous a écoutés décrire le cheminement de Pierre.

On a appris qu'on ne pouvait pas porter plainte d'une manière officielle, puisqu'on n'était ni majeurs ni l'un de ses deux parents. Mme Aubin nous a conseillé de parler à mon oncle, et j'ai dû lui expliquer qu'il était pratiquement toujours absent.

— Et de plus, si oncle Martin intervient, Pierre va sûrement le rejeter. Quant à sa mère, elle est malade et ne saurait s'en mêler... C'est pour ça qu'on doit le tirer de ce mauvais pas. Parlez-nous du mouvement éodien.

— C'est une secte polymorphe. Je l'appelle l'«Hydre». Par dérision, peut-être. J'en viens à imiter ceux que je poursuis.

Constatant notre incompréhension, Mme Aubin a précisé que la mise à mort de l'hydre de Lerne était l'un des douze travaux qu'Eurysthée avait imposés à Héraclès pour expier ses fautes. L'hydre était un serpent qui ravageait la région de l'Argolide.

— Le monstre avait sept têtes mais, chaque fois qu'on en coupait une, une autre repoussait à sa place. Héraclès réussit pourtant à en brûler six. Il coupa et enterra la dernière, puis trempa ses flèches dans le sang empoisonné. Le mouvement éodien ressemble à cette hydre: je tranche une tête, et il en naît une autre!

— Vous semblez bien connaître les Éodiens.

— Trop, hélas! Depuis trop longtemps. Mon fils a été l'une de leurs proies, il y a deux ans.

— Deux ans? Et maintenant, comment...

— Il s'est suicidé. Il n'a pas survécu à leur lavage de cerveau. J'ai réussi à l'arracher à cette secte, mais il n'avait plus le goût de vivre.

Antoine m'a serré la main très fort, puis il a présenté ses condoléances à Mme Aubin.

— C'est la pensée de mon fils qui me soutient, nous a-t-elle confessé. Je ne veux pas que sa mort soit inutile. La vengeance n'est même pas le moteur de mon action; je tiens seulement à circonscrire les ravages des sectes.

Alexis s'est enflammé:

— Pourquoi est-ce qu'on n'a pas interdit le mouvement éodien?

— Parce qu'il change de nom sans arrêt. Polymorphe, comme je vous l'ai dit. Et qu'il est difficile de distinguer une secte d'une religion. Il y a plusieurs centaines de groupes religieux au Québec. Et on n'exerce aucun contrôle sur eux, à moins que des plaintes ne soient déposées... pour fraude, par exemple. On étudie alors le dossier. Mais c'est très difficile d'avoir des preuves solides qui permettent de condamner une secte. Nous vivons dans un pays démocratique, où chacun est libre de choisir sa religion...

— Mais une secte, ce n'est pas pareil! a protesté Eugénie.

— Je sais, a fait Mme Aubin. Toutefois, les gouvernements ne se penchent pas tellement sur ces problèmes.

— Comment sauver Pierre?

— Et Gordon, a ajouté Eugénie. Lui aussi est malheureux...

J'ai failli rétorquer que c'était Gordon qui avait entraîné Pierre, mais je ne voulais pas paraître mesquine.

— Vous devez gagner la confiance de vos amis. Conserver des relations avec eux. C'est quand ils coupent les liens avec leur entourage que les gens deviennent des membres à part entière d'une secte. Ils veulent se créer une nouvelle famille. Une famille où on les accueille à bras ouverts, où on les flatte. Les dirigeants donnent à leurs proies l'impression qu'elles sont importantes, qu'on a absolument besoin d'elles dans le groupe. Et, bien sûr, on promet le bonheur et la vérité à ces nouveaux membres.

— Mais ils doivent finir par se rendre compte que personne ne détient la vérité, ai-je dit.

— Ils sont fragiles quand ils entrent dans le groupe. Et on ne fait rien pour que cela change, au contraire. On épuise les membres afin qu'ils n'aient pas assez d'énergie pour réfléchir, pour réagir. Il y a parfois des rites exténuants, des règles sévères ou des mises en scène impressionnantes qui déstabilisent les victimes.

— C'est criminel!

— Oui, mais le code pénal n'a rien prévu pour les sectes. Je vous le répète, pour aider Pierre, vous devez rester près de lui.

— Il me fait confiance, ai-je révélé à Mme Aubin. Je lui ai raconté que je voulais entrer dans le mouvement éodien.

— Il voudra des preuves que vous croyez réellement au groupe. S'il constate que vous lui mentez, vous représenterez le démon, l'ennemi à abattre...

Mme Aubin a soupiré et a tenté de nous

persuader d'en parler aux parents de Pierre. On a répété que c'était impossible. Mon oncle était capable d'envoyer Pierre étudier dans un autre pays pour qu'il échappe à leur emprise. Mais où qu'il aille, Pierre serait seul. Et ferait de nouveau une cible excellente. Des sectes, il y en a partout.

— Je vais vous donner toute la documentation que j'ai amassée sur les Éodiens, a conclu Mme Aubin.

— Savez-vous qui a incendié le local d'Exsecte?

— J'ai mon idée...

— Est-ce le mouvement éodien?

— C'est possible. J'ai reçu des menaces anonymes ces dernières semaines. Maître Myria, de son vrai nom Réjean Drolet, ne m'aime pas tellement. Évidemment, je n'ai pas de preuves. Les policiers analysent présentement les lettres qu'on m'a envoyées et j'ai fait appel à un détective privé pour m'aider à trouver les coupables.

— Vous connaissez un détective privé?

— Oui, Sean Corrigan, un vieil ami. On ne se voit pas souvent, mais je sais que je peux me fier à lui. Il me rappellera dès qu'il aura trouvé une piste.

On a souhaité bonne chance à Mme Aubin,

après lui avoir promis de la tenir au courant de nos efforts pour ramener Pierre et Gordon à la raison.

En me raccompagnant chez moi, Antoine m'a répété qu'il n'aimait pas mon travail d'«infiltration». C'était beau de vouloir sauver Pierre, mais pas à mes risques et périls; si les dirigeants devinaient que je les espionnais, ils seraient sûrement furieux.

J'avais un peu peur, mais je n'en ai rien montré à Antoine. Je ne pouvais pas faire marche arrière et abandonner Pierre.

Chapitre 6

Une réunion étrange

La fin du jour s'accordait avec mon état d'esprit: mélancolique et sombre. Les rues étaient verglacées, et j'ai failli glisser plus d'une fois. J'avais hâte qu'il neige, car le paysage désolé de la fin de l'automne me démoralisait. Pierre était beaucoup plus joyeux que moi. Mais c'était une gaieté trop étrange pour que je l'envie. En fait, mon cousin était surexcité, fébrile, quand je l'ai rejoint pour manger. J'ai même eu peur qu'il ait pris de la drogue.

J'ai pensé qu'il était pour se fâcher, mais il a éclaté de rire quand je lui ai demandé si les membres du mouvement éodien prenaient des stupéfiants.

— On n'en a pas besoin. Notre sang est de plus en plus pur. On flotte sans consommer de cochonneries chimiques. Je ne me suis jamais senti aussi bien. Tu verras...

— J'ai hâte.

— Tu seras étonnée! Dans deux heures, tu auras le bonheur d'assister à ta première réunion.

Le bonheur?!

Terreur serait un mot plus adéquat. Je pense que j'ai serré les dents durant toute la rencontre pour les empêcher de claquer.

Imaginez une centaine de personnes vêtues de bleu, chacune accroupie sur un petit tapis en forme d'étoile, qui chantent dans une langue qu'elles ne comprennent même pas. Une langue inventée par Maître Myria, qu'ils regardent tous avec dévotion.

J'avais l'impression d'avoir autour de moi des chiens dressés qui s'assoyaient, s'agenouillaient, s'accroupissaient, se relevaient au moindre battement de cils du Maître. Ils ont chanté pendant près d'une demi-heure, puis un des bras droits de Maître Myria a invité les pécheurs à se confesser.

Un homme s'est dirigé vers l'estrade et s'est agenouillé sous le plus gros spot. Il a tendu ses mains au Maître en le priant de l'aider à se corriger de ses impuretés. Le Maître a pris une barre de métal et lui a donné sept coups sur les avant-bras. L'homme ne cessait de fixer le Maître avec une expression extatique, comme si son bourreau le caressait au lieu de le battre. Il l'a ensuite remercié. Puis un autre homme est venu subir la même punition, puis un troisième, un quatrième.

J'avais peur que mon cousin ne les suive, mais le Maître a écourté la séance en ordonnant aux membres de continuer à chanter tandis qu'il discuterait avec ses arthroédiens.

— Ses quoi? ai-je chuchoté.

— Arthroédiens. Ses lieutenants, si tu préfères. Ça vient de *arthro* qui signifie «articulation». Les aides du Maître sont ses articulations en quelque sorte. N'est-ce pas lumineux?

Lumineux? Pas autant que les guirlandes de projecteurs qui réchauffaient la salle. L'air commençait à se raréfier et je me demandais combien de temps durerait encore cette réunion. Je connaissais maintenant les refrains de toutes les chansons, même si je ne pouvais les déchiffrer, et je les ânonnais pour montrer ma bonne volonté.

Gordon m'a tapée sur l'épaule en me disant qu'il avait hâte que je sois des leurs et qu'il me présenterait à ses parrain et marraine à la fin de la séance.

J'ai balbutié des remerciements avant de lui demander où je rencontrerais ces gens.

— Ici même. Plusieurs postulants sont dans cette salle. Ils verront d'abord les chefs, qui les présenteront au Maître s'ils croient à leur foi.

— J'espère qu'on m'acceptera, ai-je trouvé à dire.

Gordon m'a tracé un petit X sur la joue:

— Ça te portera chance.

Les chants se sont enfin terminés, et le Maître est revenu dans la grande salle. De petits groupes se sont formés puis les chefs, pardon, les arthroédiens se sont dirigés vers ces cellules. J'ai reconnu le couple qui avait assisté au concours. Je leur ai souri du mieux que j'ai pu, mais il me semblait que mon aversion était palpable.

Non. Quand je leur ai raconté que j'admirais le génie de Maître Myria, ils m'ont souri à leur tour avant de me prier de m'asseoir et de répondre à leurs questions.

J'avais lu la documentation de Mme Aubin avec beaucoup d'attention. Je crois que c'est ce qui m'a permis de passer le test. J'ai fait semblant d'être timorée et d'avoir besoin d'appartenir à un groupe pour vivre. Je leur ai dit que j'avais une grande soif de vérité, car j'en avais assez de souffrir.

J'ai parlé de mes parents qui ne me comprenaient pas, d'une sensation de vide à l'intérieur de moi-même. J'ai même raconté que j'avais pensé au suicide. Puis j'ai ajouté que je n'en avais jamais parlé. Même pas à mon cousin. Mais je voulais obtenir l'aide du mouvement éodien. Allait-on me la refuser?

Non.

Le couple m'a assurée de son appui et, quand le Maître s'est arrêté devant nous, ils m'ont décrite comme une excellente candidate. Maître Myria m'a fixée durant une minute interminable, et il m'a demandé mon poids. J'ai répondu à cette question incongrue malgré ma surprise, puis il a posé sa main sur ma tête: j'étais acceptée comme novice.

J'ai tout de suite annoncé que je voulais acheter le costume bleu réglementaire. Le Maître a refusé; les membres du mouvement éodien n'avaient pas à dépenser de l'argent. C'est lui qui les vêtait et les nourrissait.

Je ne comprenais plus rien! J'ai remercié

le Maître avec humilité, mais j'étais pressée de rentrer pour discuter de cette anomalie avec mes amis. On avait lu assez de documents pour savoir qu'il y avait toujours des magouilles financières dans ces organismes. Les membres devaient verser une partie, sinon tout leur salaire à la secte. Pourquoi le mouvement éodien semblait-il différent?

Qui payait les dépenses du groupe? Et comment? Ne serait-ce que la location de la salle de réunion... Il y avait bien la vente de gadgets et de livres pour les fidèles, mais ce n'était pas suffisant pour subvenir aux besoins de Maître Myria. J'avais remarqué qu'il portait de grosses bagues et j'aurais parié qu'il se déplaçait dans une voiture luxueuse.

Pour montrer ma bonne foi, j'ai acheté une chandelle à l'une de mes «soeurs». Cette Uradienne m'a expliqué qu'elle les fabriquait selon des procédés ancestraux et que Maître Myria les bénissait. «Ces bougies favorisent la méditation», a-t-elle ajouté. J'ai payé une somme dérisoire et j'ai remercié ma «soeur» en souriant. Béatement. On sourit toujours béatement dans le mouvement éodien.

Pierre a tenu à me raccompagner chez moi. Il ventait si violemment que les panneaux indiquant le stationnement étaient tous renversés. J'aurais tant aimé que les rafales pénètrent l'âme de Pierre et emportent au loin, au large, au bout du monde, toutes les folies qui y avaient poussé comme de la mauvaise herbe.

Cependant, je devais continuer à jouer mon rôle. J'ai montré beaucoup d'enthousiasme en parlant de la réunion, tout en tentant de lui soutirer des informations additionnelles sur le fonctionnement du mouvement, ses origines, ses buts.

— Nous ne posons pas de questions au Maître, Nat. Il nous dit ce qu'il doit nous dire quand il le juge opportun.

— Mais comment fait-il pour savoir que c'est le bon moment pour faire des révélations?

— Il le sait, c'est tout, a rétorqué Pierre sur le ton de l'évidence. C'est le Maître.

Je me demandais comment cet homme avait pu impressionner à ce point mon cousin. Il n'avait rien d'exceptionnel, et ce ne sont pas ses flatteries qui m'auraient convaincue d'adhérer à sa secte. J'avais peine à croire à la naïveté de tant de gens.

On avait discuté avec quelques personnes à la sortie de la salle de réunion; il y avait un ingénieur, des professeurs, des hommes d'affaires, un journaliste, des comédiennes. Ils avaient tous déjà entendu parler des ravages des sectes. Pourquoi ne se rendaient-ils pas compte qu'ils étaient des victimes?

— Maître Myria est vraiment charismatique, ai-je dit. Et nos parrains sont formidables. Je me demande pourquoi Alexis méprise tellement un mouvement qu'il ne connaît pas.

Dénigrer Alexis faisait partie du plan de notre quatuor; je devais gagner la confiance de Pierre. Dénoncer des pseudo-ennemis y contribuerait peut-être.

— Alexis se moque du mouvement?

— Plus ou moins. Il me trouve stupide de m'y intéresser. Je pense qu'il t'en veut encore d'avoir joué seul au concours. D'autant plus que tu l'as remporté. Mais tu le méritais! C'est vraiment merveilleux quand on pense que M. Jackson présidait le jury. Il s'ouvre enfin à un autre genre de musique. Dommage qu'il ait démissionné tout de suite après le concours; les élèves auraient pu profiter de son savoir encore longtemps.

— Oui, c'est vraiment triste. J'étais étonné qu'il vote pour moi!

— Est-ce que tu joues parfois pour nos

amis du mouvement éodien?

Pierre a secoué la tête. Non, on ne le lui avait jamais proposé.

— C'est curieux, ton parrain et ta marraine avaient l'air d'apprécier ton talent lors de la finale. Ils étaient fiers de te féliciter.

Pierre a éludé ma question en expliquant qu'il y avait des membres du groupe qui étaient plus doués que lui.

— Ça m'étonnerait, ai-je rétorqué.

— Je dois me corriger de mon orgueil, Nat. Et tu devrais m'imiter.

Pour qui se prenait-il? Je détestais ce ton pontifiant! J'ai failli lui river son clou, mais j'ai réussi à baisser la tête avec humilité. Il fallait vraiment que je tienne à lui pour vouloir encore le sauver.

— Alors Alexis rit de nous? a questionné Pierre.

— Il ne nous connaît même pas. Son dédain ne peut pas nous atteindre, non? Je le vois un peu moins depuis quelque temps; il est superficiel. Je continue à travailler en équipe avec lui, mais je n'aime pas qu'il nous juge.

J'insistais sur le «nous» pour montrer que je faisais vraiment partie du groupe. En même temps, si j'enfonçais Alexis, je devais justifier nos rencontres au cas où Pierre nous croiserait dans les corridors de l'école.

— Alexis est un ignorant. On n'a rien à faire d'un ignorant. Et je...

Ses dernières paroles ont été couvertes par le tonnerre. Un éclair a déchiré le ciel, et j'ai sursauté en entendant un autre coup de tonnerre.

— Tu es bien nerveuse, a remarqué Pierre.

— Trop d'émotions dans la même soirée, je suppose.

— Avec le mouvement, tu vas apprendre à contrôler tes émotions. Moi, il n'y a plus rien qui me dérange.

«Comme si tu étais mort», ai-je pensé.

La pluie s'est mise à tomber dru. Elle était glacée, entêtée, et j'allais courir quand une auto s'est arrêtée à notre hauteur.

— Montez, a lancé Déïon, notre «parrain».

— Ce n'est pas nécessaire, ai-je répondu. On va mouiller vos sièges.

Je trouvais que cette voiture arrivait à point nommé. Trop. Ils nous avaient suivis. Logiquement, ils auraient dû nous dépasser depuis longtemps. Où allaient-ils nous amener?

— On va vous déposer chez vous, a annoncé Damia, la «marraine».

Pierre m'avait expliqué que tous les couples étaient rebaptisés par le Maître et que l'homme et la femme avaient toujours les mêmes initiales pour favoriser leur osmose.

— Merci, a fait Pierre en montant dans la voiture. Vous me gênez, vous venez toujours me reconduire.

— On t'a cherché, mais tu étais déjà parti.

Ah bon? Les deux Éodiens le ramenaient après chaque réunion?

— Monte, Nat.

Avais-je le choix? Après tout, on n'avait pas entendu parler d'enlèvements par une secte ces derniers jours, seulement d'un incendie criminel...

Heureusement, ils m'ont laissée devant la porte. Maman s'est inquiétée en voyant mes cheveux mouillés. Tout en me tendant une serviette, elle m'a demandé pourquoi Pierre n'était pas entré avec moi et qui nous avait reconduits.

— Tu es trempée, ce qui veut dire que vous êtes montés dans cette voiture après avoir goûté à l'orage. Qui s'est arrêté pour offrir de vous reconduire?

Maman est trop futée!

— On est allés à une conférence sur les

religions, ai-je répondu. Et il y avait des professeurs qui nous ont vus marcher sous la pluie.

Je ne mentais pas tout à fait; j'avais beaucoup appris sur le sujet ce soir-là. Et il y avait effectivement des professeurs, même s'ils ne nous enseignaient pas.

L'étonnement de ma mère était manifeste.

— C'est pour un travail avec Antoine, Eugénie et Alexis.

Maman a pensé que je parlais d'un projet étudiant. Je pensais, moi, à Héraclès et à ses douze travaux; ce héros aurait-il su tirer Pierre des griffes de Maître Myria?

La nuit, j'ai rêvé aux cavales de Diomède, qu'avait domptées Héraclès. Les chevaux étaient tout bleus mais, comme dans la légende, ils se nourrissaient de chair humaine. Dans mon cauchemar, les bêtes suçaient le cerveau de leurs proies. Pierre était attaché à un autel et Maître Myria s'approchait de lui pour lui trancher la tête afin de l'offrir aux juments.

Je me suis réveillée en sueur. Et je ne me suis pas rendormie tout de suite; j'avais trop peur de refaire le même rêve.

**

En me levant, j'avais des picotements dans la gorge et un affreux mal de tête. Quand je suis descendue pour boire mon jus d'orange, papa m'a conseillé d'aller me recoucher.

— Tu fais sûrement de la fièvre, je vais t'apporter des médicaments.

— Mais je dois aller à l'école!

— Tu n'aimais pas autant les études quand tu ne sortais pas avec Antoine, a dit mon frère.

— Ça n'a rien à voir!

Et c'était vrai. À 75%. Je voulais surtout raconter ma soirée avec les dingues. Mais mon père a été inflexible quand il a vu grimper le mercure.

— À 39 °C, on reste couché. Tu parleras à ton ami ce soir quand il reviendra de ses cours. Nicolas va l'informer que tu es malade.

Mon aîné a acquiescé en souriant.

— Je lui raconterai que tu es à l'agonie et que tu n'as rien à envier à la Dame aux camélias: peut-être qu'il t'apportera des bonbons?

— Nicolas! Cesse de taquiner ta soeur, elle est malade.

Je me suis enfoncée sous les draps en espérant que je ne rêverais pas de mon frère!

En fin d'après-midi, maman est revenue

de son travail et m'a apporté un bouillon de poulet. Je me sentais encore faible, mais je voulais tout de même parler à Antoine et à Alexis.

— Tu n'es pas raisonnable, a jugé maman. Il n'est pas question que tes amis viennent ici ce soir. Tu n'as qu'à leur parler au téléphone.

J'ai boudé un peu, mais j'ai dû m'incliner. J'ai relaté ma soirée avec Pierre à Antoine, puis à Alexis, qui s'est chargé de tout répéter à Eugénie. Ils ont promis de joindre Mme Aubin pour parler du mystère entourant le peu d'intérêt de Maître Myria pour l'argent.

— Vraiment étrange, a murmuré Antoine. Les dirigeants des sectes ont tous le goût de l'argent. Maître Myria doit être très riche pour s'en moquer... Alors voici la question qu'on doit se poser: comment est-il devenu si riche?

— Il faut que vous enquêtiez sur cet homme.

— Je vais faire comme toi avec Pierre: je vais le suivre.

J'ai protesté: c'était trop dangereux! On ne savait rien de ce type!

— Il ne m'a jamais vu; il ne se méfiera pas de moi. Et cette filature se fera en alternance avec Alexis. On ne peut pas rester les bras croisés!

— Je serai debout demain! ai-je promis.

— Je m'ennuie de toi, a chuchoté Antoine.

— Moi aussi.

Mais le lendemain, je faisais encore de la fièvre et j'avais mal aux oreilles. J'entendais une sorte de bourdonnement très énervant. Papa m'a appris que les gens qui souffrent d'acouphènes entendent un son de ce genre en permanence.

— C'est parfois pire, comme un sifflement. Et ça ne se guérit pas. C'est ce qui arrive à ceux qui écoutent la musique trop fort. Comprends-tu pourquoi on te conseille régulièrement de baisser le volume de ton baladeur?

Si papa avait raison, j'allais suivre son conseil. J'ai cherché «acouphène» dans le dictionnaire médical. C'était encore pire que ce que papa m'avait décrit... Quand je dirai ça à Alexis, il sera découragé! Mais pourquoi avons-nous des oreilles si fragiles?

Je n'allais pas demander aux dieux pourquoi l'humain était imparfait à ce point, mais je ne pouvais m'empêcher de songer que celui ou celle qui nous avait créés devait être assez distrait ce jour-là.

Pierre m'a téléphoné et m'a appris qu'il y avait une réunion le soir même, mais je lui ai expliqué que j'étais couchée.

— Je suis navrée de ne pouvoir t'accompagner, ai-je menti. Salue bien Damia et Déïon pour moi; je serais encore plus malade s'ils ne nous avaient pas reconduits.

— On sera déçus de ton absence.

Il y avait un léger reproche dans sa voix. Il s'est tu un petit moment, puis il a ajouté que de voir le Maître m'aiderait sûrement à recouvrer la santé.

— Il dégage une telle force!

— Mes parents ne me laisseront jamais sortir. Tu les connais!

— Quand on veut vraiment voir quelqu'un, on y arrive.

— Pierre, ce n'est pas si simple!

— Bon. Je vais t'apporter du sirop, demain. Un sirop spécial qui purifie le corps. J'en prends chaque fois que je me sens fatigué. C'est un sirop qu'on fabrique expressément en Asie pour Maître Myria.

— Je serai en meilleure forme en me réveillant. Je te rappellerai pour que tu me racontes la soirée.

Au réveil, je dois admettre que je pensais seulement à Antoine; ça faisait cinquante-deux heures que je ne l'avais pas vu. On n'avait jamais été séparés aussi longtemps. J'avais hâte d'entendre sa voix, de caresser ses cheveux noirs, de me blottir contre lui. Bien des élèves nous taquinaient en nous voyant toujours ensemble, mais je devinais une pointe de jalousie...

J'avoue que j'étais contente d'être enviée par Julia Mancini, qui plaisait aux neuf dixièmes des garçons du collège et qui aurait bien voulu avoir *aussi* une liaison avec mon amoureux. Mais Antoine ne semblait même pas la remarquer, malgré ses chandails hyper-moulants et son rouge à lèvres qui aurait fait honneur à un camion de pompier.

Il faisait beau quand je suis sortie. J'ai mis un chapeau et j'ai pris des gants pour faire plaisir à maman, qui aurait préféré que je reste une journée de plus chez nous. J'ai quitté la maison plus tôt que d'habitude, car j'avais envie de marcher après toutes ces heures passées au lit. J'ai vu le pic mineur atterrir sur le bouleau des voisins, puis j'ai entendu rire des mésanges qui se poursuivaient d'une branche à l'autre.

Il faisait froid, l'air était humide, et il régnait une odeur annonciatrice de neige. Je respirais à pleins poumons quand je me suis aperçue que j'avais échappé un gant. Je me suis retournée, je l'ai ramassé. Et j'ai continué à marcher. Puis j'ai pris conscience que j'avais vu une voiture marron en faisant demi-tour.

Cette voiture ressemblait à celle de Damia et de Déïon...

Chapitre 7

Une mort suspecte

Ces Éodiens me suivaient!

J'ai ressenti un long frisson. Et ce n'était pas le froid qui en était la cause. J'ai continué à marcher jusqu'à un arrêt d'autobus. Tout ce que je souhaitais, c'est que des passagers l'attendent et que je puisse me glisser parmi eux pour échapper à la surveillance des Éodiens. La chance m'a souri; l'autobus est arrivé au moment où j'atteignais l'arrêt. Je suis montée. J'ai vu la voiture s'arrêter, puis repartir en sens inverse.

J'ai ensuite demandé au chauffeur quel était le circuit du bus: il n'allait pas en direction de l'école. Je suis descendue à l'arrêt suivant et j'ai pris un taxi pour m'y rendre.

Antoine semblait inquiet quand je suis arrivée.

— Où étais-tu? Ça fait quinze minutes que tu devrais être ici.

— Je me suis trompée d'autobus, ai-je dit sans fournir d'autres explications.

Je ne voulais pas qu'Antoine sache qu'on m'avait suivie; je préférais en parler à Alexis.

Je m'étonnais moi-même de ne pas me confier à Antoine. Après tout, j'étais amoureuse de lui... Mais j'étais amie avec Alexis depuis si longtemps. On se connaissait tellement bien; on avait vécu plusieurs aventures ensemble.

Quand j'ai confié à Alexis ces sentiments, il m'a avoué qu'il ressentait la même chose envers Eugénie:

— Je suis fou d'elle, mais notre amitié est plus... plus simple. Les filles sont compliquées, tu ne peux pas savoir.

— Et les garçons! Ils sont tellement bizarres.

On a éclaté de rire.

— Il y a plus étrange, ai-je ajouté en reprenant mon sérieux. Je pense qu'on m'a suivie.

— Les Éodiens? Tu crois?

— Oui. J'ai cru reconnaître la voiture de Damia et de Déïon.

— Mais pourquoi? Ils savent que tu étudies à la même école que Pierre. Qu'est-ce que ça leur donne de t'épier?

— Je l'ignore. Je sais seulement que je déteste être observée de la sorte.

— Crois-tu qu'ils ont des espions ici?

Je n'avais pas pensé à cela. Un professeur ou un élève de la fin du secondaire était peut-être chargé de me surveiller.

— On doit faire semblant de travailler ensemble, Alex. Et ce serait préférable qu'on se parle moins souvent quand il y a des témoins. Il faudra être vraiment prudents désormais. On se téléphonera plutôt.

Alexis a acquiescé, puis il m'a raconté que l'enquête sur Maître Myria était ardue.

— Je te dirai tout au téléphone ce soir.

La journée m'a paru interminable. J'étais lasse. J'aurais dû écouter ma mère. J'entendais à peine le prof de maths et j'ai failli m'endormir durant le cours d'histoire. Pourtant, j'adore ce cours! Antoine a proposé de me raccompagner jusque chez moi.

— Tu as vraiment l'air malade.

Il m'a flatté la joue, puis m'a embrassée dans le cou.

— Fais attention, tu vas attraper ma grippe.

— Ce n'est pas un petit microbe qui va m'empêcher de t'embrasser, a-t-il répondu.

À la maison, maman lui a offert un chocolat chaud, mais il l'a refusé.

— Je suis déjà en retard. Prends soin de toi, Natasha.

Antoine était le seul à m'appeler Natasha. Je trouvais ça plus romantique que Nat. Il avait l'air triste de me quitter; ça m'a flattée, et je me suis glissée dans mes draps en me félicitant de ma chance.

C'est le téléphone qui m'a réveillée. J'étais seule dans la maison. Mes parents étaient allés au théâtre, et Nicolas devait être chez son amie. J'ai couru pour répondre.

— Allô? Allô?

Rien. On a raccroché sans même s'excuser. Je déteste ça. Ce n'est tout de même pas difficile de dire: «Je me suis trompé de numéro!»

Je m'étais installée dans un fauteuil avec une couverture pour regarder un film, quand le téléphone a sonné de nouveau. C'était Alexis.

— Mme Aubin n'avait pas d'autres informations que celles qu'elle nous a données au sujet de Maître Myria. Cet homme est une énigme: on ne sait pas d'où il vient, ni comment il a amassé sa fortune. Mme Aubin a toujours cru qu'il exigeait de l'argent de ses disciples; elle est très étonnée qu'on ait refusé ton fric.

— J'aime autant ça. Y a-t-il des développements au sujet de l'incendie de son bureau?

— Non.

— Son ami ne l'a pas aidée?

— Ce n'est pas ça: elle n'a pas réussi à le joindre. Je crois qu'elle s'inquiète pour lui, même si elle m'a affirmé que Sean quittait souvent Montréal pour ses enquêtes et qu'elle restait de longs moments sans recevoir de ses nouvelles. Je pense qu'on devrait raconter notre histoire à M. Chanteclerc. Il pourra peut-être nous donner un coup de main? Il nous avait bien aidés lors de notre aventure à Québec, et on est restés amis.

Bonne idée; Horace Chanteclerc connaissait des tas de gens dans le monde des affaires. Quelqu'un saurait peut-être d'où venait la fortune de Maître Myria.

— De son vrai nom Réjean Drolet, me suis-je souvenue avant de pouffer de rire. Comment peut-il se faire appeler Maître Myria sans se sentir ridicule?

— Quand on se voit dans la peau du Maître du monde, on a probablement l'impression que personne n'osera rire de nous...

J'ai téléphoné tout de suite à M. Chanteclerc. Il semblait très content qu'on fasse appel à lui. Malgré son calme, j'ai senti qu'il bouillait intérieurement en apprenant la métamorphose de Pierre.

— Il est pourtant intelligent! ai-je dit. Mais il doit être plus influençable que je le pensais.

— Il est surtout plus sensible. Plus seul et plus malheureux.

— J'ai toujours été amie avec lui!

— Tu n'as pas à te justifier, Natasha. Tu es fidèle, certes, mais tu es bien dans ta peau.

Est-ce que je devais m'en plaindre? Et est-ce que j'étais si bien?

— Tu sembles toujours en pleine possession de tes moyens. Tu es débrouillarde, sociable, vive, dynamique. À côté de toi, Pierre s'est peut-être senti fade et sans intérêt. Il n'a pas réussi à prendre sa place.

— Il n'avait qu'à se faire d'autres amis!

J'étais blessée; je faisais tout ce que je pouvais pour mon cousin, et Horace Chanteclerc m'apprenait que j'étais la cause de ses malheurs. C'était trop! Mon interlocuteur a deviné ma colère et m'a apaisée en me répétant que Pierre était incapable de poser un jugement sensé.

— Il est obnubilé par ce mouvement. Je vais me renseigner sur son gourou et te rappeler.

— Je ne veux pas vous déranger.

— Ça me fait plaisir d'être utile. Et je m'ennuie de votre gang...

J'étais rassérénée en reposant le combiné; j'avais bien fait de raconter mes soucis à M. Chanteclerc. Il aurait sûrement des informations à nous donner bientôt.

Je n'ai pas rêvé cette nuit-là et je me suis levée en grande forme. J'aurais pu escalader une montagne. Je chantais à tue-tête en beurrant mes rôties, et mon père m'a taquinée en disant que l'amour me donnait de la voix. J'ai rougi, mais j'ai continué à chanter. Je me demande pourquoi tous les parents ont tant de plaisir à agacer leurs enfants à propos de leurs amours. Est-ce qu'ils ne se souviennent pas combien ça les énervait quand ils avaient notre âge?

Papa a ouvert la radio. On prévoyait quinze centimètres de neige.

Super! On aurait peut-être un Noël blanc. C'est si triste de décorer un arbre planté dans du vieux gazon décoloré et d'être obligé d'ajouter de la neige artificielle pour faire «vrai». Je me réjouissais de cette première chute de neige quand j'ai entendu le présentateur dire que le cadavre de l'homme qu'on avait repêché dans le port de Montréal était identifié.

Il s'agissait de Sean Corrigan, un détective privé.

Sean Corrigan, l'ami de Mme Aubin.

Notre histoire commençait à sentir vraiment mauvais. Subitement, je n'avais plus faim. Quand mon père s'est inquiété de me voir quitter la maison sans manger, je lui ai expliqué que j'avais oublié un rendez-vous à l'école pour un travail en équipe.

— Attends, je vais te déposer.

Durant le trajet, papa m'a parlé de Pierre. Il n'aimait pas son attitude.

— Il se renferme en lui-même; ça ne peut pas être bon. J'espère qu'il se confie un peu à toi.

— Parfois.

— Que se passe-t-il? Crois-tu qu'il aurait besoin de consulter un spécialiste? Je peux en parler à son père. Je m'entends bien avec Martin.

— Quand il est là.

— Je sais que ses absences sont trop fréquentes, mais ton oncle ne tient pas en place. Il a toujours été comme ça. À l'université, il commençait déjà à organiser des voyages. Ce n'est pas pour rien qu'il possède l'entreprise la plus importante aujourd'hui. Vous avez été contents, Pierre et toi, de profiter de billets d'avion à prix réduit... pour ne pas dire gratuits.

— Ça fait longtemps qu'on n'a pas voyagé, ai-je répondu. Peut-être qu'un séjour à l'étranger distrairait Pierre.

— Pour les vacances de Noël?

J'ai hoché la tête, même si je n'avais aucune envie de quitter Montréal durant les fêtes: je ne voulais surtout pas être séparée d'Antoine. Mais je devais meubler la conversation et je disais n'importe quoi.

— À moins, bien sûr, qu'Antoine se joigne à nous?

Ce serait le rêve! Je me voyais déjà à Venise ou à New York. Ou dans un petit chalet douillet à la montagne. Avec Alexis et Eugénie. Et Pierre qui serait redevenu normal et qui aurait rencontré une fille super en arrivant dans ce joli village du Vermont.

— Nat? Tu es dans la lune. Tu es arrivée.

Papa s'est penché vers moi pour m'embrasser et me souhaiter une bonne journée.

Antoine, Alexis et Eugénie n'étaient pas encore arrivés. J'ai eu le temps d'aller acheter un journal pour en apprendre davantage sur la mort de Sean Corrigan.

Sean Corrigan a été formellement identifié hier soir par un de ses neveux, James Corrigan. Sean Corrigan travaillait depuis huit ans comme détective privé; cet emploi l'obligeait à de fréquents déplacements, mais sa famille et ses amis se sont préoccupés de son absence avant-hier midi, au moment où il devait participer à une grande fête familiale. On a signalé alors sa disparition.

James Corrigan a déclaré aux journalistes que son oncle s'était noyé. Un accident? Sean Corrigan aurait-il souffert d'un malaise cardiaque à la suite duquel il aurait chuté dans les eaux troubles du port? Personne ne l'a vu se débattre, personne ne l'a entendu crier.

Vu la nature de son travail, les enquêteurs ont exigé une autopsie afin d'en apprendre davantage. On n'exclut pas l'hypothèse d'un meurtre. Toute personne ayant des informations à ce sujet est priée de téléphoner à Police Ports Canada.

Mes amis n'étaient pas au courant de cette tragédie. Je leur ai tendu l'article que je venais de parcourir avec consternation. Ils l'ont lu en silence.

— Devrait-on présenter nos condoléances à Mme Aubin? a demandé Alexis.

— Il y a sûrement des policiers chez elle pour l'interroger.

— Ils ne savent peut-être pas qu'ils sont amis, a dit Eugénie.

— Nous la connaissons très peu, ai-je protesté. Si j'avais de la peine, je n'aimerais pas que des inconnus frappent à ma porte. On ne peut rien pour elle. On devrait simplement lui envoyer un mot.

— Il faudrait pourtant savoir si Mme Aubin a obtenu des renseignements sur les Éodiens par Sean Corrigan, a objecté Antoine.

— S'il suivait une piste concernant ce mouvement, a ajouté Alexis.

Mes amis avaient raison. Eugénie s'est chargée d'appeler Mme Aubin pour lui demander si on pouvait la revoir quelques minutes.

— Elle a l'air découragée, mais elle a accepté.

Eugénie nous a ensuite rapporté la conversation qu'elle avait eue avec M. Waresky. Il avait quitté sa femme, Jeannine, quand elle était entrée dans une secte et n'avait jamais eu de ses nouvelles depuis. Il ne pouvait rien nous dire de plus.

Après les cours, on s'est arrêtés chez un fleuriste et on a acheté des fleurs à Mme Aubin. Pas pour qu'elle les mette sur la tombe de son ami, mais pour la réconforter. Mme Aubin a paru touchée par notre attention. Elle nous a appris qu'elle avait confié une mission concernant les Éodiens à Sean Corrigan.

— Il devait filer Réjean Drolet.

— Qu'ont dit les policiers?

— Que Sean enquêtait sur plusieurs dossiers à la fois et qu'on ne pouvait accuser personne pour l'instant. Mais ils surveilleront discrètement Drolet. Je me demande ce qu'il cache pour s'adonner maintenant à des activités criminelles. Ce n'est pas courant dans les sectes. Les lavages de cerveau, oui, les abus de pouvoir, oui, s'approprier les biens des fidèles, oui, mais le meurtre? C'est inhabituel. Je l'accuse peut-être à tort, mais je ne crois pas.

— Vous n'avez aucune idée du but que vise Drolet?

Mme Aubin a secoué la tête en soupirant.

On a promis de revenir la voir. On n'osait pas lui demander si elle avait un mari ou un ami, quelqu'un pour s'occuper d'elle. On l'espérait sans trop y croire.

La neige commençait à tomber quand on a quitté Mme Aubin. Le ciel était bas, lourd de flocons qui s'amusaient follement à tourbillonner jusqu'au sol. J'ai ouvert la bouche pour en manger. Il paraît que la neige est polluée, mais c'est tellement tentant d'avaler les premiers flocons. J'avais trop envie d'être de nouveau une petite fille et de n'avoir d'autre projet en tête que la création d'un bonhomme de neige. L'enfance me semblait bien loin...

Pourtant, quand Antoine m'a serrée contre lui, j'ai pensé que mon âge avait aussi ses avantages. Alexis et Eugénie marchaient devant nous en silence, comme si des paroles pouvaient briser la magie de la première neige. On s'est séparés devant chez moi. Si la neige nous faisait penser à Noël, elle nous rappelait aussi que les travaux de fin de trimestre exigeaient notre attention.

Je rédigeais un plan pour un exposé oral quand Pierre m'a appelée; il y aurait une réunion le soir même pour fêter la neige. Je n'ai pu m'empêcher de m'étonner:

— Je n'aurais jamais cru qu'il y avait un dieu grec de la neige. Je pensais que c'était réservé aux héros scandinaves, comme Thor, Odin ou Freya.

— En Grèce, il y a de la neige au sommet des montagnes. Et ce n'est pas la mythologie grecque telle que les Anciens la concevaient qui nous intéresse. Il faut que tu apprennes à ne pas trop coller à un classicisme ancestral. Il faut que tu t'ouvres à l'avenir. Nos actions vont nous projeter dans un monde nouveau où seuls les audacieux et les visionnaires se retrouveront.

— Nos actions?

— On a des projets. Je ne peux pas t'en parler maintenant. Il faut que tu franchisses trois étapes avant de devenir un membre à part entière. Tu devras te soumettre à une épreuve.

Une épreuve? Je n'aimais pas cette idée. Je ne pourrais pas commettre un acte illégal si on me le demandait. Mais si je refusais, je perdrais la confiance de Pierre et des Éodiens. Comment éviter ce piège?

La neige m'a tirée provisoirement de ce mauvais pas; après le souper, la visibilité était nulle. Des rafales de vent aveuglaient les automobilistes, la chaussée était glissante et mes parents refusaient que je sorte pour affronter la tempête.

— Tu viens tout juste d'avoir la grippe; il n'est pas question que tu retombes malade.

Pierre a boudé au téléphone, disant que je manquais de culot et qu'il se demandait si le mouvement avait besoin d'une personne aussi craintive que moi. Et aussi ingrate.

— Ingrate?

— On t'a reçue à bras ouverts, mais tu n'es venue à aucune des réunions suivantes. Je passe pour un idiot qui veut faire entrer n'importe qui dans le groupe. Ça me nuira si je veux de nouveau présenter quelqu'un.

— Mais je t'assure que je ne peux pas faire autrement.

— C'est ta deuxième chance, Nat. Tu ferais mieux de considérer attentivement la troisième. Sinon, on croira que tu t'es moquée de nous.

J'aurais aimé rétorquer: «Et alors?» Mais le ton de cet avertissement m'en a dissuadée. J'ai répété que je regrettais, j'ai juré que je serais présente à la prochaine réunion et que j'étais prête à faire amende honorable.

— Ne t'inquiète pas, on l'exigera.

Chapitre 8

Les secrets de Maître Myria

Au collège, tout le monde était excité. La cour était d'une blancheur de crème quand on est arrivés. Elle ne l'est pas restée très longtemps: on s'est mis à se lancer des balles de neige en criant jusqu'à ce que la cloche annonce le début des cours. À midi, j'ai tenté de rencontrer Pierre pour l'inviter à manger avec moi, mais il était invisible.

J'ai eu un petit frisson en me demandant s'il avait disparu lui aussi. Puis j'ai chassé très vite cette idée. Pourquoi Réjean Drolet aurait-il voulu se débarrasser d'un disciple aussi docile que mon cousin? C'était une idée ridicule! J'ai attendu Pierre à la fin de la journée, en vain. Pourtant, un de ses professeurs m'avait assurée qu'il avait assisté à son cours. Il était donc présent durant l'après-midi. Je suis allée à l'auditorium et à la bibliothèque; il n'y était pas. Pierre s'était volatilisé.

Comme Antoine devait aller chez le dentiste, je suis rentrée seule chez moi. La douceur de la neige m'a apaisée et j'ai marché très lentement pour profiter du trajet. J'ai pris le temps de m'arrêter dans un parc pour regarder les écureuils et j'ai rêvé d'aller me promener sur le mont Royal avec mon amoureux durant la fin de semaine. Puis je me suis souvenue que le concert rock avait lieu le samedi; j'essaierais plutôt de filer mon cousin.

Était-il encore en colère contre moi? Le resterait-il longtemps? Jusqu'à ce que je me soumette à une épreuve? Je ne savais comment me sortir de cette impasse. J'ai fait une boule de neige que j'ai lancée de toutes mes forces contre un mur; j'avais l'impression d'être cette boule. Pierre était ce mur que je ne parvenais pas à ébranler. Je m'effritais contre lui, je n'avais aucune prise.

Je me suis retournée deux ou trois fois, car j'avais l'impression d'être suivie, mais c'était sûrement le fruit de mon imagination; il n'y avait aucune voiture marron dans les parages. De toute façon, avec les détours que j'avais effectués, Damia et Déïon auraient eu du mal à m'espionner.

J'ai cependant poussé la porte de la maison avec un certain soulagement; il y avait trop d'éléments inquiétants dans cette enquête pour que je réussisse à faire taire mon angoisse. La manière dont Pierre avait remporté le concours, l'attitude de M. Jackson, l'incendie du bureau de Mme Aubin, la mort de Sean Corrigan, l'étrange détachement de Réjean Drolet face à l'argent, tout tourbillonnait dans ma tête. J'en avais la nausée.

Sur la table de la cuisine, Nicolas avait laissé un mot:

«Nat, M. Chanteclerc va te rappeler après le souper. Parents à un vernissage. Suis chez ma blonde. N.»

J'ai avalé une soupe puis je suis montée dans ma chambre pour réviser mes notes d'histoire.

J'essayais vainement de retenir les dates et les lieux des traités militaires quand Antoine m'a téléphoné.

— Nat, Pierre te surveille!

— Quoi?

— Je ne voulais pas t'affoler ni avoir l'air de te surprotéger — je sais que tu n'aurais pas apprécié —, mais j'ai vu qu'il te suivait.

— Antoine!

— J'admets que je t'ai menti. Je ne suis pas allé chez le dentiste. Je t'ai filée. Au cas où des Éodiens auraient voulu s'en prendre à toi. Et j'ai vu Pierre t'espionner. Il n'y avait aucun doute.

— Mais pourquoi?

— Je pense que tu as perdu sa confiance... Heureusement que tu n'avais pas donné rendez-vous à Alexis. Il aurait été persuadé de ta trahison. Je suppose qu'il voulait seulement s'assurer que tu rentrais bien chez toi sans rencontrer des «ennemis». Tu es fâchée contre moi?

Je ne savais pas trop; je détestais le mensonge, mais j'étais touchée qu'Antoine s'inquiète pour moi.

— Non, je me demande simplement comment agir dorénavant avec Pierre.

— Sois naturelle. Appelle-le. Dis-lui que tu le cherchais après les cours.

— Je vais attendre d'avoir parlé avec Horace Chanteclerc; il va me téléphoner tantôt. J'espère qu'il aura quelques informations à nous livrer.

Il en avait.

Mais je n'ai eu aucun plaisir à en prendre connaissance.

— Ce Réjean Drolet est un vrai caméléon, m'a raconté M. Chanteclerc. Il change d'identité avec une aisance stupéfiante.

— Mais on n'a pas le droit de changer de nom comme ça! C'est illégal.

— Je sais. Il ne change pas son nom comme tel. Mais il a des tas de sociétés qui ont des tas de noms différents. Il peut toujours prétendre que ce sont des filiales. Ces raisons sociales lui permettent d'avoir des antennes dans toutes sortes de milieux: du monde médical au monde artistique, en passant par le sport ou les affaires. Des affaires très secrètes. M. Drolet a des fréquentations assez douteuses.

— Douteuses? Pourquoi n'arrête-t-on pas ses complices?

— Ce n'est pas si facile; ces gens sont protégés. Il faut des preuves très solides. Mon amie Louise qui est avocate m'a conseillé la prudence.

— Qui sont-ils? ai-je questionné.

— Je l'ignore. Fais attention. Ne retourne pas à leurs réunions. Sous aucun prétexte.

— Mais Pierre va bien finir par se douter

de quelque chose!

— Ne prenez pas de décision sans m'en parler. J'ai ta parole?

J'ai promis. Je savais que M. Chanteclerc appellerait mes parents s'il pensait que je pouvais commettre une imprudence. Il n'était pas un mouchard, mais tout de même un adulte... responsable, comme il me le répétait souvent.

Jusqu'ici, il avait réussi à nous aider sans mêler nos parents à nos aventures, mais il nous avait avertis, Pierre, Alexis et moi, qu'il se réservait le droit de consulter nos parents s'il le jugeait nécessaire. Cette «clause» ne nous plaisait guère, mais on aimait bien Horace Chanteclerc. Et il connaissait tant de monde! Dans tant de domaines! Il était lui-même un vrai puits de science, une mine de renseignements.

— J'aurai d'autres informations d'ici deux jours, a ajouté M. Chanteclerc. Je suis tellement furieux d'être cloué au lit!

Il avait fait une mauvaise chute et s'était brisé une hanche; il ne devait pas bouger durant plusieurs semaines.

— C'est long, ai-je compati.

— Quand on a de vieux os comme les miens, ça prend plus de temps...

— Vous n'êtes pas vieux! ai-je protesté.

— Assez vieux pour te répéter d'être prudente! Je te rappellerai demain à la même heure. D'ici là, pas de décision hâtive, pas d'impulsion regrettable.

J'ai eu bien de la peine à retourner à mes manuels d'histoire. Le monde contemporain me suffisait amplement! Je n'avais aucune envie d'apprendre les guerres du passé, les alliances militaires et autres faits d'armes qui se répétaient inlassablement de siècle en siècle. L'univers était imparfait depuis toujours, et rien n'annonçait des changements.

Impossible d'être totalement heureuse: j'étais amoureuse d'Antoine, mais Pierre me causait les plus graves soucis. Et je ne pouvais me réjouir pleinement d'assister au concert rock quand je pensais que, ailleurs dans le monde, des filles de mon âge fuiraient des bombes au même moment.

Je détestais le téléjournal. Chaque fois que je le regardais, j'y voyais des horreurs. Parfois, je comprenais un peu Gordon, qui avait eu envie de mourir: on ne nous présentait pas souvent un avenir radieux. En même temps, les nouvelles scientifiques étaient si fabuleuses que j'étais contente d'appartenir à un siècle où le progrès était manifeste.

J'étais un peu perdue. Et je ne savais pas à qui en parler. Je n'osais pas me confier à Antoine, de crainte qu'il me trouve trop compliquée.

J'ai toujours entendu papa dire que les hommes détestent les femmes qui font des chichis. Je ne voulais pas qu'il me trouve trop sensible; il était tombé amoureux de moi parce que j'aimais l'aventure et le mystère. Pas le romantisme. Pas la fragilité.

J'étais fragile, pourtant. Comme tout le monde, j'imagine. Et les longues soirées où je parlais en toute franchise avec mon cousin me manquaient terriblement.

Ces temps heureux reviendraient-ils?

J'ai regardé la neige tomber durant un long moment avant de m'endormir. J'aurais tant aimé me réveiller dans un monde aussi douillet et pur que cette belle nappe blanche.

J'ai rêvé d'un pique-nique et je me suis levée de très bonne humeur. Avec un appétit féroce. Mon père a applaudi quand il m'a vue faire des crêpes.

— Quelle belle surprise! Tu dois t'être levée à l'aube.

— J'en avais trop envie, j'en ai rêvé.

— Je croyais que tu rêvais à Antoine, a dit papa.

Était-ce vraiment inévitable? J'ai retenu un soupir pour m'épargner d'autres commentaires du même genre. Je me suis demandé si on taquinait autant Antoine chez lui. Il fallait qu'on s'aime pour supporter toutes ces plaisanteries!

Juste avant le début du cours, Eugénie a eu le temps de me dire qu'elle avait vu Pierre une heure plus tôt à l'auditorium.

— Qu'est-ce que tu faisais là? lui ai-je demandé.

— J'avais promis à Adélaïde de lui faire répéter son texte, mais elle n'était pas encore arrivée. Je suis allée aux toilettes et, quand je suis revenue, j'ai entendu la voix de Pierre. J'ai fait le tour pour passer par les coulisses afin de mieux voir son interlocuteur: il m'était inconnu, mais il était habillé en bleu. Même ses gants étaient turquoise. Je n'ai malheureusement saisi que la fin de leur conversation; ils se sont serré la main d'une drôle de façon, puis ils se sont séparés, après que le «bleuté» lui eut remis un paquet.

— Un gros paquet?

— Non, de la taille d'un dictionnaire. Le «bleuté» a demandé à Pierre s'il savait ce qu'il avait à faire, et ton cousin a hoché la tête en disant: «J'ai hâte au concert. Ils seront très contents de moi.» L'homme a tapé dans le dos de Pierre en lui disant qu'il était formidable. Adélaïde a poussé la porte à ce moment; Pierre ne l'a même pas saluée. On aurait dit qu'il ne la voyait pas! Il tenait le paquet contre son coeur. Que peut-il renfermer de si précieux?

— Rien de bon, je te le garantis!

Le prof nous a priées de nous taire, puis il a distribué les copies d'examen. Ma mémoire m'a beaucoup aidée, car j'avais du mal à raisonner; j'étais obnubilée par le mystérieux colis. Comment savoir ce qu'il recelait?

J'étais persuadée que ce n'était pas un disque laser, ni un livre, ni un instrument de musique, même si ce colis avait un lien avec le concert.

Maman m'a proposé d'aller magasiner avec elle dans la soirée, mais je ne pouvais pas rater l'appel de M. Chanteclerc. J'ai décroché à la première sonnerie. Je savais pourtant que notre ami n'aurait pas de bonnes nouvelles.

— Drolet a des liens avec des groupes terroristes.

— Quoi?

— Ce sont eux qui le financent. Ce mouvement n'est qu'une couverture. Les recrues des terroristes se mêlent aux innocents qui croient aux balivernes de Drolet et qui participent à ses réunions. L'information circule ainsi par microfilms, par disquettes...

— Est-ce que ce ne serait pas plus simple s'ils se rencontraient dans un endroit discret plutôt que d'assister à toute cette mascarade?

— Ils ont sans doute leurs raisons.

— Mais si votre amie Louise est au courant de tout cela, pourquoi la police ne l'est-elle pas?

— Les autorités en savent sûrement autant que nous. Peut-être qu'un agent de la GRC réussira un jour à infiltrer le mouvement.

— Mais on n'est sûrs de rien! Pierre est en danger. On lui a remis un paquet ce matin, et ce ne sont certainement pas des chocolats! On essaie de le mêler à quelque chose; il doit y avoir un lien avec le concert.

— Ça vous laisse deux jours pour vous emparer du paquet, vérifier son contenu et le rendre à Pierre.

— Il ne s'en séparera pas. Il doit y tenir plus qu'à la prunelle de ses yeux.

— Vous devrez trouver une solution. Je vous fais confiance. Je te donne le numéro de Jean Lavallée, un ami qui habite à Montréal et qui a déjà travaillé pour... la police. Appelez-le dès que vous aurez le colis; il vous aidera.

— Merci, monsieur Chanteclerc.

— Horace, appelle-moi Horace. J'ai un prénom qui s'harmonise à votre enquête. Même s'il s'agit de mythologie romaine.

— Pardon?

— Les Horaces et les Curiaces; trois frères romains qui se sont battus contre trois frères natifs d'Albe la Longue. Mais c'est une autre histoire...

La nôtre me suffisait amplement! J'ai relu le numéro de téléphone de M. Lavallée en me demandant quel avait été exactement son rôle au sein des forces policières. J'aurais aimé qu'Horace m'en dise plus. J'ai souri. Est-ce que je m'habituerais à son prénom?

J'ai informé Alexis des recherches de notre ami. Il a réagi promptement:

— On n'a plus le choix! Nous allons nous introduire chez Pierre pour chercher le paquet tandis que tu le distrairas.

— Ah oui?

— Tu as une meilleure idée?

— Non.

— Tu as les clés de chez lui?

Oui, je les avais. Comme Pierre avait les clés de notre maison. Depuis que nous étions petits. On nous surnommait «les jumeaux». Je n'aimais pas mes traîtrises, mais mon cousin nous laissait-il le choix?

— Oncle Martin part tôt le matin et ma tante est en Floride. Et Pierre n'aura peut-être pas le paquet avec lui. De toute façon, on fera sûrement des découvertes.

***

En traversant le parc qui donne sur la rue où habite Pierre, j'ai été saisie par la beauté de l'endroit. Le crépuscule irisait la neige, et on aurait cru que des millions de minuscules opales tapissaient le sol. J'aurais aimé m'asseoir pour contempler les lieux, mais on devait arriver chez Pierre avant la nuit. Eugénie avait apporté des modifications au plan initial:

— On ne peut pas s'introduire comme ça chez ton cousin, Nat. Même si tu nous prêtes la clé. C'est illégal. Si quelqu'un signalait notre présence dans cette maison, on aurait bien du mal à expliquer ce qu'on y faisait.

— Mais on doit pourtant trouver ce paquet! avait alors protesté Antoine.

— Je sais. Mais c'est toi qui entraîneras Pierre à l'extérieur. Il faut le persuader de te rejoindre au café, tandis que Nat, Alexis et moi pénétrerons chez lui. Si jamais son père revenait, Nat pourrait lui expliquer qu'on est entrés pour attendre Pierre.

— Mais Pierre me connaît à peine...

— Invente ce que tu veux, mais convaincs-le de te retrouver et retiens-le au moins une heure.

Antoine avait téléphoné à Pierre et avait prétendu que mon comportement le fascinait; il devait lui en parler.

Dès qu'on a vu Pierre quitter la maison, on a sonné à la porte pour s'assurer qu'il n'y avait personne. On a attendu quelques secondes puis on est entrés. Eugénie, qui n'était jamais allée chez Pierre, s'extasiait sur la beauté des lieux, leur richesse, mais Alexis et moi n'étions plus impressionnés. On pensait plutôt à notre mission.

On s'est dirigés tout de suite vers la chambre de mon cousin, tandis qu'Eugénie restait dans le salon pour faire le guet et nous avertir si Pierre ou son père revenaient plus tôt que prévu.

Alexis a failli tomber à la renverse quand il a poussé la porte de la chambre de Pierre: un ordre impeccable y régnait. Mon cousin nous avait habitués à un capharnaüm digne d'une ville après un raid aérien. Je ne suis pas, moi-même, une maniaque du ménage, et ma mère m'ennuie constamment à ce sujet, mais ma chambre avait toujours été plus rangée que celle de Pierre. Qu'est-ce qui l'avait décidé à nettoyer cette pièce?

— Il a enlevé ses posters de John Coltrane et des Rolling Stones! s'est écrié Alexis. Il va vraiment mal.

On a jeté un coup d'oeil à sa bibliothèque; il y avait plusieurs titres qui m'étaient familiers. J'avais vu ces livres à la réunion des Éodiens.

À la fin de la séance, près de la sortie, des livres étaient étalés sur une table. Ils traitaient de la conscience spirituelle (est-ce que la conscience peut être autre que spirituelle?), de l'approche optimale du bonheur, du retour aux sources antiques, des projets d'un monde meilleur.

J'en ai pris un et je l'ai ouvert. Une photo de Maître Myria est tombée par terre.

— Oh non! a gémi Alexis.

— Comment peut-il croire en ce pantin?

On a continué nos recherches en silence, atterrés par nos découvertes. Il y avait évidemment les bougies du mouvement éodien, mais Pierre avait caché dans ses tiroirs les décorations et les diplômes qu'il avait reçus quand il montait en grade dans le mouvement.

— Il est déjà au stade 4. Ça me paraît bien rapide pour quelqu'un qui est entré dans le mouvement il n'y a même pas deux mois.

— Tu as raison, Nat. Pourquoi admire-t-on autant ton cousin?

— Et s'il avait participé à l'incendie d'Exsecte?

— N'exagère pas. Je te l'ai déjà dit, Réjean Drolet ne pouvait pas lui faire confiance si tôt. Des membres plus anciens et plus âgés doivent s'être chargés de cette mission. On ne confie pas un tel travail à un nouveau.

— Oui, mais on apprécie pourtant les ados dans ce mouvement. Il y en avait plusieurs quand je suis allée à la réunion. Et rappelle-toi les néo-nazis à Paris. Ils faisaient faire leur sale boulot par des gens de notre âge.

Alexis a soupiré:

— Cette secte ne vaut pas mieux que les organisations nazies, mais je ne comprends toujours pas le but du mouvement éodien.

On a cherché durant une heure, sans succès; le paquet n'était pas dans sa chambre. Malgré notre gêne, on a fouillé sommairement les autres pièces. Le colis n'y était pas.

On avait pourtant vu Pierre sortir de chez lui les mains vides. Où avait-il caché son trésor?

On a quitté la maison le coeur lourd, découragés. J'ai glissé sur la dernière marche du perron. Je ne me suis pas fait mal mais, alors que j'étais allongée sur le sol, mon attention a été attirée par la forme bizarre d'un sac d'ordures. On devinait une boîte carrée à travers le plastique vert.

— Ça va? m'a demandé Alexis.

— Beaucoup mieux.

Mes amis m'ont dévisagée en se disant sans doute que j'avais perdu la boule en tombant.

— Regardez ce sac. Dans le coin gauche. On dirait qu'il contient une boîte.

Alexis m'a aussitôt lâché le bras pour ouvrir le sac. Il a froncé le nez, mais il a vaillamment poursuivi sa fouille. Il a poussé un cri triomphal en extirpant une boîte noire. Du papier d'emballage bleu ciel était toujours collé à ses côtés.

— C'est la couleur du papier et la grosseur de la boîte, a souligné Eugénie. Mais Pierre l'a vidée de son contenu.

— Il n'avait même pas de sac à dos quand il est parti tantôt. Ce qui signifie que l'objet que renfermait ce paquet ne devait pas être très gros. Mais fragile: il y a beaucoup de papier de soie.

Que trimballait Pierre?

— On devrait conserver cette boîte et l'apporter à l'ami de M. Chanteclerc, ai-je suggéré. Il y a peut-être des indices, des empreintes qui pourront nous aider à savoir quel est ce maudit objet!

— Quand je pense qu'Antoine est assis juste à côté et qu'il l'ignore.

— Espérons qu'il aura remarqué quelque chose d'inusité, ai-je fait sans trop de conviction. Antoine est très observateur.

— Je sais que tu l'aimes, mais ses beaux yeux ne sont pas des rayons X qui voient à travers la matière, a dit Alexis.

J'ai failli riposter et le traiter de défaitiste, mais je n'étais pas beaucoup plus optimiste que lui. Et Alexis, hélas! avait raison: Antoine n'avait rien noté de particulier.

— Sauf, bien sûr, le discours de ton cousin, Natasha. Pierre est vraiment persuadé d'être investi d'une mission qui lui vaudra l'admiration de ses pairs. Je lui ai dit que, grâce à toi, je m'étais intéressé au mouvement éodien et que je voulais en savoir plus, mais il a répondu que son groupe n'appréciait pas tellement tes absences aux réunions. J'ai plaidé ta cause. J'ai même dit que tes parents t'avaient punie parce que tu leur avais tenu tête. Il a fléchi et a promis qu'il parlerait de moi à la prochaine rencontre.

— Quand?

— Elle aura lieu juste après le concert. Réjean Drolet, pardon, Maître Myria sera dans de bonnes dispositions, m'a dit Pierre. Il paraît qu'il adore le rock.

— Ce n'est pourtant pas ce qu'on entend au cours des réunions.

— Il semble que Drolet ait pris Pierre en affection à cause de ses talents musicaux.

— Pierre m'a pourtant assurée qu'il n'avait jamais joué pour lui.

— Mais ton cousin a remporté le concours; il sera habillé en bleu au concert. C'est une bonne publicité pour le mouvement. Peut-être qu'ils gagneront d'autres étudiants à leur cause. Drolet montre un goût pour la musique et parle de voyages; ça peut intéresser bien du monde.

— Pas moi, en tout cas.

— Pierre m'a quitté pour aller répéter la pièce qu'il jouera demain, a ajouté Antoine.

— Je ne suis pas certaine qu'elle me plaira, ai-je lâché.

— Ce n'est pas grave, le concert a lieu juste après la remise du trophée. On devrait tout de même passer une bonne soirée au Stade olympique. C'est la deuxième fois seulement que j'y vais.

— Mais Antoine et moi, nous ne pourrons pas nous asseoir avec vous, ai-je précisé à Eugénie et à Alexis. Pierre doit croire que nous sommes ennemis.

— Cette histoire est pathétique, a gémi Eugénie. J'ai l'impression qu'on n'en verra jamais la fin.

Comme elle se trompait!

Chapitre 9

Le concert rock

Le lendemain soir, j'ai tenté de joindre Pierre au moins dix fois et, quand je l'ai eu au bout du fil, il était dans une colère indescriptible. Il a fini par se calmer et m'a appris qu'il avait été attaqué chez lui par un homme masqué qui l'avait attaché et l'avait laissé là.

— Qu'est-ce que tu me racontes?

— Je n'ai pas apprécié du tout. Je devais voir Maître Myria cet après-midi. J'ai à peine le temps de me changer pour aller au concert.

— Mais qui a pu t'agresser? Quelqu'un qui est jaloux de toi?

— Si on avait voulu m'empêcher de jouer, on m'aurait brisé un doigt. Non, c'était pour me voler.

— Te voler?

— Cent dollars. Il m'a enlevé mes vêtements, est sorti de la maison et il me les a rendus quand il est revenu, quatre heures plus tard.

— Mais pourquoi n'a-t-il pas pris ton argent plus rapidement? Je ne comprends rien...

— Moi non plus, mais je n'ai pas le temps de chercher à éclaircir ce mystère maintenant. Damia et Déïon seront ici dans une demi-heure. Sois ponctuelle.

Tout en me rendant chez Pierre, je me demandais qui avait attaqué mon cousin. Je devinais toutefois qu'on avait «emprunté» ses vêtements parce qu'on y cherchait un objet précis. Eugénie n'était donc pas la seule à avoir vu un Éodien remettre un paquet à Pierre.

Quels étaient les ennemis des Éodiens? Qui voulait subtiliser l'objet dont Pierre refusait de se séparer? On ne le lui avait pourtant pas volé: mon cousin aurait été atterré, et il semblait seulement excédé. Alors?

Antoine nous attendait devant la porte

centrale du Stade; il s'était habillé en bleu pour manifester son intérêt envers les Éodiens, et cette attitude semblait leur plaire. Encore une fois, j'ai été étonnée d'entendre Damia demander à Antoine combien il pesait, après lui avoir parlé de futurs voyages en Amérique centrale. Je me rappelais qu'on m'avait posé cette curieuse question. Quel rapport y avait-il entre notre foi et notre poids?

Alors que d'autres Éodiens nous rejoignaient, Antoine m'a fait remarquer que notre groupe devait être très visible pour les autres spectateurs. On était une cinquantaine, tous vêtus de bleu.

— Tout le monde nous remarque, a murmuré mon amoureux.

— Si au moins on avait de bons billets. Je pensais que les Éodiens avaient des contacts avec les organisateurs et qu'on serait mieux placés.

— Oui, c'est bizarre. Alexis et Eugénie ont plus de chance. Je ne sais pas ce qu'on verra sur la bande vidéo.

Antoine avait apporté le caméscope de son père avec l'intention de filmer les moments importants de la soirée. C'était pourtant interdit, et j'allais lui demander comment il avait pu entrer avec l'appareil quand les lumières se sont éteintes puis rallumées, très vite. Les vedettes du groupe rock sont apparues. J'étais si loin de la scène qu'elles me paraissaient minuscules. Je n'ai pu m'empêcher de me tourner vers Damia:

— On ne peut même pas reconnaître Pierre à cette distance.

Damia m'a souri sans me répondre.

Après coup, je me suis souvenue que son sourire n'avait rien de béat, ni d'illuminé. Mais à ce moment, je pensais à mon cousin: était-il aussi nerveux que moi? Quel rôle jouait son paquet dans la rencontre avec les rockers? L'organisateur du spectacle a annoncé le nom du groupe qui jouerait en première partie, puis il a ajouté qu'on remettrait un prix à un jeune musicien avant la seconde moitié du show.

Je pense que les Bums étaient bons, mais j'avais vraiment hâte qu'ils en finissent et que Pierre reçoive son trophée. J'espérais que ce prix lui donnerait confiance en lui et lui ouvrirait les yeux; il avait beaucoup de qualités et n'avait aucunement besoin du mouvement éodien pour s'épanouir.

Ce n'est pas Réjean Drolet, après tout, qui lui avait appris la musique et qui avait développé son talent.

J'ai senti un mouvement chez mes voisins immédiats quand Drolet s'est levé pour mieux voir Pierre, qui s'avançait sur la scène. Puis le gourou s'est assis en faisant un signe de tête à Damia et à Déïon.

Je n'ai pas du tout aimé ce geste trop discret pour être honnête. En regardant Pierre tendre son saxophone au chanteur, j'ai senti mes entrailles se nouer. Pourquoi mon cousin éprouvait-il le besoin de présenter son instrument de musique? Attendait-il une bénédiction? Est-ce que ces rockers étaient aussi des Éodiens?

— J'ai peur, ai-je chuchoté à l'oreille d'Antoine.

— Ne t'inquiète pas. On a les choses en main.

J'ai dévisagé mon amoureux: que voulait-il dire?

— Je t'expliquerai après.

Je n'ai pas eu le temps de demander «après quoi». On a entendu une explosion, il y a eu des étincelles, des flammes, des cris, puis une sirène d'alarme a retenti. Réjean Drolet ne paraissait pas du tout effrayé, au contraire. Les gens s'agitaient, quittaient leurs sièges, hurlaient, et lui semblait se réjouir de la tournure des événements.

L'instant suivant, il ne souriait plus du tout. Un policier s'était emparé d'un micro pour annoncer aux spectateurs qu'un attentat venait d'être évité. On ne comptait aucun blessé, car on avait réussi à désamorcer la bombe à temps. Toutes les issues du Stade étaient surveillées. On procéderait à des arrestations, et le concert reprendrait dans une heure. L'homme demandait aux fans d'être patients.

Durant l'intervention du policier, Antoine filmait Réjean Drolet, qui blêmissait et regardait le plafond du Stade comme s'il attendait un miracle. Puis il s'est aperçu qu'Antoine l'enregistrait et il a claqué des doigts; deux Éodiens se sont emparés du caméscope.

— Ce n'est pas grave, a dit Déïon derrière nous. Nous aussi, on a filmé la scène. Mais les acrobates que vous aviez engagés n'ont pu grimper sur le toit aussi haut que prévu. La fête est terminée.

Déïon?

Réjean Drolet a empoigné sa voisine, qui s'est mise à hurler.

— Je la tue si vous faites un geste.

J'ai alors vu briller le canon d'un revolver dans la main de Déïon.

— Vous êtes en état d'arrestation. Tout ce

que vous direz pourra être retenu contre vous.

Drolet s'est rendu compte qu'il ne sortirait pas du Stade et il a lâché son otage.

J'avais l'impression d'être dans un film... mais d'en avoir manqué le début!

— Que se passe-t-il? Antoine?

Des policiers en civil emmenaient Drolet, Damia et trois autres Éodiens selon les indications de Déïon. Antoine m'a expliqué qu'il avait fait la connaissance de Déïon, ou plutôt de l'agent Michel Morin, quelques heures auparavant.

— Mais comment?

— Alexis et moi, nous détestions l'idée que tu accompagnes les Éodiens au concert. On ne savait pas ce que contenait le paquet, mais on ne pouvait pas oublier qu'Horace Chanteclerc avait parlé de terrorisme. Que font ces types habituellement? Ils posent des bombes. Aujourd'hui, elles sont très sophistiquées. On a remis à Pierre un petit morceau de métal très particulier. Il devait ajouter cette pièce à son saxophone. Dès qu'il en jouerait, il exploserait.

— Quoi? Pierre?

— Pierre ignorait tout, évidemment. On ne lui a pas lavé le cerveau au point d'en faire un kamikaze.

— Je ne comprends rien.

— Allons rejoindre Alexis et Eugénie; ils doivent avoir retrouvé ton cousin maintenant.

Il régnait une atmosphère très étrange dans les coulisses. Les rockers parlaient avec les policiers et Pierre. Ce dernier était livide et il tremblait comme une feuille.

— Je ne pourrai plus jamais jouer, déclarait-il à l'un des musiciens.

— Ce serait dommage, tu n'as pas remporté le concours sans raison.

— Ils ont triché pendant ce concours, je le sais maintenant. On a tout fait pour que je gagne.

— Mais ça n'aurait pas été vraisemblable si tu n'avais pas eu de talent, ai-je dit en m'approchant de Pierre. On a abusé de ta confiance, mais on ne peut pas t'enlever tes dons...

— Je veux rentrer à la maison, Nat.

J'ai hoché la tête. Mille questions s'agitaient dans mon esprit, mais Pierre était si pitoyable qu'il valait mieux remettre les explications à plus tard. On a pu quitter le Stade juste avant le début du concert. On a accompagné mon cousin chez lui. Heureusement, son père était absent. Dès notre arrivée, Alexis a téléphoné à Mme Aubin et à

M. Chanteclerc pour leur raconter le dénouement de notre enquête.

Puis Antoine et lui ont daigné nous instruire sur les événements des dernières heures.

— J'ai appelé l'ami d'Horace, a dit Alexis. Ce paquet nous inquiétait trop.

— Mais pourquoi ne nous en avez-vous pas parlé? a demandé Eugénie.

Antoine a rougi et a expliqué qu'Alexis et lui avaient décidé ça très vite, mais j'ai compris qu'ils voulaient nous protéger, nous, les pauvres filles. On réglerait ça plus tard...

— Bref, nous en avons discuté avec Jean Lavallée. Ce paquet l'inquiétait lui aussi. Il a décidé de fouiller Pierre. Il a trouvé le mystérieux objet et l'a fait inspecter par ses collègues. Ils ont découvert que c'était une partie d'une bombe et ont averti la GRC, qui a prévenu son agent dans la secte. Ils ont désamorcé l'engin, puis Lavallée l'a remis dans le pantalon de Pierre. Tu n'as rien remarqué, non?

Pierre a secoué la tête. Il n'avait pas prononcé un mot depuis qu'on avait poussé la porte.

— Ils avaient concocté une fausse bombe, et il y a eu une mini-explosion au moment prévu. On avait cependant besoin de piéger

Drolet. Sa tentative de prise d'otage prouvait son implication dans cette histoire. Ça, plus les aveux des acrobates qu'il avait engagés pour lâcher des pétards dans le stade afin de porter l'affolement à son comble.

— Et le témoignage du faux disciple Déïon, a ajouté Alexis. Il travaillait sur cette affaire depuis longtemps; il a accumulé bien des renseignements...

— Mais pourquoi voulait-on faire sauter une bombe au Stade? a fait Eugénie.

— Le groupe s'apprêtait à financer une campagne anti-secte.

— Pourquoi?

— Parce qu'on le leur a demandé, tout simplement. «Ils plaisent aux jeunes, nous a dit l'agent Morin. Vous leur faites confiance, vous les admirez. Ils devaient tourner une série de pubs pour dénoncer le danger des sectes. Ils sont très courageux. Ça leur amenait un bon paquet d'ennemis.»

— On aurait pu se débarrasser d'eux autrement.

— Ils se méfiaient. Ils savaient qu'ils gênaient. Drolet a imaginé qu'ils feraient confiance à Pierre et à son saxophone...

Je me suis tournée vers mon cousin, puis j'ai téléphoné à mes parents pour leur dire que je resterais à dormir chez Pierre. Je ne voulais pas le laisser seul. J'ai tenté de lui faire manger une bouchée, mais il a même résisté à mon offre de crêpes. Il était bouleversé et se murait dans un silence angoissant. Je me suis couchée dans la chambre d'amis, mais je me suis réveillée plusieurs fois. À l'aube, des plaintes m'ont tirée du lit.

Mon cousin pleurait ses illusions.

Je l'ai consolé du mieux que j'ai pu. Eugénie, Alexis et Antoine nous ont rejoints dans la matinée. On a tenté de distraire Pierre, mais il était vraiment perdu. Le resterait-il longtemps? Il semblait terriblement fragile. Même sa démarche avait changé durant son séjour chez les Éodiens: il était voûté et ses pas étaient mal assurés. Mme Aubin nous a conseillé d'être patients.

— Pierre a tout de même échappé au pire, m'a dit Antoine, et des dizaines de personnes aussi.

***

On revenait du cinéma où on avait vu une comédie. Je n'avais pas beaucoup ri et ma tristesse n'avait pas échappé à Antoine.

— Je sais. On n'aurait jamais imaginé

que Drolet était aussi dément.

L'agent Morin nous avait appris que non seulement Drolet était en cheville avec les terroristes qui avaient incendié les locaux d'Exsecte et assassiné Corrigan, mais qu'il trempait dans un trafic d'organes. Des organes comme le foie, les reins, les poumons, qu'on prélevait chez des jeunes en pleine forme. Ces jeunes qui étaient entrés dans le mouvement éodien et à qui Drolet offrait, dès leur majorité, un beau voyage dans le Sud pour rencontrer d'autres Éodiens.

Ils rencontraient plutôt le scalpel de médecins sans scrupules. S'ils survivaient, ils n'avaient plus la force ni le courage de porter plainte contre les organisateurs du voyage. Certains étaient faibles et conditionnés à un point tel qu'ils croyaient nécessaire de sacrifier leur corps aux dieux. Les organes prélevés étaient revendus à des cliniques où de riches patients qui attendaient des greffes les accueillaient avec bonheur, ignorant ou voulant ignorer d'où ils provenaient.

Je comprenais maintenant pourquoi on nous avait interrogés sur notre santé. Et Alexis nous a expliqué qu'il est plus facile de manipuler les disciples quand ils sont affaiblis par un manque de nourriture.

— Au moins, Pierre n'est pas parti à l'étranger, a conclu Antoine.

— Oui, c'est merveilleux.

Quelques jours avant Noël, le coeur de mon cousin s'est remis à battre normalement, c'est-à-dire très très vite, quand Adélaïde l'a invité à un concert. Antoine avait tout raconté à son amie d'enfance et celle-ci avait décidé qu'elle tirerait Pierre de sa morosité.

J'espère qu'elle y réussira.

Table des matières

Achevé d'imprimer
sur les presses de Litho Acme inc.